THE LAST

Book Three of the Nameless War Trilogy

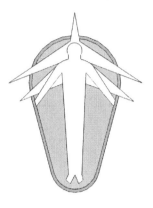

By Edmond Barrett

First Print Edition

This is a work of fiction. Names, characters, places and incidents are either the product of the author's imagination or are used fictitiously, and any resemblance to actual persons, living or, business establishments, events or locales is entirely coincidental.

ISBN:1501045822
ISBN-13: 978-1501045820

With thanks to my parents for their support, to my test readers Phil and Peter, my editor Jan, Sorcha for her encouragement and to Anne for that idea.

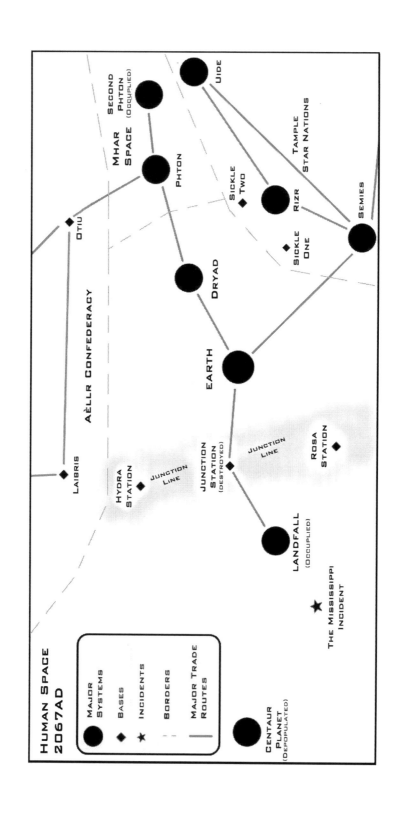

Human Space 2067AD

Major Systems ●
Bases ◆
Incidents ★
Borders - - -
Major Trade Routes ──

Uide

Second Phton (Occupied)

Mhar Space

Phton

Tample Star Nations

Sickle Two

Rizr

Semies

Sickle One

Otiu

Aèllr Confederacy

Dryad

Earth

Laibris

Hydra Station

Junction Line

Junction Station (Destroyed)

Junction Line

Rosa Station

Landfall (Occupied)

The Mississippi Incident

Centaur Planet (Depopulated)

CONTENTS

Ladies and Gentlemen, good morning to you all and thank you, wherever you are, for joining me. Today, I do not speak to you as the President of United States or even as an American citizen. We have reached a moment, in our shared history that transcends mere nationality. So instead, I now speak to you all, as a fellow member of the human race.

Eighteen months ago the alien race we still know only as the Nameless launched a war of conquest upon us, overrunning our outer defences and seizing the colony world of Landfall. At great loss their opening offensive was halted and forced back at Alpha Centauri. Since then, the ships of Battle Fleet have been engaged in combat against the Nameless along a series of fortified systems known as The Junction Line. Their efforts were aimed at buying us time to rebuild and replace that which was lost in those first terrible weeks.

A few hours ago, I was informed that the Line has been breached. The Nameless are now advancing upon Earth. While our fleet is contesting each solar system in turn, its commanders believe there is no prospect of forming a new defensive line. Direct assault upon Earth is now at most only a few weeks away.

The days ahead will without question be both dark and difficult. But I believe no matter how dark those days are; if we stand ready with our strengths, our skills, our hopes and our prayers, we can emerge victorious. God Bless you all

Chapter One

Disposable Heroes

10th November 2067

On their star charts the solar system went by the catchy name of two eight three dash two seven three dash four zero three. The captain of the Spanish ship, which had performed the first and only survey of the system, had attempted to give it a name, but with nothing of any great interest or value in the system, it hadn't stuck. The three Predator class destroyers coasted along in a vertical triangle formation, with fifty kilometres of separation between them. In the centre of the triangle, formed into a loose circle, were ten A class missile boats – vessels that were little more than a standard courier ship, with a launch rack of anti-ship missiles welded onto the dorsal hull. Finally, out twenty kilometres ahead, were two gunboats – another variant of the A class that had swapped the missiles for a quad point defence battery. Usually they would be their missile-armed brethren's only support. Consequently, and not without good cause, they were often referred to as the Forlorn Hope.

Since the collapse of the Junction Line the missile boats had been assaulting the advancing Nameless forces – some times against the space gates their supply ships relied on, sometimes against the enemy fighting ships. On their own, there was no prospect that they would stop the Nameless, but if they delayed them for even a single hour, then that was another hour for Earth to prepare. The Nameless had responded with ships and fighters and while losses had not yet been severe, they were creeping towards unsustainable. So this raid would go in supported by what for the strike boat crews was the reassuring bulk of supporting destroyers.

Reassuring for the boat crews, Commander Carol Berg thought to herself as she looked around the bridge of the *Mantis*, but not so reassuring for her or the rest of the men and women crewing the destroyers. There were too many things out there that could turn *Mantis* into chaff with a single hit – and they were heading towards three of them. The formation of ships had been approaching the space gate and its defenders for three days. Relative to the target, they'd dropped back into real space behind the planet's smallest moon. Before they came out from behind the moon's shadow, they'd made several discrete course corrections, then cut power and gone ballistic. Since then it had been a waiting and watching game. With missiles that outranged the weapons of any human ship by a wide margin, encounters with the Nameless were always about getting close enough to fire, without being crippled or destroyed on the approach. But if a human ship did get to gun range, then the advantage shifted decisively in their favour. Compared to the heavy plasma cannons of a battleship, *Mantis*'s four guns were peashooters. But if a Nameless ship was to find itself within fifty thousand kilometres of the destroyer, then there was nothing the aliens had yet fielded that *Mantis* couldn't shoot full of holes. The trick was getting there. Using their jump drive to drop in on top of the target was a high-risk tactic that both sides had occasionally used, but since ships spent most of their time close to planets where the gravitational effect known as the mass shadow prevented a ship from jumping in or out, that option wasn't available very often. Again the Nameless had an advantage; their drives allowed them to jump about a third closer than their human counterparts. So that left the raiders with only the discrete insertion and a slow, nerve-wracking approach.

Berg suddenly yawned and her helmet visor fogged up for a moment before her survival suit's environmental control kicked in and compensated. Standard doctrine called for most of a ship's compartments to be depressurised before combat to reduce secondary damage if they were hit, so survival suits were a necessary evil. The fleet's suits were in theory able to keep a person alive for three continuous days, twice that if their electrical systems were plugged into the ship's power grid and assuming you'd had time to put in place the necessary plumbing. Still it wasn't many people's first choice and after a few hours, personal performance would tend to degrade. Looking at her watch Berg realised she'd been on the bridge for nearly six hours, enough time for fatigue to become a factor.

"Lieutenant Mintz, I'm going below for a while." She didn't bother adding: 'call me if anything happens.'

"Yes, Captain."

Popping the seat restraints she floated out of her chair and pushed off towards the rear hatch. Moving down the passageway she noted that at least one off duty crewmember had opted to sleep in his bunk, in his survival suit rather than one of the few crew compartments that still had pressure – probably one of those occasional oddballs who claimed survival suits were comfortable. After waiting for the airlock to cycle, Berg pulled herself through into the sickbay.

"Hello, Skipper. Is it business or pleasure that brings you to my door?" asked Surgeon Lieutenant Norrett.

"Just stretching out, Doctor," Berg replied as she opened her visor. "Just before I hit the bunk for a few hours."

"Of course. Do you need anything?"

"No, if I took pills to go to sleep I'd need pills to wake up again," she replied with a slight frown. "Are many people using them?"

"No not really," the Doctor replied mildly. "Although modern pills don't have those kinds of side effects, not if the dosage is worked out with sufficient care."

"Any other problems I should be aware of?"

"Nothing unusual, although from my point of view things would be a good deal easier if we could spin up the centrifuge. Certain operations are tricky enough without worrying about having to stop bits from floating out," he replied.

"I'm sure it does, but having a spun up centrifuge would also make it more likely you'd have casualties to treat. We'll be entering their missile range in another four hours, the attack goes in another hundred minutes after that."

"I'm all ready for it here, Captain," Norrett replied with a nod.

Privilege of rank meant Berg's cabin still had pressure. Operational realities meant the temperature was set below the point of comfort. But after six hours on the bridge, it was still a relief to be able to take off her helmet and neck dam. Peeling away the top half of her suit, she strapped herself into the bunk. *Mantis* had been home for nearly two years and by now Berg should have been expecting to take the next step in her career, probably a six months tour as second-in-command on board a cruiser or battleship, before being offered the captaincy of her own cruiser. However, that was a peacetime promotion track. Wartime was different and Berg had been fighting this war longer than most.

As second-in-command on board the cruiser *Mississippi*, she'd been there when they first encountered the Nameless. Her career survived the subsequent enquiry and she'd then been appointed to

Mantis and dispatched to the frontier base of Baden – just in time for the Nameless assault that no one had seen coming. *Mantis* came out of those first desperate battles with barely a scratch and since then had served on the Junction Line right up to the day the Nameless cracked it open. Some of the crew had taken to calling their destroyer 'Magic-Man', but to Berg that seemed like tempting fate. One should never call attention to luck when she shows favour, just in case she took offence. If Earth made it to the end of the spring, she probably would get her captaincy. The odds were though that she'd be staying in *Mantis* unless filling a dead man's boots somewhere else.

They were six and a half hours from contact, assuming their arrival in the system hadn't been detected. If that assumption was wrong, then the Nameless could well be waiting for them and that was why this strike group was composed of small, relatively expendable ships. It was also why there probably wasn't a single commanding officer present that had slept properly in days. Berg settled for cleaning her face with a wet wipe, brushing her teeth and trying to force a brush through her dirty and matted hair, before pulling a blanket around herself and attempting to sleep. She managed to doze for a few hours – enough to feel sharper. On the bridge nothing much had changed except that the countdown had dropped to two hours.

"Any movement at all?" she asked Mintz as she buckled herself in.

"None, Captain," he replied with a quick shake of his head.

On the main holo, stationed around the space gate, were three Nameless escorts. All sitting at rest relative to the planet, they were the reason for the strike group's slow approach. If the gate had been left unattended, then a quick flyby would have been enough to destroy it or force its self-destruct systems to fire.

But the presence of the escorts offered both threat and opportunity. Three of them were enough to stand off the missile boats, but by throwing *Mantis* and her two squadron mates into the mix, they might be able to take out both the gate and the escorts. Of course the Nameless would replace both within a day, but if they had to leave more ships behind to protect the gates, then they would have that many fewer ships available to assault Earth.

"Any ideas on the new design features?" she asked, nodding towards the holo.

"None," Mintz replied

About a day earlier they'd noticed that two of the Nameless

escorts appeared to be slightly different from the standard pattern. There was a blister on the side of the hulls facing them and they assumed there was a matching one of the other side.

"It's not a question of resolution," Mintz continued. "We're getting good quality visuals but there isn't much to see."

He tapped a control and brought up a close-up of one of the escorts.

"We can see some welds but there isn't much more. A retrofit of some sort, but it could be anything from a mounting for a death ray to more space for the captain's drinks cabinet."

Berg smiled slightly at his heavy attempt at humour

"Anything from the *Scorpion*?"

"No. I guess Captain Liv doesn't believe he has anything to add."

Berg made no comment. There wasn't really much to say. Any news about the Nameless tended to be bad, but without some kind of information there wasn't much that could be said or done. Quite certainly, they couldn't break off an attack just because they saw something that might be unknown. In fact, quite the opposite – if they did, then they had to try to find out what it was. If that meant the hard way, well, that was just the way it had to be. At least she was on a destroyer – a real ship – and not one of those poor suckers on the missile boats.

"We've started running a firing solution plot," Mintz said after a long silence. "I know it's a little early but..."

"It doesn't do any harm," Berg cut him off, "just as long as we keep an eye out for anything else."

An hour and half later, Berg was starting to nod off again when a report came in on the command channel.

"Bridge, Sensors. Power spike! The gate is going active!"

In an instant Berg was fully alert. With a quick sweep of her eyes she covered the main holo and the countdown display. At current velocity they were still twenty-five minutes away from gun range and closer to forty for missiles. By going full power on the engines those figures would drop to ten and twenty. But the cap ship missiles of the three Nameless ships, would easily reach out this far. The *Mantis*'s four light plasma cannons were better at shooting down missiles than the larger versions mounted on cruisers and battleships, but they were still a poor alternative to the flak guns which were steadily superseding the heavy calibre railguns carried by the battle line ships. If the Nameless started shooting now, they might still push through to firing range, but it would likely cost them.

"The escorts?" she demanded.

"Negative movement. Missile ports are still closed."

"Bridge, Sensors. New contacts. Ship jumping in, bearing zero, zero, one, dash zero, one, one..."

Another voice cut across the first.

"Bridge, Sensors. Ships are coming through the gate!"

Berg felt adrenalin sizzle through her blood, blowing away her fatigue. On the holo, a dozen plus new contacts appeared, some around the gate and others filing through it. Berg flicked her intercom to ship wide.

"All hands! Close on stations!" she called. "Engines and Fire Control stand ready."

Then she switched back to the command channel.

"Tactical, give me a count and classifications. Now!"

"Confirmed, Captain. Working."

Berg clenched and unclenched her fists as she waited for the Tactical and Sensors Sections to work their way through a mass of new readings.

"Tactical, Bridge. Provisional count – thirteen new contacts, two cruisers, three escorts, eight gateship transports."

"Oh, hell," someone muttered across the command channel. They were right to curse. They had just gone from facing three cap ship missile launchers and twelve light launchers, to ten and thirty-two respectively. In terms of firepower, things had just decisively shifted against them.

"Must be a supply convoy coming through," Berg said through gritted teeth. "God damn their timing!"

"Coms, Bridge. Laser signal from *Scorpion*."

"My screen, Coms," Berg replied.

On the small screen of her command chair, the faces of Captain 'Bull' Liv and Commander Dorsey of the *Puma* appeared.

"Commanders, we're in the shits," Liv coarsely began. "We're in too close to break off. If we try it, we'll be taken apart before we can make it over the Red Line and jump away. So we'll have to plough straight though, lay down the hurt and hope we cause enough havoc to get clear. And when I say straight through, I mean straight fucking through. Stand by both of you for full orders."

The screen blanked out again before Berg could reply.

"Yes, sir," she muttered to herself but without rancour. Liv wasn't wrong. Unfortunately.

"Guns, stand by for direction," she ordered across the command channel. "Plan A just went out the airlock. Plan B is a frontal charge, then bug out in the confusion."

"Fire Control, Bridge. Understood."

On the holo the newly arrived ships were still milling around, but the three original escorts hadn't moved. With so many new arrivals at close quarters, their detection equipment might have been overwhelmed by the mass of engine emissions at such close quarters. Or their operators might be distracted, assuming they even had operators in any sense a human could recognise.

The movements of the convoy appeared to be dictated by the transports. They were circling round the space gate in a line astern formation.

"Sensors, Bridge. The space gate is moving. We are reading active thrusters. It is turning, three, four... stabilising at a turn of three degrees to port, vertical climb of two degrees."

The transports were definitely lining up on the gate, preparing to use it to jump away. In thirty minutes at most they would be gone again. After more than a year of war, they were still no closer to understanding how those damn gates, or Nameless jump drives in general, worked. After a jump, a human, or any of the other three known races, would be extending radiator panels, dumping waste heat they'd had to store in heat sinks during their time in jump space as fast as possible. But the Nameless ships, both transports and warships, had much smaller radiators. Since heat build up didn't appear to be a factor in their drives, why they seemed to hit the wall in terms of jump distance at about four point seven and a half light years was a mystery. God only knew what happened to the gateship transports when the gate they were to use got destroyed. They probably had to either divert to another or circle waiting for it to be replaced.

"Bridge, Coms. Download from Flag."

"My screen."

Mintz looked over her shoulder as she quickly skimmed down through it. There wasn't much — there hadn't been time for anything complicated. Still Berg read down with a growing sense of unease. When she glanced up, she could see matching alarm in Mintz's eyes.

"Captain Liv is clearly a man of his word," she observed as calmly as she could manage. "Bridge, Fire Control. I'm sending you firing instructions. Stand by to engage."

There wasn't time or the means for discussion, Liv was the man in charge and he'd made the call. Now they had to see how well it would work.

"Receiving," replied the gunner over the intercom.

"Depressurise all compartments. Lieutenant Mintz, you'd better get to Damage Control," Berg ordered as she tightened her seat restraints, "All hands, stand by for contact."

Another twelve minutes crept past, until finally the human formation crossed the imaginary line in space where their gun entered effective range. On the bridge of the *Mantis* no order was given, the commands having already been programmed into the computers. The four guns of each destroyer fired simultaneously and a split second later the engines crash started. If the Nameless got any warning from their Faster Than Light sensors, it wasn't enough. Four plasma bolts slammed into and through each of the two cruisers, while the third salvo smashed into the gate, just as a gateship passed through and started to fade away as it jumped.

"Target, heavy damage!" shouted Tactical.

On the holo, Berg could see that the Nameless ships had been thrown into confusion. The four gateships, which had been queuing to make their jump, were taking frantic evasive action as the shattered gate tumbled back towards them. The one that had been mid-jump when the gate was smashed somehow seemed to crash back into real space, disintegrating as it did so. But if the convoy escorts were thrown into disarray, the gate guards turned to bear.

"Missile ports opening, infrared spike. Contact separation, we have incoming!"

A cloud of new missiles appeared on the holo as the gate guards launched their cap ship and dual-purpose missiles.

"Stand by, Point Defence," Berg ordered through gritted teeth as their ship accelerated and the G load pressed her into the seat. *Mantis* could probably survive a hit or two from the smaller dual-purpose missiles, but a direct hit by a cap ship missile, would reduce any destroyer to vapours. But the destroyer guns weren't coming to bear on the approaching missiles, not yet. Instead their second salvo stabbed out at the three escorts that had arrived with the convoy. The gate guards would need at least two minutes to reload their smaller missiles, longer still the larger tubes. In that same time the convoy escorts could add to the fire against the approaching human ships if they were allowed to. In the trade off between attack and defence, Liv chose to attempt to kill ships rather than missiles.

An alarm sounded across the command channel as the Nameless missiles accelerated in.

"Point Defence, commence, commence, commence!" Berg barked out. "Countermeasures, full spread!"

Out in front of the formation, the two gunboats started to fire, laying down a barrage the approaching missiles would have to come through, while behind them the missile popped chaff to confuse the missile homing systems. Some missiles detonated as point defence found its mark, others lost their lock and veered away. Some got through.

One of the missile boats took a direct hit from a cap ship missile that was only marginally smaller than its target. The missile boat disappeared in a flash that consumed both the boat and one of its neighbours. The contact was so fast Berg barely had time to register their loss before the icon for *Scorpion* started blinking.

"Coms, Bridge. We've lost link up with *Scorpion*!"

"*Puma*?"

"Still online, Captain," Communications replied.

Berg glanced away from the holo and switched her screen to one of the external cameras. With the ship going full burn there was a lot of vibration, but she could see that *Scorpion*'s guns were still firing, as was point defence. But there was a ragged gouge in the hull that intersected with one of the centrifuges folded down pods. The ship wasn't turning or making any evasive manoeuvres. Instead it looked to be locked on the last set of programmed instructions. As she watched, the destroyer's main guns fired again. So hurt but not fatally, either the bridge or its personnel had been knocked out and as the next most senior officer...

"Coms, inform *Puma* I am in command." Berg snapped out as she looked back at the holo.

Liv's plan had called for the formation to make a slight turn to cross just astern of the Nameless ships. That manoeuvre could already be pre-programmed into *Scorpion*'s helm, However, chances were it needed activation, because if there were personnel losses or command lines cut, then they might not be able to turn. So if the rest did, then *Scorpion* would be left isolated and vulnerable. As it was, with *Scorpion*'s coms down, the three destroyers couldn't cross-link their fire control to ensure no overlap, so their firing effectiveness was already degraded.

"Helm, cancel course change. Maintain current heading."

Someone on the command net drew breath sharply.

"Skipper," said the helmsman, "that is dangerously close to…"

"Noted helmsman!" Berg cut him off, before adding quietly, "be ready to take evasive action."

If the helmsman replied she didn't hear him as her attention shifted to fire control. Quickly she assigned targets for the two destroyers and the missile boats.

"Coms! Upload to all ships' missile targets. Execute in twenty seconds."

"Understood, Skipper. Gunboats report fifty percent ammunition expended."

"Order them to fall back behind the missile boats to cover the retreat."

The timing was beyond tight. The two gunboats slid through the formation of the surviving eight missile boats just as the human ships crossed into missile range. Each boat salvoed off four missiles, while between them *Mantis* and *Puma* added another eight from their internal launchers. The missiles spread out as they bore down on the alien starships. The dual-purpose missiles that the Nameless now launched weren't aimed at the charging human ships, instead they homed in on their opposite numbers. In front of *Mantis*, missiles started to smash together

"Bridge, Sensors. New contacts, those escorts have just launched fighters! Two each!"

That answered the question, but Berg didn't have time to worry about it now. The two groups of ships were about to intersect. The Nameless vessels were still barely moving but no two of them were moving on the same track. The bridge collision detection warning started to scream.

"Helm, go manual!" Berg shouted.

The strike group flashed through the milling confusion of the Nameless ships.

"Cut power. Helm! Reverse face. Fire Control, fire at will!"

The bridge crew clung to their seats as the destroyer spun through one hundred and eighty degrees.

As *Mantis* coasted backwards, firing into the swiftly receding targets, Berg took stock of the situation. The first thing she noticed was the number of friendly blips was wrong.

"Sensors, I'm not seeing one of the gunboats. Where is it?"

There was a pause as the officer at the sensor control checked, then he wound back the computer records before turning back towards her with a downcast expression.

"I think they went into one of the gateships, Skipper," he said.

"Shit," Berg muttered.

On the holo, several Nameless ships were also missing. It looked like they'd got one of the cruisers, a couple of the escorts and all but one of the gateships. The four fighters seemed to be the only Nameless units attempting to actively engage them. The velocity at which the strike group had flashed past had left them floundering astern. With the human ships moving directly away from them, any missile their ships fired would be left trying to make a stern chase. They'd exhaust their fuel long before they reached their targets. The fighters were actively pursuing but it would take a lot more than four crude Nameless fighters to inconvenience two undamaged destroyers. But there were more vulnerable targets than the destroyers. The surviving gunboat only carried a single weapons mount, with limited ammunition. Even just four of those crappy fighters would overwhelm the gunboat, chase down the otherwise unarmed missile boats and gut them.

The Nameless tactics were continuing to evolve. At least this time the surprise hadn't been a painful one.

"Skipper, signal from *Scorpion*, voice only."

"Put it on," Berg ordered.

"Commander," Liv's voice crackled across the link, "we've recovered helm control from the engine room. We took splinter damage, which severed the control runs and internal communications. Update me on the situation."

"We've destroyed the gate, sir, and several enemy ships, with most of the remainder damaged. We're now outbound..."

"Can we go around for another pass? Finish them before they can jump?"

"Negative sir," Berg replied. "We've lost a gunboat and the enemy have put fighters up. The missile boats need *Mantis* and *Puma*. Without us the fighters will take them apart."

Even more pressing, they needed to get the damaged *Scorpion* clear of the combat zone but put that way, the Bull would probably insist on going back in, to prove some kind of point.

There was silence on the link.

"Alright, Commander, lead us out," Liv eventually agreed, but grudgingly.

Ten hours after Mantis and her strike group left, a reconnaissance boat made a prearranged pass through the system. It found the gate had already been replaced.

Chapter Two

The Few

15th November 2067

"Do you have anything else to add, Captain?" Admiral Clarence asked as he accepted her report.

"No sir, I don't believe so," Captain Faith Willis replied with a slight shake of her head.

A woman of average height and slender build, she presented the very image of a professional military officer. The three rings on her uniform sleeve had the shine of a new promotion.

"All right, Captain."

Clarence glanced at the computer screen and scrolled up and down aimlessly before sighing tiredly.

"Is there anything I can do to help? I might be able to lay my hands on a few more experienced ratings."

"Thank you sir, but I don't think so. Any newcomers at this stage would just add integration problems. Although if you have any experienced petty officers..."

Clarence shook his head.

"We'll manage then. Thank you, sir."

As she rose to leave, the Admiral spoke.

"As I think I've said to you before, Captain, good luck out there."

The shuttle trip was a short one but from Willis's position in the passenger compartment there was a lot to see. Earth's lower orbit was clogged with the ships of the fleet, planetary defence starforts, construction platforms of the orbital industries and scores of civilian vessels seeking the protection of their home world. If the grapevine was to be believed, certain government figures were using civilian ships to transport their families to the safety of the Dryad system. However as someone who'd nearly had her arse shot off there, Willis severely doubted it. No, if there was any place of safety at all, it was here on Earth.

The shuttle homed in on one of the smaller construction platforms and a few minutes later Willis was pulling herself along the station passageway. As she went, both her own personnel and those of the dock itself pushed past, carrying equipment and supplies. Passing a viewing port that faced down into the dock, Willis caught sight of the harshly lit vessel within. Although there was a lot to – God there was a lot to do – she pulled up at the port and pushed herself down until her boot magnets locked onto the deck plating. Leaning down on the rail she stifled a sigh.

There within, lay The *Black Prince*, second ship of what Headquarters had originally called the Emergency Construction Programme, before boldly rechristening them 'Warrior Class Cruisers.' Most ships within the fleet collected at least a couple of nicknames during their time, but the Warriors hadn't even gone into service before receiving their first. The crews and now even officers were already referring to them rather more accurately as 'Austerity Class Cruisers.' To an experienced eye like Willis's, it was easy to see why.

The first weeks of the war had seen losses more savage than even the most pessimistic planner had allowed for. The fleet's pre-war workhorse, the Myth Class, had on average each taken three and a half years to build. Their successors, the Statesman Class, required nearly four. But those planners had made allowances for at least some losses. Any war would likely be won or lost before a like-for-like replacement could be got into service. So instead, the fleet had constructed a number of basic space frames that could be finished much more quickly – in essence vessels that could be brought into service fast. But such speed of construction came at a price.

Black Prince wouldn't be the equal of the vessels she replaced. In terms of plasma cannons, a Myth class ship had four double gun turrets, while the Warriors got two triples. They did at least have flak guns – one double mount on each of the dorsal and ventral towers between the plasma cannons and the radar masts – which at least gave far better fields of fire than the Myth's sponson mounts. The planned missile launchers had been deleted with the internal volume given over to more magazine space for flak gun ammunition. So on paper they were packing about two thirds of the armament of a Myth with a matching reduction in ship size. But Willis thought to herself as she pushed off from the deck, bald statistics never told the whole story.

In time of war or peace, no military ever got everything it wanted and for the internationally funded Battle Fleet, that was especially true. There was a joke both inside and out of the fleet that during the Contact War, when the fleet closed on the enemy, it was to save money by getting its ammunition back. Certainly it was true to say that in peacetime, something had to be pretty much comprehensively broken before the fleet discarded it. When ships went in for maintenance and upgrade cycles, any equipment removed was stockpiled on the Moon. With the start of the war, those stockpiles had been opened and used to turn the stock hulls into functioning warships in a little over a year.

Black Prince's engines had originally belonged to members of the Continental class cruisers. Her six plasma cannons had been removed from the Myths during their first upgrade cycle, while the radar and passive sensor arrays had originally belonged to two entirely separate classes of destroyers. Not everything was old – the reactors at least were new constructions. Hell, if they'd tried to stick in second hand reactors, then God and all his angels could not have got her aboard. The armour plate was also new but the thickness was unspectacular and, with it attached to the surface of the hull rather than integrated into the structure, they weren't getting as much protection as might otherwise have been achieved for the mass. There was a part of Willis, specifically that part of her that loved new gadgets, which wanted to go into a corner and have a little cry when she thought about her new command. But then another part of her would sternly point out that compared her last command – the elderly cruiser *Hood* – *Black Prince* was a formidable warship.

Obviously alerted to her return, her two most senior officers were waiting for her at the personnel access hatch. Between them they summed up the duality in *Black Prince*'s crew. Her first officer, Lieutenant Commander Chuichi, was new to her and recently promoted. He seemed competent if slightly glum by nature. David Guinness, her Chief Engineer, was by contrast an old hand and veteran of the fighting around Dryad. He'd kept *Hood* going until the day the old ship was shot to pieces around them. Willis had always had suspicions he was overage for frontline service, but he was good at his job and what she didn't know, she didn't have to report. He along with about half the survivors from *Hood* had followed her to *Black Prince*. Chuichi was looking even more dour than usual. With his computer pad tucked under his arm, Guinness looked far more cheerful.

"Captain," Chuichi said as they both saluted.

"Gentlemen. Follow me please," Willis replied as she pulled herself past.

Climbing down into the centrifuge, they headed for officers' row.

"I've been informed that as of oh nine Hundred hours, we are formally on strength," she continued as she closed her cabin hatch. "Talk to the cook. We can't manage much of a commissioning ceremony, but ask him to do his best. The crew has worked hard up to now and they'll have to work even harder from here on in."

If such a thing was possible, Chuichi looked even gloomier.

"That's asking a lot," he said. "The crew are still getting used to the equipment."

In response, Guinness patted his computer pad, on which he had uploaded a copy of the ship's tech 'bible'.

"But Commander," he said, "the advantage of old equipment is it doesn't have any surprises to throw at us. All the kinks have been seen and we have the fixes on record, not to mention that a lot of my lads are used to older tech than this."

Chuichi let out a non-committal grunt.

"What about the rest of the squadron?" he asked.

"*Cetshwayo* and *Saladin* are also being commissioned. We are to be designated Cruiser Squadron Twenty Three. Commodore Dandolo on *Saladin* will be squadron commander and we are joining the Home Fleet."

"It is a lot to ask of any crew," Chuichi said morosely, "to go from commissioning to combat inside a few weeks."

"I know, Commander, but we aren't the only ones and well... a few weeks from now, we will be shot at. We can do it out there where we can shoot back or we can be sitting here where we can't. I know which one I would prefer."

The flak cruiser *Deimos* hung in geo stationery orbit over Mar's equator. Around her in matching orbits were another dozen ships, mostly civilian. There was a continuous cycle of shuttles leaving the ships, being passed on their way by those climbing away from the planet surface. Five years old and designed with a projected operational lifespan of twenty-five years, she should have been in her prime. But *Deimos* was now a hard used warhorse. Many hull plates showed the scars of minor strikes, others dished inwards from the force of near misses and a few were paler and cleaner – new plates covering repairs to major damage. On board, Commodore Ronan Crowe was making his way down to his cabin when a furious bellow erupted from the compartment ahead.

"For the love of sweet Jesus! Would you shut your yap hole! People are trying to fucking sleep!"

As Crowe passed through he caught sight of a couple of shocked civilians and a tired and irritated looking petty officer leaning out of a sleeping alcove. One of the civilians caught sight of Crowe and by his expression clearly expected him to discipline the petty officer. Crowe kept walking.

The ship's Bosun was waiting at the hatch to his cabin.

"Come in Benson," Crowe said as he passed. "So what have you got for me?" he added, as he threw his cap onto the bunk before absentmindedly scratching his balding crown.

For years he had wondered which he'd do first – go grey or bald, but it looked like his receding hairline would carry the day.

"We've found places for everyone so far, sir," Benson reported as he stood at parade rest, "but a couple of compartments are starting to look like tins of sardines."

"We won't have to put up with them for much more than a day Bosun."

"Sir, how many more are we getting? It's just that we are overtaxing life support as it is."

"How much redundancy do we have left?"

"The book says we can take another twenty warm bodies, but the book also says that we're badly overdue a full system purge and overhaul. If we suffer any kind of failure," Benson paused, "well then things will get a bit interesting, sir."

"In which case we'll declare an emergency and either head to Earth or offload them on someone else," Crowe replied as he checked his computer for any other messages. There were a few from Headquarters and one from his wife. He moved it to be looked at later, then winced as he noticed the previous one still showed as unread.

"A lot of the civvies have non-standard survival suits – cheap rubbish, which won't mate with our systems, sir," Benson persisted. "If we have to depressurise, we can't link them to a flow system. Some of them have small O2 tanks that give as little as twenty minutes..."

"Bosun, I appreciate your concerns, but we won't be in action before we drop them off. Our presence here is no more than a precaution. Lieutenant Shermer is due to bring another dozen from the surface, then that's us full."

"Yes, sir," the Bosun agreed in the resigned tone of a man who didn't agree but knew there was nothing to be gained by further argument.

"Still a few precautions won't hurt. Get a few hands to do carbon dioxide checks. Make sure we don't have foul spots. These people with cheap suits, make sure they are moved to sickbay if we have to depressurise."

When the Bosun was gone Crowe sat back in his chair and heaved a long sigh. It had certainly come to something when orbiting around Mars – pretty much Earth's back yard – was enough to leave some of the crew feeling exposed. But this crew had seen a lot, maybe even too much. The Massacre at Baden, Kite String, the defeat at and retreat from Junction – they been in the thick of it – and all in little more than a year. They'd seen the Nameless spring surprise after surprise on them: jump in capability far closer to a planet than any human ship could manage, FTL sensors, mass driver missiles and most recently fighters. It was no wonder that in the minds of too many, the Nameless were becoming less a military opponent and more an all-powerful bogeyman. We need a victory, and we need it soon, Crowe thought. He then smiled unhappily to himself. The next battle would be fought in the skies above Earth and if they didn't win that one – well, that would be the end of all humanity's problems.

Turning his chair, Crowe stared at the hologram being projected against the cabin wall. The powerful cameras mounted on *Deimos*'s outer hull could make out robots far below, hard at work darkening the surface and pumping out CO_2. There weren't many people on Mars – less than two thousand, all part of what was usually referred to as The Great Experiment. But now as the human race contracted inwards, back towards the world of its birth, it was being abandoned. Around Saturn the forces of planetary defence were being strengthened, while the orbital hydrogen processing facilities were being evacuated of all but the few brave souls willing to remain behind to form skeleton crews. The rest headed for Earth to be with their families.

Family; Crowe glanced toward the photo of his wife. Was it wrong that he felt no regret that if the end came, they wouldn't be together? No, he'd been the one to start this and he would be here for the end. *All I ever wanted was to explore.*

"Lieutenant Shermer, ma'am, we have a slight problem in the main habitat," the voice of the senior petty officer crackled across the radio.

"What kind of problem, PO?" Alanna asked as she stood with her back to the compound, enjoying the stark beauty of the Martian landscape, where a dust devil briefly swirled before collapsing again.

"Well, it's a bit political, ma'am," came the reply.

Out of my pay grade, Alanna mentally translated.

"Alright, PO, I'm on my way," she replied.

Political complications were exactly why junior officers were sent on these kinds of jobs. Nodding to the shuttle pilot who was busy prepping for take off, she set out across the compound.

The walk wasn't far, but in the unfamiliar Martian gravity only one third of Earth's, Alanna was breathing heavily by the time she reached the main personnel airlock. The settlement, sited in the shadow of Olympus Mons, was the administrative and maintenance centre for terraforming activity in this quarter of the planet. She probably could have, probably should have insisted they just drop everything and get into the damn shuttle. But they wanted to make sure anything that could potentially go wrong in the next few weeks was either dealt with or shut down. Various flyers, flimsy things that would never be able to fly in Earth gravity, flitted about, moving materials into the central compound.

Mostly the evacuation had gone quietly. The researchers and technicians accepted that on a planet with no orbital defences, it was the only choice. If the terraforming worked as claimed, then someday Mars might be a garden world on which a person could stroll about in nothing but their skin – if the notion took them. But that was decades away and in the here and now, Alanna waited patiently as the habitat's airlock cycled.

"Alright," she said to the two men waiting just inside the lock as she pulled off her helmet. "What's the problem?"

"This gentleman," the petty officer said before the civilian could open his mouth, "wants to remain here. He even has a couple of others persuaded. He also has a piece of paper."

The PO's tone suggested this last point was the most heinous crime of all.

"Lieutenant," the civilian said with a polite smile, "I am Professor Scalzi, the head administrator of this outpost. Could I prevail upon you to be allowed to speak privately?"

He was an elderly man, with sparse white hair and a friendly smile.

"Alright, Professor. But it will have to be quick."

"Of course."

Scalzi led her to what was clearly his office and waved her towards a chair before pushing his own from behind the desk next to her.

"Lieutenant, what your man told you was fundamentally correct. I and two of my colleagues would like to remain behind."

"I'm sorry, Prof..." Alanna began.

"Please, hear me out at least."

Alanna settled back into her seat as he continued.

"I'm aware that the orders from your superiors and mine are for the complete evacuation of Mars, but I would ask you to in part set those orders aside. Lieutenant, I don't know whether you have had the opportunity to follow our work, but I would like you to understand that the terraforming of the planet is at a delicate phase. We are approaching the tipping point at which the process starts to become self-sustaining. We only have to get the atmosphere a little thicker and a little warmer, for bacteria to be able to work. But at this moment the process still needs monitoring and adjustments. If we all up sticks and leave, what we have achieved so far will start to degrade. We could lose ten years of work in months."

"It's not likely to be as long as months. If we drive..." Alanna bit her lip. "When we drive off the Nameless, you can return here. It should be no more than weeks."

"Oh, Lieutenant, I don't doubt that the battle for Earth will be over in weeks at most, but in its aftermath, I don't believe getting anyone back to Mars will be a priority. That is why I and my colleagues wish to remain – as a skeleton crew if you will."

"Professor, do you understand, you won't be safe here? I don't know the exact plans, Professor, but I can say with certainty that the fleet won't defend Mars and that there is no planetary defence here. If you put out a Mayday, there won't be a response."

"I understand that. Battle Fleet made it very clear that we are trusting to good fortune. But I want to make something equally clear to you. I have been on this planet for the last nine years of my life and I gave another ten before that in preparation for coming here. I fully expected, even before this war, to be buried here. I know the odds you and your courageous comrades are facing. We have to put as brave a face as possible on this, but I know they aren't good. If the worst happens, well, being on Earth won't change anything."

"Sir, is there no one there you would want to be with?" Alanna asked quietly.

"No, there isn't. This world became home a long time ago," Scalzi replied, before adding, "not to mention that after nearly ten years in one third Earth gravity, I'd probably break a hip within an hour of landing." He handed over a neatly folded sheet. "This is the piece of paper that so offended your man. It is to confirm that I and three of my colleagues have decided of our own free will, not to evacuate and we absolve Battle Fleet of any responsibility with regard to our safety."

Alanna sat for a moment, thinking, then reached out and took the sheet.

"My commander won't be happy," she said. "I don't have the authority to force you get on that shuttle. But I strongly advise you to do so."

"I – we, choose not to."

Alanna sat back in her seat and opened the sheet. At the bottom were three neat signatures. "All right Professor," she eventually said. "I wish you luck."

"Thank you, Lieutenant. I hoped you would understand."

"Maybe a little, Professor, but I've got out of the habit of thinking long-term," Alanna replied with a sigh. "When we leave, go dark. Don't wait for the Nameless to arrive. If you wait until they do, it will be too late. Shut down all transmitters, beacons and reactors, if you can. Just run at the very minimum. With a little luck, you won't look like you're worth a missile."

"Why did you let them stay, ma'am?" one of the shuttle pilots asked as they climbed away from Olympus Mons. "The Council gave us full authority to evacuate."

As the shuttle had lumbered down the runway, she'd seen three tiny suited figures standing outside the compound waving.

"When this is over, Lieutenant," Scalzi said as they stood at the

21

edge of the compound, "come back here. I'll give you the full fifty-dollar tour. I'll make sure you see the real Mars, what it is and what it will be, not just the tourist nonsense."

"Because he thinks we can win," Alanna replied quietly, "and I don't want him to be wrong.

Lost in thought, his cold blue eyes staring into space and his spare frame ramrod straight, Admiral Paul Lewis stood on the very spot where, a little over two years before, he had watched the cruiser *Mississippi* limp home after that first fateful encounter with the Nameless. A year after that, he'd led the Home Fleet out for the great clash at Alpha Centauri. As the Home Fleet repaired and rebuilt, he had seen many ships set off to fight only to return as broken vessels.

Two years and yet not enough time, not close to enough time.

The last twelve months had seen dozens of new defence projects started, as Battle Fleet attempted to adapt to the war it now found itself desperately fighting. Some of the projects – the jump missiles and parasite fighters – held great promise. But others, such as the cold plasma shielding, were so wildly ambitious that Lewis couldn't help but wonder what the hell their proponents were thinking. But it didn't matter – two years wasn't enough time for a project to go from concept to development, then through production and into service.

Turning, Lewis looked into the brightly lit space of the shipyard. The battleship *Warspite*, his flagship, lay in the most distant berth, her refit finished. She was now completing her final loading and would within hours be moving out to join the fleet. Alongside her lay one of the few new projects to reach fruition, the barrage ship *Minstrel*. Built on freighter chassis, each side of the hull disposed forty short, low velocity railguns. At maximum rate of fire, *Minstrel* could lay down a box barrage no missile could get through and empty her magazines in less than eight minutes.

No, when the Nameless arrived, there would be no new wonder weapons. Battle Fleet would have to fight with the same armaments that had come up short so many times before.

"The breakthrough at Junction Line three weeks ago, has resulted in a drastic change in the strategic situation that is not in our favour," Admiral Wingate told the Council. An African-American in his mid-sixties, he was the fleet's senior military officer. Despite the faded scars of old burns and a maimed hand, until two years previously he had looked like a man ten years younger. Now the reverse was true. "Unlike their opening advance last year, this new the Nameless offensive has been methodical rather than a blitzkrieg."

The Council chamber was near silent, disturbed only by the hum of the holograms. On the far side of the table sat the hologramatic forms of the heads of United States, Argentina, India, China, Japan, Great Britain and France. In the two years since the first contact with the Nameless, this room had seen many briefings. The means by which the war would be prosecuted had been subject to both discussion and argument. All the while as the war ground on, humanity's position weakened.

"While we cannot be sure of their exact strength, or their timing, we can be certain that within the next three weeks the Nameless will arrive in this solar system with a fleet that will outnumber and outgun our own," Wingate continued. "Ladies and Gentlemen, I will not lie to you. What we face is a strategic nightmare and what may well amount to a tactical, no-win scenario."

"So," asked President Clifton, "can we expect an immediate direct attack on Earth?"

"No, Madam President. I do not believe Earth will be subject to an immediate frontal assault, something I say with considerable regret," Wingate replied. "With the combined strength of the Home and Second Fleets, plus the starforts and ground-based planetary defence fighters, such an assault could be stood off. In fact, given the relative fragility of Nameless warships compared to our own, a direct assault would give us the best chance of winning a decisive victory. This is something we have to assume the Nameless themselves are well aware of. While they have never demonstrated any reluctance to suffer casualties, it is unlikely they will seek a battle that plays to our strengths."

"So what do you believe their strategy will be?" British Prime Minister Layland asked quietly.

"To a certain extent, sir, it depends on what their long and short term objectives are," Wingate replied. "If our swift eradication is their primary objective, then they may be willing to take a more forceful approach to destroy Battle Fleet and our planetary defences. Once they control Earth's orbit, orbital bombardment will sterilise the planet within days. If they want Earth with a still functioning biosphere, then the intensity of any bombardment must be reduced. However, with control of orbit, none of the national militaries could mount an effective defence for long. Any large troop formations could be picked apart by orbital fire. This approach would expose the Nameless to a more long running campaign with higher casualties."

"So there is a chance of them getting bogged down in an insurgency type conflict?" someone asked.

"No, not really," Wingate said shaking his head. "A classic insurgency has fighters operating within and concealed by a civilian population. As we know from the Centaur planet, any civilian population controlled by the Nameless would be liquidated. Military forces that could survive would have to remain hidden within wilderness regions."

"So in other words, most of the population of Earth would be slaughtered, with a few survivors running for the rest of their lives," Clifton said sombrely.

"Yes, ma'am. If the Nameless achieve Earth orbit, then we have already lost. But direct assault is probably not the way they will choose to go. I and my staff believe that for the Nameless, unless they are subject to time constraints we are not aware of, siege is the most likely strategy."

"Saturn. Cut us off from Saturn, you mean?" Clifton asked.

"Yes, ma'am," Wingate replied. "Over three quarters of Earth's power is now generated by hydrogen harvested from Saturn. Currently jump-capable tug ships are moving slow-boat tankers to Earth. How much information the Nameless have on the infrastructure of this solar system, is currently unknowable. But once they have units in the system, it will be impossible to conceal."

"If the starforts around Earth and Saturn could hold off a direct assault, could we run convoys in and out?" the Indian Prime Minister asked.

"Sir, while we believe that the planetary defence units around Saturn could stand off all but the heaviest assault, we also believe that the Nameless will be reluctant to put such a force into a mass shadow as deep as Saturn's, since to do so, would run the risk of being caught by our mobile units where they couldn't jump away. Unfortunately, they don't need to take out the harvesting facilities. Earth – with its much shallower Mass Shadow, they could assault. Therefore the majority of our mobile units will have to remain around Earth to provide close defence. That would leave only a small number of ships free for convoys and the Nameless would see any convoy climbing out of the Mass Shadow. They would have all the time needed to intercept it. To guarantee their safety, we would have to send the whole fleet – the same ships also needed to defend Earth. Just cutting us off from Saturn will be enough."

Wingate shifted uncomfortably, then continued.

"Battle Fleet's strategic fuel reserves will last no more than thirty days under normal usage. But that figure will drop sharply when those ships are engaged in combat. If we have access to the various national reserves, that figure can be extended, but once we are cut off from Saturn, Earth and the fleet are living on borrowed time."

"So they can wait until Earth is protected only by a fleet of powerless hulks," the Chinese representative said. "Therefore, we must ask – how does the fleet propose to avoid this?"

"Yes, we clearly have a window after the Nameless arrive during which we can meet their fleet with our own," Clifton said. "How does the fleet plan to use that window?"

"Unfortunately, ma'am, that is where the situation becomes nightmarish," Wingate said in an uncompromising tone. "We know that heavy casualties hold no fear for the Nameless. We also know that their economic strength is such that they can replace a lost fleet. We can't. This means that simply charging out to meet them in a mutual massacre of our fleets, would make our destruction inevitable a year or two later. If we are to win, then it has to be a crushing victory. Something we have so far been unable to deliver."

"What does Battle Fleet propose to do then?" Clifton asked.

There was silence on the military side of the table.

"We won't lie to the Council," Wingate said heavily, "we are still actively considering all possible options. We are currently massing the bulk of the fleet around Earth. A few elements are being retained at Rosa and Hydra Stations to harass the flanks of the Nameless breakthrough. Several others are being withdrawn from Dryad."

It was a non-answer that the career politicians of the Council recognised, but they also realised there was nothing to be gained by pointing it out. The militaries of individual nations were being mobilised, states of emergency had been declared and martial law was already in place in a dozen cities. If changes to the leadership of Battle Fleet could have achieved anything, that time had come and gone.

"I appreciate your candour, Admiral," Clifton said. "So I need you to answer this question: what are our odds?"

Wingate didn't reply for moment.

"The truth is... the truth is that we will need to beat the odds to be still here in six months."

There was a kind of collective sigh in the chamber.

"Is there anything we can do to improve those odds?"

"Anything that can be done is being done. The only thing I can add is that I have faith in the officers who will lead this fight. They are the best that are available to us."

"I see," Clifton said before looking up and down the Council side of the table.

"I assume you remember the discussion of three months ago?"

Wingate took a long, slow breath.

"The Lazarus Protocol, ma'am?"

"Yes. I believe the time has come to activate it." Clifton again looked up and down the table. "Does anyone here object?"

"Is there sufficient time?" the President of France asked quietly.

"Yes, sir, there is," Wingate replied. "The preparations have been made. The ships needed have been moved to their start positions. Detailed orders are ready to be issued to the necessary officers."

"Is there any knowledge of this outside your office?"

"No, Madam President, but they will need to be told."

"No earlier than they absolutely have to," Clifton snapped before sitting back. "I'm sorry, Admiral, we know your concerns. We know that they are valid ones, but this... this will be a very difficult thing for the public to swallow, so it will be announced at a moment of the Council's choosing."

"Very well, ma'am," Wingate said. "I have made my objections, ones I continue to stand by, but I will not waste the Council's time repeating them."

"There is one final matter," Prime Minister Layland said.

"I'm not sure that..." Clifton began.

"With respect, I am," Layland said, before turning back to Wingate. "Admiral, it has been agreed among the industrialised nations that whatever else happens, we will not suffer the same fate as the Centaurs. The human race will not be marched into extermination camps. If the Nameless make planetary landings, those landing zones will be hit with all means still at our disposal – up to and including nuclear weapons. If the Nameless take this planet, then all they will gain is a radioactive wasteland."

Chapter Three

Ghost Ship

20th November 2067

Crowe glanced up briefly in response to the tap on the hatch. "Come in."

Alanna entered and came to attention. "You asked to see me, sir."

"At ease, Lieutenant," Crowe said looking up from his work. As usual her face was completely blank. The last time she had been in this cabin was when he'd chewed her out for leaving the civvies on Mars. He'd expected to receive orders to go back and drag them out, but it appeared that higher authority had decided they'd made their bed. Instead *Deimos* had received something completely unexpected and, in its own way, just as unwelcome.

"Lieutenant, we've received orders from Headquarters that relate to you," he started. "With immediate effect you are being transferred off *Deimos*. This was not a transfer I requested."

"I see, sir," she replied. "Where am I going?"

"You've probably heard about the new light carriers being rushed into service."

"Yes sir," Alanna replied.

There was a slight tension in her stance now as she guessed at what might be coming. Crowe plunged on.

"Now they've been commissioned, fleet is trying to put together fighter groups for them. We are considered a lower priority for fighters, so we've been ordered to hand over our most experienced crew, which obviously includes you. You'll be replaced by a rookie crew just out of training."

Alanna looked puzzled for a moment, then surprised.

"Lieutenant?"

"I'm sorry sir. I'm used to thinking of myself as a newbie," she said.

"Sorry, Lieutenant, but you are a long way from that now."

"Where am I to report to, sir?"

"You're to report to the Aldrin Lunar facility at oh ten hundred hours tomorrow," Crowe replied. "You're also taking your fighter and weapons controller with you."

"I see, sir, thank you for telling me. I'll start to make preparations."

"There is one last thing, Lieutenant."

Crowe paused. He wished he'd been enough of a coward to leave out this part and let her find out for herself.

"One of the new carriers – the one you're assigned to – was christened *Norge*. Headquarters has decided to change her name. From tomorrow, she will be the new *Dauntless*."

Alanna made no reply, but he saw the muscles in her arms tighten and guessed that behind her back, she had clenched her fists.

"Is the transfer permanent, sir?" she asked after several moments, in a tightly controlled voice.

"As permanent as anything is," he replied, observing her closely. "I will be requesting your return but realistically, you're now too experienced for this post."

Crowe stopped there, genuinely unsure of what more to say.

"Thank you, sir, for telling me. I appreciate it. Lieutenant Malm... he... he can be counted on to look after the new pilot," she stopped and then abruptly put out her hand. "It has been a pleasure to serve with you and I wish you good luck, sir."

"Thank you, Lieutenant," Crowe replied as he stood to shake the proffered hand. "You've done well here, Lieutenant, and I'm sorry to say someone down in Headquarters appears to have been reading my reports. This is a step up for you and I wish you good luck on your new ship. You are dismissed."

She should have saluted before leaving and clipped the edge of the hatch as she went out. Neither was lost on Crowe.

The concern he had been trying to keep from his face was now plainly apparent. He'd felt the tremble in her grip. Fifteen months ago, during the first Nameless offensive against Earth, a green as grass Lieutenant Alanna Shermer had been finishing her final assessments aboard the fleet's elderly training carrier *Dauntless*. After the battle of Alpha Centauri, when the dust settled, *Dauntless*'s fighter group, the carrier herself and even her escort, were all destroyed. Of the hundreds of men and women that made up the crews, the Lieutenant was the sole survivor, pulled out of the wreck of a shattered fighter.

God knew, there had been days where Crowe felt he was only just holding it together. But in the year plus that the Lieutenant had been under his command, Crowe had always sensed that for her, that was what every day felt like. Now some arsehole in Headquarters had decided to put her onto a ship named after the very one on which she had probably experienced the worst days of her life. He'd put in a complaint, but it hadn't fitted into any neat box, so by the time someone with a brain looked at it, she would be on *Dauntless*. He could contact her new captain, but Crowe shook his head as he rejected the thought. He couldn't do that, not when all he had were his reservations. Reservations weren't enough to call into question the courage of a fellow officer who had already served with such distinction. No, all he could hope for was that she could keep holding it together.

Alanna slammed her fist into the cabin wall just hard enough to hurt. Leaning forward, she pressed her forehead against the wall, feeling the cool of the metalwork.

"It's just a ship, just another fucking ship," she whispered to herself.

Through the metal she could feel the distant throb of the generators and the hum of the atmospheric recyclers. She squeezed her eyes tightly shut, but it did nothing to block out the memories. The fighter squadron on *Dauntless* hadn't just been colleagues – they'd been comrades and friends, the centre around which her world orbited. They'd been the people she'd watched die, unable to do anything to save them and in the end, she'd failed even to join them.

Alanna straightened sharply as she heard the hatch start to open and turned towards her packing, which also put her back to the hatch.

"Oh hello, Alanna," said the gunner as he side slipped into the tiny cabin. "Thought you were second watch today?"

"No, I've been taken off the rotation."

"Oh?"

"I'm being transferred out."

"That so? Well good luck with that," he grunted as he pulled off his jacket. "A lot of last minute transfers going through, before the shit hits the fan."

Of all the officers on *Deimos* she found the gunner the easiest to deal with. He'd always seemed to accept she didn't want to get to know people. Either that or he was just terminally uncurious.

"Do you know where you're heading yet?" he asked, as he flopped onto his bunk.

"Yes. One of the new carriers."

"Nice. Back among your own kind."

Alanna made no reply.

"I'll miss old *Deimos*," Petty Officer Kristen Schurenhofer said conversationally as their Raven class fighter, *D for Dubious*, climbed out of the Moon's gravity well. "Still, Skipper, a change is as good as a rest."

"If you say so," Alanna replied morosely.

Buzz Aldrin base had been a hive of activity, with transfers to and from various fleet ships, national military personnel transiting to planetary defence installations around Saturn and evacuated civilians en route back to Earth. Alanna and Schurenhofer had spent an uncomfortable night in a converted exercise hall with three score others. The time had both dragged and seemed to fly past far too fast. Now they were on their way, orbiting around the Moon on a course that would bring them onto an intercept.

"Well, on a carrier we're likely to be flying more than escort missions," Schurenhofer said. "Not to mention I won't have to listen to jokers in the petty officers' mess claiming I'm not doing anything because I spend half my time in a fighter."

"You never said anything about that before."

"Not the business of an officer. Besides, it sort of stopped after Kite String. The shit I was getting the most attitude from was in the hangar when they pulled what was left of poor old Racklow out of his fighter."

Their conversation was interrupted by a beep from Schurenhofer's control panel.

"Entering *Dauntless*'s approach lane," she reported.

Alanna responded automatically. "*Dauntless* flight control, this is fighter *D for Dubious*, transfer in. Request approach authorisation and docking instruction."

"*D for Dubious*, this is *Dauntless* flight control. Approach authorised. Dock at Hangar Four. Over."

Alanna made no reply.

"*Dubious*, are you receiving? Over," the radio repeated.

Schurenhofer glanced over at her and then activated the radio.

"*Dauntless* control, this is *Dubious*, Hanger Four we are on approach. *Dubious* over and out," she responded. "You know, Skipper, if a cigar is sometimes just a cigar, then a name is sometimes just a name," she added, before glancing again at Alanna.

"I didn't ask for your opinion, Petty Officer," Alanna responded coldly.

"And I didn't ask for a pilot with survivor guilt issues coming out her ears, but hey, here we are," Schurenhofer replied. "Believe me I would happily kick the ass of whoever assigned us to this ship, but if you decide to zone out because of a name, you'll get yourself killed and more importantly, me to. You've done a decent job of keeping us alive so far and I'd rather you keep it that way."

"You don't know what it was like out there," Alanna snapped at her. "You weren't there!"

"Nope, I sure wasn't," Schurenhofer agreed. "The fact that I'm still alive is proof of that. But I know what it's like out here now. I know I've got a whole bunch of plans that sort of hinge on me staying alive."

"You done?"

"Possibly."

"Will you turn the cockpit voice recorder back on then?" Alanna asked.

"Only if I'm sure I don't have to say anything else that could get me court martialed."

"Well, that would be one way out of this fighter."

"True," Schurenhofer agreed, "and probably into one flown by some rookie with both a brain and penis, but only enough blood to run one at a time."

The navigation panel gave a beep as they started their final approach.

"A cigar is just a cigar? Where the hell do you get this stuff?" Alanna muttered as she switched *Dubious* to manual. "But if you do find out who assigned us here," she added, "you hold him, I'll hit him."

As the hangar door closed, Schurenhofer busied herself putting *Dubious* through the shut down sequence. Outside a couple of deck hands were getting magnetic couplings into place. Alanna hadn't wanted to look much at *Dauntless*, but it was hard not to look at a ship you were actively attempting to dock with. From what she could see, the new *Dauntless* bore only the most passing resemblance to her lost predecessor. Her basic hull had been taken from pre-war stock, which was also being used for the new Austerity class cruisers. Human fighter carriers had always gone for individual box hangars attached externally to the main hull. Unlike a launch bay built into the main body, it meant in theory no single hit could cripple the carrier's entire launch and recovery capability. *Dauntless* was no exception in that regard, but she did show her cruiser roots. Just forward of the main radar towers, there was a second pair, each mounting a flak battery. The old *Dauntless* had carried only a limited point defence grid, relying instead on either her escort or distance to keep her safe. But this ship was meant to survive getting into harm's way.

As Alanna and Schurenhofer climbed out of *Dubious*, the ship's bosun met them.

"Lieutenant," he said as he saluted, "the Squadron Commander wants to see you straight away, if you would follow me please."

"Alright," Alanna replied, "Kristen?"

"Got it, Skipper," Schurenhofer replied as she took Alanna's pack. "I'll go find out where flight crews live on this tin can."

Another officer was waiting outside the Squadron Commander's office when Alanna arrived. The bosun tapped on the door.

"Sir, they're both here."

"Send them in."

"Lieutenant Alanna Shermer reporting as ordered, sir," she said, saluting.

"Lieutenant Nikolai Udaltsov," said the other in a strong Russian accent.

The Squadron Commander gave them both a baleful look, before nodding them towards a pair of spare chairs.

"First welcome aboard the *Dauntless*," he said in a decidedly unwelcoming tone. "My name is Squadron Commander Jules Dati. I am your new commanding officer and that is as much time as we can spare for pleasantries."

Alanna wanted to look to see what Udaltsov made of the bizarre welcome, but forced herself to keep her gaze front and centre.

"I expect you are both aware this ship is newly commissioned. However, the Headquarters has informed the Captain that we are expected to report ourselves as combat worthy within the next two weeks."

Alanna heard a sharp intake of breath beside her. Dati flicked towards Udaltsov with all the precision and warmth of a weapons fire control system.

"You have something to say, Lieutenant?" he asked.

"That will be a very tough schedule to meet, sir," Udaltsov carefully ventured.

"Yes, it is," Dati replied almost mildly, before frowning. "However if *Dauntless* is not ready it will not be because my fighters have come up short. Are we entirely clear on that?"

"Yes sir," Alanna and Udaltsov choroused.

"Good," Dati said. "The rest of the squadron will arrive in six hours. They are all newly trained pilots, from the training carrier Kiev Flyer."

"I'm sorry, sir? New pilots?" Alanna interrupted. "I thought I was joining an established squadron."

"What on earth made you think that, Lieutenant?" Dati replied coldly. "The fleet does not have enough fighters or crews. Headquarters is not willing to strip half a dozen cruisers of their integrated fighter complement to fill *Dauntless*'s hangars. It is as much as I have been able to achieve to get you two to serve as flight leaders. The rest of the squadron are new pilots and they will be looking to you for leadership. You are both temporarily promoted to Lieutenant Commanders, effective immediately. But be certain that if you come up short I will make sure you regret it." Dati looked at his watch. "You have a few hours of liberty before the rest of the squadron arrives. I suggest you use them to familiarise yourself with the ship. You are both dismissed."

"Lord mother," Udaltsov muttered as Dati's door closed behind them. "When they commissioned the *Yorktown* Class carriers, it was a year before they were considered combat worthy."

Alanna shrugged as she started to walk down the passageway.

"I was just wondering," Udaltsov continued as he followed behind. "At the end of the Great Patriotic War, when the Red Army closed in on Berlin, is this what it felt like for the defenders?"

Alanna looked up at him. His tone wasn't defeatist, more one of honest curiosity.

"Alanna Shermer," he then said, half to himself. "Where do I know that name from?"

"I'm the only survivor from the last *Dauntless*," she replied.

Udaltsov gave her a blank look for a moment – then started to look deeply uncomfortable. "Oh I see."

"You'd have heard about it soon unless the grapevine suffered one hell of a breakdown. More recently I've been on the *Deimos*. You?"

"I'm formerly of the *Cerberus*. We only arrived back from Rosa Station three days ago. It is fair to say my captain was not pleased at my removal."

"I think mine wasn't sure whether to be pissed off or relieved. I was senior pilot on *Deimos*. How about you?"

"I've been senior for the last four months."

Alanna nodded – a dead man's boots promotion like so many.

"So we're supposed to be leading flights of four, but both of us are only used to flying flights of two." Alanna paused and sighed. "I guess we might as well see what we have to work with," she said, opening a hatch into the ships galley. "Err... I think we've taken a wrong turn somewhere."

During the night *Dauntless* broke lunar orbit and set course down into Earth's gravity well. By midday the carrier was settled into a high Earth orbit waiting for its new fighter complement to arrive.

Alanna, Udaltsov and Dati were all on the bridge, watching the new squadron arrive. It was the first time Alanna had been up on the bridge or met Captain Philippe Durane. A reservist, Alanna guessed. An elderly man with a round friendly face, he looked more like a favourite grandfather than a military officer. Alanna had caught Dati give him a look of pure contempt and wondered what that was about.

The fighters formed up and landed, it was all pretty smooth but then a pilot who couldn't land on a carrier that was neither manoeuvring nor accelerating, had no place in a Raven. In turn, each fighter docked with an armature and was drawn into the hangar.

"Too slow, too damn slow," Dati snarled. "We could have been hit by a dozen missiles in the time it has taken to get them in."

"Early days, Commander," Durane replied calmly. "Nothing is perfect from the first."

"Yes sir," Dati replied coldly before turning to Alanna and Udaltsov. "You have your assignments, now get down there and take command."

Schurenhofer had corralled the three newly arrived crews and herded them to a briefing room. Alanna paused on the threshold, remembering the day she had arrived on the old *Dauntless* in the last days of peace. New pilots on their first starship, they'd been like children on a school trip and she'd dreaded seeing that again. But as she walked into the briefing room, that dread, along with any sense of familiarity, faded away. These weren't pilots expecting to serve in a fleet at peace. They knew exactly what they were getting into. The atmosphere was funereal and she felt herself relax.

Alanna nodded to Schurenhofer.

"Attention on deck!" Schurenhofer barked. Everyone snapped sharply to attention as Alanna walked slowly to the head of the room and looked around.

"My name is Lieutenant Commander Alanna Shermer. I am the only survivor of the last Dauntless and I am your new flight leader. My job here is to keep you alive long enough for you to learn how to do yours."

Chapter Four

Farwell to Convention

20th November 2067

Ship Senior Oadra paced slowly around the bridge of the Aèllr cruiser. The normally busy corridors of the great ship were almost deserted. With all non-essential crewmembers landed, now all that remained on the ship was a small diplomatic detail, those needed to navigate, to maintain and if it came to it – fight. That last part was what frightened Oadra and if she was any judge, also most of her crew. She turned back towards the main command display. There was little to see, just an ancient star, three worthless planets... and a human starship. No, not a starship, a *warship*, and not just any ship. Oadra recognised it immediately. Decades previously, during the war between Earth and the Aèllr, that very vessel had hunted the space lanes of the Confederacy. Now it was silent, dark and, like Oadra, waiting.

On the display another indicator appeared, a starship jumping in. Alarm rippled around the bridge.

"Senior, a vessel has transited inwards. It is human, a diplomatic vessel."

"Senior," a communication operative said quietly behind Oadra, "the diplomatic vessel has signalled us."

The operative passed over a computer pad.

"Senior, the human warship, it is activating its engines," called out a sensor operative. "It is moving away."

The warship had accomplished its role, demarking a border that had now, perhaps, ceased to be.

Oadra read the signal. It was as she had expected and dreaded. She reread the last line, irrationally hoping it would somehow change. But no, it continued to read 'follow me.'

"Helm, bring us in astern of the diplomatic ship."

Oadra looked around her bridge and smiled weakly.

"Communications, dispatch a drone to Laibris Base, inform them we are en route to Earth."

27th November 2067

The magnetic surface in the heels of Admiral Lewis's boots made a tap-tap sound as he strode down the hospital corridor. His brow was furrowed as his mind worked. Turning into one of the wards, he nodded to the duty nurse. By unwritten rule, rank was largely in abeyance here on wards. While none of the patients in the corridor saluted, those who saw him still straightened into as close to attention as they could manage. Lewis nodded to individual men and women but didn't pause. The ward wasn't large — it didn't need to be. The reality was that in space combat, it was easier to get killed than it was to get wounded. Those who ended up here were in many ways the lucky ones. Lewis paused at the door to remove his cap and knocked before entering. Stepping around the door, he sighed.

"You're supposed to be in bed," he said in a mild tone that might have surprised some of his subordinates.

"I was uncomfortable," his wife replied, looking up from her reader. "Of course I'm not comfortable in this bloody chair either. Did you get everything?"

"Believe it or not I can manage the odd task without my staff officers," he replied, passing over the bag. "How are you feeling?"

"Better. Over of the worse of it the doctors say," Laura replied as she rummaged through the bag, while Lewis pulled up the room's other chair. "But then in the next breath they say God forbid I insist on acting healthily."

Until its destruction, Admiral Laura Lewis had been the commanding officer of Junction Station. During its evacuation she'd been subject to smoke inhalation and on return trip to Earth, a predatory infection had taken advantage of the damage to her lungs. By the time they reached their home world, she'd had to be stretchered off the ship.

"While I don't object to a visit," Laura commented, "I do understand you have other things on your plate at the moment."

"The understatement of the century," Lewis replied dryly. "Admiral Fengzi and his staff are testing a number of new tactical deployments and, frankly, I needed to get out for a while."

"You don't have much faith in Fengzi?"

"Not at the best of times and this is far from the best of times. I thought things were bad eighteen months ago. Now though – the problem appears intractable," Lewis admitted. "We can assume they don't have the strength to make a direct assault – if they did it wouldn't have taken them a year to break through the Junction Line. But they don't need to. They can cut us off from Saturn and once they do, then it is just a matter of time."

Lewis shrugged to emphasise his point.

"The media is claiming that fuel convoys will be run in," Laura said.

"Which proves again why journalism is reserved for people without the skills to make it in the fast food industry," he replied sourly. "With their Faster Than Light sensors and FTL transmitters, they'll only have put out a picket around Earth and Saturn to be aware of any move we make in virtual real time. We on the other hand will be dealing with the lags inherent to light speed transmissions. So sending out anything less than the entire fleet to escort one of those convoy's guarantees that the convoy will be intercepted and we will suffer defeat in detail…"

"And if you send out the entire fleet, that will leave Earth exposed," Laura finished.

"General Westenlake of Planetary Defence has admitted that without the fleet, the best they can hope to achieve is to slow them a little, bleed them a bit, but not stop them."

Lewis stopped as he stared into space. Long used to him, his wife let the silence stretch out.

"Has any progress been made?" she eventually asked.

"A little. The lighter units operating out of Rosa and Hydra are continuing to strike at the enemy supply lines. So far the Nameless don't appear to be willing to take the time to destroy either of those bases. Not that they need to."

"This is no time for defeatism, Paul!" she exclaimed. "God knows there's enough of that going around already!"

The intensity of Laura's statement was offset by a sudden fit of coughing. He hurriedly passed her a glass of water.

"The problem and solution are what they always have been," Lewis said after a long silence. "The Nameless can engage with missiles from far beyond plasma cannon range. Plus, given that they can jump a good deal deeper into a Mass Shadow than we can, it's difficult to see how we can close the range without a degree of co-operation from them. If however, our ships do succeed in getting into gun range, then the advantage switches decisively to us. The question always has been – how to get there."

"Fighters?"

"Possibly; depending on serviceability, between us and Planetary Defence we can field maybe thirty five squadrons, but getting them on target is still difficult," Lewis replied staring into the middle distance. "Although now that the Nameless have fighters – even primitive ones – that means a portion of any strike will have to carry anti-fighter rather than anti-ship missiles. Right now, I am sorry to say, our best hope hinges on them making a serious mistake. And that isn't much of a plan."

The room once again lapsed into silence.

I shouldn't be here, Lewis thought to himself. *I shouldn't have to do this, not again*. The day before Lewis had made one of his infrequent visits to his assigned office in Headquarters. Mostly he preferred to run his command from *Warspite*, even when she was in for refit. But in the office, pinned to a wall, was a calendar, one which some unknown individual had continued to flip the pages. On yesterday's day's page was a note that Lewis had himself scribbled more than a year before. It had been the day scheduled for him to hand over command of the Home Fleet and end his time as space-going officer. All that remained would have been a two-year ground posting, in which he would provide oversight for weapons development and figure out what to do in retirement. He glanced at Laura. He could remember those days after the last war, when any trip out of port was a journey into the unknown. The universe back then had seemed like a bright and wonderful place. How had it come to this?

Finally Laura spoke. "Unless I'm dead I will discharge myself by the end of the week."

"Are you sure that's…"

"I'm going to Brian's," Laura cut him off. "I sometimes think we didn't spend enough time with him when he was growing up. If the worst comes to pass, that's where I want to be."

"His house is well away from anywhere that's likely to be the target of any first strike," Lewis said distantly.

"Paul!" Laura said sharply before continuing more softly, "if you get a chance, please speak to him."

"If I possibly can I will, but if I can't… tell him…"

"I will. You'd better go. Your mind isn't here. Either get some sleep or get back to work."

Lewis's return to *Warspite* was subject to a detour to one of Earth's smaller orbital dockyards, to view yet another weapon system being frantically rushed into service. He'd already seen several that were at such a technologically immature state that they were probably more dangerous to the user than enemy. Still, the presence of Commodore Tsukioka, the fleet's intelligence chief, indicated this one at least might be of some use. Looking down into the enclosed space of the yard, Lewis saw what appeared to be rows of the fleet's standard emergency message drone. Some had been joined together in groups of three by a central housing.

"Alright Commodore, give me the run down," Lewis said

"This, sir, started out as a planetary defence project," Tsukioka said, nodding to General Westenlake. "It was designed to give a stand-off strike capacity to the defence grid and to support to the fighters on sorties beyond Earth's orbit."

"The fruits of our labours," said Westenlake. "Unfortunately it could have done with more time to be ripened."

"We're calling them torpedoes," Tsukioka continued. "The drones use what is basically a cut down starship engine. Such an engine doesn't have the high-end performance of a missile drive, but unlike a missile engine, these can run for several days. The original plan was for something more ambitious, but as an expedient to allow us to use existing production lines, the engineers have modified the basic Mk Thirteen Emergency Message Drone. The jump drives have been removed and space used for a basic sensor package and a warhead. The navigation software had to be completely replaced – the original package was designed to avoid running into things as its first priority."

"And the role they are intended for?" Lewis replied, turning back to the two men. "The profile I'm looking at doesn't seem fast enough for anti-ship purposes."

"Sir," the Commodore said. "These torpedoes aren't intended to function as a standard missile. They haven't the acceleration to close like a missile, but they are capable of accelerating for hours."

"Endurance rather than sprint capacity," Lewis said.

"The role envisioned by Planetary Defence was to fire off several hundred torpedoes in the opening stages of an engagement, to flank and hem in an opposing force."

"A blocker, rather than a striker," Lewis murmured. "A semimobile minefield."

"Yes, sir," Tsukioka replied. "The ones with the extra casings, that's primarily fuel. They can accelerate for up to three days. The torpedoes probably won't land many hits, but they carry too much punch to be ignored. However, the rushed development has caused problems."

"Oh?"

"A thirty percent failure rate is projected. We have three hundred torpedoes, which are tied into the Planetary Defence Grid. Production means we're adding another four a day to the available units."

"Could they be tied into our ships?"

"Sir?"

"These torpedoes, they match the physical dimensions of the Mk Thirteen. The next battle will be fought inside this solar system. We will have no requirement for message drones."

Tsukioka glanced towards one of the developers.

"Yes, sir, I believe so."

"It gives us another card to play," Lewis said as mentally he started to slot the new weapons into his plans.

30th November 2067

Lewis lay on his bunk on *Warspite* staring up at the deckhead, his mind drifting from one possible deployment to another. The great battleship was now out of dock and holding in a high Earth orbit with the rest of the fleet. Nothing new was coming to mind and nothing they'd already considered would stand even the smallest chance of success. All options were on the table, from fielding untested weapon systems to using untried tactics that would have seen a first year cadet kicked out of officer training for even suggesting during peacetime. None of it would work – the Nameless simply possessed all the advantages. If there was an answer to their dilemma, Lewis couldn't see it. His eyes started to flicker shut as he drifted off.

The main alarm went off with a banshee like scream. Lewis was up and out of the bunk instantly, simultaneously trying to ram his intercom earpiece into place.

"Bridge, report!" he shouted.

"Sir, an alien ship has just jumped in!"

Christ, I thought I had a few more weeks, Lewis thought desperately as he reached for his survival suit. *We aren't ready!* Then the officer on the other end of the link said what Lewis did not expect.

"Sir, it's not the Nameless. It's... Aèllr?"

The voice on the other end sounded confused. Lewis didn't reply; he was out of his cabin and heading for the bridge.

"Report!" he barked as he stepped onto the bridge.

"It's confirmed – contact is an Aèllr Province class heavy cruiser," called out a bridge office. "It's one light second beyond the Red Line and at rest relative. Engines are at standby, her gun turrets are trained fore and aft, they are not powered up."

"The fleet is coming online. We have tactical uplink from all squadrons," added Captain Sheehan, his chief of staff.

Lewis stepped towards the bridge's main holo. The red blip for the Aèllr was blinking slowly, but beside it was a second blip, this one green.

"What's that?" he asked.

"Transponder is showing it as the diplomatic cruiser the *Mandela*, sir. She jumped in at the same time as the Aèllr contact. She isn't moving. Records say she should be at the Mhar home world."

"The *Mandela* is transmitting, sir," reported a communications officer. "Diplomatic encryption sir... Sir, we do not have the key for that encryption."

"Sir, signal from Headquarters. Priority One, we are ordered to... ordered to... we're ordered to stand down."

"Confirm that!" Lewis demanded.

"Sir, that's confirmed. We are ordered to stand down. The whole fleet is ordered to stand down. Orders on the authority of Admiral Wingate."

The bridge went silent. Looking around, Lewis could see confusion on some faces, alarm on others and fear on a few, both officers and crew. Whatever else, a crew needed to think their commanders were in control. On the display the Aèllr cruiser was slowly moving towards one of the outer markers.

"Very well," Lewis said, forcing himself to speak calmly. "Captain Holfe, please have a shuttle prepared. I may need to return to the surface."

By the time the shuttle was ready orders had arrived from Headquarters instructing his return. As soon as he landed, Lewis was escorted to Wingate's office. The atmosphere had changed in the few days he had been away. From one of fatalistic gloom, to something uncertain; junior officers and ratings watched Lewis pass, searching for some clue to indicate whether this development could be viewed as good news or bad.

When Lewis was shown in, Wingate was standing at the window, while Admiral Fengzi was sitting frowning. Wingate held a glass of something in his maimed left hand. They'd never been friends as such, always superior and subordinate, but Lewis had known Wingate for a long time. He knew that those days when his superior poured a very small measure of whiskey into a glass were never good ones.

"Sit down, Paul," Wingate said without turning. "Gentlemen, I expect you are aware of the new arrival."

"Yes, sir," Lewis replied. "Clearly they were expected, sir. So why are they here?"

"Well it's not to join us," Wingate said heavily. "Although God knows we wouldn't turn them down if they did."

"Then why are they here?" Fengzi asked.

"A few months ago the Aèllr Confederacy unexpectedly contacted our diplomatic mission on the Mhar home world. They made clear that they knew how vulnerable we are. They also made clear that they regard the Nameless as a serious threat to the Confederacy. Because of that, they see no advantage to themselves if we get wiped out. Much of the information we have on the Nameless comes from them."

"Yes, we're both aware of that," Fengzi said impatiently.

"What you won't be aware of is that with the opening of a direct line of communication to central government of the Confederacy, the Council decided to explore whether they could be persuaded to offer material assistance."

"From the Aèllr!" Fengzi burst out. "Good God! What the hell..."

"I'm not finished," Wingate cut across him.

He raised the glass to his lips then lowered it again.

"The answer was a very firm no. Apparently, there are senior elements in the Confederacy's central government that would favour at least offering logistical support, while we could still carry much of the burden. But it has become equally clear from various Mhar sources that those elements could not carry the Aèllr home world, much less their various colony worlds. For them, this is a war being fought a long distance away, by people they don't care much about."

"But something has been agreed," Lewis said, "or that ship wouldn't be here."

"Yes." Wingate paused to put down the untouched glass. "That ship is here as part of a project codenamed The Lazarus Protocol. While the Aèllr are unwilling to get actively involved at this time, those central government elements are willing to make concessions and the Council has struck a bargain. On behalf of the Council, the President of the United States will be making an announcement in about twenty minutes. She will be informing the planet that a convoy of personnel transports is being formed. Five thousand colonists have been selected from the major nations, who are being lifted into orbit as we speak. Once they're on board their ships and in hibernation, they will be escorted to the Confederacy border by the Aèllr cruiser. There they will wait for the Battle of Earth to be decided. Should Earth fall, then they will continue on to the Aèllr colony world of Ptioet, on the far side of Confederacy space. It is the newest of their colony worlds, which they only started to settle twenty years ago. One of the planet's continents has yet to be opened for settlement. We've... bought it."

Lewis and Fengzi exchanged looks of amazement.

"The colony will be an Aèllr protectorate. They have offered guarantees on internal independence, which the Council regards as acceptable," Wingate continued as he sat down. "Thanks to their position on the far side of Aèllr space from the Nameless, they will be a protected outpost of humanity."

"The Aèllr? The race against which we fought a war: a war in which they attempted to box us in onto our own planet."

Fengzi's tone was no longer angry, but one of utter disbelief. "Last year the Council kept good ships pissing around on the Aèllr border when Dryad was nearly taken from us!"

"And they're doing this out of the goodness of their hearts?" Lewis asked in a matching tone.

"Politicians take time to adjust to new conditions," Wingate shrugged. "Once they do, they can go in unexpected directions. No, the Aèllr are not acting out of some newly discovered fondness for us. Our ships will be carrying a database of our ship designs, technical plus tactical manuals and every piece of military writing from the last two hundred years. That is the price we have paid for their agreement."

"We can't give the..." Fengzi started to exclaim.

Wingate slammed his hand down.

"That decision has been made!" he shouted, before continuing more calmly. "The agreement has what is in effect a standby proviso. If we succeed in repelling the Nameless, then the convoy will return without handing over any information. That much I was able to add to the deal."

"And we really think the Aèllr can be trusted?" Fengzi asked, aghast.

"The Council do and that's what matters," Wingate shrugged. "If Earth falls, then our military secrets are valuable only as currency. Our political masters have made the decision and we do as we are bid. The Council is doing what it thinks, what it hopes, is for the best. That isn't our problem; our problem is making sure this doesn't break the morale of the fleet."

"What about Dryad?" Lewis asked.

"Publicly, nothing will be mentioned. If asked, the Council will state that since the Mhar cannot offer any meaningful military protection and none of the Tample can be trusted, the policy towards Dryad is as it always has been – to defend it against all comers. However when Admiral Melchiori was ordered to send the *Resplendent* home, he was also instructed that in the event of Earth falling, he is authorised to seek political union with the Mhar Union. The three cruisers under his command should provide a sufficient sweetener for such a deal."

"With us gone, the Mhar would likely seek full alliance with the Aèllr," Fengzi said, now in a calmer tone.

"Yes. Which since the Aèllr seem to sincerely believe that war with the Nameless is coming, would likely not be refused," Wingate agreed in a tired voice. "So even if Earth falls, something will remain of humanity. Even if is only as a subordinate species."

He pulled himself to his feet again and, picking up the glass, returned to the window.

"I think that's all gentlemen. You are both dismissed."

The two Admirals lingered for a few moments outside Wingate's office before, by unspoken agreement, they headed towards the Flag Officers restaurant. Fengzi irritably waved away one of the service staff as he sat down heavily.

"Subordinate species," he muttered, shaking his head. "To even think it makes me gag. Why did we even bother all those years ago just to roll over now? God damn gutless worms of politicians!"

"It puts the human race's eggs in more than one basket," Lewis said. "Not a bad plan as far as it goes."

"Except it depends on the goodwill of people who don't have much reason to have any towards us!" Fengzi observed darkly, before shaking his head again. "To have come to this!"

The two sat in silence for a while.

"How is the latest set of tactical simulations looking?" Lewis eventually asked.

"Every damn thing we can think of has been tried," Fengzi replied. "While some aspects get good results, the overall ratio of our losses to theirs is still coming up short – Far too short. I mean we have some things going for us. In as near as we can tell, they can only jump within a solar system. So they can't hide their support ships outside the system. Also, since the Nameless ships have to be close to stationary to jump, if we get into gun range we could knock them off like ducks in a row. Problem is there just doesn't seem to be a way to manoeuvre the fleet into contact without them seeing us coming. Even getting from the highest orbit to the edge of Earth's mass shadow takes too damn long."

The both lapsed back into silence, each man lost in his own thoughts.

"Why an entire fleet?" Lewis murmured.

"What?"

"Why are we thinking about getting the entire fleet in," Lewis said in a still distant tone. "Get into gun range and even a small force could inflict disproportionate damage."

"Because there is no material difference between getting a small fast force in or a larger slower one. Plus, if they didn't get into gun range, then they'd be overwhelmed. Don't get me wrong, there is a role for detached elements – most of the carriers can be more productive carrying out hit and runs from the edge of the solar system than they would be sat in Earth orbit."

Lewis was still staring into the middle distance and it was doubtful whether he had even heard Fengzi.

"The Nameless cap ship missiles can fire from over a light second out, but to put in serious weight of fire, they have to get within three quarters of a light second of the target so they can use the smaller dual-purpose missiles. So to put in an assault against Earth, they have to get inside the mass shadow."

"Which still gives them a margin of a good quarter of a light second to play with," Fengzi said. "If we try to move towards them, then they can slow down fast enough to be able to jump away before we reach gun range."

"Not if something bottles them up. If by the time they know they're in contact they're already under fire, then even if our force is only a few ships we could inflict major casualties on them. They have to come to a near halt and become sitting ducks, as you put it, or try to run in real space, where they possess no acceleration advantage and we could chase them down."

"Yes, yes! That's all lovely but we've looked at this!" Fengzi replied in exasperation. "The only ships we can reasonably expect to get to gun range are fighters and strike boats. Even with them the only ones to get there will be from our carriers operating from beyond the heliopause. If we used all our carriers, that gives us only six squadrons of space fighters and two dozen strike boats. Even if we got them into position, they could not hold! The Nameless would push them aside, not without loss to themselves, but not enough loss!"

"Then we need something more substantial than fighters. A fast division of line warships," Lewis replied. "The Nameless would have to cross through their gun range to escape."

"And how the hell are you planning to get this fast division into this happy position?" Fengzi asked sarcastically. "The Nameless will not put themselves in a vulnerable position knowing there is a force wandering around somewhere in the solar system. This fast division will be chased down and crushed, or forced to retreat to Earth or another mass shadow."

"The fast division would have to be concealed. The Nameless cannot seek what they do not know exists," Lewis wondered, half to himself.

"Where?" Fengzi asked, returning to his exasperated tone. "Both my staff and yours have looked at that thoroughly! The only place we could 'hide' a squadron would be out beyond the heliopause in interstellar space and that's no use. As soon as they arrive, the Nameless will jam the FTL frequencies. That will limit this fast division to light speed communications and sensors. If the Nameless do move into this position of vulnerability, the fast division won't even know until *hours* afterward."

"Then we hide them inside the solar system."

"Hide! There is nowhere we can hide an entire squadron! One or two ships might be able to go silent and not be spotted, but unless the Nameless suddenly become complete idiots, they'll do a complete sweep of the system and get close enough to Earth to compare whatever we have in orbit with their force projections of us. Except for

Saturn's lower rings, there is no orbit into which we can put a force of ships where they won't be spotted – and that's in an even deeper mass shadow, so no use."

"Then don't put them in orbit," Lewis said slowly. "Land them."

"What!"

"Put the ships down and cut to silent running. The remaining heat profile can be masked by the surrounding material."

"Exactly which ships are you planning to do this with?" Fengzi demanded. "We only have a couple of dozen strike boats that are even capable of landing on the Moon!"

"I wasn't thinking of Earth's moon. I was thinking of Mars's – either Phobos or *Deimos*. The transmission lag between Earth and Mars is about thirty minutes."

Fengzi opened his mouth to retort, but then stopped and looked thoughtful.

"Mars's mass shadow is shallow and Phobos is small – escape velocity is what… ten to fifteen metres per second?" he said after a moment.

"About that. Mars has been evacuated. It would need to be a strike group, fast enough to get into contact and strong enough to do damage when it got there," Lewis replied.

"What ships are you thinking of?"

"Hmm, *Warspite*, a flak cruiser and maybe half a dozen Statesman class cruisers – or a batch of three Myth class ships, plus destroyers."

Fengzi raised an eyebrow, "*Warspite*? Surely it would be better if it was a ship other than the Home Fleet Flagship."

"On full burn, *Warspite* can nearly match the acceleration curve of a heavy cruiser. The only other battleship we have that can match *Warspite* for pace is old *Fortitude* and she doesn't have even nearly the same firepower. No it would have to be either *Warspite* or no battleship at all, and it would need a battleship."

"That leaves you with a problem of a missing ship. They've seen *Warspite*, when they don't see her here, that will be a giveaway."

"No. Her sister ship…"

"*Yavuz Sultan Selim*? She's not ready, they're still building her."

"She's mostly done, currently she's missing several engines. Planetary Defence is already due to take her over and use her as a crude starfort, but what's important is that a vessel with the correct silhouette will be visible," Lewis said.

"Well, that still leaves you with a lot of ships to hide and you haven't explained how you plan to land ships that were built in orbit and were never designed to put down."

"In classic rocket ship fashion – tail down. We'd have to put a landing gear onto them, but with Phobos's gravity even a very flimsy structure would be adequate."

"There's a lot of ifs and buts in all this," Fengzi said after some thought, "and at the end of the day, what would it get us?"

"At best," Lewis replied simply, "it gives us one heavy swing from a direction they don't expect. But under the right conditions, that might be enough."

"Well," Fengzi said eventually, "that's good enough to justify taking a detailed look. See where the devil is in this detail."

5th December 2067

"This region on the Phobos's Stickney Crater is the most extensively surveyed part of the moon – ice mining began ten years ago," Staff Captain Sheehan said, as he gestured towards a chart of the moon.

The briefing room was crowded with the fleet's senior officers and they all studied the chart carefully.

"The surface is approximately eight part rock to two parts ice and although there is a certain porosity, computer models indicate that under Phobos gravity, the three point landing gear outlined by engineering should be sufficient. The force we have slated for this fast division is *Warspite*, *Deimos*, Cruiser Squadrons Twelve and Fourteen..."

"Should?" Wingate interrupted, "Should seems sketchy, Captain. We are talking about a significant number of ships. Nose up, tail down – that's the most unstable possible posture. What happens if one of the cruisers – or God help us – *Warspite*, puts a landing pad down on one of these pores?"

Sheehan looked unaccountably flustered. Not surprising, Lewis thought. Sheehan didn't believe in the plan, but his Chief of Staff was a professional and knew his job was to try to make Lewis's decisions work. The past three days had seen his staff run ragged as they attempted to plan for a scenario never before considered. The men and women who had designed the ships were drafted in to provide their input and as they did, the plan Lewis had sketched out was refined and developed.

Designs for the landing gear were hastily put together and various orbital dockyards were already fabricating them. The destroyers were dropped when no hard points could be found that would support their landing gear. Civilians familiar with the Martian moons were also brought in to provide their expertise, while the chosen starships were moved up to the space docks, ready for the conversion work. They had now reached the point where to go any further would mean formal permission.

"Sir," Lewis cut in, "the very worst case scenario would be a ship tumbling. But given that Phobos's escape velocity is very low, if a ship fails to find firm footing, any of them, including *Warspite*, can pull away. The biggest danger would be if a ship came down too hard and one or more of the landing gear struts collapsed."

"So we could lose a ship before the fight even begins." Wingate persisted.

"Yes, sir, we could," Lewis replied. "Such a ship would be recoverable but not in time for the battle."

"You're not selling this well, Paul."

"We can't mount a conventional defence, not successfully," Lewis said. "Sooner or later the Nameless will close in on either Earth or Saturn. When they do, they will enter a mass shadow. If it is Earth, then we can pin them with this fast division on one side and the rest of the fleet on the other, with fighters and these new torpedoes sealing the flanks. If it's Saturn, then we jump in behind them and hem them in until the rest of the fleet joins us. But for us to stand any chance of doing this, we have to come from a direction where they don't see us coming."

Wingate's eyes flicked towards Fengzi.

"We have looked at every other possibility, sir," Fengzi said. "They will not work. This piece of off-the-wall thinking stands a chance, just not a very good one."

"But *Warspite* and you: both away from Earth?" Wingate asked.

"I can't be the anvil sir. I need to be the hammer. We have to achieve gun range and I believe this is the way to do it."

Wingate stared at the display.

"The Council will not like this," he said eventually.

"The Council has handed over a chunk of the human race to the fucking Aèllr," Fengzi replied. "We've been off the wall, they've done the unthinkable."

"I may not word it that way Admiral, but you're right. We've already given up on conventional thinking," Wingate replied before turning. "Admiral Lewis, you are authorised to proceed."

Chapter Five

Digging In

12th December 2067

"I'm just saying sir, we've got problems brewing," said *Deimos*'s Chief Engineer. "The Bosun has got teams doing ultrasounds along the rest of the longitudinal beams, but I'm expecting more of the same."

"Unfortunately, I expect you're right," Crowe replied, looking up from his computer pad. "I'm not sure what they are putting us into dock for at this late hour, but I want this brought to the dockyard's attention. We may as well try to get something out of this."

There was no doubt that when the shit hit the fan they would be in the middle of it. *Deimos* had a well drilled and by now experienced crew, but that didn't mean they couldn't have their focus buggered up. The news about the Confederacy was bad enough and they'd had their two message drones swapped out for the new torpedoes. He wanted the crew to be ready, not pissing around with new equipment they wouldn't have time to master. This was not the time to start rearranging deck chairs on the Titanic.

Currently, *Deimos* was holding position five hundred metres outside the Gemini construction platform, waiting for a tug to assist with the final approach and docking.

"This isn't something to be dealt with on the fly," the engineer warned. "This is major overhaul stuff and even then, the ship might still have problems," he ended with a shrug.

Crowe looked back at the pad. The inspection results were bad, but far from unexpected. *Deimos* had been designed to escort larger slower vessels like fighter carriers and support ships, protecting them from enemy fighters, strike boats and destroyers. With no requirement to match the rapid movements of more nimble ships, she was relatively lightly built. But in this war, *Deimos* had found herself in a battle line role more stressful than that envisioned by her designers. Along the way she'd absorbed two heavy blows and numerous minor hits, all of which were taking their toll. The diagram now in front of Crowe showed the ship's main structural beams, with red markers indicating where micro fractures had already been detected in the ship's structure. *Deimos* wasn't an old ship but war was wearing her out fast. To stand any chance of stopping the rot, she needed a major refit – a refit that she would not get. So why were they heading into a dock where the heavy cruisers *De Gaulle* and *Michael Collins* had already been moored? Something was up. He could feel it and he knew he probably wouldn't like it.

The briefing room was almost silent as the officers who had been gathered there departed. Some looked shell-shocked and some bemused as they filed out. Crowe remained in his seat, furious. He'd barely had time to get *Deimos* to her berth before running for the shuttle to *Starforge*. Once there, he'd been escorted to a briefing room with a dozen other commanding officers – some of the fleet's best. These were the men and women expected to provide the next generation of admirals and fleet commanders. As a man who before the war had happily taken the role of a driver for civilian exploration missions, this was not company Crowe had either expected or wanted to find himself in. When Admiral Lewis had walked into the room, he'd known it would be bad. He hadn't been wrong.

When the other commanding officers had left, he approached the Admiral. Lewis remained seated as he organised his papers.

"Commodore Crowe," he said calmly as he looked up. "Is there a reason you are still here?"

"Yes, sir," Crowe replied, "my ship, *again?*"

"Yes, Commodore. Have you a good reason why I should not assign *Deimos* to this?"

"Because we covered the retreat from Junction Station. Before that we were in Kite String and before that we barely made it out of Baden."

"You feel you've done enough?" Lewis replied in a dangerously calm voice.

"My crew are tired, my ship is wearing out and now…"

"And now, Commodore, you have been given your orders," Lewis replied coldly before he glanced back at his Chief of Staff.

"Captain," he prompted.

"Yes, sir," Sheehan replied before leaving the room.

"I am aware of *Deimos*'s war record, Commodore," Lewis continued as the hatch closed, "just as I am aware of yours. I have a lot of respect for your efforts from the Mississippi Incident to the present, which is a large part of the reason I am tolerating this conversation. No one will get a chance to sit this one out Commodore. You know that as well as I do."

Crowe changed tack.

"Sir, my ship badly needs a complete overhaul," he said. "Another ship another Luna class..."

"A marginally more relevant factor," Lewis interrupted. "But the fact that *Deimos* has seen hard use is not a negative point. It's one that made the choice simpler."

"My ship was chosen because it is expendable," Crowe said in a hollow voice.

"All warships are expendable to some degree," Lewis corrected. "Even if the Fast Division gets into position, even if it achieves what we hope it can, there is no guarantee that the ships of the division that survive will be fit for further service. Your ship was chosen because the Luna class as a whole have been hard used. *Deimos* may not be fit for further service no matter what position I place her in, so I must instead make best use of her now."

"You're thinking of the next battle," Crowe said. "The one after this."

"Yes," Lewis replied simply. "A victory here merely staves off defeat. It doesn't win the war. And win the war is what we have to do."

For a moment Crowe saw through the facade of command, seeing not the cold blooded, uncaring officer he was familiar with. Not the one who had thrown men and women into the furnace of battle without hesitation, but the man behind the uniform. Old, tired, determined and yet desperately afraid that nothing he could do would be enough. This plan, this insane plan to land starships, was the product of a man who, if not grasping at straws, was getting close to it.

"Desperate times, Commodore," Lewis said quietly. "If the price of getting the Home and Second Fleets into gun range is the loss of *Warspite*, *Deimos* and a half dozen first class cruisers, then that price is acceptable. If you have no further questions, Commodore, then you are dismissed."

In the last sentence the Admiral's tone changed. It regained its certainty and Crowe knew that he had reached the end of the old man's tolerance.

By the time he got back to the Gemini platform, dockworkers were already crawling all over the outer hull of *Deimos*, closely watched from one of the observation platforms by the cruiser's deeply suspicious chief engineer.

"Sir," he said as Crowe approached, "some kind of work has started on the ship, but I've not been informed of the details, which is completely in breach of regs."

"And subject to the orders they've received from Headquarters," Crowe replied, as he pushed himself down until his boot magnets locked onto the floor. "Is anyone else off the ship?"

"No. A staff officer turned up just after you left with orders for all personnel to remain on board. I've only got this far because the Commander argued that I need to be aware of what changes are being made to the ship."

"Well, get yourself back on board, Chief," Crowe replied. "I have to give you all a briefing."

"Yes, sir," the Chief replied, turning away from the viewing port just in time to miss the first of three structures being swung into place over the cruiser's drive section.

Deimos's wardroom was only big enough to just about accommodate all of her officers. Some had been with the ship since before Crowe took command. Others had arrived as replacements for those killed, wounded or in all too few cases, transferred off. But as a pair of ratings set up a holo projector, it struck Crowe that this ship – his ship – had developed an oddly unique esprit de corps in the form of a weary resignation that whatever was about to hit the fan, they'd be in the middle of it and, at the same time, a confidence that they'd come out the far side.

"Gentlemen, we've received our assignment for the coming engagement," Crowe started, "and I will admit it is not what any of us are expecting.

He turned on the holo projector. It showed *Deimos* herself, as she would appear once the dockyard workers were done.

"What in hell's name?" exclaimed Lieutenant Colwell from the back as a general mutter went round the room.

Crowe couldn't blame them. Three spindly legs were mounted at one hundred and twenty degrees to each other, at right angles to the longitudinal axis of the ship. They gave the ship a landing platform, which would allow the cruiser to stand upright on her tail. But it looked like the ship had been forcibly crossbred with an old Apollo moon lander.

"Quiet please. As you will have figured out, our mission will be unorthodox. We have been assigned to a new force to be designated as the Fast Division. It will consist of our own ship, the *Warspite* and the heavy cruisers *De Gaulle*, *Churchill*, *Michael Collins*, *Hades*, *Hermes* and *Athena*. As soon as our new struts are complete, we will break Earth orbit and head for the Martian moon of Phobos. Once there, we will land on the surface of the moon."

There was another babble of voices. This time Crowe let them continue for several moments before rapping on the table.

"We will land there, secure ourselves, power down and make sufficient arrangements to allow us to dump our remaining waste heat into the surface of the moon."

"What on Earth is the purpose of this, sir?" asked Commander Bhudraja.

"We are the counter attack element. If or when the Nameless make a move against either Earth or Saturn, our job will be to jump in behind them and pin them inside a mass shadow until the rest of the fleet can join us. We will be the cork in the bottle. Our role is obvious — we are here to protect the other seven ships during the run into plasma cannon range."

"Eight ships versus a fleet?" asked the gunner.

"Eight good ships," Crowe replied.

"More like seven plus us," Colwell said. "No one has ever landed a starship the size of *Deimos*! Not even on a low gravity moon!"

"Gentlemen," Crowe interrupted, frowning at Colwell as he did so, "we can stop the debate right here. The bottom line is we have been given our orders. Headquarters thinks this is our best shot at getting a force into gun range, so that's what we will do."

"There are no existing navigational system programmes to allow for landing," Colwell said unhappily.

"Headquarter has promised landing programmes for the helm, but frankly we aren't counting on that. So you and the helmsman have two days to come up with some," Crowe replied.

"What about our aft firing arcs?" the gunner asked. "Those legs will block our firing astern. How can we remove them once we've taken off again?"

"We're being supplied with shaped charges to fit once we've landed. Those should be able to remove them. But as a redundancy, we are being supplied with a half dozen rounds for the flak guns, which will be solid shot rather than explosive."

"You mean…"

"Yes. If necessary, we'll shoot them off."

Colwell was still shaking his head in disbelief.

"Look at it this way. The Americans managed to make the first moon landing in a vessel so primitive we'd be afraid to get into it. Let alone fly it."

"Yes sir, but Neil Armstrong at least had the luxury of a purpose built ship!"

"Well, Ladies and Gentlemen," Crowe replied turning off the holo, "as the saying goes, if you can't take a joke, then you shouldn't have joined!"

Forty-eight hours later, *Deimos* emerged from docks with her three spindly legs to join the other seven ships of the Fast Division. If they looked ridiculous on *Deimos*, on the imposing bulk of *Warspite* they were truly absurd. Colwell had come up with a landing programme and at least in simulation it appeared sound. But then again, as the old saying went: garbage in, garbage out. Simulations were only as good as the data they were based on and Colwell hadn't been wrong when he pointed out that no one had ever landed a starship. It was certainly true that Phobos was a low gravity moon, so low in fact that one could probably achieve escape velocity with a pushbike and a ramp. Even so, if they came down too hard, the landing legs would give way and if that happened – well it would be interesting to watch, but only from a safe distance.

Crowe looked up from his desk as his intercom buzzed.

"Yes, what is it?"

"Sir, Communications. We're receiving a transmission from Headquarters. We're ordered to put it up ship wide."

"Very well. I'll be up to the bridge in a moment."

The grapevine must have kicked in because more of the ship's officers were hanging around than had any legitimate reason to be there. Crowe listened to the message, then nodded to the communications officer.

"Men and women of the fleet," Admiral Wingate's voice echoed through *Deimos* and every other ship in the fleet. "A short time ago we received word from our reconnaissance ships that the leading elements of the Nameless fleet have now reached Alpha Centauri. We believe their arrival in this solar system is days or perhaps only hours away. I will not lie to you. The battle ahead will be the hardest we of the fleet have ever fought and the odds are now against us. But this is what we have trained for, what we have prepared for and what we have sworn to do – to stand between Earth and all that would threaten it.

"Our task has often been hard and frequently thankless, but now more than ever it is essential. Shortly your ships will be taking their final positions and I need not tell you that from here, there will be no retreat. Defeat here will mean the end of Earth history. But should the worst happen, we can draw comfort from the convoy that will leave for the Confederacy. So even if it is without Earth, the human race will go on. I wish you all good luck. Admiral Wingate out."

Crowe looked around his bridge. Officers and ratings avoid eye contact, both with him and each other.

"Well, now we know," he said. "I expect we will shortly be receiving orders to take our position. Commander Bhudraja, I want all officers to make final checks of their sections. I will be conducting a personal inspection of all compartments. That ought to give everyone something to think about."

The replies to his instructions were low and mumbled.

Within an hour, led by *Warspite*, the convoy of transports had broken orbit and were heading for the Red Line, joined by the other seven ships of the Fast Division plus three of the fleet's fighter carriers and their escorts – all en route to their own positions out beyond the heliopause. At the outer marker the personnel transports and their thousands of hibernating colonists were handed over to the Aèllr cruiser. It was something that two years previously would have been unthinkable, but now passed almost unremarked. There was too much to do. Messages of good luck were passed back and forth as ships prepared to jump. The carriers were the first to go, and then *Deimos* made her jump.

"Commencing descent," the helmsman muttered nervously as *Deimos* completed the turn over and began to slowly drop towards the surface of Phobos.

He wasn't the only one who looked worried, Crowe thought to himself as he surreptitiously tightened his seat restraints. At the last minute, Headquarters had sent up a landing programme for helm. Crowe had looked it over and decided that when it came to it, he would put his faith in the crew that knew *Deimos* as a real ship, rather than a sterile computer simulation. A hundred kilometres to port, the cruiser *Michael Collins* was starting to roll as the rest of the formation came in behind. A battleship and seven cruisers, slowly dropping towards the centre of the Stickney Crater, all of them hoping the hastily welded struts would take the shock of landing. As the ship with lowest mass, *Deimos* would be best able to pull away at the last moment and so would lead them in.

"All hands, this is the Bridge. No crewmembers are to move until instructed by the Bridge. Everyone brace for landing," Crowe ordered across the main intercom channel, before adding to himself: "never thought I'd say that on a starship."

When a couple of the bridge crew briefly looked towards him he realised he'd spoken across the bridge channel.

"Never thought we'd hear you say it, sir," someone replied.

Crowe gave a brief grin.

"Helm, be ready with the throttle," he ordered. "If the struts give or we don't find firm footing, then we need to go full burn. But await my order."

"Yes, sir."

With Phobos's weak gravitational pull, the approach was painfully slow. As *Deimos* took a tail down posture, range finding lasers swept the surface of the moon below and the computer compared the readings to the charts of Phobos.

"We're slightly off course, compensating," said the helmsman tersely.

"We are seven minutes out from landing zone," Colwell called out. "Radar confirms landing zone is clear and level. We are clear for final approach."

"Thank you, Lieutenant," Crowe replied, before switching intercom channels. "Commander Bhudraja, are your tether teams ready?"

"Confirmed, sir. Airlocks have been flushed, we are ready," Bhudraja replied.

The bridge lapsed into silence as *Deimos* continued to slowly drop towards the surface. The occasional firing of the manoeuvring thrusters was enough to keep the descent under control as the computer ran through the landing programme. At twenty metres up, the main engines pulsed for a split second, enough to arrest their momentum completely and send dust billowing up from the surface. In the low gravity some of it had probably achieved escape velocity.

"Radar has lost the surface!" Colwell barked out. "Too much dust!"

"Steady!" Crowe shouted. "We still have it on visual!"

On the main holo the camera in the stern suddenly got a clear view of the surface – coming up fast!

"Thrusters, all full!" Crowe, shouted. "Brace, brace, brace!"

A shudder ran through the *Deimos* as she settled.

Then she shifted.

"We're tilting!" someone shouted, but Crowe's own senses had already told him that. The cruiser's centrifuge had been closed down for the landing and they positioned the bridge so it had the same arbitrary 'Up' designation as the areas outside the centrifuge.

"Activate the jacks on Strut One!" Crowe shouted.

Deimos seemed to hesitate for a moment, then reversed the tilt and settled.

"Lieutenant?"

"We're … zero point seven nine degrees off the vertical."

Colwell looked up from the computer panel. Even across the bridge and through his helmet visor, Crowe could see the relief on his face.

"We're within tolerances, Commodore," he announced.

"Thank God for that!" Crowe said in an explosive breath. "Coms, Bridge. Activate the beacon for the rest of the squadron. Commander Bhudraja, get your teams out there."

Outside crewmembers went shinning down the flanks of the cruiser into the dust that was still billowing around them. Others tossed down cables and soon the radio channels were crackling with voices as the landing parties began to hammer steel tethers into Phobos's grey surface that would keep them stable. Above them, the rest of the Fast Division lined up for their own approach.

Over the next hour Crowe watched the rest of the ships slowly descend and settle on the moon's surface. Some came down dangerously close to one another, while others, like *Deimos*, tottered for a moment before finding firm footing. But each made it down safely, successively throwing up more and more dust. Finally *Warspite* lumbered down and once again Crowe found himself holding his breath. A brief pulse of her engines threw out more dust than had any of the previous ships and completely blotted out the landing zone. Totally blinded, Crowe could only wait until Communication reported the battleship's beacon had activated.

With the last of the warships down, an orbiting support ship released its drop pods. Threading their way through the landed ships to put down safely and with their tethers in place, crewmembers were soon hooking their ships up to the fuel supplies within the pods.

"Sir."

"Yes Commander?" Crowe replied without turning from the main holo.

"I've finished the inspection of the tethers and they are all secured," Bhudraja reported. "We are hooked up to the extra fuel tanks and the Chief reports he'll have the lines to the heat dumps dug in within the next three hours."

"The reactors?"

"Number One is going into shut down and will be cold within two hours. Number Two is at minimum power."

"So that means we have up to six weeks of endurance. That's good, Commander, that is good. I want you to pass along to the crew that they have done very well. Do you know about the rest of the Squadron?"

"According to radio transmissions they're okay, but the dust we've thrown up means we can't get a communications laser hook up," Bhudraja replied.

"So I see," Crowe replied. The holo in front of him was set for visual mode, but with all the dust flying around in the moon's low gravity environment, it was like looking into a blizzard.

"It should clear…" Bhudraja started.

"I hope it doesn't," Crowe interrupted. "Unless the Nameless have accurate scans of the solar system, they'll likely assume this is natural. Ground returns will mean we're lost to radar. Once we have the lines from the radiators dug in there won't be a heat profile and this dust will conceal us even from visuals."

"I wonder whether the Admiral thought of this?" Bhudraja asked.

Crowe turned towards him.

"Who knows sir," he replied. "But at least we've successfully completed the first step."

20th December 2067

The intercom above Crowe's bed buzzed.
"What is it?" he muttered as he rubbed his eyes.
"Sir, it's the Nameless. They're here."

Chapter Six

Day One

How much do they know about us? Are we as much a mystery to them as they are to us? Lewis thought to himself as he stood on the bridge of *Warspite* following the main holo as it played again through the readings. *I doubt it.* This, this was too potent a show of strength to be anything other than planned. To win the psychological battle before even a single shot was fired.

None of the ships of the Fast Division could see the Nameless directly. The mass of Phobos blocked direct line of sight. Instead they were getting readings from a small observation satellite orbiting Mars and transmitting a signal via laser. It introduced an extra element of risk for the Fast Division, but Lewis had to be able to see. On the holo, row after row of Nameless ships dropped into real space. Escort ships at first, then cruisers, carriers and finally capital ships, slowly, methodically dropping into real space between the orbits of Mars and Saturn. Clouds of fighters deployed outwards into a protective sphere around the fleet. For the first time in over a quarter century, an alien fleet was entering Earth's solar system; and no Battle Fleet ships were engaging them.

Looking around the *Warspite*'s bridge, Lewis could see the effect it was having. Officers and ratings were glancing over their shoulders at the holo. Their confidence was being shaken and if they were to stand a chance, he needed them sharp.

"Tactical, what's the count?" he asked.

"Bridge, we have one hundred and thirty-three escorts, seventy-four cruisers, thirty-one capital ships and twelve carriers. Support ships are still jumping in, sir.

"Two hundred and fifty ships," Captain Sheehan whispered, "Sweet Jesus!"

Between them, Home and Second Fleets could come up with a combined strength of under one hundred ships of all types.

"They're light in carriers," Lewis grunted. "So at about sixty fighters per carrier, that gives them about seven hundred and twenty, plus perhaps another sixty flying from escorts, less whatever they lose due to serviceability issues. That's against the four hundred or so that Planetary Defence and we can come up with, so odds of less than two to one. Unless their fighters have got a lot better than they were a few weeks ago, then we have the advantage there. Interesting."

"What do we do now, sir?" Sheehan asked.

"We, Captain? We, Captain, do nothing. The first move belongs to our colleagues and good luck to them." Lewis turned towards *Warspite*'s captain. "Captain Holfe, I would like to invite you and your officers to dinner this evening."

Prior to jump technology interstellar space had represented the final barrier to human expansion, an empty gulf of near nothingness separating Earth's sun from its nearest neighbour. Before first contact, science fiction writers had imagined vast colony ships setting forth on centuries' long one-way journeys, their crews either hibernating through countless centuries or entire generations living out their lives in ships that would be the only world they knew.

Those imagined futures became obsolete the day that first alien ship force landed on Earth, the day humanity seized jump drive technology and made it their own. From that point, interstellar space changed from barrier to irrelevance. As soon as a ship cleared the mass shadow of its home planet, it could jump away, free to travel without ever passing through the great emptiness. This was no place for humanity.

Yet humanity was here.

The carrier *Dauntless* and her three escorting destroyers hung silent and motionless, all but invisible in the darkness. Nearby, three support ships waited in equal silence. In front of them, so distant that it was just one speck among countless others, was Earth's sun.

Alanna took a deep breath, adjusted her grip on the bar and made the lift in a single smooth motion. As her arms locked straight, she began to count under her breath.

"One-one thousand, two-one thousand, three-one thousand..."

She continued the count to ten, then, slowly lowered the weights back down. Sitting up from the bench she frowned to herself. To be able to lift and hold that amount was acceptable, but acceptable wasn't the same as good. Fighter crews could expect to be subject to major G loads in combat. Raven fighters might be fly-by-wire and in theory the control column could be worked with a fingertip, but in a tight turn the pilot's hand might weight as much as his or her torso did in Earth gravity. So muscle building wasn't so much a choice as an occupational requirement. On top of that, there was the problem that went all the way back to the earliest days of the space age: muscular dystrophy. What with everything else happening on board, she hadn't had a chance to do as much exercise as she would have liked.

Most of the *Dauntless*'s flight crews were in the gym along with a few other members of the crew. But aside from heavy breathing, the room was silent. The cause was in one corner of the gym, exercising on one of the rowing machines. Even as he worked the machine, Commander Dati's eyes swept the room and stopped on Alanna. Aware of his gaze, she wiped the back of her neck and took a very slow drink of water.

"Are you done, Miss Shermer?" Dati boomed in a sarcastic tone.

Alanna glanced around the silent room.

"Yes, sir, I am," she replied, before getting up and walking out. She could have done with more time, but equally she could see several of her own flight crew were pushing themselves too hard. If exercise was necessary, over-exercise was dangerous. But once one person left the gym, others would quickly follow. Dati's displeasure, however, would focus on the first one out. But she could take that.

Pausing briefly to pull on her flight suit, she climbed up and out of the centrifuge, then made her way to *Dubious*'s hangar. Schurenhofer was sat in the pilot seat working her way down through the checklist. The deck crew signed off on a fighter when any maintenance work was done, but Alanna hadn't lasted this long by relying on a signature. When you were out there on your own if something broke, it was your problem. Alanna worked her way round *Dubious*, checking control surfaces and thruster assemblies. Satisfied she pulled herself aboard.

"Hello, Skipper," Schurenhofer said as Alanna sat in. "Nearly done."

"Everything okay?"

"So far: perhaps the age of miracles has not yet passed," Schurenhofer replied. "How are things upstairs?"

"Tense," Alanna replied.

"So everything's normal then," Schurenhofer grunted.

"I have to say it, but this was not what I was expecting," Alanna said as she stretched out. "I expected to find things tough here, but not like this. I have a bunch of newbie pilots that I have to shield from their own C.O."

"Yeah."

There had been numerous drills since *Dauntless's* hurried commissioning, some in the simulators but most in live flight. Considering the majority of the pilots were just out of training and strangers to each other, they weren't doing badly. In fact, they'd started out pretty well. If a hanging focused the mind, then preparing for combat tempered that focus into something that could cut steel. But that wasn't good enough for Dati. Each debriefing turned into an hour-long torrent of abuse as every tiny imperfection was put under a microscope and scorn heaped upon some unfortunate crewmember. Not yet into combat and Alanna could see morale dropping. She'd started speaking up, countering Dati and pointing out that many of the flaws he'd highlighted were irrelevant in the context of combat operations. She'd even dropped the odd clanger in simulations just to draw Dati's wrath away from other members of her flight. Much as he might rage, there was one factor Dati couldn't either ignore or dismiss. Alanna had over a year in frontline service. The fact she was still alive proved she knew her job.

Dati wasn't subjecting Udaltsov's flight to the same treatment though. It wasn't his fault really. With a couple of extra years of service on her, he seemed to have military obedience more thoroughly rooted in him and hadn't yet managed to get his head round the idea that a superior officer was someone you had to work around.

"Heard something interesting about the good Commander," Schurenhofer said as she ticked the last box on the checklist.

"Oh?"

"He was stationed on the *Yorktown* when the war started."

"Well that's bullshit," Alanna said dismissively.

When the Nameless started their war on humanity it had been with a surprise attack on the Fleet base at Baden. In a day of disasters, the *Yorktown* was one that stood out. Caught at her mooring, the big carrier was destroyed without striking a single blow in her own defence. As far as Alanna had ever heard, there were no survivors.

"He supposedly wasn't on her when the Nameless hit – away on compassionate leave," Schurenhofer expanded.

Alanna made no reply. That story was sufficiently short on frills to be plausible. Being the only survivor of a ship, to be the only one to have come back was bad enough when you had been there, when you *knew* that you had done all that you could. How much worse could it be if you hadn't been there? Could that anger turn outwards rather than inwards?

"Why would anyone put someone like that in charge of a squadron?"

"Why would anyone put someone like you in charge of a flight, Skipper?" Schurenhofer replied giving her a sidelong glance. "Not enough flight crews to go round."

Before Alanna could make any reply, her intercom beeped.

"All flight crews to the briefing room, all flight crews to the briefing room," squawked an automated message.

The entire Squadron waited. Some were still pulling on their flight suits and there was a low background murmur of conversation that even Dati's frown couldn't silence. When Captain Durane walked into the briefing room they came to attention. The imminence of the combat didn't seem to worry him. If anything, it seemed to put an extra spring in his step.

"Ladies and Gentlemen," Durane began as he took his place at the head of the room. "A few minutes ago we received an FTL transmission from Earth. The Nameless have begun to jump into our solar system. As previously agreed, a fighter and strike boat attack will be put in as they deploy. This is an opportunity to put them off their stroke, make it clear that we are not about to roll over or surrender the initiative.

Given the enemy's position and composition, Headquarters has ordered we use Plan Welcome One. Forty minutes from now, we will jump back into the solar system, approximately inside the orbit of Neptune. From there you will launch, making your own jump to reach the combat zone. Flights One and Two will be armed with a mix of anti-fighter and anti-ship missiles."

Nodding to Alanna, Durane added: "Flight Three will carry a pure anti-fighter load out. Your objective will be firstly to draw out and engage the enemy fighters to clear the way for our strike boats. Your secondary objective will be to engage and destroy either support ships or carriers. Commander Dati will now give you your detailed briefings. Good hunting to you all and give them hell!"

With their respective weapon controllers starting up the four Ravens of Flight Three and the deck crews finishing the arming, Alanna gave her final briefing.

"Alright, whatever else happens, make sure you wingmen stick close to your leader," she told them. "I don't want to find myself floating around out there on my own. Remember, we'll have a tech advantage, but they'll definitely have a numerical one. So our first pass will be with missiles so that we can thin the herd a bit, before closing to gun range. Even so, we'll have to be careful to avoid being mobbed. Above all else, we have to be sure we don't get boxed in,"

"I don't get why Planetary Defence is only putting in half of their fighters," complained Lieutenant Ponta of the fighter *B for Bold*.

"Basic strategy," Alanna replied. "Don't let the enemy get a good idea of your strength unless you have to. If they've only seen half the fighters we have, then that should leave their force projections way off."

Ponta nodded unhappily.

"Unless someone pulls a death ray out of their ass, we aren't going to win this today, even if we deploy every fighter we have," she added. "This is opening night stuff. Oh and by the way, the rest of us will be buying the drinks for the first one to make ace."

"All hands, brace for thrust! All hands, brace for thrust!" squawked the intercom.

"Get to your planes, folks. This show is about to hit the road."

Alanna watched them go and felt old and sad as she wondered to herself how many of them would still be alive a week from now. The first five combat sorties were statistically the most dangerous for new pilots. Trained but not experienced, if they got through those five, then their chances of survival shot up as they learned to react without conscious thought. She'd tried not to get to know them, so it wouldn't hurt as much when they started dying. But they went and said things that made them into people rather than just names and ranks. Ponta was a devout Catholic who always wore rosary beads under his shirt. Jacka was engaged to be married to her girlfriend and had tried to arrange the ceremony before shipping out, but bureaucracy had defeated her. Finally there was Andrews, an Australian and as devoted to rugby, as Ponta was to God. These were just a few fragments from their lives, but far more than Alanna wanted to know about any of them.

The fabric of space peeled open ahead of *Dauntless* as the jump conduit formed and the carrier lunged back into Earth's solar system.

With the distance so short the time in jump space was only seconds before the vessel and her escort dropped back into real space. As the *Dauntless* crossed the portal threshold, the hatches of the hangars were already opening. The twelve fighters were pushed sideways, out on their docking armatures, then in a single smooth ripple they launched. As the fighters accelerated away, the carrier was already turning. Within minutes she would jump away, back beyond the heliopause until it was time to return to recover her children.

As *Dauntless* disappeared, the Squadron cut power and coasted. With radio silence enforced, each crew was left to their own thoughts. Alanna found hers turning inwards and darkening. Once more unto the breach and she wondered how many more times she could do this. She should have been rotated out of the line months ago. But the early war losses meant there weren't enough pilots to go round. New pilots and the transfers from the national militaries, who had to be trained to land on starships, weren't keeping pace with losses. So people like her had to keep flying until the day they died or burnt out – usually at the same time.

Rather than carry on down that path, Alanna checked her watch and navigational data again. Schurenhofer raised an eyebrow but made no comment. There were three fighter carriers deployed beyond the heliopause, *Dauntless* and her sister ship *Huáscar*, the older armoured carrier *Illustrious* and orbiting Earth was *Akagi*. There were fighters deployed on the various battleships and cruisers of the gun line, and finally there were the ground-based squadrons of Planetary Defence. That added up to a lot of fighters coming from a lot of different directions, with different distances to cover. Consequently, the *Dauntless* group had to wait to allow time for the fighters from Earth to climb out of the planet's mass shadow. This strike would likely be the only combined strike the fleet would manage. Once the Nameless jammers came online, *Dauntless* and the other carriers would have to launch and recover strikes based on sensor readings taken from millions of kilometres out and, as such, hours out of date. Orders from Earth would be limited to either light speed radio transmissions or message drones that might be shot down or aimed at the wrong bit of interstellar space. Her watch let out a beep.

"No updates?" she asked.

"Nope. Looks like the Nameless haven't moved yet. Pity, if the heavies could get in this would be over real quick."

"Yeah well, if they'd seen the fleet move you can be sure they would have to," Alanna murmured. "Okay, here's hoping everyone else is in position."

"Charging jump drive," Schurenhofer said. "Tally-bloody-ho."

As they re-entered real space, Alanna threw *Dubious* into a fast series of evasive manoeuvres.

"Contacts," Schurenhofer reported. "Multiple contacts, confirmed as hostiles."

"Friendlies?"

"Negative friendlies," Schurenhofer replied. "No one else here, Skip. I think we're early."

On the display, at a range of eighty thousand kilometres, the Nameless fleet was formed into a sphere with the carriers and support ships at the centre and successive smaller ships making up each layer with fighters at the outer surface.

"Reading two to two-fifty fighters," Schurenhofer said flatly.

"Oh Christ," someone said across the radio.

"Who the hell said that?" Dati's voice roared across the net.

Alanna ignored it.

"Fight Three! We stick to the plan. Follow me!" she ordered, as they accelerated in. The other two flights formed up behind.

On the display she could see that a blob of at least seventy fighters had broken away from the fleet and was accelerating towards them, while behind them the enemy carriers launched yet more. Schurenhofer hunched over her console.

"Acceleration curves and energy outputs match previous observations. I think we're looking at the same type of fighters we've seen before," she said after a minute.

"Alright, Flight Three, stand by to engage with missiles."

Schurenhofer swiftly tagged two targets and cross referenced with other fighters' targets. With both groups of fighters accelerating directly towards one another, the range was dropping so fast that the descending numbers on Alanna's display became a blur.

"Flight Three," Alanna ordered. "On my mark, fire and break left. Mark!"

Dubious shuddered as two missiles detached from their pylons and streaked away. Six more from the rest of the flight all raced towards the Nameless. Alanna pulled to the left and up. As Flight Three pulled away, One and Two fired in turn. The Nameless fighters were caught between trying to pursue and defend themselves from the approaching missiles. They tried to do both and did neither well. Alanna rolled *Dubious* and in the distance saw brief tiny flashes.

"Eighteen hostiles down," Schurenhofer said.

Someone else in the Squadron must have come up with the same count and got overexcited.

"Oh yeah! Eat that!"

It must have been someone in Flight Two as she heard Udaltsov shout at them.

A smattering of new contacts appeared as the Nameless fighters launched their own missiles. *Dubious*'s threat detection system ran a swift analysis. They were the same dual-purpose missiles the Nameless had been using since the start of the war, slightly too small for anti-ship work and slightly too heavy for anti-fighter. With the Ravens curving round the edge of the enemy fighters, the missiles weren't able to build up speed and those that reached them were picked off. As Alanna turned them in for another pass, another speckle of green dots appeared at the edge of her display.

"I see them," Alanna said, "about time."

For twenty minutes human fighters swirled around the Nameless formation. Although enemy fighters were steadily picked off, their carriers kept feeding fresh units in. As gaps opened in the fighter screen, the Planetary Defence and Battle Fleet squadrons darted in to strike directly at the fleet and ran into a hail of counter fire. The battle became a swirl of chaos as individual flights and even separate fighters fought and died. Flights One and Two pressed on into the sphere of starships, while Alanna and Flight Three provided top cover. As both sides exhausted their supplies of missiles, the fighting closed to gun range and the Nameless weight of numbers started to tell. Some moments *Dubious* was the attacker, pouncing on slower, less manoeuvrable opponents, then seconds later she would frantically twist and turn to avoid getting boxed in. Her wingman stuck gamely on position, but clearly overwhelmed, his fire came only in spasms. An American Cobra fighter streaked past *Dubious*, close enough for Alanna to see with the naked eye, one engine ablaze and with four enemy fighters in pursuit.

"Live bait," she said as she pulled in behind and took down two before they realised she was there. Her wingman potted the third and the fourth fled. The American gave a brief wing waggle as he headed for safety.

"Second lot of strike boats are arriving," Schurenhofer reported. Alanna couldn't remember the first lot. But this time she was close enough to see the strike go wrong. A large group of Nameless fighters broke off from the dogfights and accelerated towards the strike boats. Human fighters tried to intercept but were blocked and engaged. The strike boats launched their missiles at long range and broke off. The fighters caught them and the gunboats succumbed while bravely attempting to protect their strike boat comrades. Only half survived long enough to jump away. As Alanna dodged *Dubious* around successive passes by Nameless fighters she could see the icons for the strike boats blink out and was glad they didn't share a radio channel.

"Flight Three, this is Squadron Leader," Dati's voice came through. "We've exhausted ordnance. Prepare to disengage."

"Understood Squadron Leader," Alanna replied. "Standing by to cover you. *A for Abbey, B for Bold* – close on my position."

Pulling *Dubious* up she aimed into the nearest formation of Nameless fighters, throwing them into confusion. Flights One and Two flashed through the gap and before the Nameless could reorganise. Alanna gathered her flight and followed them at full power.

Dauntless jumped in ten minutes after the squadron arrived at the rendezvous point. Time enough for Alanna to see that both Flights One and Two were missing a plane each and that two of hers were showing damage codes on their transponders. The landing was ragged, taking nearly twenty minutes, but this time there was no public abuse from Dati as he waited his turn. Alanna was among the last to land and leaving Schurenhofer to deal with shutdown, she left the hangar to find her troops.

Ponta was out of his fighter by the time Alanna got into the hangar. He and his weapons controller were looking up at the damage. With the hangar still pressurising, they were both still helmeted, but despite that Alanna could see their grim expressions. The vertical stabiliser had been shot to pieces. Not necessary for space flight, but if *B for Bold* tried to fly atmospheric; she'd be as airworthy as a brick.

"Ma'am," said the weapons controller when he saw her.

"What happened?" Alanna asked looking at the stump of the stabiliser.

"I was going after a pair and they sucked me into a mob of them." Ponta said with a shake of his head. Unconsciously his fingers rubbed at the front of his flight suit, where the rosary beneath pressed up against his skin.

"They would have got us, but for the fact another squadron engaged them. Americans, I think."

"Someone up here... Someone *out* here was looking after us," his weapons controller added.

"Yes, something like that," Ponta said, still rubbing the rosary.

"Go," Alanna ordered, "the computer will have finished downloading your logs. The intelligence officer will be waiting to debrief you."

"Yes ma'am," Ponta replied, after taking a last look at the damage.

At first glance the fighter *A for Abbey* didn't appear damaged, but the deck crew gathered around the crew access hatch indicated otherwise. As she pushed off from the deck, Alanna could see weapon strikes on the fuselage and, most ominous of all, two panels of the cockpit canopy were shattered. Alanna dreaded to think what damage had been inflicted within.

The deck chief saw her coming.

"They're both still alive," he said, "though their guardian angels must have racked up one hell of an overtime bill on this one."

As he spoke, the deck crew started to stand back from the access way as the first of the crew pulled themselves out. There was something odd about the flight suit and it took Alanna a moment to work out what. The chest area and helmet were a darker grey, almost a black, with all insignia gone. Alanna abruptly realised what it was – the flight suit was scorched. When they were hit, something had come close enough to burn but not kill. The first figure in the now anonymous suit reached back to help as a shaky hand reached out to feel around the hatch.

"Where are the fucking medics?" Jacka's anguished voice came from the first suit to emerge.

"Down here, Lieutenant," the Chief replied. "Easy now."

As the injured weapons controller was taken into the medics' care, Alanna took a quick glance inside the cockpit. Almost every surface showed evidence of heat damage, with the exception of the seats, protected by the bodies of the crew.

"We took a direct hit, ma'am," said Jacka from behind her. Turning, Alanna found Jacka floating beside her, holding herself steady with one hand on the wing. If they'd been in gravity, Jacka probably would have collapsed. Her visor was darker than it should have been – the polarisation must have been damaged. If her suit had looked bad before, up close if was frightening. It must still have been airtight to get her this far, but Alanna guessed she'd have to be cut out of it. She took Jacka by the arm and pushed them back towards the airlock out of the hangar. Catching sight of her weapons controller being strapped to a board for transport, Jacka resisted weakly.

"What can be done is being done. He'll catch up with you at sickbay," Alanna told her.

As the sickbay, orderlies cut through the scorched suit while Jacka talked.

"They nearly got us as we were disengaging. We took a hit from the port side. I didn't even see them coming. It was a passing shot, so they only landed a couple of hits, but the first one hit the canopy. It must have caught us at a right angle because it went straight through – in one side and out the other, without hitting anything else."

Alanna felt sick. The bolt from a plasma gun was held together by a magnetic field. The cockpit canopy obviously hadn't provided enough resistance to disrupt that field. If it had hit anything else on its way through, it would have lost integrity instantly and quite simply burnt out everything in the cockpit.

"But James was looking in the direction of first hit."

Jacka cast her eyes towards the section of the sickbay where curtains had been pulled and the lights turned down low.

"Afterwards, he said he couldn't see," she added in an anguished voice.

"His helmet visor probably over polarised and locked. Let's not panic. Let's wait until the Doctor is done, then if we have to panic, well, we'll panic with precision."

"Lieutenant Commander Shermer?" said a rating from the hatch.

"Yes?"

"You're wanted in the briefing room."

"Alright," she replied, before patting Jacka on the arm. "I'll be down again as soon as I can. Try to get some rest."

Dati was waiting for her.

"Where were you?" he demanded, but for once without any real anger.

"Sickbay, sir."

"And?"

"Lieutenant Jacka is pretty shaken, but will likely be okay. Her weapons controller is probably permanently blinded though," Alanna replied tiredly, as it all just seemed to catch up with her.

"Sit down before you fall down," Dati grunted. "Intelligence is still compiling but at a rough count, we took down maybe thirty odd fighters, a couple of escorts and damaged a cruiser. They shot down most of our anti-ship missiles."

"Not a bad start."

Dati sat down beside her.

"This was our big strike and I don't think we hit anything the Nameless gave a rat's ass about." Dati shook his head. "Each member of the Squadron is the product of years of training, yet here we are on day one and four of them are dead and one might as well be for all the use he'll be to us. When I think what the old *Dauntless* did with obsolete fighters."

"I was there sir," Alanna replied.

Dati looked at her sharply. Then, realising who he was talking to, he turned away.

"More than half of us didn't come back and that was when the Nameless didn't have fighters or know how to fight them," Alanna reminded him.

"Well they do now. They activated their FTL jammers a short while ago. The last transmission we got from Earth was that Nameless support ships had been observed jumping in and delivering new fighters. Next time, we'll have to go in the under strength until Earth can get replacements to us."

"Lieutenant Shermer. I'm ready for you now."

It was the intelligence officer. As Alanna got up to follow him to the hatch, Dati called after her.

"Good work, Lieutenant, you did well with your flight. Pity it didn't amount to anything."

Chapter Seven

Tightening of the Noose

25th December 2067

Crowe instinctively ducked under the hatchway as he made his way up to the bridge and walked into the paper streamer that was unexpectedly hanging in the way. Made from cut-up paper manuals, it wasn't the most colourful of decorations, while the next one manufactured from lengths of platted coloured wires was even less festive. But for the moment they added some much needed cheer to the grey confines of the crew quarters, even if engineering would in due course have to recover and return them to stores.

"Whoops, sorry sir," a petty officer apologised as Crowe attempted to disentangle himself without ripping the streamer. "I'll tighten that up a bit."

"And Merry Christmas, sir," he added, as he lifted it out of Crowe's way.

"And you PO? Have you eaten yet?" Crowe asked.

"No sir," the petty officer said with a shake of his head. "Looking forward to my first ever Christmas dinner."

"Well don't let me hold you, the Cook has done well."

"Thank you, sir,"

The petty officer was a native of the Indian sub-continent and, if Crowe remembered his file correctly, it listed him as a Hindu. By its nature the fleet had always been a multinational and multicultural organisation. In the early days that had been something of a challenge, but at the same time, this aspect offered some significant advantages in terms of the day-to-day operations. With most ships having at least a sizeable minority of non-Christians, it was possible to give most of Christmas Day off to those who were. In turn, the important days of other religious groups and cultures could be given their days with little difficulty.

On board *Deimos* this Christmas was different, with a palpable desire by the crew to celebrate something – anything. The ship's Christian contingent had extended the season's greetings and invited the rest of the crew to Christmas dinner. Even if quite a few of them were a bit vague as to what was involved, there had been few refusals and the crew had thrown themselves into decorating the ship with whatever they could lay their hands on. Somehow, the ship's purser had managed to get hold of some real turkey meat before they left. Despite the fact, because there were so many mouths to feed, no one would get more than a taste of the big bird, the day had definitely lightened the mood.

God knows they needed it. The arrival of the Nameless fleet dropping into the system had been a hard blow. Watching the fighters and strike boats throw themselves into the fight, only to recoil as their enemy gave as good as they got, was harder still. Crowe still considered himself to be at heart an explorer rather than a fighting officer, but still, not to steer towards the metaphorical sound of gunfire felt like a betrayal. Stepping onto the bridge, Crowe crossed from a world of determined festivity into one of demanding professionalism. Mostly. Someone seemed to have stuck a paper star above the main holo. Commander Bhudraja was sitting in the command chair and rose as soon as he noticed Crowe. The duty watch were all there, leaning over their passive sensor consoles, looking out for anything that might indicate Nameless ships in the vicinity.

There had been a heart-stopping moment a few days earlier when a Nameless scout dropped into real space close to Mars. It actually got inside the orbit of Phobos before jumping away, evidently satisfied nothing of consequence was present. Since then they'd mostly been relying on three discrete passive sensor satellites orbiting the Red Planet, which lasered their readings to a pick-up some distance from the Fast Division's position on the surface. The dust from their landing was still slowly swirling around with the result that laser connection was occasionally lost for several seconds. But between that and radio transmissions, they stayed well informed.

"Commander, anything to report?"

"No sir," Bhudraja replied. "We observed the *Illustrious*'s fighter group put in a strike about an hour ago. The Nameless jumped after that and have yet to reappear. So they're either far enough away that the first light speed emissions haven't reached us yet or there is a solar body between us and them."

"How many fighters?"

"Sensors think about a dozen," Bhudraja replied. "The *Illustrious* should have eighteen fighters, so if they dispatched a dozen, then that was all they had to send."

Crowe glanced towards a display showing outside the ship. The floating dust still blotted out almost everything, but it was very slowly settling, allowing Crowe to just about make out the looming dark presence of *Warspite* in the distance. Every day they made a status report via laser to the flagship. Every day they received an automatic acknowledgement and nothing more. Did Admiral Lewis know uncertainty? Did he wonder whether the time for the Fast Division to make its move would ever come or worry whether he would recognise the moment? Impossible to know – the Admiral was as inscrutable as a sphinx.

"Do you think, sir," Bhudraja asked, "we were right to mark Christmas? There was no Christmas out there."

"We're not out there," Crowe replied. "I know what you're saying, Commander. We're celebrating while others are fighting and I did wonder about it. But we're doing what we have to. Our job is the easy one, right up to the moment it suddenly becomes very, very difficult."

"Yes, sir. I have a few thoughts on keeping the crew busy; after today."

"Good. We'll try to use this as productively as we can. We can't allow people time to over-think this."

The two of them stood silent for a while.

"I got something called a Brussels sprout on my plate," Bhudraja commented.

"They're a bit of an acquired taste."

"I don't think I'll bother."

12th January 2068

Willis had just pulled herself through the engine room hatch when the main alarm went off. As she swung herself around, she heard Guinness mutter something like 'here we go again.'

"Bridge, report!" Willis snapped into her intercom as she pulled herself back the way she'd come. Behind, she heard the pitch of the generators change as they spun up to full power.

"Captain, an enemy force has just jumped in – ninety ships. Two carriers, five cap ships and twenty cruisers with escorts and scouts," the duty officer replied.

"Shit," Willis muttered half to herself. Ahead, the off-duty engineering shifts came pouring down the passageway.

"Make a hole!" Willis shouted as she accelerated towards them. Ratings pulled themselves towards the sides as Willis shot down the middle. At the reactor room bulkhead, she let out a grunt of pain as she clipped the edge of the hatch.

"Captain, should we bring the Number Two Reactor online?"

Orders had come up from the surface for all ships to minimise fuel expenditure. *Black Prince* could run, even fight, on one reactor, but it left her dangerously underpowered and exposed to damage or equipment failure. But bringing a cold reactor online was a twenty-minute, fuel intensive process.

"Bring it online," she confirmed.

"Yes, Captain."

By the time she reached the bridge, the battle station's crew had already arrived and changed into their survival suits. On the status board, sections were rapidly turning green as they reported in as ready for action. Willis tossed her jacket into one corner as she pulled on her own suit.

"Alright, Guns," she said to the duty officer, "I've got this."

He nodded before heading for the hatch and his own station, nearly colliding at the hatch with Lieutenant Commander Chuichi.

The Commander had his suit on but helmet under his arm.

"They're not even trying are they," he said nodding towards the main holo.

"No, they aren't," Willis replied, as she sealed up her suit. "Bastards!"

"Bridge, Coms. Orders coming in from Squadron Command."

"My screen," she replied.

There was nothing unexpected in the orders from *Saladin*. Positioned on the right flank of the fleet, they were to sweep forward. There were gaps in the formation that would allow Planetary Defence's forts to fire through in support. A faint chime came across the intercom command channel as the last section reported it was ready for action.

"Decompress all sections," Willis ordered before turning to Chuichi, "You'd better head aft, Commander."

"Yes, Captain," he replied, before pulling himself to the hatch, back towards his post in Damage Control. There was no haste in his movements. There didn't need to be, he could predict just as easily as anyone else in the fleet how the next couple of hours would go.

"Helm, bring us to heading one zero three dash zero eight seven and bring engines to forty percent."

The engines fired and Willis felt herself being pushed back into her seat as *Black Prince* and the rest of the fleet started to climb up and out of orbit. Ahead, Planetary Defence fighter squadrons led the way, accelerating away from the more sluggish starships.

"Bridge, Sensors. Contact separation, we have incoming."

On the main holo Willis saw a mass of new contacts appear as the Nameless ships launched a wave of large missiles down into Earth's gravity well. *Black Prince*'s computer started to work out whether any were specifically aimed at them. Positioned as they were on the extreme right flank of the combined fleet, they probably weren't, but assumptions made for corpses. A mass of lines appeared on the screen as the computer extrapolated the course of each missile and established that most were aimed at the centre of the fleet.

"Bridge, Fire Control. Prepare for Fire Plan Baker," she ordered.

As the approaching missiles crossed through the half light second mark, some began to disappear. The orbital forts were already scoring a few hits with their big laser cannons, but most of the disappearing missiles weren't being destroyed. They were big mass driver missiles, firing before they reached flak range, each one sending a metal lump weighing several kilograms indiscriminately barrelling towards Earth. With so much else flying about, *Black Prince*'s radar couldn't pick them up yet. When the range closed, they would re-acquire and then try to knock a few off course with plasma cannon fire, while the ships in the centre manoeuvred to avoid them. The orbital forts would have to deal with whatever got through. A few made it pass both the fleet and Planetary Defence, but most struck the atmosphere at the wrong angle to make entry. They either burned up or more likely skipped off Earth's atmosphere. The only one that made it down plunged into the mid North Atlantic, but even that caused flooding of the Western European and Eastern American coasts.

"Contacts entering firing range."

"Flak guns commence firing."

In their dorsal and ventral mounts, the two flak guns started to track and fire, eliminating those missiles that entered *Black Prince*'s defensive zone. Even as the first wave of missiles died, the Nameless launched a second, which went the same way as the first, as did the third. They began to retreat slowly away, staying well under the maximum velocity at they could jump. As the escorts exhausted their supply of cap ship missiles, the weight of successive salvos diminished. The Nameless fighters that had deployed, began to fall back and land on their carriers and then with five minutes to go before the human fighters reached effective missile range, the enemy ships began to jump away.

On her bridge Willis went through the motions, giving the orders that needed to be given for *Black Prince* to metaphorically march to the top of the hill, then march down again. An hour and a half after the first jump in, *Black Prince* was back in position, with only diminished fuel and ammunition to show for it.

I could have done the whole damn thing from my bunk, Willis thought to herself when she finally made it off the bridge. Next time maybe she would, she thought only half in jest. Nostalgia was a terrible thing, but she was starting to miss old *Hood* and more particularly, Dryad Station. She'd been in over her head and stared defeat in the face, but at least she'd been able to make some kind of running. Here she was just one more cog in a giant machine that wasn't achieving very much. It wasn't anything anyone could be blamed for, but that didn't make her feel any less useless. It had been the same for nearly the last three weeks. Every two or three days a sizeable chunk of the Nameless fleet would jump in and put in what amounted to a bombardment. No ships had been lost, but every time the fleet had to react, it had consumed fuel they couldn't replace. Guinness was standing at the door of her cabin. For a moment Willis wondered why he was there, before remembering that she had wanted to talk to him before the bombardment.

"You have those figures?"

"Yes, Skipper," he replied offering a pad.

"Twelve percent?" Willis said with dismay as she scanned the list.

"Sorry, Skipper," Guinness replied, "but yeah, each one of these little jaunts costs us about twelve percent of our fuel."

"That isn't even close to the fuel efficiency the book says we should get."

"The book wasn't written with our combination of equipment in mind, ma'am," Guinness said. "We didn't get a shakedown cruise, so we didn't get a chance to find the optimum setting either, which isn't helping. But mostly ma'am, I think whoever signed off those engines as reconditioned, did the fucking bare minimum and figured the job's a good 'un. Pardon my language."

They were already getting some pointed messages from both Headquarters and the flagship of the fleet. Guinness was damn a good engineer, but he had his limits.

"If we could get a bit of downtime – proper downtime, then there's a lot I could do."

"What's proper downtime, Chief?" Willis asked.

"Two weeks."

"Chief, that isn't even worth asking for," she replied. "Is there anything you can do while we're in the line?"

"Section three in the report, Skipper."

Willis skimmed across it.

"Alright, proceed." She hesitated as she considered what to say next. "Chief, I want you to take a really close look at Number One Reactor. Make sure it has no problems."

"Sure, I can do. But it hasn't..."

"We aren't bringing Number Two online when the Nameless turn up next. We'll just have to chance it."

Guinness's expression tightened.

"Okay, Skipper, I'll give it a double check."

18th January 2068

Alanna climbed wearily out of the cockpit of *Dubious* and signed over the fighter to the deck crew. She glanced over at the scorch marks on the port wing and shook her head. Schurenhofer didn't even glance as she pulled herself towards the hatch out of the hangar.

"Skipper, you want me to..." she started to ask.

"No. No point both of us. Just go," Alanna said, more sharply than she meant to. Schurenhofer looked for a moment, as if she was about to make her own steely reply, but shrugged instead.

As she cleared the airlock Alanna pulled off her helmet and loosened the neck dam. She had maybe three hours before *Dubious* needed to fly off again. Debrief for this mission, briefing for the next and prep would eat up an hour of that – at least. So how best use the time? Eat, sleep or wash – pick any two.

"Get anything?"

It took Alanna's tired brain a moment to realise someone had addressed her. It was Udaltsov, his helmet on but visor up. He looked just as tired as she felt.

"Swing and a miss," she replied. "They didn't have fighter cover and jumped away as soon as they saw us."

Udaltsov shrugged and carried on down the passageway. Conversations had gone that way. No one had the energy for anything beyond the bare minimum. They were three days into a four-day cycle. *Dauntless* jumped into the system, well clear of any of the planets. After the first day the Nameless hadn't stood still and let Earth throw its entire fighter force at them. Instead their fleet jumped back and forth across the system, maintaining the siege, without giving the defenders a solid target to aim at. Sometimes a chunk of the fleet would break away and rendezvous with support ships. That need to resupply was potentially their Achilles heel, but the Nameless knew that too. Their supply ships always stayed at least two light hours away from Earth. By the time the fleet sensors detected them, they'd already jumped away to a new position. The three carriers stood more of a chance. Jumping around the system, they could get closer and be subject to shorter light speed lags. Sometimes they were sent out as squadrons, but mostly as individual flights. Something like two out of every five sorties resulted in contact. When that happened, it was short and sharp as the Ravens attempted to knife through the fighter screen to get into range for anti-ship missiles. But the hunt wasn't just one way. Nameless cruiser squadrons hunted the carriers. They'd come close to making an interception several times and on the last such occasion *Dauntless* was forced to break for interstellar space, which had at least confirmed the long held suspicion that the Nameless drives were strictly for system to system jumps. Interstellar space was a no-go zone for them.

Climbing up and into the centrifuge, Alanna walked into the debriefing room and dropped her helmet on the intelligence officer's desk.

"Well?" he asked.

"Nothing at our primary target," she said as she flopped into a chair. "We sighted support ships at the secondary, but they jumped away just as we arrived. Are you writing this down?"

The last part she said in an exasperated tone.

"I'm waiting for your weapons controller."

"She isn't coming – I told her not to. You don't need to hear the same damn thing in stereo."

"You're supposed to both be here for debrief," his voice rose angrily.

"And you're supposed to put us onto a target," she shouted back "not have us farting around out there for hours on end!"

"All hands! Brace for in system jump! Brace for in system jump!" the intercom system suddenly announced. Both of them gripped the table as the carrier jolted in and out of jump space. He gave her a disgusted look and hurried away. With the shift in position the intelligence section would be taking stock of the readings from the passive sensors. Udaltsov's flight would be launching to provide cover if something was too close, while Dati's would be ready to fly off on a strike mission.

She should probably have waited for the intelligence officer to return and complete his debrief, but that wasn't about to happen. Picking her helmet up, she headed for the mess.

Schurenhofer was already eating by the time she arrived. Alanna joined Jacka in the queue for food. The other pilot had been a rookie when she arrived on *Dauntless*. Now she was a veteran and fighter ace several times over. Aside from Alanna and Schurenhofer, she was the only member of the original flight still around. Andrews disappeared on day ten, when they got involved in a dogfight over Neptune. No one saw what happened to him. Ponta's fighter lost its jump drive close to Saturn. It was fifty-fifty but he might have made the real space passage to one of the orbital forts before the fighter's environmental support packed up. Two replacement crews had reached them. One was lost within a day of their arrival.

With food on her plate Alanna found a seat and started to eat. There wasn't much talk in the canteen. It might not have been as tough for the carrier crew as the flight crews, but they weren't having it easy either. If nothing else, it wore on their nerves, spending days in enemy territory, in which a hostile force could jump in at any moment.

"Hey, you're supposed to eat it, not sleep in it!"

Looking round, Alanna saw Jacka, further down the table, her eyes closed, her head slowly dropped and settled into her plate.

Someone guffawed and Jacka jerked upright. A piece of mushroom dropped off her chin. She glared around the room with red-rimmed eyes filled with belligerence. The compartment went silent, the humour of the previous moment lost. Jacka threw down her cutlery and stalked out. The Lieutenant's weapons controller looked to Alanna, clearly wondering whether he should go after her. Alanna shook her head. People returned to their meals. Such incidents were now too common to be worth mentioning. Exhaustion did funny things to people. Normally easy-going individuals became snappy, ready to take offence where none was intended. Two other pilots on Udaltsov's flight were close friends, but now, every time they spoke to each other, they did so with studied politeness, as if they were afraid that their last words in this life might be ones of anger.

The intelligence officer walked into the mess and started towards the food service area, only to alter his course towards Alanna as soon as he saw her.

If he whines about briefing I'll... Alanna thought. She could feel herself getting hot as her temper began to go.

"Lieutenant," he said, "we just picked up a transmission from the American starfort *Cold Harbour*. Lieutenant Ponta made it."

It took her a moment to work out what he was talking about.

"I didn't think he would," she replied, as the heat of her anger dissipated.

"They cut oxygen flow to the point where it was just enough to keep them alive provided they didn't move," he said before shrugging. "Even with that, they only landed with less than an hour of air left. Still they made it."

Alanna smiled for what felt like the first time in years.

20th January 2068

Snow crunched underfoot as he stepped out through the small door onto the flat roof. Europe was experiencing its hardest winter in twenty years, although compared to what he'd seen in some parts of the States, it was barely worth mentioning.

"Oh yeah," said Jeff Harlow as he set down the camera tripod and sat-phone case. "This is the spot."

"Why don't you leave that determination to the professional there, champ?" said his camerawoman Marie, as she laboured up the stairs. "And more to the point, would you mind shifting your overpaid self out of the way?"

Jeff did as he was told and Marie stepped onto the hotel's flat roof and looked around. It wasn't a very tall building, but then London wasn't a very tall city. The sun was setting fast and the metropolis was already lit up.

"You've got to wonder why they waited until this time. Surely it would have been better to do it during the day?" Marie asked, as she carefully set her camera bag down.

"With the Brits, God knows. Union rules or an attempt to drum up the spirit of Dunkirk," Jeff replied as he rubbed his shoulder. The six months he'd spent in deep space covering the fighting on the Junction Line had definitely caused some muscle loss. He should have done more exercise, but he'd never been much good at that. Not much point in saying anything though. Marie was twice his age but built like a brick shithouse – so much mockery would ensue. He wasn't about to make that mistake, not twice anyway.

"Spirit of what?"

"Never mind."

"Well let's get this set up. They won't wait for us," she grunted as she kicked open the camera tripod.

"Yeah," Jeff replied, looking out across the city, "This will be first take stuff. Mind you, when you've done filming in combat..."

"Yes! Yes! YES!" Marie cut in with mock exasperation. "I know about your war heroics!"

Jeff grinned. Something landed in his hair.

"Snowing again," he observed

"Good. It adds to the ambience."

"Oy! Is anyone up there?" came a shout from the stairs down into the hotel.

"Yeah, Richard, we are," Marie shouted back.

There was the thump of feet on the stairs and Richard, the film crew manager, emerged onto the roof.

"I wondered where you'd got to," Jeff said. "Where's Jennifer? Time's a bit short if we're to get those shots."

"Guys, can you put everything down for a minute," Richard said.

His tone immediately got Jeff's attention. When he'd been with the fleet, it was always bad news when people talked like that.

"Richard, where's Jen?" Marie asked trying to look past him. Jennifer was their makeup girl and gopher – and she wasn't on the stairs behind Richard.

"I got a phone call about an hour ago from the airline. Our flight and our tickets have been cancelled."

"What!" Jeff exclaimed. "But they were supposed to run until Tuesday!"

"Yeah," Richard said grimly. "The thing is, a couple of governments have started requisitioning fuel from their airports. It looks like the crews got scared that they would find themselves stranded in the ass end of nowhere – probably right to be. Our plane is being used to get flight crews and embassy staff back to the States."

"When!" Jeff asked

Richard glanced at his watch. "About twenty minutes ago."

"And you didn't call us!" Marie shouted at him furiously.

"Look! They were only prepared to give us one seat," Richard shouted back. "Just one! And the plane was taking off as soon as it was full. You two weren't there so the only choices were me or Jen." He paused before continuing more calmly. "Jen has a young family so I threw her into a cab to Heathrow. She made it, just about." He looked back and forth at the two of them. "I made a call guys and I think I made the right one."

"Well shit!" Marie said in a tone now more disgusted than angry.

"So where does that leave us then?" Jeff asked, as Marie circled the roof cursing and kicking. "Any chance of getting another flight?"

"Not a prayer," Richard said shaking his head. "Even airline staff that live here are being told to go home."

"You told them we are a film crew?"

"Oh yeah. But that was no currency."

"So... what now? The embassy?"

"Probably closed and we've got a better option," Richard said, shaking his head. "I ran into the hotel manager on the way up."

"I thought he said he was closing up," Jeff said.

The hotel mostly catered to business customers. In the past three days the place had become increasingly quiet as guests left without being replaced. This morning, there had only been one other person at breakfast and Jeff had seen him check out afterwards. The same was true of the staff – there appeared to be only one or two still around. In fact the city as a whole was shutting down. Most shops had pulled down their shutters more than a week ago and the supermarkets were mostly cleaned out. Only the shops that sold camping and survival gear still seemed to have trade and even they were closing now.

"He's offered to let us stay – for free as long as we take care of the place. I think he expected the janitor to still be around, but he was the first to fuck off. I know it's not perfect but..." he trailed off.

They'd been in Dublin covering updates from Fleet Headquarters as the battle was fought out there in the solar system. But as it ground on without resolution, a world that had become used to reliable energy suddenly discovered what happened when the hydrogen flow was turned off. The network wanted coverage from a major European capital. They could have used a local reporter but they wanted one of their own. A couple of other networks were prepared to pay syndication fees to use the footage, which sweetened the deal. They'd offered every available news team huge bonuses to stay in Europe a little longer. Jeff's crew was an amalgamation of those few prepared stay.

Fool's gold, Jeff thought to himself. If missiles started raining down, then the health of anyone's bank balance would count for exactly jack-shit. But what would he have done if he had been home? If this was the end of the world, where did he want to spend it? Rattling around in an apartment that wasn't home, but just a place where he kept his stuff? He could have gone to his parents and spent his last days with them and his family. *I'd rather step out of an airlock in my birthday suit*, he thought to himself. Richard and Marie both had spouses, who they pretty soon would not be in a position to contact, let alone get home to.

"Well, we knew we were taking a risk," Jeff said.

"Yeah, we did," Richard agreed. He shook his head and Jeff realised with embarrassment there were tears in the other man's eyes. "I'm up to my ears in debt but what the hell will money be worth soon?"

"If the fleet wins – then the same as it was last month."

"If it was going to win, it would have done so by now," Marie abruptly put in. "Here we are at the start of the end of days providing *expert* coverage for people back home that by now probably don't have electricity to power their screens."

In the distance, at the visible edge of the city, an entire section of lights went out.

"Shit! It's started!" Marie exclaimed as she sprang towards her camera.

Jeff pulled off his jacket and smoothed down his hair.

"And... go," she muttered as she got the camera settled.

"Tonight, Ladies and Gentlemen, in the great city of London, I am witnessing something not seen in over a century. Tonight, Ladies and Gentlemen, all over Europe the lights are going out."

21st January 2068

On the main holo, the blip with multiple damage codes wavered and vanished.

"Bridge, Sensors! *Illustrious* has jumped."

Berg was too busy shouting orders at Helm and Fire Control to have time to acknowledge.

"Helm! Give me sideslip to port! Guns! Target all missiles on contact FC1 and fire!"

Mantis shuddered as she coughed out four slammer missiles towards the enemy fighter carrier. There wasn't a hope in hell any of them would make it through, but if it forced the Nameless to use several of their own to intercept them, then that was a good enough trade off. Off to port, *Puma* was still breaking up as she was wracked by explosions. As the closest ship to the enemy when the four Nameless cruisers jumped in, she hadn't stood much of a chance. But she thinned much of the first wave of missiles and mauled one cruiser with gunfire before she herself was torn open. *Wasp*, her armament gutted by two direct hits, was running for her life as the crew frantically tried to get the jump drive back online. Off to starboard, there was a swirling melee of fighters. One of the carrier's flights had been flying escort when the Nameless arrived. They'd stopped the cap ship missiles aimed at the carrier, but couldn't deal with all the dual-purpose ones that followed. The standby flight was taken out on the deck. Then a Nameless carrier jumped in and disgorged its entire complement. All the Ravens could do was to attempt to tie up the enemy fighters.

"Coms. Anything from *Wasp*?" Berg demanded.

"Only that they need more time."

Berg looked towards her screen. There was an open link to Captain Liv on *Scorpion*.

"We can't stay here much longer," she said as *Mantis* jolted violently.

"We *have* to give them a little more time," the Bull replied tightly.

The two destroyers were accelerating backwards away from the Nameless. They kept their guns bearing on the enemy but any hit could take out either ship's jump drive. Weaving, dodging and copious amounts of chaff was the only thing keeping *Mantis* and *Scorpion* alive. But they were playing Russian roulette and the Nameless only had to be lucky once.

"Sir, we're crossing the line between courage and stupidity!" Berg called. The incoming missiles thinned and she turned and snapped at fire control.

"Guns, switch target – two salvoes at target C3."

One bolt struck home and on the holo the computer highlighted fragments blasting clear. A second later a Nameless missile got through *Mantis*'s point defence fire. A gouge was ripped in the port engine nacelle and coolant began to vent as the hull was peppered with missile fragments. Berg spun towards the damage control display. Several sections were blinking red and two thrusters had gone dark. A second later one came back online as the Lazarus systems found a working connection.

Berg opened her mouth to shout at Liv again, when she was cut off.

"Bridge, Sensors. *Wasp* has jumped!"

"Navigation, give me jump calculations. Helm, stand ready to make the turn," she barked.

There was no signal from *Scorpion*. The Bull knew that for this manoeuvre, the captain had to rely on his or her own judgement to choose the moment to spin the ship around so that the jump drive would face in the direction of travel. It was an action that would also turn all their heavy weapons away from the enemy. Berg leaned forward in her seat, staring intently at the holo. Another missile burst close enough for *Mantis* to be hit by fragments. There was a gap between one salvo and another. Was it enough for *Mantis* to turn and engage her jump drive?

"Helm, now!"

With damage to the port side thrusters, the helmsman didn't attempt to spin and instead flipped *Mantis* vertically. From the bows came the whine of the drive spinning up. Point defence continued to blaze away but the plasma cannons now had no target and the destroyer's course steadied as she prepared to jump. Two Cap Ship missiles locked on and powered in.

"Jumping!" shouted the Navigator as the jump portal opened ahead of them. *Mantis* lunged through into safety.

"So much for the opinions of those who thought we should have stripped the armour off," said Captain Chothia of the *Illustrious* across the laser hook up. "That first hit would have crippled us if we hadn't had the plate to stop it."

He looked exhausted. Designed before jump drives for fighters had been developed, of the pre-war carriers *Illustrious* uniquely had cruiser level armour. It had saved her, but only just. All the hangars on one side were wrecked and half the engines were bleeding coolant or plasma.

The expression on group commander Rear Admiral Paahlisson's face suggested that at best he regarded this as cold comfort. With the task group returned to the safety of interstellar space, it was time to take stock and the picture was not pretty. The conference screen was segmented to show the face of each ship's commander. The *Wasp* had lost power shortly after arriving and, now mostly evacuated, she hung from the side of the support ship *Samuel Clemens*. So the screen was now split only four ways.

"Yes, Captain," Paahlisson said. "But unfortunately the level of damaged sustained is well beyond what we can repair ourselves. It was brave work by Commander Liv, covering *Wasp*."

It was foolish, Berg thought to herself. There was no way *Wasp* could be repaired in time to be of any use in this fight. But they'd nearly thrown good after bad trying to save her. The Admiral's chilly tone suggested he thought the same. But somehow, even misplaced bravery had to be congratulated.

"What condition are your ships in?" Paahlisson continued. "Are they combat worthy?"

"In our case no," said Liv. "Fire Control took a hit just as we made our jump. We may be able to…"

"And you, Commander Berg?" Paahlisson cut him off.

"We have some damage, sir, which we can repair from our own resources. My ship can still fight."

"Good. I want you to resupply your ship from the *Samuel Clemens*. You will then escort our ammunition ships, first to the resupply point for *Huáscar*. You'll leave one of the ammunition ships with them. You are then to proceed to the *Dauntless* Task Group and attach yourself to them. We're out of this fight but we have to get whatever we can back in. Commander Liv, your ship will remain here to provide *Illustrious* with close escort."

"Sir, I would like to suggest we transfer some flight crews to *Mantis* before she leaves," said Chothia. "We now have more crews than we have fighters to put them in."

"Make it happen," Paahlisson said.

A day later *Mantis*, her damaged hull freshly patched, led the two ammunition ships away from the mauled carrier.

22nd January 2068

Staff Captain Sheehan tapped on the hatch before stepping through. A quick sweep of the cabin's work and sleeping areas was enough to establish the Admiral wasn't there. Sheehan sighed to himself – that left only one other place he would be.

Not many of the crew were around. With the battleship landed and shut down, there wasn't anything like enough real work to occupy the entire crew. The ship's internals were now gleaming from stem to stern, so even the make work exercises were exhausted. Passing through the crew areas, Sheehan could hear an argument going on. Looking into the ratings' mess, he could see a pair of then swearing at each other in at least two different languages. In the corner of the mess, half a dozen other ratings were playing cards, totally ignoring the noise behind them. A petty officer was standing just inside the hatch and gave Sheehan a sheepish look before stepping forward to separate the two. Arguments had become common and unless they became physical, the ships NCOs were inclined to let people blow off steam.

There was the old cliché that the wait before battle was the worst bit. Having seen actual combat, a month ago Sheehan would have called that bullshit. But now, after landing on Phobos and weeks of listening to the radio signals of those doing the actual fighting, he was starting to reconsider. Several times they'd observed the Nameless fleet approach Earth and the Fast Division had stood ready to take off. But each time, the Admiral decided the position wasn't good enough. Either there weren't enough Nameless ships, or they weren't deep enough into Earth's mass shadow. Each time the crew had to stand down, it got harder.

Stepping onto the bridge, he immediately sensed the tension. The officer in charge sat rigidly in the command chair, while around him and seated at their posts, the duty watch were all as still as statues. Off to one side, at the communications section, Sheehan found Lewis. He had an earpiece on and was sitting, one elbow rested on the console, his chin on his hand, staring into the middle distance.

"Sir, the supply report for the Fast Division," Sheehan said, handing over the computer pad. The information could have been sent directly to the Admiral's terminal, but there were some things that required the personal touch.

Lewis took off his earpiece and cast his eyes over the report. There was nothing especially new or interesting, just a list of fuel reserves, maintenance levels and crew conditions. The daily report had barely altered in weeks, aside from the inevitable downward creep of their fuel supplies. As Lewis read, Sheehan could hear whispering voices from the earpiece.

"*Illustrious* was intercepted," Lewis said without looking up.

"Sir?"

"The *Illustrious* – she got jumped by an enemy cruiser squadron within the orbit of Saturn. The transmissions reached us about an hour ago."

His tone was so even he could have been commenting on the weather, but Sheehan felt his blood freeze. His niece was stationed on the carrier.

"Survivors, sir?" he asked after swallowing hard.

"*Illustrious* wasn't destroyed, Captain," Lewis said glancing up. "But she was badly hit. Half of her hangars and most of her fighters were knocked out. Thanks to the efforts of her escort the Nameless didn't manage to finish her off, but *Puma* was lost and *Wasp* badly damaged. So the *Illustrious* task group is off the board."

Lewis returned to his reading.

And that was it. One ship and probably its entire crew gone and another two damaged to an extent that guaranteed heavy casualties, all condensed and diminished into a single sentence. Sheehan knew Lewis well, but had never known anyone else who could compartmentalise so ruthlessly. In the three and half years he'd served as the Admiral's Chief of Staff, he'd rarely known him to speak on any personal matter. Now more than ever, he had apparently focused himself entirely on the job. Sheehan wondered if Lewis allowed himself to think about his family, even in the privacy of his own mind.

"We have fifteen days," Lewis said quietly, so quietly Sheehan doubted he had intended to speak at all. He turned toward the main holo at the centre of the bridge. "We daren't push any further – we wouldn't have the fuel to either fight or run. The question will be whether to break for Earth, for Saturn or beyond the heliopause and meet with the carriers. A powerful and mobile gun squadron might make life difficult for the Nameless but unless they are having logistical issues we are not aware of, they can simply play safe."

The Admiral lapsed back into silence, still staring at the holo. Sheehan waited patiently for the next order. As he did, a thought occurred to him that he had never expected to have. Could the Admiral make the decision? Two years ago he would have laughed at the suggestion that a man like Lewis could be frozen into indecision. But now – now he genuinely wondered. The Admiral was an old man and maybe a tired one. He'd given the fleet most of his life, had sent not just people, but friends to their deaths. Had he reached his limit and if so, what could be done? Finally Lewis moved, but only to put his earpiece back in place.

"Sir, perhaps some time away from the bridge would be useful," he ventured.

The Admiral's cold eyes turned on Sheehan.

"And go where, Captain?" he asked calmly.

"Perhaps some sleep sir, a walk around the ship or just a few hours off. There is nothing that comes in here that can't be got to you in seconds."

Lewis made no immediate reply.

"My cabin, Captain, is not a place I wish to spend much time," he replied eventually. "It has four walls and a lot of old ghosts."

Sheehan wondered how to reply to such an uncharacteristic statement. But Lewis carried on speaking.

"I will take a tour of the ship in a while. There is no need to inform the officers or crew. Having an Admiral suddenly appear among them will give them something to focus on. You are dismissed, Captain."

Sheehan nodded and left. Although he tried to conceal it, Lewis could see his chief of staff was troubled. He wasn't the only one. The Fast Division simply wasn't getting the opening it needed and Lewis was starting to doubt it ever would. The lag resulting from the distance between Mars and Earth was simply too great. By the time the light speed transmissions and emissions reached *Warspite*, the Nameless were already leaving. For weeks his mind had churned, searching for an answer, but one didn't seem to present itself. For the past few days, he'd found that all he could do was scan the civilian radio bands, listening to Earth slowly shut down.

Reaching out he touched a control and reactivated the communications console. Randomly he chose a radio channel.

Loyal Listeners, the Federal authorities have just informed us that this station will no longer be supplied with power. In a couple of hours' time, we will be cut off and this I can tell you blows. But despair not listeners. Our management has managed to secure a backup generator. We will be on air at Six PM Eastern Central Time for as long as we can. Now that this serious business is dealt with, we have a couple of hours until shutdown. So we are going to give you the best of Alternative Rock from the past three decades! And all totally ad free — because if this is the end of the world, then we ain't going quietly!

31st January 2068

Admiral Wingate wrapped his hands around the mug and waited for the heat to thaw out his fingers. Although Fleet Headquarters had its own power supply, independent of the local grid, the output had been dropped to the barest minimum to conserve fuel for as long as possible. The heating had been shut off the same day the Nameless arrived, as were the lifts and everything else now viewed as a luxury. Wingate had abandoned his office located at the top of the building and moved down to the ground floor, which was also more convenient for the main control room and the Council chamber. But as the heat leeched out of the building and Europe plunged into the worst winter in decades, even in the centre of the building it became bitingly cold. Finishing his drink, Wingate headed for the control room. The picture was the same as it had been for over a month now. A cluster of red blips hovered between Mars and Saturn like a sore. Speckled across the entire solar system were other red dots; the Nameless Fleet and its outlying scouts. With the information based on light speed sensors it was all out of date. The only green blips were around Earth and Saturn. Occasionally they caught sight of the three carriers operating from the edge of the system, but currently none were visible. With Nameless jammers online their Faster Than Light transmitters had been rendered useless most of the time and radio transmissions far too slow, so there was no way to exercise tactical control from Earth. As he always did when he came into the control room, Wingate darted his eyes to Mars and silent Phobos. Their supposed ace remained up their sleeve, yet to be played and perhaps unplayable.

"Carol," he said as he walked back into his office. "Is everything organised for the briefing?"

"No, sir," his chief of staff replied.

Bundled up in a heavy jacket, with a red nose, she looked miserable.

"We've been informed sir, that we will have a lot of non-sitting governments listening in as observers. Some governments though are having problems making the connection. The Council have agreed to delay the start by three quarters of an hour."

"Will that be enough?"

"Probably not sir," she replied with a shake of her head. "The governments of Singapore, New Zealand, Finland, South Africa and Argentina currently can't find sufficiently secure internet connections."

The Internet, possibly one of greatest structures of the late twentieth and early twenty-first century, was already starting to crumble as one server after another lost its power supply. As soon as the lifeblood of hydrogen had been cut, the governments of the world had begun to cut power to the least important parts of their electrical grids. As hydrogen supplies failed and strategic reserves ran dry, one country after another started to shut down everything judged non-critical. Even for a man like Wingate, who understood on an intellectual level how little really counted as 'critical', it was still shocking to see entire cities go cold and dark. Aside from a few official vehicles, little was moving on the streets outside. All economic activity had ceased as the population of planet Earth battened down the hatches.

Everyone in the room stood as the holograms of the Council chamber shimmered into life. The Presidents of the United States and Brazil, and the Prime Ministers of China, Israel, France, Germany, India and Australia all appeared. On the military side of the Council table, General Westenlake of Planetary Defence and Admiral Fengzi were also represented in hologramatic form. On the other side of Wingate stood Secretary Daniel Callahan, the fleet's political head, who since the start of the war had worked hard to protect the fleet from internal threats. Now he looked worn and tired.

"Please, gentlemen," President Clifton said, waving them to be seated. "Admirals, I know you have prepared us a briefing, but I have no interest in hearing it because I can predict what you will say. The Nameless remain out there, the fleet remains here. The brave fighter pilots of the Fleet and Planetary Defence continue to beat themselves against the enemy and all the while out fuel stocks diminish."

Clifton paused and looked around the chamber.

"Admiral, we are at crisis point. A few minutes ago I signed an executive order that will allow for the shut down of power supplies to all users, including hospitals. In essence, I have just signed the death warrants for hundreds of Americans currently lying in hospital beds across the nation. But worst of all, that's not enough! In less than two weeks, America will be down to the trickle of power that comes from wind and wave energy. The USA has handed over fuel to the fleet and Planetary Defence, but we are now only days away from having no fuel to give."

"The same is true of us all," said the Prime Minister of India. "You speak of crisis, but we are now beyond that. I am informed that my country is now only seventy-two hours from final shut down. If the fleet is to successfully defend this planet, then the window of opportunity in which to achieve this is closing."

"Admiral Wingate, your strategy of waiting for the Nameless to make a direct assault has failed," Clifton finished flatly.

Wingate pushed his briefing notes to one side.

"Yes Madam President, you're correct. It has."

The admission visibly shook some of the Council members. Wingate ploughed on before anyone could speak.

"We had estimated that to sustain a fleet of their size across such a distance would place such a logistical burden on the Nameless that they would be forced to attempt to bring the siege to a premature end. Whether because their supply system is stronger than we expected or our elements at Rosa and Hydra have been unable to inflict sufficient losses on them, this has not occurred. We have equally come to the conclusion that a more high risk approach must be considered."

"You have a proposal, Admiral?" Clifton asked.

"Simply charging the fleet out there is no more practical than it was a month ago. Our objective must be to lure the Nameless deep enough into a mass shadow so that they cannot jump away. The Fast Division remains our trump card."

"How can you be sure of that, Admiral?" the German Chancellor asked. "The Nameless have entered Earth's mass shadow several times and still Admiral Lewis has not moved!"

"And he has been right not to," said Fengzi before Wingate could reply.

This coming from a man who had frequently and openly clashed with Lewis in the past that cut the Council off.

"Mars is currently about as far from Earth as it gets. Speed of light transmission means Admiral Lewis only sees the Nameless near Earth, nearly twenty minutes *after* they arrive. He requires a minimum of twenty minutes to heat engines, start reactors and get his ships off the surface. To get outside the Mars mass shadow and make the jump takes another twenty."

"So, an hour's delay between their arrival and his response,"

Clifton said heavily. "Can we improve on that?"

"No," Wingate replied. "We can send radio transmissions, but those have no speed advantage over the readings Lewis can get from his own passive sensors. The Nameless have too many FTL transmitters that are better than ours. We can't punch through. If we used message drones or a courier ship, it would compromise the Fast Division. No, what we believe we must do is keep the Nameless close to Earth for longer, at a time when Lewis can be alerted beforehand and be ready."

"How?" asked the Indian Premier.

"Live bait," said Fengzi.

"In essence that is correct," Wingate said. "What we propose is to send a convoy to Saturn. Using six of the fastest tankers we have available, we intend to run in with a light escort. Six tankers worth of fuel will extend the endurance of the fleet by another three weeks. We are offering the Nameless a target they cannot refuse. We can make Lewis and the carriers aware of where the convoy will be, which will avoid some of the inherent delays."

"Why haven't we tried this before?" Clifton asked.

"It's a high risk. By sending out a small force, we will give the Nameless an opportunity to cut out a section of our fleet. Previously such a course would have been suspicious. Previously we wouldn't have been in an obviously desperate enough position to risk it. The Nameless can see that Earth is shutting down. If we don't get that fuel through we won't have a fleet. This is our last chance to pull the Nameless in while the fleet is still operational. We are calling it Operation Gauntlet."

Chapter Eight

Running the Gauntlet

5th February 2068

Shattered metal work, white like bone, severed cables that bled and in her ears, the screams, the screams of the dead.

Willis woke with a start and for a moment thought she was back on the *Hood*. But the cabin was too big and the last time she'd seen hers on *Hood*, it was after a Tample laser had sliced straight through.

The intercom above her bunk buzzed again and recollection finally kicked in. She was on board *Black Prince* and it was the intercom rather than the main alarm that had woken her.

"Willis here, what is it?" she asked.

"Officer of the Watch; I'm sorry to wake…"

"What is it?" Willis repeated, struggling to keep the snap out of her voice.

"Captain, we've been ordered to break formation and drop down into low orbit. You are ordered to attend a briefing at *Starforge Three*."

"When?"

"Ninety minutes, Captain."

Willis pushed herself upright as she rubbed her eyes and tried to think what this could mean. Her tired brain refused to cooperate.

"Manoeuvre us as ordered and prep the shuttle. I'll be up in a few minutes."

"Christ, Faith, you look rough," said Commodore Dandolo as Willis came into the briefing room. A yawn had chosen the precise moment she walked through the hatch to force its way out.

"With all due respect, sir," Willis replied as she slumped into a seat, "you're no oil painting yourself at the moment."

"You asked for that," Captain Ozo of the *Cetshwayo* said from his seat, arms folded across his chest and his eyes closed as Dandolo grinned at Willis. The briefing room was one of the smaller ones. Someone had put a plate of sandwiches and a large thermos container of what was presumably coffee on a small table to one side of the room. Willis really, really wanted coffee, but she also really wanted to stay in her chair and go to sleep. Dandolo dropped himself into a seat before she could work out whether asking a superior officer to pour the drinks was pushing it.

"Our own damn fault for having a war with people who seem to have a nineteen hour cycle," he said.

Fighter strikes were the latest move by the Nameless. One of their carriers would drop in as close to Earth as they could manage, launch thirty to forty fighters and jump away. The fighters would then make a fast run through before being recovered on the other side of the planet. The raids had achieved very little in terms of damage, but they were occurring two or three times a day, putting the entire fleet on alert each time, costing precious fuel and disrupting everyone's sleep patterns.

"Any idea what we've been called for?" Ozo asked.

"My guess is we'll be redeployed and split up for close defence of the main orbital platforms," said Dandolo. "Well, commanding a squadron was nice while it lasted."

"They've already got the starforts for that," Willis said. "In fact, that's what they're there for."

"What else could it be?" Dandolo asked as he looked towards the coffee and then at Willis, probably wondering whether he could get away with ordering her to pour.

"Hello? Are we in the right place?" said somebody in the hatchway.

Looking around Willis saw a commander standing in the hatch, with at least two more officers behind him. The rings on his sleeve were shiny and new, so a recent promotion.

"Where are you trying to be?" Dandolo asked.

"The briefing at eleven hundred."

"I think you've found the right place. Since you're on your feet Commander, could you pour the coffee?"

He took the order with good grace.

"Thank you, Commander...?" Willis asked, as he handed her a cup.

"Valance, of the *Minstrel*," he said, glancing down at her jacket and the medals hanging there. "I recognise you, Captain. I'd like to thank you."

"You're welcome, but what for?" she asked.

"I have relatives out in Dryad, working in the water industry. If you hadn't kept the Tample out, it would have gone badly for them."

The other officers who'd come behind looked at her curiously. All junior commanders and, like Valance, recent promotions.

"We're from the Twenty-Second Destroyer Squadron," one of them said .

"Emergency constructions?" asked Ozo.

"That's us, first of the new Town Class – *Olstyn*, *Obernai* and *Humaita*," the speaker nodded to the female officer. "Jessica's *Humaita* is the flak gun armed version."

Willis grimaced. The Towns were the destroyer equivalent of the Warriors – emergency construction on stock hulls. A few of them had sacrificed their plasma cannons and missile launchers for just two flak guns and magazine space for ammunition. No wonder they were being called the Toothless Terrors. Willis, Ozo and Dandolo exchanged a look.

"Uh-oh," Willis said.

"I don't think we're here to protect orbital platforms," Ozo commented. Behind, another three captains were walking in.

Guinness and Chuichi were waiting at the airlock. The faces of both men fell when they saw Willis's expression. She nodded for them to follow.

As her cabin hatch clunked closed behind them, Willis settled into her seat with a sigh.

"Well the good news is that we're effectively off strength for the next two days," she said.

"And the bad news?" Chuichi asked.

"That we've been handed a task, which comes with a guarantee that valour medals will be handed out with a shovel, but odds are most of them will be awarded posthumously," she replied grimly. "The fleet has decided to run a convoy to Saturn and we're to be part of the escort."

"Supplies?" asked Guinness

"Mostly empty tankers. We'll be bringing back fuel for the fleet."

"Oh, Jesus!" Guinness exclaimed.

"With respect, Captain, but who did you annoy?" Chuichi asked tersely.

"The joys of being in a cheap ship," Willis replied with an exasperated wave of her hand. "We are more expendable. There will be heavy cover in the shape of the battleship *Fortitude* and a couple more cruisers, but they won't be going into Saturn's mass shadow. Based on what I've seen so far, we can get to Saturn. The difficult part will be to get back out of her mass shadow with loaded tankers before we get taken apart."

Both men looked grim. They could appreciate the difficulties she was referring to. Saturn's mass shadow was nearly five times 'deeper' than Earth's. The Nameless would have hours in which to see and react to the convoy's move towards the edge.

"However, that isn't the important bit," Willis added. "This is the part that will not be spoken of outside this cabin until we are on our way back from Saturn."

That got their attention.

"The fuel is basically a red herring. Assuming we manage to get all six tankers back in one piece, they would provide enough fuel to run the fleet for three weeks or perhaps half that if we fuel the starforts as well. Our real objective is to provide a target the Nameless can't ignore at a known time and place, so that the Fast Division can spring its ambush. Obviously we need the element of surprise. There aren't many civilian radio transmitters left on air, but Headquarters doesn't want some bloody journalist blabbing. God knows what, if anything, the Nameless understand of human communication, but why take risks?"

"Why indeed, but does Fleet think we'll make it far enough for a return journey?" Chuichi asked.

"Yes. More by accident than design the Nameless haven't seen *Minstrel* in action yet. They will most likely first attempt to stop us with light units supported by a few mediums. We should be able to stand that off. So the next time the Nameless will either have to let us through or pile in en masse."

"I would have thought this was a job for more sophisticated ships, like a trio of Myths..." Chuichi trailed off.

Willis drummed her fingers on the desk while staring into space.

"Captain, did you..."

"Object?" Willis cut him off. "No. This is not a volunteer operation. The fine detail of this plan is still being put together, but if the price of making it work is the loss of our entire squadron, then

Headquarters will pay it."

She looked up at them, her face twisted into a bitter smile.

"It's not as if they're wrong."

Chuichi and Guinness parted ways at the hatch, both seeking time to process what they had just been told. Guinness made his way out of the centrifuge and aft to his own 'kingdom' in the engine rooms. Only the duty shift was around and various inspection work was underway. Guinness pulled himself into the small space he called his office.

"I am getting too old for this," he said to himself.

He caught sight of his reflection in a metal storage hatch – white hair, not too many wrinkles, but then spacers didn't get to absorb that much UV light.

"You stupid old fart, you *are* too old for this."

He'd been here before. More than thirty years ago in the last war, as part of a fleet with its back to the wall, staring defeat in the face. Had he been frightened back then? He didn't think so. Too young and too stupid – well maybe not young but certainly stupid. He'd never had much taste for gambling and to his mind that was what a tactical officer had to be – pushing chips onto the table, hoping to get them back, but willing to accept some might be sacrificed for greater advantage. As an engineer he understood that things could happen in an engine room, bad things. But since then he'd witnessed events such as the *Mississippi*, Alpha Centauri and Dryad, watching good lads and girls die at their posts. Maybe it would be better to go back to the Skipper's cabin and tell her he couldn't do it, not again. Tell her while there was still time to replace a frightened old man.

Looking around his eyes fell on a photograph – him, her, the two boys, each with a huge ice cream in their hand, all of them beaming into the camera. For the life of him he couldn't remember where it had been taken. It had been a family day trip somewhere, back when the lads were both wee. Wherever it was, it had been a great day, one of the best. He hadn't been around as much as he'd wanted when they were small. But he'd been out here, protecting them all and that was what he was still doing. If he were able to leave, where would he go? Go home to an empty house? Kissing his finger he put it on her face.

"Might be seeing you soon girl," he whispered.

8th February 2068

The next few days were a whirl of activity on board *Black Prince* and the rest of the squadron. As ammunition ships and tankers queued to offload, the cruiser's tanks and magazines were filled to the brim. Several times work was interrupted by Nameless raids, but the aliens never got close to low orbit and work quickly resumed. Willis handed responsibility for loading to Chuichi, while she spent most of her time at *Starforge Three*, helping to thrash out the fine detail of the forthcoming op.

"So we can't actually be sure Admiral Lewis and the Fast Division will turn up?" asked Commander Valance.

"Well not a hundred percent," said one of the Headquarters staff officers. "He's on radio silence, but we have been sending him radio updates. We've been careful to keep the amount of radio traffic at a constant level so if the Nameless can hear it, then it looks like the same level of updates we've been sending the carriers since December."

"Lewis is days away from breaking for Earth or Saturn," Dandolo commented. "In his shoes, I'd rather make my move when all hell is breaking loose than when things are nice and calm."

"Still seems a bit of a weak point to me," said the captain of the *Humaita*.

"Not one we can fix, Jessica," Willis replied as she flicked at the pages on her data pad. "We have to roll with what we can alter and work around what we can't."

With her own history of having to plan a defence largely based on guesstimates, no one would argue too hard.

"Y'know, there are already odds being given on whether we'll make it back in one piece," Ozo said.

"So what are the odds on us?" Dandolo asked, as he studied a chart of the solar system.

"Pretty long."

"Put me down for fifty," said Jessica.

"They might want cash up front," Ozo pointed out.

"If I don't make it sir, I won't have much need for money," she replied with a smile. "If I do, well then that's the celebratory booze up paid for."

"Mines, torpedoes and random zigzags," said Willis.

The conversation stopped as everyone looked at her.

"Want to expand on that one, Faith?" Dandolo asked.

"When we jump in at Saturn, drop mines astern. With them falling into Saturn's gravity well, they can't follow from directly astern. If we put the torpedoes above and below us that will leave just the flanks open, from where *Minstrel* can bring her main battery to bear."

"Sound fairs," said Ozo. "Where do zigzags come in?"

"Random zigzags will stop them from getting into an optimum firing position."

"With the amount of warning they'll get, they can spread out and fire from all angles," said Commander Valance. "*Minstrel* can put down one hell of a wall of fire, but only across a very limited arc."

"If they try spreading out that much, they'll have no mutual support," said Dandolo. "The *Dauntless* and *Huáscar* will operate in support. If they spread out then our fighters will chop them up."

"Especially if we make a couple of dummy runs out," Ozo added.

"Okay," Dandolo said, turning to one of the staff officers, "let's try running this through Sims and see what happens."

13th February 2068

The Nameless escort had been holding position inside Earth's mass shadow, providing its fleet with a forward picket. Although they were within the Red line, they had to remain far enough out so that their jump drives could still function – watching the orbiting ships and the planet below as the lights went out. When there was a flicker of light from astern as four human fighters jumped in right on the Red Line and powered down towards it, the Nameless reacted instantly. It was a race between the alien ship jumping clear and the accelerating fighters trying to get to within effective missile range. The Nameless ship won the race, disappearing to safety. As the four fighters peeled off, on the opposite side of the planet, another four were jumping in close to the picket's second ship. Like the first, it retreated to safety, but the Nameless forward screen had suddenly evaporated.

On board *Black Prince* Willis tightened the straps of her seat restraints as the cruiser accelerated up and out of Earth's orbit.

"Coms, Bridge. Signal from the *Dauntless*'s fighters: the door is open. Also general signal from Fleet Command: God Speed."

Willis nodded tensely. On the main holo the blips for the convoy were separating from those of the rest of the fleet. The ten warships were formed up around the six tankers, two ammunition ships, a pair of general transports and one of the fleet's FTL communications ships, all accelerating up and out of the gravity well, at the pace of the slowest ship. Two squadrons of American fighters formed an outer perimeter.

"This is too slow," Chuichi muttered across the command channel

The Commander was standing on the bridge, ready to head aft to damage control once the action started, but until then maintaining his present position so that he would be aware of the tactical situation. Willis made no reply. It was slow, but equally it was exactly what they expected. This was as good as loaded transports could manage. If only there had been time to do as someone had suggested and strap on a set of old fashioned chemical rockets. The Nameless picket ships would return to station within minutes, sight the convoy and call for back up. How far could they get before that happened? Minutes crept past as the convoy continued to accelerate. On the main holo their ships crossed a dotted green line. Willis flicked her intercom to ship wide.

"All hands, this is the Captain. We have just crossed the abort line. We are now committed. That's all."

In the port side engine room, Guinness did as he always did when the Captain's voice came across the intercom and glanced towards the bows. Stupid really, as there was never anything to be learned from the engine room bulkhead, but it was something he still did. The wait was agonising, would they get clear or not get out at all?

"Committed?" asked one of the engineering ratings.

"Weren't you listening at the briefing?" Guinness reprimanded him, glancing at the forward bulkhead again. "Even if the transports go all astern, they're carrying too much velocity to stop before they go over the Red Line. Now shut your yap."

Damn, this was cruel! The reactors were ready to go to one hundred percent. The engines were barely going at fifty percent and only the flak guns were drawing power. She might be a jigsaw of a ship but *Black Prince* desperately wanted to stretch her legs. He could practically feel it. Guinness took a sip from his water reservoir and immediately regretted it as he suddenly wanted to urinate. He couldn't. There wasn't anything in his bladder to be pissed out. To distract himself he cycled through the system displays on his screen. Reactor One: okay, Reactor Two: okay, Engines One through Four: yes, yes, yes and yes, Jump Drive: okay, Computer: okay, Power Display..."

Across the main channel the action alarm went off. His display beeped as the cruiser's six plasma cannons started to draw power.

Guinness looked down the engine bay.

"Okay, lads! This is it!"

"Bridge, Sensors. Contact! Contact jumping in, bearing zero seven three dash three zero five. Contact is... scout."

"Understood, Sensors," Willis replied as she checked her straps again. On the holo the American fighters wavered, their course diverging from the convoy for a moment before someone decided they couldn't get to the scout fast enough to matter. The Americans settled back into their screening formation.

"Navigator?" Willis murmured.

"We are seventeen minutes from the Red Line. Jump calculations have been made."

"Confirm the jump drive is ready?"

"Confirmed Captain."

In the lead it would be *Fortitude* to open the jump portal. But if she was taken out or damaged, each ship had to be ready. Overhead she heard the whine of A Turret training out to starboard and the distant alien ship. The scout began to move, as always the newly arrived ship was nearly stationary, but started to accelerate, running parallel to the convoy. Those damn FTL sensors of theirs were undoubtedly probing to find the composition of the convoy.

"Bridge, Coms. Enemy FTL jammers are powering down. C band is opening up. The enemy scout is transmitting."

"How the hell do they do that?" Chuichi growled, shaking his head. The jammers were dotted about the solar system. The Nameless used the same six transmission bands humanity had access to, but they also seemed to have access to another, which judging by effect seemed to allow them to shut down the jammers without the lag of radio transmitters.

"Not important, as long as they stay predictable," Willis replied before turning towards the communications lieutenant to give him a questioning look.

"Groundside and orbital FTL transmitters are going active," he confirmed.

The fleet had learned that from the lost colony of Landfall. There were three FTL transmitters on Earth and the fleet had another pair in orbiting communication ships. All of them had been waiting for this. The scout's transmission was distorted and swamped as all five commenced the electronic equivalent of screaming across the same band. One band at a time, the distant jammers shut down as the scout tried to find a clear connection. Seconds then minutes were wasted as the scout tried to get the word out. All the while the convoy closed on the Red Line. Finally all six bands were open. The five human transmitters tried to follow and swamp the scout's transmitter, but it could change band far quicker than its human counter parts.

"We've just picked up what seems to be an enemy reply to the scout," the communications officer reported.

Willis nodded. The word was out.

"Seven more minutes to jump out," said the Navigator, pre-empting her next question.

"Best head aft, Commander," she said to Chuichi, "that's the build up done."

"Yes, Captain. See you at Saturn."

The main hatch closed behind the Commander and the bridge went silent. The clock continued to count down.

"Three minutes to jump out."

"Bridge, Sensors. Contacts! Multiple contacts bearing zero seven two dash three zero seven. Reading one cap ship, seven cruisers, eighteen escorts."

"I see them," Willis replied. "Fire Control, stand ready for instructions."

"Understood."

"Bridge, Coms, signal from the *Saladin*. It's the Commodore."

"My screen."

Dandolo's face appeared.

"Captain, I believe we can hold out for three minutes, so we'll keep *Minstrel* in reserve."

"Bridge, Sensors. Contact separation, we have incoming!" the voice of the speaker rose sharply. Two-dozen new contacts appeared on the screen and began to accelerate towards the convoy. Willis looked around her bridge. The old hands who been with her on *Hood* were calm, but the new ones –

"Steady people, they only outnumber us two to one. Helm, roll to port and present broadside."

The first salvo couldn't be much more than a probe and there wouldn't be time for a second before the convoy crossed the Red Line.

As she spoke, the plasma cannons started to fire methodically up at the approaching missiles. Two vanished as plasma bolts slammed into them. As it approached them, the American fighters thinned the salvo considerably. The flak guns started to track and fire, the thump of the guns reverberating through the ship. None of the missiles made it as far as point defence range.

"Contact heading change, they're coming to…"

"I see it," Willis cut him off. The Nameless squadron was turning towards Saturn. They'd guessed where the convoy was heading. Not too much of a feat.

"Bridge, Navigation, we're crossing the Red Line now. *Fortitude* is jumping."

"Helm, take us in," Willis ordered.

The respite of jump space lasted no more than a few second before *Black Prince* thumped back into real space. Ahead Saturn loomed large and the gas giant's ring of starforts appeared on the holo along with the planet's extensive network of moons. The closest, Enceladue, with Chinese surface fortifications on each of its poles, formed Saturn's outer perimeter and was five hours away at best speed.

"Captain, the *Dar Pomorza* is dropping mines."

Willis had always doubted the Nameless would attempt to drop in directly behind them. Missiles following up the convoy's wake would have the slowest possible approach speed. Still there was no point taking chances and the idea of a Nameless squadron blundering into a minefield was always a pleasant one.

Black Prince's sensors caught a brief glimpse of them before they dropped below the sensor threshold. The American fighters that had followed them down the jump conduit redeployed into screening positions, while ahead new blips appeared as the squadrons based around Saturn launched. There was also the Nameless picket, holding position well clear of the Saturn defences. It began to transmit immediately and this time the distant Earth transmitters weren't able to significantly block it. *Fortitude* and the cruisers *Loki* and *Osiris* began to angle way from the convoy, as they prepared to jump away out past the heliopause to wait.

"Bridge, Sensors, contacts jumping in, bearing zero, six, nine dash zero, zero, nine, range one, one, zero kay."

The cluster of red blips appeared off to starboard. Slightly ahead of the convoy and outside of their gun range, they were close enough for the Nameless to put down maximum weight of fire.

"Okay, we're about to find out if *Minstrel* lives up to the billing," Willis said to no one in particular.

"Contact separation, we have incoming."

The speaker was calmer this time, but this salvo was a mix of small and large missiles. That meant scores of them were coming in, more than three cruisers and three destroyers could hope to stop, especially with lumbering transports ruling out evasive action.

"*Minstrel* is firing, Captain," Sensors reported.

Willis flicked her screen to an external camera trained on the barrage ship. If this didn't work out, then things were about to get very bad. As that thought crossed her mind, a glittering flash ran down the *Minstrel*'s flank. The muzzle velocity was only about fifteen hundred metres per second, low for any kind of railgun. With the projectiles set to burst at thirty thousand kilometres, transit time would be twenty seconds unless they met something first. The projectiles were small, but *Black Prince*'s radar was getting a good read on them as they slowly diverged from each other in a flat wall in front of the incoming missiles. Then they simultaneously detonated. A rectangular area of space became a mass of overlapping flashes just as the missile plunged in. Barely a quarter of them made it through only to run into the *Minstrel*'s next wave of projectiles. This time there was a rippling flash as the proximity fuses on some of the projectiles registered the missiles ahead and fired. The flak guns on board *Black Prince* remained silent, as the entire first salvo of missiles was obliterated.

"Bloody hell!" Willis exclaimed. She hadn't realized she'd been holding her breath. *Minstrel* continued to fire methodically as the Nameless threw three more big salvos at them, all with an equal lack of results.

There were further exclamations across the command channel. As the Nameless fire spluttered out, there were cheers on the bridge.

"Can we go off duty now, Skipper?" the gunner asked. "I think *Minstrel* has got this."

Willis let the crew enjoy the moment for a few minutes before re-establishing command.

"Okay folks, let's calm it down. It's not as if these bastards have ever had problems with adapting," she ordered.

Still, *Minstrel*'s performance had clearly taken the wind out of the sails of the intercepting Nameless. Pulling up the communication display on her screen, she could see FTL transmissions going back and forth from the intercepting squadron and the rest of the Nameless fleet. As they discussed, the convoy was getting further and further into Saturn's mass shadow, while behind them fighters from the two carriers were jumping in. The window of opportunity for the Nameless was closing.

"So they made it in?" Captain Holfe, *Warspite*'s Commanding Officer, asked.

"So it would appear," Lewis replied as he drummed his fingers on the edge of the main holo.

The entire plan was high risk, but to have put the austerity cruisers into the role instead of more capable vessels struck him as tactical stinginess. If this was the last big throw, then there was no point holding back. Frustratingly, the relative positions of Mars and Saturn meant the Fast Division couldn't really see the convoy directly and were instead relying on radio transmissions.

"The problem is," said Sheehan, "they had to play their best card to get that far. *Minstrel* blew off the guts of eighty percent of her ammunition before they reached the outer perimeter."

"But they can reload?" Holfe asked. "They brought ammunition ships with them."

"Yes, but *Minstrel* will need several hours of downtime to do that, so no use in combat."

"Yes, *Minstrel* has some glaring flaws and I don't doubt the Nameless will be working them out," Lewis said thoughtfully, "But their principal focus will be on the fact that by the time the convoy crossed the perimeter, a single ship held off – what, fifty of theirs?"

"Roughly that," Sheehan agreed.

"So the Nameless now know they'll have to throw in a significant number of ships to overwhelm the convoy defenders," Lewis continued in the same thoughtful tone. "That's most, if not all, of their ships."

"Getting out of Saturn won't be as easy as getting in. And I don't know if they can do it," Sheehan said in a tone of grim finality.

"We could assist," Holfe suggested. "Make Saturn the point we engage."

"I think that's throwing good after bad," Sheehan replied, crossing his arms. Both of them turned to Lewis. He stared into the holo, lost in thought.

"No," he said eventually. "We will not engage at Saturn. We would likely maul a squadron or two, but even under the most favourable conditions we couldn't destroy or pin down a fleet. No, this is someone else's script and we will, if given the chance, play the part laid down for us."

"What if the convoy doesn't make it?" Holfe asked. "We've got only a few more days of fuel."

Lewis sighed and turned to face them.

"We take off and make for Saturn, Captain." He smiled bitterly. "Unlike our colleagues around Earth, we will at least then be able to make our last stand with charged weapons."

The pipes pulsed in unison as hydrogen fuel pumped into the tanker Dos Amigos. Lifeblood, Willis thought to herself as she peered through the large viewing port. Beyond, Saturn dominated the view. A fuel skimmer slowly made its way down towards the planet. Although Saturn had been cut off, the fuel industry had continued to work gathering hydrogen. With only skeleton crews on any single facility, the pace had been slow, but with no fuel leaving for Earth or anywhere else, it had been enough to fill every one of the storage tanks orbiting the planet. *Black Prince* was docked on the other side of the station, filling her own tanks and Willis had taken the opportunity to stretch her legs under the excuse of paying her respects to the facility supervisor.

"Won't be long now, Captain," said a passing civilian worker.

"Pardon?"

"Another day to fill the tanks and you'll be ready," the man said cheerfully.

He was dressed in standard work overalls, but the flashes on his shoulders indicated he was a junior supervisor. His round face gave him the look of a man permanently enjoying a joke.

"I'm telling you, those bug-eyed bastards must have been raging, watching you guys waltz through with barely a pause. They know they're bollixed now."

Willis smiled blandly.

"Well, better be getting on. Don't want to be the dickhead that causes a delay. Thanks again," he added before bustling off. Willis kept her fixed smiled until he pulled himself round a corner and disappeared from view.

"Ignorance is bliss," she muttered to herself.

"Not to be awkward, but when you decided to come here, you did have a plan to get back out again?" asked Colonel Bunton.

As the most senior officer present the American was currently in command of the various orbital defences under the umbrella of Planetary Defence. He'd called the meeting on the Starfort *Cold Harbour* to confirm the defender's role in the breakout.

"We're playing this one a little bit more by ear than anyone is really happy with," Dandolo said. "If we'd got in clean, then we'd have had the option to simply make a straight run for the Red Line. Given that the Nameless have seen *Minstrel* strut her stuff, that's now off the table."

"I still don't get why *Fortitude* and her cruisers didn't stay with you," Bunton replied. "I mean the firepower they could bring to bear…"

"The Nameless could bring more," Dandolo cut him off. "But now that she's outside any mass shadow, she's harder to predict or monitor and far too powerful to ignore. She might be our smallest battleship but if she jumps in on top of them she could still make a mess."

"Well don't get me wrong, I can understand why Earth didn't want to transmit the entire plan ahead of time, but we've got to the point where I need to know what you're doing so I can organise our support. Y'know there are only so many ways out of Saturn to make a direct run at Earth," Bunton said.

"Happily we won't be heading direct to Earth," Willis replied. When Bunton gave her a questioning look she continued. "We'll head out past the Heliopause. Give *Minstrel* – and the rest of us – a chance to rearm and link up with *Fortitude*, before we make our run to Earth.

Bunton looked thoughtful for a moment then shrugged. "That's all well and good but getting out of Saturn's mass shadow will take those tankers at least fifteen hours."

"It's the last five that actually count," Willis said. "That's the point at which they can jump in around us, but we can't jump out. So that's why we won't fly in a straight line."

"The Nameless will see us make our move hours before we reach a position they can fire on." Dandolo turned and looked out into *Cold Harbour*'s control centre. On the main holo a dozen red blips were visible, scouts now forming a tight picket around the planet.

"The carriers will start pegging at those bastards in a few hours," he continued, "which will keep them jumping – literally as well as metaphorically. With gaps in their coverage, their fleet will have to be ready to move for an extended period. When we make our move the Home Fleet will move closer to the Earth Red Line. That will mean they have to be careful about getting in too deep, especially as the coms ship we brought with us isn't coming back. It will stay here and keep a running commentary on where any Nameless units are."

"We'll spiral out from Saturn," Willis said. That had been her idea. "Since we stay on the inside of the turn it will be hard for them to stay level for any great length of time. We'll re-launch our torpedoes before contact and put them on station so that they'll screen ahead and behind us. That combined with your fighters and *Minstrel* will make a close range jump in wildly dangerous. Basically we're going do our level best to turn this into a marathon rather than a sprint. *Minstrel* has problems with ammunition but the same is true of them. There are only so many missiles you can shoehorn onto any ship. We'll make our final break past the moon of Tethys."

"Hopefully, they won't expect that because in its current position Saturn is between Tethys and Earth," Ozo said.

"And the European fortresses at the poles can give covering fire," observed Bunton.

"That too," Dandolo agreed.

"There is one thing I've been wondering about," Valance said. "It didn't come up in the planning, but so far I've been rearming from just the *Remarque*. I'll pretty much empty her, but I wonder whether we should balance the load across the two ammunition ships, just in case one..." he trailed off.

Neither the captains of the ammunition ship or the tankers were present as observers at the meeting. All were Battle Fleet officers ,but in the support units rather than combat wings.

"No," said Willis before Dandolo could reply. "The empty ship can be kept on the engaged side of the convoy as we move out, to protect the other." She glanced at the captain of the *Remarque*. His eyes had widened, and he looked to Dandolo. The Commodore didn't meet his gaze. Up to this point the ammunition ships along with the coms ship had been the critical ones to get through to Saturn so they'd been positioned at the heart of the formation.

"Yes. We'll do that. The empty ammunition ship will join the two general transports. They will form an outer column on the threatened side of the convoy. The remaining ammunition ship will stay in the central position."

Willis saw the face of the officer drop. He should have expected this, but equally they should have spelt it out beforehand. The general transports were civilian ships crewed by Battle Fleet personnel for this mission. But as vessels never intended to be put directly into harm's way, the ammunition ships had their usual crews. The man should have had time to prepare himself, but instead he'd been allowed to think his part was done.

Their eyes met and she saw a man who knew he'd likely been handed a death sentence.

"Well," Bunton said after an uncomfortable moment, "I can assure you Planetary Defence will not let you down. Although I still think you should aim to get to Earth as fast as possible. I know your barrage ship will likely be empty if... when, you reach the Red Line, so likely will the Nameless. Heading out past the Heliopause to rearm sounds more beneficial to them than us."

"Headquarters thinks otherwise," Dandolo replied blandly.

"Okay. Both my fellow American officers and those of the Chinese installations have contacted me. They are proposing dinner before you leave."

"Thank you," Dandolo replied, "we'll be there."

As they left *Cold Harbour*, Ozo murmured in Willis's ear.

"The dinner offer would be nicer if you weren't left with the feeling the Americans think it would be rude not to give the condemned a last meal."

16th February 2068

As the recorded words of Admiral Wingate echoed through *Black Prince*, Guinness looked around the engine room. They hadn't depressurised yet, so no one had their helmet on and he could see their faces. Some looked shaken, other excited, most looked like they were still processing what they'd heard.

"You knew, Chief?" one of his deputies asked.

"Yes," Guinness replied.

"Wow!" The young man pondered it for a moment then smiled. "Well if we're going out, we're going out epic!"

God bless the young, Guinness thought to himself.

"Well, this will be painful," Willis remarked as *Black Prince* accelerated at thirty percent of maximum. With the six tankers fully loaded this was the best sustainable speed for the slowest ship. The captain of that ship reckoned he could maybe get up to thirty five percent of *Black Prince*'s best, but not for more than an hour.

"On the positive side, at least the Chief won't shout at me for damaging his engines."

That at least got a smile on the bridge. Willis glanced again at the Holo. Knowing what was coming, the crew of each ship would be coping with the next few hours as best they could. They'd made all possible preparations. Every ship system had been checked and doubled checked. The medical dispenser of each crewmember's survival suit had been stocked with the generally detested wake-up shots, but facing into an engagement that might last days, there was no choice. As they began a build-up that would test the nerves of even the strongest of them, as captain, she had to lead by example. At times like this, that amounted to looking like everything was under control.

"Commander," she said standing up, "I'm going below for a nap. Tell the galley I want the crew fed in eight hours."

Chuichi nodded in agreement.

"And make sure you get some rest yourself," she added.

Willis didn't go directly to her cabin; instead she made a quick tour of the ship, to the immediate consternation of the ship's non-commissioned officers. Having a commanding officer running loose certainly distracted the ship's petty officers as they tried to get ahead of her to make sure anything she shouldn't see was removed from sight. Willis allowed her attention to be drawn so other things could be cleared away behind her. Finally though, her slow circuit brought her to her own cabin.

She lay down on her bunk with hands beneath her head. Her first year in the fleet had, as with all officer candidates, been spent as a rating. In those early days, her immediate superior had once told her that a good officer needed to learn how to sleep. Young and confident, she'd thought it foolish at the time, but as the years, particularly the last two, passed the more she'd come to appreciate that Petty Officer Joseph Taylor had known what he was talking about. He was probably retired by now, but as a man cast from the same mould as her own engineer, he might have wriggled his way back in. If he had, hopefully he was still alive out there somewhere.

Willis looked around the small cabin. Space on board a starship was at an extreme premium, even for the captain. Her cabin on *Hood* hadn't been a home, just a place to sleep. But here on *Black Prince*, she'd at least tried to add a few homey touches. Willis's glaze fell on the picture on her desk. One of her in the uniform of a junior lieutenant with arm around the friend she'd left forever at Dryad. To say there was no such thing as an atheist in a foxhole had always been wrong. What was true was that there was no such thing as an agnostic in one, because when it all hit the fan, a person would pretty quickly come down on one side of the fence or the other. Willis wasn't a religious or spiritual person, but she hoped there was something beyond this life and that if she saw him again, she would be able to say his sacrifice had been worth it. Then like a good officer Faith Willis dozed off.

Going to action stations was far more casual than usual. The ship's cook excelled himself with a greater selection than was usually available. The wardroom attendant arrived at Willis's cabin with a plate of her favourite – macaroni cheese with bacon – and despite her nerves, she'd enjoyed it greatly.

"All sections have reported in as closed up and ready for action," Chuichi said. The Commander was standing with helmet settled on his hip. He and Willis were now the only ones not wearing their helmets. It gave the opportunity for a last few words without being overheard. Willis nodded absent-mindedly in response to his report as she looked around her bridge. The atmosphere was tense but not fearful. They were sharp and ready. Just like her crew had been on the old *Hood*, before the little cruiser was shot to pieces around them. She gave her head a brief shake, as if it could dislodge the memory.

"Commander, when this starts, it might be very sudden so I want you to head for Damage Control as soon as we decompress."

Chuichi nodded patiently.

"There is one last thing I want you to understand in case the bridge is knocked out and you have to take command. *Black Prince* will not disengage under any circumstances, short of the ship being abandoned. Even if we don't have a working gun left or we can't keep up with the convoy, *Black Prince* will *not* retreat."

Willis looked at the main holo. Ahead was the Blue Line, the closest to Saturn that the Nameless could jump in. Beyond, three enemy scouts were visible half way between the Blue and Red Line. Further on still a flight of human fighters was visible.

"If we don't get out of Saturn, then everything else falls apart."

Chuichi nodded grimly.

"See you over the line, Captain."

"And you, Commander."

"Bridge, Coms, signal from *Saladin*: prepare to turn in succession at mark."

"Understood, Coms. Helm, stand ready. Tactical, decompress the ship. Let's get on with it."

Right on the Blue Line the entire convoy turned in succession through ninety degrees and started to travel along the line. Willis smiled slightly as communications reported a sudden flurry of FTL transmissions from the watching scouts. Then a few minutes later came the slower FTL pulses from the Battle Fleet communications ship Outreach, still orbiting Saturn and now being fed information from the starforts.

A little later, *Black Prince*'s communications centre reported FTL transmissions from Earth. As the visible Nameless scouts turned and started to shadow the convoy, there were several brief flares as torpedoes were launched from warships moving onto station ahead and behind the convoy. Each time the Nameless scouts stopped transmitting, their jammers came back online. But finally a transmission from Earth got through. The Home Fleet was in position close to the Earth Red Line. Once again the convoy turned, angling out and away from Saturn.

For another hour and a half the convoy slowly opened the distance between them and Saturn. Two squadrons of fighters from the starforts rendezvoused. The distance was such that the fighters could only spend about an hour with them before starting the journey back to their bases. With the long climb out of the gravity well and the dive back, even for something as quick as a fighter, each squadron could make only one sortie in a day. Each of the Saturn squadrons was set to meet them in sequence during the long climb, so there would always be a few fighters with them, if never very many.

"Contact!" The command channel warning made Willis jump. "Multiple contacts jumping in bearing two, zero, nine dash zero, one, seven! Range: one hundred thousand!"

"Reactors to full. Tactical, give me a read," Willis responded as the action alarm sounded.

"Provisional count: two cap ships, five cruisers and nine escorts. Their formation is tight, looks optimised for anti-fighter."

The Saturn fighters were already moving onto the port side of the convoy, getting ready to engage their missiles.

"Coms, Bridge. Signal from *Saladin*, we are to hold on the disengaged side."

"Acknowledge," Willis replied as she gripped the armrest of her chair. A hundred thousand kilometres put them at the very limit of cruiser scale plasma cannons. But against the unarmoured Nameless ships even a plasma bolt losing final coherency would do damage. The three cruisers were formed in a triangle, vertical to the direction of travel. With *Black Prince* positioned on the bottom right, they currently could only see the Nameless through the convoy. Ahead, the three destroyers also formed in a triangle and rotated around the convoy to allow their single flak gun armed vessel to present its weapon.

"Contact separation, we have incoming," Sensors reported.

"Sensors, keep a sharp eye on your scopes," Willis ordered. "Do not get hung up on those missiles – they are someone else's problem."

At the head of the convoy *Minstrel* started to fire, only slowly this time to conserve her ammunition, as *Saladin* and *Cetshwayo* began to fire both plasma cannons and flak guns. Two missile salvos burned in while on the main holo, one of the enemy cap ships flashed as the computer registered hits. Willis frowned as she studied the holo. This was... kinda tentative. With those ships tightly packed to fend off fighters, their own fire was coming down a single axis, which gave the human ships the best possible chance of stopping everything they threw. She glanced at the weapons display. Their plasma and flak turrets were both pointed towards the distant enemy ships. Just like everyone else's guns.

"Bridge, Fire Control. Go fore and aft on all guns!"

There was no question or confusion from the gunner as the turrets began to swing round, but then another voice cut across the command channel.

"Contact! Multiple new contacts are jumping in at multiple bearings!"

"Oh Christ!" Willis muttered. Not a cluster, not this time, or even at the edge of gun range. Instead a curved line was forming a quarter circle, running from dead ahead round to starboard between the convoy and Saturn. Beyond them several more contacts had appeared fifty thousand kilometres ahead. The holo blinked as it reset the scale.

"New contacts, range ten thousand and closing!"

They'd wondered whether the Nameless would dare commit to a short-range jump in. The aliens were nearly stationary for the jump and the convoy was seconds away from spearing through their line. Close range favoured the gun armed human ships, but with the element of surprise and short flight time, the first salvo of missiles could overwhelm the target. It would probably cost the Nameless ships, but with two thirds of the escort and all of the fighters already engaged, it might gut the convoy. With their enemy still phasing in, Tactical didn't yet have any indication as to what they were. It could be ten capital ships or ten scouts. By the time they knew, the Nameless would have completed their jump in and the missiles would be flying.

But *Black Prince*'s guns had already been swinging round when the jump in began and vital seconds had already been saved. There was no time to request instructions from *Saladin*. They needed to make best use of their weapons and right now that meant suppressive fire – hit them while they were still getting a fix on location and target.

The entire thought process shot across Willis's mind as she sought a solution. There was no time for subtlety or a perfect fit. *Black Prince* needed to lay down fire in as many directions as possible. The middle of the Nameless formation was the most likely location for any heavy units.

"Helm! Roll to present starboard broadside. Bridge to Fire Control, lock and fire on targets U One, Zero and U One, One with plasma cannons!" she shouted. "Flak guns, fire on U One, Two and U One, Nine. Countermeasures, full spread!"

As *Black Prince*'s turrets opened up, several of the transports started firing off their own chaff bursts. Ahead the destroyer, which, like *Black Prince*, had been on the disengaged side, volleyed off all four missiles at separate targets. On the holo the new contacts stabilised as they completed jump in and Tactical started to classify them. One of them met a salvo of plasma bolts head on, which cut through the entire length of the ship, intersecting a reactor. Willis had just registered it as an escort when it vanished from the plot, without leaving even an icon for wreckage.

"Contact separations, we have incoming!"

"Point Defence Batteries," Willis said as she tightened her seat straps, "Commence! Commence! Commence!"

The salvo wasn't a single launch or targeted at one or a small number of targets. Instead it was a staggered launch, with almost every ship in the convoy targeted. The immediate counter fire had panicked the Nameless into a premature launch and that Willis realised, gave them a chance. The holo became a mess of overlapping signals as every ship started firing off chaff rockets. *Black Prince*'s flak guns switched to picking off missiles but there were several dozen inbound. Willis realised there was no way they could even get close to stopping all of them.

"Guns! Concentrate on the cap ship missiles," she commanded. "Helm, bring us ahead two thirds, level with the ammunition ship!"

As she spoke a cap ship missile penetrated the counter fire and hammered into one of the tankers. The detonation split her in half then one after another, her fuel tanks went up. The drive section, somehow still intact but now without any control, came corkscrewing up through the convoy, forcing the clumsy transports to desperately scramble out of the way. A second tanker was hit, this time a glancing strike, but enough to rupture several of her fuel tanks. A final cap missile struck one of the empty transports. The blast cut a ragged gash across the empty cargo bays but failed to find critical systems. *Black Prince* jolted as two of the smaller dual-purpose missiles found their way through the counter fire from point defence and powered in. Another four transports on the display indicated they had taken damage as the smaller missiles found a way in.

Willis glanced at damage control but no critical systems showed as lost. On the main holo, tactical had finally identified the newcomers as five, formerly six, escorts and four cruisers. No cap ships, Willis thought, thank God! But the three still ahead were now showing as cap ships. Fire was still coming in from the opposite side, pinning the rest of the escort as the convoy raced through the Nameless line. No missiles flew. The aliens must have been reloading but now they were astern. Aside from a few point defence guns, the convoy had no weapons that could be brought to bear. There were no missile coming from the Nameless ships falling astern, which could only mean they were reloading their tubes for another big salvo, which this time, unlike the hurried initial attack, would be properly coordinated. Missiles were already inbound from the three cap ships ahead, trying to pin the defenders into facing that way.

No guidance came from *Saladin*. The fighters abandoned their position on the flank and moved to intercept the fire from the front, but with threats on all sides the defence was stretched too thin. Willis's eyes lit on the six torpedoes tracking along thirty thousand kilometres astern of the convoy. The weapons were set to engage any targets that got within ten thousand kilometres but they could take commands.

"Tactical, take control of the aft torpedoes. Target the three cruisers!"

"Understood."

"Helm, reverse our facing!" she continued to shout. "Guns, engage at will!"

The six torpedoes began to accelerate towards the escorts. Their own radar arrays were still shut down, with the guidance systems instead relying on passive sensors and returns from the radar pulses of the surrounding ships. Coming from astern combined with their small size, the alien ships didn't appear to see them coming. At ten thousand kilometres the Nameless registered their presence and began to take evasive action. Missiles intended for attack were instead redirected to defence, but the torpedoes were something the Nameless hadn't encountered before. As each one registered a targeting radar lock on, they began to launch chaff. Two torpedoes vaporised as they met enemy missiles head on, but the other four evaded and continued to close. The starship engines that powered the torpedoes gave extended endurance a missile couldn't match, but they didn't have the same high acceleration. However, their designer had come up with a solution in the form of attached old-fashioned chemical rockets. As these fired, the torpedoes accelerated through their final run-in. The three alien escorts volleyed off the rest of their dual-purpose missiles, intercepting and destroying one more torpedo. Another clipped a frantically dodging cruiser, enough to rip a ragged gash along the entire length of the ship's upper hull. The final two, projectiles every bit as big as the cap ship missiles the Nameless had used since the start of the war, hammered straight into ships utterly incapable of surviving such a blow.

As the Nameless vessels died, their surviving ships salvoed off their loads. But the loss of three cruisers had pulled their teeth. Their weakened salvo met *Black Prince*'s counter fire. Willis felt her ship jump as another missile found its way through, while a tanker took a direct hit and exploded.

"Bridge, Sensors. All contacts are jumping out!"

On the holo the blips for the enemy ships were becoming indistinct.

"Yes, that showed them!" someone said across the command channel. Ten Nameless ships had dropped in. Six had survived to jump out.

Willis looked at the holo, on the opposite side of the convoy, the first group of enemy ships was also falling back.

Willis had barely time to draw breath before the next call came.

"Bridge, Coms. Signal from *Saladin*, convoy heading change to two, eight, zero, dash zero, zero, zero turn in succession."

"Acknowledge and proceed," she replied. Her hand bumped against the visor of her helmet as she unconsciously tried to rub her eyes. Commodore Dandolo's move was a good one. There was likely to be a break before any further attack and by turning the convoy to move directly away from Saturn, they were gaining maximum distance before that could happen. In his seat, she doubted she would have made that decision as fast. Too many things were demanding her attention and she was being reminded that even after a year in command of not just a ship, but the defence of a star system, this wasn't the type of war she had experience of. On the damage control panel several sections were flashing. It was time to find out what surviving thus far had cost them.

Battle Fleet Headquarters

"How do you think it's going?" Secretary Callahan asked quietly.

Wingate made no immediate reply. The two men were standing at the back of the fleet command room, watching the giant hologram as the battle played out at an agonisingly slow rate.

Wingate didn't reply immediately. Instead he mentally tried several possible answers, *as well as can be expected, too early to say, inside projections*.

"We're on the cusp of failure," he said quietly. When Callahan turned sharply to look at him he continued. "Two tankers are down, all the rest are damaged to some extent. Probably less than half the cargo remains. The Nameless might judge... might correctly judge, that they have done enough."

Wingate paused as he continued to stare up at the main holo. On it were a handful of green blips just entering the gun range of the forts on the moon of Tethys. Of course with the picture based on light speed transmissions, it was about eighty minutes out of date. Every twenty minutes or so, an FTL band would open as the Nameless scouts sent an update and the coms ship still orbiting Saturn attempted to get its own message through. Based on that information, a second set of green blips showed something closer to the convoy's real time position, now past Tethys and heading almost directly for the Saturn Red Line.

"How will we know?" Callahan asked, "I mean, whether the Nameless think that?"

"They took this seriously. Their close range jump in with the inevitable casualties proved that. But if they don't put in another contact before the convoy can jump, then we have probably failed."

Wingate motioned with his maimed hand towards a large group of red blips close to Earth. The main Nameless Fleet, a light minute out from Earth, facing the Home Fleet, which was now holding position just inside the Earth Red Line. In their relative positions the two fleets were for the moment effectively neutralising each other, neither allowing the other the freedom to act. Which left the field open to the smaller vessels on each side. The fighters from Earth were preparing to fly to Saturn, as were those from the carriers *Dauntless* and Huascar, all to support the last push.

"There has to be one more serious assault and the convoy has to get through it without significant extra damage."

"What if..." Callahan's question trailed off.

"We don't have the fuel to try this again," Wingate said.

The convoy continued to accelerate away from Tethys. A few shots from the heavy laser cannons mounted on the surface had been enough to persuade the shadowing Nameless scouts to keep their distance. For an hour Willis and the rest of the crew had been able to relax – a little.

"We've lucky so far," Dandolo said across the coms link, "although God knows we're within our rights not to feel it."

"I know I'm not," Ozo said.

"We haven't lost any of the escort," Dandolo continued, "and we haven't lost the ammunition ship. For that we can give thanks to which ever higher power looked out for us."

Willis winced. The fully loaded ammunition ship *Numancia* was supposed to have been on the disengaged side of the convoy, but in the chaos of battle she had found herself directly in the line of fire. Before *Black Prince* had come alongside her, a missile had smashed into an almost full ammunition bunker. By some miracle, it had failed to cause any secondary detonations. With all hell breaking loose, no one realised it until the shooting stopped and the *Numancia*'s very frightened looking captain reported in. Given that the distance between *Numancia* and *Black Prince* had been as little as twenty kilometres, Willis didn't like to dwell on the damage that a detonating ten thousand ton starship suddenly transformed into shrapnel might have inflicted on them.

"But now we'll have to make the last sprint," Dandolo continued, "and odds are that's exactly what it will be. Commander Valance, I know you've been trying to keep your ammunition expenditure under control, but from here on in, hold nothing back. Same goes for the rest of you."

Valance nodded.

"For the record sir, my magazines are now at forty two percent," he said.

"Understood Commander," Dandolo replied. "One last thing, I want each ship to generate its own jump solution. The transports will jump as soon as they clear the Red Line."

"That runs the risk of leaving someone behind it they lose their jump drive at the wrong moment," Ozo warned.

"I'm aware of that, but the alternative is to go down the all or nothing route," Dandolo said. "Okay, let's get this over with."

"I see them!" Willis snapped before the sensor officer could open his mouth. On the holo dead ahead, just inside the Red Line, a dozen Nameless ships, a mix of cruisers, escorts and a single carrier dropped into real space. Four fighters from the *Dauntless* were slowly cruising along the line and they immediately accelerated in. The Nameless carrier spewed fighters and within moments a vicious dogfight erupted.

"Contact separation, we have incoming."

The Saturn fighters pacing along ahead went full burn to get out far enough ahead to thin the first missile salvo. The convoy started to turn enough to present broadside and still make forward progress. On the holo, more Nameless ships started to jump in, at least twenty in total and short of turning one eighty, the convoy was on course to charge into the middle of them.

Willis had to swallow hard to generate enough moisture to speak.

"Bridge, Fire Control. Engage when ready."

There was an eruption of flame and explosions as flak rounds and plasma bolts shattered missiles and clawed them out of space. Three escorts tried to jump in behind and were set upon by the squadron of American fighters that had been pacing along astern. More fighters, some from Earth and others from the carriers, fed into the fight as more Nameless ships arrived.

One of the empty transports took a direct hit, its escape pods hurtling away as it tumbled out of formation and broke up as it went. The destroyer *Olstyn* took two hits in quick succession that wrecked her armament, but grimly held her place in the formation. Still they crept closer to the Red Line. *Fortitude* and the heavy cruisers, *Loki* and *Osiris* jumped in, their guns stabbing out even as they emerged from jump space. Alien ships scrambled clear as plasma bolts burned towards them. A Nameless carrier and a pair of cruisers were badly hit before more of their ships arrived around them and forced the battleship to jump away.

"New contacts!" the sensor officer's voice was hoarse. They were now only minutes away from jump out but every ship's ammunition magazine was all but empty. Most of the Nameless ships had jumped away, their missiles expended, several of them nursing wounds from the human fighters that had also now largely withdrawn. In this marathon they were down to the last few contenders.

Willis glanced at the navigation display; they were passing through the Red Line now. In theory, a jump was possible, but the gradient of risk from safe to suicidal was so steep that now wasn't the time. A moment later she wondered if that was true. There were six new arrivals, two capital ships dead ahead and a pair of cruisers on either flank. The cap ships were firing as they arrived. Two cap ship missiles, clearly not yet far enough into real space disintegrated. The rest along with a swarm of smaller missiles roared down as every human ship fired all available weapons and launched the last of their chaff.

Minstrel couldn't turn fast enough. Her forward defence consisted of only a few turret-mounted laser cannons, but she could lay down more chaff than even a battleship. With only moments to decide, Commander Valance didn't attempt to turn to line up a broadside and instead presented only the ship's bows and the smallest possible target cross section. On *Black Prince*, Willis saw a cap ship missile graze the barrage ship's starboard side, breaking up and ripping open the side as it went, while the impact of smaller missiles left multiple craters in her hull.

"Evasive manoeuvres, countermeasures full spread!" Willis bellowed. *Black Prince* started to jolt around violently as missiles burned past them.

"*Saladin*, this is *Minstrel*. We've taken heavy damage. The starboard side battery is wrecked." Valance was shouting directly across the command channel.

Willis spoke without thinking.

"*Minstrel*, do you still have your jump drive?" she demanded.

"Yes, thank God!"

"Turn and present your port side to the cap ships, coast in and give them everything as you go!"

"Got it," Valance replied. *Minstrel*'s engines spluttered out as her thrusters fired and, swinging on her own axis, brought the undamaged port battery to bear. Approaching side on, she opened fire. The second salvo from the cap ships ran into a wall of fire it could not penetrate as the cruisers held off their counterparts on the flanks. One of their surviving tankers blinked out as it jumped. Within seconds the other survivors disappeared, leaving only the escort. A break between salvos was enough for them to make their own escape.

―――――――――――――――――

D for Dubious coasted slowly along the starboard flank of the cruiser *Black Prince*, the fighter's spotlight playing across the hull. Each time they came across significant damage, Alanna would pause the beam.

"*Black Prince*, are you getting this?" she asked.

"Confirmed *Dubious*, the laser hook up is stable."

"Jesus, what a mess," Schurenhofer muttered.

Alanna nodded in agreement. The starboard side had taken the worst of the onslaught, its armoured belt punctured and scored. The wing on that side was reduced to little more than the underlying lattice, covered by the frozen remains of non-critical supplies that had been stored within, all of it ending in the shattered remnants of the wingtip manoeuvring engine. The coms officer on board the cruiser must have heard Schurenhofer.

"Looks worse on the outside than it does on the inside. Armour kept most of it out."

"Did you lose anyone?"

"Three in sickbay, two in the morgue. Looks like the starboard side belt armour will have to be replaced, but at least with an Austerity class ship that won't be too hard."

"Provided you get back to a ship yard," Schurenhofer reminded him.

Whoever he was, the coms officer seemed to have regained his calm pretty quickly. Two hours earlier Alanna had been on the bridge of

Dauntless when the convoy started appearing on radar. Separate jumps meant they were scattered across fifty thousand kilometres, in response to which the carrier's fighters and destroyers had rapidly set out to shepherd them back together. Not that it was entirely necessary. Like scattered ducklings, the transports were already beginning to cluster back together for protection when their escorts started to arrive.

A few minutes after completing its jump, the crew of the *Olstyn* abandoned ship as the destroyer lost power. Priority for Alanna and the rest of the fighters became external surveys of the surviving ships.

"Just as well the bastards don't seem to be able to come after us out here," the coms officer said as *Dubious* continued to move along the flank.

"Yep," Alanna replied, "although they bloody try to compensate by chasing us around while we're in-system."

That had been a hot topic of conversation on the carrier between those who wondered why and those who were just glad of it.

"A bit of peace and quiet will do us good before it's time for 'once more unto the breach dear friends,'" continued the blasé coms officer.

"When it happens, we'll be right behind you," Alanna said as *Dubious* passed the end of the cruiser. "That's it *Black Prince*, I'm moving on." She hesitated for a moment before adding: "Look me up when we're all back on Earth and we can share stories."

"Just as long as its' only stories. Otherwise my fiancé might object. Look after yourself, *Dubious*. This is *Black Prince* over and out."

Willis had overheard the conversation between her coms officer and the departing fighter and let it pass without comment. After the intensity of combat, the crew was experiencing what she always thought of as the high of survival. It would fade pretty quickly, but there wouldn't be time for survivor's guilt, not before they went in again.

"How bad is it, Commander?" Dandolo asked across the conference link.

On the screen, Valance looked like he'd come off second best in a bar room brawl. One eyebrow was being held together with glue stitches and he had a black eye.

"Multiple ruptures in the outer hull, so about forty percent of internal sections are no longer capable of holding pressure. Our structural integrity is not compromised though – chalk that one up as the advantage of a freighter hull. Where it gets bad is with the armament. The starboard side battery is basically cabbaged. My gunner reports we have just twelve of our original forty guns. But to be honest, the whole thing took such a jolt I have no confidence in the automatic loaders."

"What about your port side?" Dandolo said. "And your engines?"

"Two guns down to port, but the rest definitely still work. Our engines took some damage, but I can keep pace with the transports."

"Alright Commander, patch her up as best you can. We'll just have to try to favour the enemy to port. Anything else, anyone?"

"Yes," Captain Ozo replied, looking deeply unhappy. "I've got problems with one of our reactors. I don't know whether it's damage or a construction problem, but it keeps losing coolant pressure."

"Can you fight?"

"Yes, sir, we can. Or at least we can get to the fight."

"That will have to do. Faith, what about you?"

"The armour of my starboard belt is in bad shape and I've lost several point defence guns on that side. Like *Minstrel*, we'll need to present our port side whenever we can."

"I understand, Captain. We'll be changing sides, so everyone gets a chance to balance their damage if nothing else."

It was a weak joke but it got a few smiles.

"We've got twenty hours before we make our run in and I'm sorry to say but getting in clean is not an option. All right everyone, replenish your magazines and get some rest. Captain Willis, can I have a private word?"

Willis kept her face impassive, but internally winced.

"I expect you know what this is about – issuing orders directly to *Minstrel*."

"Yes, sir, I'm sorry, I..."

"It was the right order to give," Dandolo interrupted, "but skipping the chain of command like that, could have seriously bollixed everything up in the middle of a firefight. That's something they beat into us all in training. That said, success justifies a hell of a lot."

He paused and gave her a sympathetic smile.

"I know that on your last posting you were effectively a Commodore, just without the rank or pay, so I appreciate it's hard to step down when you've been used to making the tough calls. Just know when to show initiative and when to toe the line. The other thing is I've had a signal from *Fortitude*. Her coms section has taken a knock and can't be relied on from here. You have more experience than either the captains of the *Loki* or *Osiris*, so you're next in line of command for the squadron."

"Commodore?"

"Hmm?"

Crowe looked up from his reading and saw Commander Bhudraja was standing in the hatch with a computer pad in his hand.

"Are you running post?" Crowe asked.

"A chance to straighten my legs sir," Bhudraja replied as he passed the pad over. "Signal from *Warspite*. The convoy made it out."

"Thank God for that," Crowe muttered. "They should have sent a proper flak cruiser, not ships made up of spare parts."

The dust thrown up by their landing had finally settled, but in doing so had completely coated the panels of the passive sensor arrays. Even keeping the communications lasers operational so they could get downloads from the orbiting satellites had meant sending out a man in a suit with the radio physically deactivated. Once they powered up, they could run a charge across the hull to repel the particles, but until then *Deimos* was basically blind.

Crowe read down the orders from *Warspite*. His frown deepened as he worked his way down.

"What does the Chief say about cold starting the reactors?" he asked, looking up.

"Since he's been alternating them, twenty minutes," Bhudraja replied. "He also said the reactors aren't the biggest problem. The engine control surfaces have been in deep cold for over a month. They need thirty minutes to warm before we dare go full thrust."

"No crash starts then?" Crowe asked.

It wasn't really a question. The thermal shock of a crash start was more or less guaranteed to cost a ship a couple of control surfaces. But for a ship taking off, even in such low gravity, the effect on directional control could be disastrous. A ground loop by a starship would undoubtedly be interesting to watch, but only as long as it was happening to someone else!

"The Chief said you can try it, so long as he can sit in an escape pod when you do."

"Not that we'll have to," Crowe tossed the pad down onto the desk. "The Admiral has decided we're only to arrive at Earth thirty minutes *after* the convoy jumps in."

"That'll keep them heavily engaged for an extended period before..."

"Before any help turns up," Crowe finished for him. "The rest of the fleet can't move up to support them without tipping our hand and leaving the Nameless free to attack Earth on the opposite side of the planet. Those poor bastards are being thrown under a bus to get the Nameless to go deep enough into the Earth's mass shadow to get pinned. And the odds are most of them are smart enough to know it to."

"We'll be in deep ourselves, sir," Bhudraja said quietly.

"Yes I know," Crowe sighed, "but for once I don't think we've been hit with the shittiest available end of the stick." Crowe pulled himself out of his chair. "I need to make a ship wide announcement – let the crew know that we're ten hours from show time."

19th February 2068

There was no point bringing empty ships, not this time. The ammunition ship and the surviving transports would remain. With their fuel tanks almost full, they would have the range to reach Dryad if Earth fell. Whether that was worth anything was a matter of opinion. The four surviving tankers were formed into a box formation, with the cruisers clustered around them, the destroyers in the vanguard and *Fortitude* bringing up the rear.

On the display Willis could see three Nameless scouts holding position a light hour away, just outside Pluto's orbit. Visible beyond them and unquestionably now somewhere else in the system, was the rest of the enemy fleet. Finally, in orbit around Earth, were the ships of the Home Fleet. With the secret of their torpedoes now revealed, dozens had been deployed at the edge of Earth's Red Line. Finally, out of sight on Phobos, the Fast Division lay in wait.

All of us are waiting for the next move, Willis thought, all of us waiting to react. The Home Fleet couldn't move up to the Red Line without leaving the Nameless free to approach and attack Earth from the opposite side. The aliens couldn't hold position close to Earth because they would leave themselves open to assault by fighters or the handful of human ships out in the system. Instead both sides had to wait in what were now starting positions. She could feel it, the whole solar system was holding its breath, waiting for the next step.

"Bridge, Coms. Signal from *Saladin*: execute jump."

Willis looked around her bridge. They'd made it this far. Humanity had needed them to, but it didn't need them to make it much further. *I'm getting really tired of being expendable*, she thought to herself.

"Navigation, send instructions to Helm. All hands, this is the Bridge, prepare for jump... and prepare for contact."

For a moment the fabric of space right on the Earth Red Line suddenly rippled, then burst open as the twelve starships dropped back into real space. As they crossed the threshold, each of the four tankers went full burn as they began to accelerate towards Earth. Below, the engines of every warship flared as they began to ascend Earth's gravity well. Fighters began to spill out from the ships and orbital forts. On the ground far below, flight crews in bulky suits ran for their planes.

The Nameless FTL jammers shut down as the scout ships began to transmit. The convoy of fuel ships, the last desperate effort of a species they were resolved to destroy, had arrived and was accelerating towards safety. The race was on.

On Phobos, undetected, eight starships prepared for lift off.

"Bridge, Sensors. Multiple new contacts bearing one, zero, one dash three, five, three."

"Strength?" Willis asked.

"One hundred and eighty plus."

They had got the result, which as an officer she had hoped for, but as a person she had feared – the Nameless were determined that no fuel would reach Earth. They'd just put in the bulk of their fleet. Could those tankers survive long enough to draw the Nameless into the trap?

"Bridge, Coms. Signal from *Saladin*, execute formation change, posture three."

"Acknowledged," Willis replied, "Helm, roll and present our port side and move us to position three."

"Confirmed."

Black Prince slid out from in front of the tankers onto the starboard side, while the battered *Minstrel* rolled round and into the gap between *Black Prince* and *Cetshwayo*, her undamaged battery facing the enemy. On the holo, the red blips of Nameless ships solidified as they completed their jump in. Tactical's analysis settled on one hundred and eighty three ships, all of them only marginally inside the Red Line. Immediately two-dozen torpedoes broke the orbit they'd been holding for days and began to home in on the alien ships.

"Contact separation, we have incoming," intoned the sensor operator as a swarm of fresh red blips appeared on the screen.

"Point Defence, commence, commence, commence!" Willis ordered.

Space erupted in flame and light as *Minstrel* attempted to fill the area ahead of the incoming missiles with shrapnel, but this time there were so many missiles that they lapped around the barrage. For its part, *Black Prince* began to launch chaff and its flak guns started to pick off missiles.

"Fire Control, concentrate on cap ship missiles!" Willis ordered as their fire lingered for a moment on a group of dual-purpose missiles, ripping them apart. Missiles burned through the formation, but with so much chaff laid down, most only locked on their targets as they passed, but *Black Prince* still jolted as smaller missiles found her. The dorsal wing was carried away and for a moment the upper radar shut down before the Lazarus systems rerouted through a working command line. On the holo a swarm of Nameless fighters came curving around *Minstrel's* barrage, then behind the alien fleet, a further two-dozen fighters made their jump in from Saturn. The enemy turned away and within minutes the fighters were engaged in their own vicious private battle. The rest of the Nameless fleet started to follow, picking up speed and moving closer to the Blue Line.

Twenty minutes after their jump in and twelve frantic minutes into the fighting, *Black Prince* and *Minstrel* still fought to hold back swarms of missiles. Torpedoes were still closing on and attacking the Nameless fleet, never in sufficient numbers to penetrate the counter fire, but enough to force the aliens to stay close for mutual protection. Two tankers had taken missile hits. Neither strike was crippling, but one of the vessels had to vent much of its fuel to avoid exploding. *Minstrel's* wall of fire was one the enemy missiles simply couldn't get through, wiping away much of their numerical superiority but all too soon the barrage ship started to show her Achilles heel. Her rate of fire slowed, then became spasmodic as Commander Valance conserved his dwindling ammunition to deal with the greatest threats. The three austerities were left to pick up the slack.

Lunar dust cascaded down the flanks of *Warspite* as the battleship lifted away from the surface. Around her, the other seven ships of the Fast Division blasted off. As the dust cleared from the passive arrays, Lewis got his first clear look at the wider solar system. Had he committed too late or too soon? A few FTL transmissions from Earth had got through, but the quality of the data was poor. More detailed information was arriving via the passive sensors, but based on light speed transmission that was fifteen minutes out of date. From this, they knew the convoy escort was heavily engaged. But that had been fifteen minutes ago, so were they still standing now? There was no real way to know, but one way or another, the Fast Division was now committed.

"Navigator, how long until we can jump?" Lewis asked.

"Sir, at current acceleration, twelve more minutes."

"We need another minute for the jump and several more to reach firing range," said Sheehan. "Those ships have to hang on for another quarter of an hour."

"Captain, if any of them are still alive when we arrive, issue them instructions to take a blocking position on the left."

"You really think they'll still be there, sir?" Sheehan asked as he looked at the distant blips on the holo.

"I'll look upon it as a useful bonus if they are," Lewis replied coldly. "But if they are destroyed in the next few minutes or the Nameless choose to disengage..." Lewis momentarily trailed off before resuming. "We'll only know once we make jump in. But there can be no hesitation; we go in as hard as we can."

Guinness let out a grunt of pain as he slammed into a bulkhead. Then *Black Prince* jolted the opposite way and he was thrown against a wall of electrical cables. A junction box jabbed him hard in the ribs as his flailing hand closed on a handhold and he managed to avoid being thrown again. Through the metal, Guinness could feel the vibrations of the hull. If there had been atmosphere in the engine room he would likely have heard the hull keening and groaning.

"Jesus, Skipper, take it easy," he half muttered before stopping. If she was throwing the ship around like this, it was because it was required.

Pulling himself from handhold to handhold, Guinness dragged himself into the starboard side generator room and stopped. The compartment was flooding. Blobs of bluish cooling fluid were floating around the compartment.

"What the hell?" Guinness began.

The engines went all astern and, in compliance with the laws of physics, the floating liquid suddenly came rushing towards him. He only had time to either brace himself or slam the hatch shut. He chose the latter.

The fluid hit him with hammer-like force, hurling him backward. Guinness lost all concept of direction. Everywhere he looked was just distorted blue. Then something grabbed him by the arm and dragged him to the 'surface.'

"Chief! Are you all right?" the generator room petty officer demanded.

"Thought I was drowning," Guinness muttered vaguely, before pulling himself together. "Where the hell's this coming from?"

"We've been holed somewhere and an entire radiator's worth of fluid has vented *inward*. We're trying to keep it out of the generator..."

"Too late!" Guinness shouted.

Behind the petty officer, Electrical Generator Number Two violently shorted out. Shoving him aside, Guinness pulled himself to the control board. More in hope than optimism, he pressed a button on the blackened panel, following which a warning icon appeared on his helmet display alerting him that electricity was shorting across his survival suit. The generator itself might be recoverable in the long run, but its control systems were toast – no one had thought a control panel on a starship would need to be waterproof! *Black Prince* could run on one generator but... Guinness pulled out his computer pad and brought up the latest reading from across engineering.

"Oh, Christ," he muttered.

"Engine Room, Bridge," Willis's voice came across the intercom. "Chief, one of the generators has just gone down."

"I know, Skipper," Guinness replied. "It's not repairable, not now. But that's not our biggest problem. We are bleeding radiator fluid on the starboard side *into* the ship. Radiator efficiency is dropping fast. The ship is already dumping heat into the heat sinks. At full military output it won't be long before we either power down or melt!"

"The radiators on the port side are mostly gone, can you transfer fluid?"

"Yes, but unless we find where it's getting in, it will simply bleed into the engineering spaces. We are already losing systems to short circuits!"

"Do what you can, Chief. I'll have Damage Control send down extra hands." Her voice was calmer than he expected. The ship had perhaps ten or twelve minutes to live, yet Willis sounded as if she was merely discussing dinner being late.

"How are we doing?" he asked before he could stop himself, so that just once he would know what was happening beyond the bulkheads.

"We've just lost *Minstrel*, Chief. Bridge out."

Now he understood. Why worry about ten minutes from now if it was unlikely they'd get that far?

"Alright, find me a fucking sealant gun and let's find that leak!"

Even with her engines at one hundred percent, the cruiser *Deimos* shook as she struggled to match the pace of the rest of the Fast Division. *Warspite* was out in front, the heavy cruisers in an arrow head formation and the fighters out on the flanks, with the *Deimos* labouring in the rear.

"Chief, have we anything extra?" Crowe asked across the intercom.

"Sir, short of our armour suddenly falling off, this is the best we can do! In fact, we are damaging the engines right now!"

"Understood," Crowe replied before turning, "Coms, inform flag we're giving it everything."

"Sir."

With no more orders to give Crowe lapsed into silence. The main holo had zoomed in on the fighting around Earth. The readings were fifteen minutes out of date but they showed the convoy escort frantically trying the hold back the Nameless juggernaut. The FTL transmissions from Earth said the Nameless were still in a position that would put them within firing range of the Fast Division within minutes of jump in. But if the Nameless started jumping out, they'd be clear before the trap could be sprung. It was all Crowe could manage not to fidget as the minutes crept past.

"Sir, signal from *Warspite*. It's a conference call from the

Admiral."

"Put it up," Crowe ordered.

The face that appeared on his screen was shocking. The Admiral's skin was almost grey with heavy bags under the eyes that suggested sleep had become a mere memory.

"Gentlemen," he said, "in five minutes we will jump as a single formation. Running order will be as it is now."

"Sir, my ship can better engage..." Crowe began.

"I know, Commodore, but if the Nameless react fast enough to put missiles out as we jump in, *Deimos* could be crippled or destroyed. Every other ship here can take a hit better. As soon as we clear the jump portal, your ship will take the lead as we close on the enemy. I'm downloading instructions for your torpedoes, which must be used to seal the flanks."

Lewis glanced away from the screen at something on his own bridge, then he turned back.

"Gentlemen we are about to jump, so I have one final order. We cannot be sure of the tactical situation, but one thing we can be certain of is that this is our last chance to inflict defeat on the enemy. Therefore, in the event that either *Warspite* or myself are lost, I leave you with one standing order: for as long as you can fight or manoeuvre, you are to close upon and engage the enemy."

Lewis glimpsed away from the screen again then looked back and attempted to smile.

"Good luck to you all," he concluded.

The screen went blank.

"Engage the enemy more closely," Crowe said to the blank screen before looking around the bridge. "All hands, prepare to jump."

Ahead of the Fast Division the fabric of space opened and they plunged down the jump conduit towards God only knew what.

Willis watched grimly as the barrage ship broke up. Even as she did so, more missiles slammed in. A few escape pods burst away, but not many. Only one of the destroyers, *Humaita*, remained, while *Cetshwayo* was now an air bleeding wreck, wobbling back and forth, her few remaining point defence guns still defiantly popping away. As *Minstrel* died, *Fortitude* pulled into her place, soaking up the abuse. While the escort slowed, the surviving tankers began to pull away. Then human fighters began to arrive from Earth. Most threw themselves at their opposite numbers, while others interposed themselves between the Nameless and the convoy, whittling down the salvoes. With *Humaita*'s magazines as bare as *Minstrel*'s had been. All she could do was take position astern of the tankers and deploy chaff.

"Captain, signal from the Commodore."

Dandolo appeared on her screen. There was no sign of Captain Ozo though.

"Captain," he said without preamble, "the tankers have just crossed the Blue Line and this is as far as we go with them. We will turn to face and make our stand here – make clear to them that they won't get those tankers without coming through us first. We don't need to hold for long. The Fast Division is on its way."

"They should have already arrived," Willis replied grimly. "Sir, if I open all radiators I have left and coast backwards, I can stay in. Otherwise my engine rooms will start melting in about five minutes."

"Alright, brake as hard as you can. We just have to hang on a little longer."

The Commodore then disappeared, his last words sounding like those of a man trying to convince himself.

Shaking her head, terrible doubt now crept into Willis's mind. They couldn't even be sure the Fast Division had even received its orders. Or that Admiral Lewis had decided to obey them. Could the fleet's iceman have decided to follow his own course and deliberately sacrifice the austerities? This was the same man who more than a year before had hung her out to dry on the old *Hood* at Alpha Centauri. No way to know. On her display she could see the rest of the Home Fleet climbing up and away from Earth, but if the Fast Division didn't arrive soon, this would be over before they could achieve firing range.

"Helm, make our facing one, two, zero dash zero, zero, zero, then go full burn on engines for ninety seconds and then cut power to them," she ordered.

"Skipper?" The helmsman's alarm was clear in his voice.

"Those are my orders. Do what you can with the manoeuvring thrusters."

Black Prince shuddered and Willis was pressed back in her seat as the engines went to max power. As they slowed, the Nameless accelerated to close the range – perhaps sensing this was a last stand by ships that knew they were about to be overwhelmed. As that thought crossed Willis's mind, *Cetshwayo* took a direct hit from a mass driver missile. Two engines were blown clear of their mountings and flame wreathed the tumbling cruiser as her last reactor scrammed. Escape pods started to blow clear of their silos as her surviving crew abandoned the doomed ship. *Black Prince* shuddered left and right as missiles struck her on either side. Half of point defence went down, while B turret and one of the flak guns went offline. Within seconds, the latter came back on as the Lazarus systems found a surviving connection. On the holo, *Saladin* flashed multiple damage codes as missiles hammered into her, then the holo shuddered and the figures disappeared.

"Bridge, Coms! We've just lost the whole coms system!"

A glance to her left confirmed the communications group was sitting in front of either blank or frozen panels.

"Understood, restore if you can," she ordered. "Report to damage control if you can't."

The communications lieutenant gave a jerky nod before grabbing his second-in-command and making for the hatch off the bridge. She turned back to the main holo just in time to see seven green blips appear on the display – right on the Red Line. Even though *Black Prince* couldn't receive transponder codes any more, she knew those blips could mean only be one thing.

"All hands! This is the Bridge. The Fast Division has arrived. We've got them now!"

There was a cheer across the intercom and Willis found she was one of the cheerers too.

––––––––––––––––––

As the ships of the Fast Division jolted back into real space, *Deimos*'s holo blanked out then started to refill as the computer absorbed more up to date information. The Nameless Fleet was still there, accelerating towards the remainder of the convoy escort. They were close to the Blue Line, still far enough out to jump, but moving too fast to do so! While a target was moving, the shooter would have to fire on several subtly distinct bearings, to cover the different deflections and compensate for any evasive manoeuvres. But with a stationary or near stationary target, instead of settling for hitting with one or two plasma bolts each time, an entire salvo could be put in. With their long-range missiles and fragile hulls, the Nameless had nothing that would survive that kind of beating long enough to jump. The tactical section was already working out whether their foe could jump before the Fast Division reached gun range. As Crowe studied the holo and measured by eye, a smile crept across his face. There were no missiles coming towards them, indicating that whatever else might be happening, the Nameless hadn't seen them coming. But how fast could they react?

As Crowe wondered, the bridge crew were already following the orders they been given before the jump. The rest of the Fast Division paused just long enough for the *Deimos* to slide up through the formation alongside *Warspite*. As their fighters deployed out in front, the torpedoes slipped clear of their silos and began to angle away into flanking positions, to box in the Nameless.

"Sir, enemy is signalling on the FTL A Band," the communications officer reported.

Pulling it up on his own screen, Crowe could see a spasm of signals coming from several of the enemy capital ships. The fire being directed at the remains of the convoy withered as the alien formation began to shift, and their ships reversed heading and began to brake hard. Even without being able to read their signals, there was no doubt that the Nameless had been thrown into confusion. But in a few minutes, perhaps even seconds, they would realise that there were a lot more ambushed ships than ambushers

"Fire Control, Bridge. Prepare to engage missiles with flak guns, but reserve plasma cannons for anti-ship fire," Crowe ordered. "Capital ships are first priority, then carriers, then cruisers."

"Yes, sir."

"Tactical," Crowe continued, "I want any ship that slows enough to jump flagged to fire control, priority as before. We can kill escorts and scouts 'til the cows come home, but the big boys are where it counts."

"Understood, sir."

On the display, the fighters that had been streaming up from Earth changed course. Instead of trying to fight their way through to the enemy starships, they were taking positions to block their possible escape routes.

"Sir, just caught a signal from the *Titan*: all ships make best speed to the enemy."

On the holo, Crowe could see the formation of the Home Fleet starting to open up as the faster ships stretched their legs. Within minutes, the fleet had broken into layers with the destroyers out front, followed by the faster cruisers, then their heavier brethren and finally the battleships lumbering in the rear. The race was on. If enough Battle Fleet ships could reach gun range, then the Nameless could neither run in real space nor stop long enough to jump.

Beside *Deimos* there was a rippling flash as *Warspite*'s heavy plasma cannons belched out her first salvo and seconds later a Nameless fighter carrier died.

"Bridge, Sensors. We have incoming."

"Fire Control, engage as directed. Point defence, commence, commence, commence!"

On the bridge of *Warspite*, Lewis eyed the holo impassively as the blip for an enemy capital ship blinked out. They had already claimed a carrier and a cruiser, but they needed another three minutes to get the smaller guns of his cruisers into range. He would get there before the Nameless could slow enough to have the option to jump. The question was what to do when he did? Turn, hold range and present broadside? No, he decided after a moment. The order given before they had jumped in remained the best option – close in on the enemy fleet and get in amongst them. At such short range, *Warspite* would inflict considerable damage before she could be overwhelmed.

Following the holo, Lewis could see whoever or whatever commanded the enemy fleet was starting to recover from their surprise. The alien fleet had commenced damage limitation and was resettling. Their escorts were braking harder than their bigger ships, causing them to move up through their fleet and into the line of fire. To come close enough to a dead stop in order to jump while the Fast Division was in gun range would result in the loss or crippling of most of their large ships. So while their engines were going full burn, *Warspite*'s computer reported that the most of enemy's ships had stopped attempting to brake. Instead, they were now attempting to reverse course in a loop that would maintain as much speed as possible. This would allow them to build up a sufficient lead on the Home Fleet to give them enough time to then slow and jump before the humans got into range. But first they had to eliminate the Fast Division.

Good decision, Lewis silently acknowledged his opposite number. Having established there was no painless way out, he, she or it had the courage or ruthlessness to follow that line of reasoning. Otherwise, they would get caught by the Home Fleet and lose everything. Coming up through Lewis's command would still carry a price, but destroying the Fast Division in the process would go a long way towards offsetting any shift in the balance of power.

"It appears they have decided their way out is through us," Lewis said calmly. "Captain Holfe, beware of ships attempting to ram."

"Understood, Admiral," *Warspite*'s captain replied across the com.

"Cruisers are entering firing range now," someone reported, as holo icons appeared showing the vessels commencing fire.

The handful of missiles coming at them had stopped as the fleet gathered itself to put in a concerted effort. Then dozens of new contacts appeared as they began to fire en masse. The ships of the Fast Division had been chosen because *Warspite* and the six heavy cruisers had traded in their big railguns for flak batteries, which now joined with *Deimos* to lay down a wall of protective fire against the approaching missiles. Dozens of them burst as shrapnel ripped them apart. None of the lumbering cap ship missiles got past, but smaller projectiles threaded their way through and *Warspite* started to jerk as missile after missile hammered into her armour.

"Admiral!"

Lewis spun his head towards the shout.

"New enemy contacts jumping in! Dead astern!"

The Fleet Command Room was near silent. Never intended to provide tactical control, it now served as an auditorium for those fleet personnel not serving on the defending ships above. Several hundred men and women lined the back wall, following the situation, knowing their presence was barely tolerated by those carrying the burden of command. When a cluster of alien blips appeared behind those representing the pitifully few ships of the Fast Division, just inside the Red Line, something like a sigh ran round the room.

"Admiral?" Secretary Callahan asked.

"It's another forty ships," Wingate confirmed. "That means that the enemy has now fed in all the ships they have in the system. As things stand the Fast Division is about to be sandwiched. Admiral Lewis will be enveloped and overwhelmed before the rest of the fleet can reach him, but they have no more ships to throw in."

"Oh my God! What can we do?"

Wingate nodded to his staff captain, before turning back to the Secretary.

"Nothing more. Our last reserves are now being committed."

As *D for Dubious* jolted into real space, an alarm sounded in Alanna's ear. She glanced down at her control panel and nearly threw up. They'd emerged a few kilometres into the Red Line. The drive had just about managed to open the conduit, but those few kilometres had been enough to total it. Schurenhofer let out a squeak of alarm as she realised what had nearly happened.

"Forget it," Alanna muttered, "we aren't dead."

But on her screen, two fighters were missing. Squadron Commander Dati had been the one to choose and calculate the jump in point. Still filled with that burning anger of his, he'd pushed too close and he and another crew had paid the price when their fighters failed to make real space re-entry. But there was no time to reflect on how close they'd come to sharing the same fate. Ahead lay their target – the Nameless reserves.

There was just one carrier and its fighters were mostly deployed, enough to hold off the twenty fighters accelerating towards them.

Pity for you bastards we aren't alone, Alanna thought as behind them *Huáscar*, *Dubious* and the escort destroyers of all three carriers jumped in and charged. They were the final elements of a line that stretched forwards through the fighters, the enemy relief force, then the Fast Division, the main Nameless fleet and finally the Home Fleet climbing up from Earth.

"Talk about the conga line of death," Schurenhofer observed.

Alanna gave her a quick grin.

"All wings, concentrate on the enemy fighters, then target the big boys!" she ordered as *Dubious* accelerated in and astern – like her lost namesake – *Dauntless* charged willingly into gun range.

Commander Berg was tossed back and forth in her chair as *Mantis* jinked left and right. The rest of the destroyers were also taking evasive action while the two carriers laid down fire from their flak guns – protecting their smaller brethren. Across the command channel, she could hear her gunnery officer swearing as he struggled to compensate. So far the fire from *Mantis* and the rest of the destroyers had been wild and ineffective. They needed to advance through this killing ground and get in among the enemy ships. The Nameless rearguard was turning to meet them and missiles were starting to fly.

"Countermeasures, full spread!" she ordered.

As she spoke, the destroyer *Cheetah* took a direct hit from a cap ship missile. The entire ship disappeared in a flash, not even leaving wreckage behind.

"Helm, prepare for the turn over. We don't want to go straight through!"

Ahead, the fighters were fully engaged, tearing into and through their enemies. Another destroyer, *Stingray*, took a heavy hit and tumbled out of control.

"Helm, now!" Berg snapped. *Mantis* flipped end over and braked hard as she matched velocity and heading with the Nameless inside their formation. Except there was now no formation – this was a melee of unimaginable scale, with each ship on its own. *Mantis* wove through, guns firing left and right, as Nameless ships attempted to escape their tormentors. The collision detector sounded urgently as an escort tried to swerve into them. Without waiting for an order, the helmsman lunged the destroyer downwards. As the escort skimmed past, *Mantis*'s point defence guns opened up, speckling the hull with punctures. Ahead there was a sudden opening and through the chaos, *Mantis*'s computer identified the largest ship of the Nameless rearguard – their carrier. Its close escort stripped away and visibly floundering, it was a target any captain would dream of finding in their sights. A quick glance to the weapons board showed all four missile tubes were still loaded.

"Fire Control, target the carrier with missiles, all tubes!"

"Roger!"

The four missiles rippled from their launchers at a range of less than one hundred kilometres. As they struck the enemy carrier amidships, it burst like an overripe fruit.

Lewis smiled coldly as the two rearguard formations smashed into one another and ceased to be a factor in the main fight. The main enemy fleet had hesitated when the carriers jumped in on top of their back up. Had the alien commander reached the limit? Certainly the average human mind could only cope with so many shocks in quick succession before it became dysfunctional. The ground-based fighter squadrons of Planetary Defence that had been held back were now joining the fight. The Nameless fighters, inferior one on one, had their numerical advantage stripped away and were now being massacred. Squadrons of human fighters, unable to find their opposite numbers to attack, now threw themselves at the fleeing Nameless ships. Strafing runs couldn't kill a starship but they could hamstring one, with the result that the Nameless fleet formation had started to break up as the lame were abandoned by the swifter. Whatever the Nameless were, they could feel panic and it was starting to show.

"Signal the squadron to come to heading two seven zero dash zero, zero, zero," Lewis calmly ordered. "We'll hold at this distance and let them come to us. They may get us yet, but by the time they do, we'll have bled them white first."

"Not just us, sir," Sheehan said, as he nodded towards a new piece of information being flagged on the display.

Bringing up the rear but armed with the biggest guns, the battleships of the Home Fleet had just reached firing range.

With its port side engine pod riddled by gunfire, the escort was locked in a slow turn as *D for Dubious* shot under it, her wingman hard on her heels. Alanna dragged her fighter's nose around to reverse its heading. One the escort's missile silos popped open as it sought swat its tormentor, just like she'd wanted it to. Alanna pressed down hard on the firing stud and three lines of gunfire stitched their way across the hull and into the silo. The missile inside blew, gouging a massive crater in the small ship. The remaining engine spluttered and failed as the escort tumbled away.

"Another one bites the dust," Schurenhofer crowed as Alanna flipped *Dubious* back over.

"What have we got ammunition wise?" she asked.

"Less than two hundred rounds on each gun," Schurenhofer replied. "But we're running out of targets just as fast."

She was right. Most of the Nameless rearguard was either destroyed, attempting to slow to jump or running in real space. Most but not all; looking as her display she could see three contacts closing on *Dauntless*.

"All *Dauntless* fighters, close in and protect mother," she ordered.

Less than fifty kilometres ahead of *Dubious*, *Dauntless* lumbered around like an elderly maiden aunt persuaded to dance a jig, her flak guns and point defence blazing away in all directions. A Nameless escort swung in and put two dual-purpose missiles into the carrier, blowing apart the hangars on one side. *Dauntless* staggered, then her flak turrets came to bear and she took savage revenge on her opponent. Closing from half a dozen directions, the carrier's children swarmed and pecked apart the other two escorts. The last of them detonated as *Dubious*'s magazines ran dry. Looking around Alanna realised her battle was over. There was no one left to fight.

Perhaps a hundred Nameless ships still remained combat worthy. Their formation was ragged but still there. Then suddenly they broke off in countless different directions as every ship went its' own way, each desperately seeking salvation. Crowe felt his jaw drop.

"My God," said Colwell, "they're routing."

It was every ship for itself.

"Sir, signal from *Warspite*: break formation, engage at will."

The battle from there became nothing more than snap shots for Crowe, as the Fast Division raced in like foxes let loose in a hen house. He saw the cruisers *Churchill* and *De Gaulle* get in on either side of the last Nameless carrier and riddle it from stem to stern. *Warspite* plunged into the centre of the expanding cloud of ships and stabbed out with her guns, claiming victims with virtually every shot. With so many targets to pursue in so many directions, some Nameless ships finally managed to slow down enough to jump out and disappear. But only small ships and a few cruisers managed to escape in this way. No enemy cap ships or carriers got clear.

They had won.

Chapter Nine

Breathing Space

28th February 2068

It was one in the morning and the White House state dinner was still going strong. In fact, one week after the last Nameless ship had fled its solar system; planet Earth was still one big party. It wasn't quite the biggest Earth had ever seen – that had been at the end of the Contact War. Lewis hadn't been on planet for the start of that, but it had still been going seven weeks later when he and *Onslaught* finally made it home.

"This way sir," said the White House aide who'd rescued Lewis from a dull conversation with two congressmen.

With a battle that should have been lost instead won, this was now the time for the men and women of power to show that they had made the hard choices and backed the winning horse. State dinners and the like were being held in all the major capitals of the world for the heroes of the hour to be lauded and politicians to claim their share of the credit. Like a military operation, the fleet had deployed its senior officers to all possible points of contact – even the one officer with a notorious lack of tolerance for the political classes.

The aide paused to tap on the door and then led the Admiral into the Oval Office.

President Clifton was standing with her back to the famous desk staring out the window.

"Admiral, I do apologise for dragging you away from the party," Clifton said as she turned around. "Please sit."

"Thank you," Lewis replied as he seated himself.

"It's unusual for the fleet to ask to speak outside of normal channels. With all respect, Admiral, it's even stranger that you should be the one to be sent here."

"There's barely a national capital that hasn't already hosted at least one of the fleet's senior officers for the celebrations, Madam President. Admiral Wingate believes it's an opportunity that can't be squandered."

"And he believes in going straight to the top in each case?"

"Yes. Time is pressing and it avoids the political hangers-on who want to be seen, but get in the way and contribute nothing useful to the discussions," Lewis replied bluntly.

Clifton smiled slightly.

"A cruel dismissal of Congress, Admiral" she said, "but please continue."

"We haven't won, Madam President," Lewis said flatly as he gestured upwards towards the stars. "This 'victory' was the best case scenario. We caused them major casualties with only light losses in return, yet it has bought us only a breathing space."

"That's a very harsh assessment of events, particularly one in which you played such an important part bringing to a successful conclusion," Clifton replied.

"It is harsh because too many people are talking this up as more than it really is. I have read the media reports and 'expert analysis.' Too many people are choosing to live in a fantasy world where we've just won the war," Lewis said shaking his head. "In the real world we've only avoided losing it."

"Most people Admiral, would at least enjoy the moment." Clifton observed.

"And were this war over, you can be sure I would be running around whooping with the best of them. But we are not there."

"Alright Admiral, say what you have come here to say."

"We wish to talk about the future and what our next step should be," Lewis replied. "What our efforts have bought us, is a momentary advantage. The Nameless fleet has been severely weakened relative to our own..."

"By the count of my own analysts, so far Battle Fleet has destroyed the equivalent of its own tonnage and that of its own manpower. How the hell can any intelligent race sustain such loss?"

"Economic strength. Immense economic strength," Lewis said. "In many respects the Nameless are in a similar position to this country more than a century ago, during the wars of the early twentieth century. It had an economy both immensely powerful and safely out of harm's way. Opponents could not directly threaten the United States homeland and instead had to hope to break the will of the American people by defeating their armies in the field. This is where the Nameless diverge from you. Before it was overrun, the reports we got from Douglas base on Landfall, indicated they used biological constructs as infantry. I suspect the crews of those ships are something similar, which is why they take such a casual attitude to losses."

"I expected you to tell me that I shouldn't expect an understandable rationale from an alien race."

"No matter what way they perceive the universe, they are subject to practical realities. They can fight a war only with the resources available to them. This is where our problem lies. Given time, the Nameless will make good their losses and they will do it quicker than we can ours. Unless we can end this war within the next twelve to eighteen months, then two to five years from now, they will be back and they won't make the same mistake twice."

Clifton's expression became graver.

"Then you don't believe Admiral, that their resolve will crumble, after losing so much?" she asked.

"No, I do not. To a certain extent, warships are built to be placed in danger and even lost if required. We have destroyed nothing they cannot replace."

"So what does the fleet propose?"

"Our problem has always been that while we've been able to fight their fleets in the field, we have not been in a position to strike at their home worlds or core worlds. In contrast as we have experienced, they have been able to attack Earth. We have been vulnerable to a knockout blow but not in a position to land one in return. We need to identify and destroy targets that will once and for all remove their ability to wage war against us. This is the first time since the attack on Baden and the Third Fleet that we haven't been under pressure. This is the first chance we've had had to seriously search for those targets."

"I know fuel supplies from Saturn have started coming in again, but with everything shut down, it will be at least six months before Earth's economic output can reach pre-siege levels," Clifton said.

"Yes, and even though damage to our forces was relatively light, ammunition expenditure was heavy. It will be months before we are ready to fight another fleet scale engagement," Lewis replied. "But we aren't looking for such a fight. Not yet. What we need to do now is to send several small squadrons out past the Junction Line, Landfall and even past the Centaur planet."

"To find the Nameless."

It wasn't a question.

"To find where we can hurt them, Madam President."

Clifton stood and returned to the window. She looked up at the night sky and pointed.

"There they are – the transports we sent to the Aèllr. We handed those people to a race we fought thirty years ago and here they are, returned to us safely."

"The Nameless are not the Aèllr; I say that as someone who has fought both of them," Lewis replied coldly. "The Aèllr sought to contain us. The Nameless will eradicate us if they can."

"You say that Admiral, but the reality is we know almost nothing about what they really are." Clifton turned sharply. "For Christ's sake, we still don't even know what they look like! What if there was a way to end this war without further bloodshed? What if we end up locked in a cycle of conflict because no one has the courage to reach out?"

Lewis made no immediate reply. Finally, he sighed.

"And what would we do if offered a ceasefire?" he asked, "Take it? Knowing that while negotiations were ongoing, the Nameless would be rebuilding their strength. That if or when those negotiations failed, the war would resume, with us in a weaker position than we had been. This is the second war I have fought in, Madam President. In the last war I survived virtual suicide missions. In this one, it has been my role to send others to their deaths. I don't advocate military solutions because I believe them to be the easy route – I've been shot at too many times for that. The Nameless have given no indication that they have any desire for peace. Perhaps this defeat will have changed that – personally I doubt it – but right now I don't believe we should even dare to pursue a diplomatic settlement, not when negotiating from a position of diminishing strength."

Clifton didn't answer and Lewis waited patiently.

"Tell me Admiral, if your fleet orbited the Nameless home world, what would you do?"

"Whatever I judged necessary to preserve the human race, which if I was granted the authority by my civilian commanders, would include bombarding that world until the rubble bounced, or holding out the olive branch of peace." Lewis said flatly. "But in my opinion, mercy is best offered from a position where it can not be mistaken for weakness."

"I do wonder Admiral, what history will say of us."

"History, Madam President, can judge me whatever way it likes, just as long as that history is written by a human."

Clifton smiled faintly.

"Admiral, this is the question that we keep coming back to. Can the fleet even achieve an outright victory? Can you win the war?"

"Do you gamble Madam President?"

Clifton frowned at the question.

"No."

"Believe me, Madam President. You and the rest of the human race are gamblers. We've had to go all-in twice just to stay in the war. If we are to win, then I can be certain of one thing. We will have to go all-in at least one more time."

.

Chapter Ten

Figures in the Landscape

1st April 2068

The object was six metres long by seven and a half wide. Its speed and apparent density would put it outside the usual parameters of a natural formation, while its current course placed it on track to intersect the planet's orbit within a fortnight. Two years previously, that last point alone would have been enough to warrant investigation. If the military established no threat was present, the orbital mining industry might have investigated to see if it might have any economic value. If they passed it over, the planetary defence grid would either have pushed the object onto a different course or used it for target practice.

That was then. There were no miners now and the defence grid was nothing more than a few orbiting fragments. Given time, the planet's new owners would likely put their own systems in place, but for the moment no one was scanning the skies closely enough to spot such a small and apparently harmless object.

So no one got close enough to make out the cylinder form, the burnt out remains of the primary thruster assembly or the stencilled lettering along the sides that read: *ESCAPE POD 037 – BADEN BASE.* Ahead was the planet Landfall, once humanity's, now lost.

Alice whistled tunelessly as she laced fresh branches up through the netting that stretched from one side of the clearing to the other. Working with her arms over her head was tiring but it needed to be done.

"You know, boss," Badie said as they finished up, "we could really do with finding a better solution than this. We use up far too much time and effort on it."

"I know," Alice replied. "An actual camouflage netting would be my favourite. This lash-up really blocks out too much light. Still, just as well Darren came up with it."

"Yes," Badie said forbiddingly. "Well, he would know about concealing fields from aerial reconnaissance. I doubt it was banana patata he was growing though."

Alice smiled but said nothing as she helped Badie put on his backpack then filled it up with the tools they'd brought with them. Despite the loss of an arm in the trenches of Douglas Base, Badie was still as strong as an ox and it definitely grated on the former policeman's nerves to use something that had been suggested by Darren their – allegedly – ex-cannabis grower. Still, that might be what would get them through the next winter, assuming a lot of other things went their way.

It was a solid hour and a half hike back to the central camp. At one time that would have been enough to leave Alice worn out. Like the netting, the long walk was another thing that burned a lot of time but again like the netting, was a necessary evil. As the two of them followed a game trail, Alice heard something, something out of place, and stopped dead in her tracks. Badie froze and then dropped into a crouch.

What is it? His raised eyebrow asked.

She heard it again, something moving down the trail towards them, something that wasn't too concerned about making noise. There was a faint pop as Alice released the catch on the holster at her hip. In what was now a practiced motion, she checked the magazine. Eleven nine-millimetre rounds remained. She chambered one of the irreplaceable bullets and motioned Badie to retreat back into the undergrowth. He nodded and slipped back, a small axe gripped in his remaining hand, while she took a firing stance behind a tree. She'd only fired the pistol a handful of times and most of those had been warning shots against animals. The weapon might be more a symbol of authority than anything else, but its weight had often been a comfort.

She could make out individual footfalls now, heavy and flat-footed – someone running hard, but only with the two feet of a human, rather than the four of a Nameless soldier drone. She half lowered the weapon just as the runner came into view. It was one of the girls from the camp, her feet thumping the ground as she puffed like an old steam train. Alice stepped out of her concealment. The runner let out a cry of surprise, jumped sideways and crashed into a shrub.

"Juliet, what are you doing here?" Alice demanded as she cleared the pistol's chamber and re-holstered it.

Juliet was still getting her breath when Badie reappeared, axe still in hand.

"William says for you to come, Boss!" Juliet said between gasps.

"What is it?"

"Something came down from the sky, Boss."

"Nameless?"

No. In that event William wouldn't be sending messages. He would know to pack up and run.

"No, Boss," Juliet confirmed. "Something big came down on parachutes. We all saw it come down. It landed over the hills to the north."

Alice glanced in the direction of the camp then down at Juliet. The girl was still sucking in air.

"Now what?" she muttered as she shrugged off her pack. "Badie."

"Yeah?"

"You and Juliet take my pack. Make your way back to camp as fast as you can manage."

"Go, we'll catch up."

When Alice reached the camp twenty minutes later, she could immediately feel an atmosphere. The sentries had been reprimanded often enough in the past about slacking. This time though, Alice heard the alert and the all clear being sounded before she even reached the perimeter. There was a smell of damp, smouldering wood from the fires at the very edge of the camp. Normally, these were placed there to distract any heat-seekers that might home in on them, but now they had been doused. Her second-in-command stood in the middle of the camp, pack on, arms crossed. Around him some people were milling about. Most were seated, but very obviously ready to go.

"William," she called out as she jogged towards him.

"Boss," he said in a serious tone. "We may have us a problem."

"Tell me."

He placed a hand on her shoulder and walked her over to the ravine that flanked the camp.

"About an hour ago," he said pointing, "we sighted something coming down. Well, I say we, but it was actually Juliet who spotted it. That girl's got eyes like a hawk. Anyway, it was coming down on a parachute and we got binoculars onto it."

"A parachute? Not rotors?"

"Yeah. A lot like the old pre-contact space capsules."

"So not a Nameless drop pod?"

"Human, boss, definitely human. It was a lander of some kind, a pretty big one by the look of it."

"How far away?"

"I think it was drifting away from us when it dropped behind those hills – so twenty to thirty kilometres maybe?"

Alice chewed her lip as she thought. When they first escaped from Douglas Base, her plan had been to keep moving and never again become sitting ducks for the Nameless. That simple plan had been enough for the first few months. They'd been able to hunt and gather as they went along. Occasionally they risked entering abandoned human settlements. A lot had already been cleaned out by other groups of escapees from Douglas, but even a single packet of dried peas could make such an expedition worthwhile. The winter had been a wake-up call though. They'd gone to ground in a cluster of caves and damn near starved. After that, the plan had changed.

"If this area was inside the range of any radar system then it can't have missed the pod coming down," William said. "The sensible thing would be to start moving now, get out of the region as fast as we can."

"And probably starve within the next six months," Alice replied, glancing up at him. "We can't bring the fields or the crops with us. If the Nameless come to investigate, they'll come by air, in which case we couldn't get far enough away to matter. And if we're on the move, we're more likely to be spotted."

"Alright, Boss. What's the plan?"

"No point sending messengers to get the people working the fields – most of them will already be on their way back. We'll go quiet for the next few days. No fires, no movement, wait to see if anything happens." She paused and shook her head. "An entire *sodding* planet and it has to land next to us."

"And if nothing does happen?" he asked.

"I need to think about that."

As the sun dropped below the horizon, Alice sat with her back to a tree watching the northern skies. One part joke to two parts reality, her nickname 'Boss' was a far cry from the Alice who had originally arrived on Landfall. She'd been a civilian language expert then, working for the fleet but really only passing through. Then the war started and five minutes in, her ride was blown away. She'd fetched up at the Fleet

Ground Base at Douglas, got drafted and assigned as a stretcher-bearer. By virtue of survival, she was judged to be command material and promoted to section leader.

When Douglas's defences began to buckle, she was assigned to lead two hundred and fifty refugees out into the wilderness to try to keep them safe. That had been more than six months ago. Since then they'd lost nearly fifty people. Most, small family clusters, simply slipped away, choosing to go it alone. A handful, weakened by the months in the underground shelters of Douglas, sickened and died. One man, a troublemaker, thief and, she suspected, a sexual criminal, she had personally driven off at gunpoint. However, survivors who joined them from other groups had replaced nearly all their losses. Going by their tales, many of those groups had been badly led. Some had been hunted down by the Nameless and destroyed, while others had turned on each other in the worst ways possible. In all that time, Alice's authority had never been seriously questioned, not because of her gun, but mostly because of the threadbare corporal's stripes still sewn to her jacket. Alice wasn't trained, but she had survived the trenches of Douglas. In the wilderness of Landfall, that made her the equivalent of the kingly one-eyed man in the land of the blind.

"I've given it a lot of thought and this is a potential opportunity," Alice told the small gathering of her most trusted lieutenants. "So we will go and look for that pod,"

For three days they'd watched the skies intently – three bright sunny days without a cloud in the sky. Obviously that didn't rule out satellite surveillance, but at what point did caution give way to paranoia?

"I don't think that's a good idea," cautioned Alan Berkly. "If the Nameless come while we're there – well God help us!"

"That is a fair point, Alan, but if they haven't come looking after three days, then odds are they won't look at all," Alice replied. "As it is, we're short of a lot of things, things that might be on that pod, and unlike the settlements we've checked in the past, it won't have been picked over by someone else first. Hell, one first aid kit would be worth it. Obviously we'll take precautions, just in case. William, I'll lead this myself. You're in charge while I'm away. Minimum movement and keep the fields well hidden."

"Okay, Boss."

"The most likely result," Alice added as she stood, "is that we won't even find the damn thing. That's thick woodland and God only knows how many square kilometres it could have come down in. I'll be looking for volunteers because if we are spotted then we aren't coming back here – we'll lead them as far away as we can."

For all Alice's grim words, there was no shortage of volunteers, allowing her to select six dependable individuals, several of whom had been witnesses to the original descent. Leaving at first light, it took them a full day to reach and crest the hills the pod had disappeared behind. Examining the trees below, Alice identified several likely points where something large might have crashed through the forest canopy. After taking a bearing, they started down.

That was the start of three frustrating days crisscrossing the forest, more than enough time for Alice to wonder whether the whole idea was a stupid mistake. All of this extra walking was burning calories that, unlike working in the fields, did not promise any return on the investment. She was within perhaps an hour of giving up when a shout came from the far end of their search line.

"I've found it!"

"Are you sure?" she shouted back.

"Oh, yeah!"

I just hope it hasn't got stuck up a tree, she thought as she made her way in the direction of the voice.

On that count at least, she wasn't disappointed. The pod was much larger than the drop pods she'd seen before. Over seven metres wide, it appeared to have landed on and pulverised one tree on the way down. The red and white parachute had snagged on another tree and it was that splash of colour, which had helped Brahimi find it. As William had said, it was clearly human, confirmed by Brahimi as they gathered around, pointing mutely at the lettering on its side.

"Oh God, it's from Baden Station!" Alice breathed.

"How the hell can it be here?" one of the women asked.

"These things don't have jump drives, Sue," said Brahimi. "It must have spent the last eighteen months in real space getting here."

They all stared up at this symbol of defeat. The great space station of Baden and the fleet that called it home, had been Landfall's outer defence. An invisible bulwark that the inhabitants of the planet had mostly never thought about, they'd simply expected that Baden would always be there. But the Nameless swept it aside in less than two hours and that had been the start of the train of events that had led them here, hiding in the untamed and barely charted wilds of a world in which they had once been masters. Alice felt sick. Despite herself, she'd hoped the object would be something positive and new, a sign that somehow things were about to change for the better. It had been a foolish hope. Instead, all they had found was a distant echo from a golden past.

"Well, let's crack it open and see what or who is in there," she eventually said. "Then get on our way again."

The impact of landing had bent flat most of the metal ladder up to the hatch, so it took a certain amount of scrambling to get up to it. Once there though, opening it was simple, as in spite of their name, airlocks didn't actually have locks. There was a hiss as the pressure equalised before the hatch swung inwards and Alice half scrambled, half fell into the pod. It was dark and there was a kind of deep cold that suggested the interior had been frozen for a long time. She shivered and stepped closer to the hatch, where warmer air was flowing in.

"What have we got, Boss?" someone called as Sue scrambled up after her.

"Good question," she replied looking around. There were twelve capsules lining the curved walls. Nine of them stood empty, three were closed and small lights glowed. Rubbing at the frosted glass she peered into one of the capsules. Inside was a man in fleet uniform. There was a control panel and she tapped the space bar, which brought up a display for the three capsules.

"One of them is dead," she said grimly. "According to the computer, he or she died six months ago."

"The other two?"

"Alive and in hibernation. Erm... if I'm understanding this, their condition is stable. I wonder how we wake them up?"

"I wonder should we?" asked Sue, "I mean they're safe in there aren't they?"

That was a good point, Alice thought to herself. She'd heard these pods could sustain people for several years and if she was reading the display right, the pod's power reserves were well inside the green, even after months in space, suggesting that the capsules could keep the two men alive for years to come. So they could simply be left there. As she pondered the question, Brahimi levered himself up and in.

"Computers!" he exclaimed. "Come to me, my sweet digital children!"

"Brahimi, find out if we can open these," Alice said before

turning to look at them. "But don't do anything until I say so."

"Alright," he replied. Then after a moment he added: "Hey, this thing is transmitting a distress beacon."

"What!" Sue and Alice simultaneously exclaimed.

"No wait, the pod's trying to transmit, but the aerial has been damaged. Nothing is going out."

"Jesus, if you do that again I'll slap you!" Sue admonished him.

"Switch it off," Alice ordered. "Sue, find what we've got while I get this thing concealed."

"Did you hear that?"

Alice paused as she reached up another branch to the man standing on top of the pod. They'd found a muddy puddle and dragged the parachute through to mute its colours, now they were using branches and whatever else they could get hold of to break up the profile. If a Nameless aircraft did cross overhead, she didn't want them to have any reason to investigate the area.

"What did you ..." Alice began.

She couldn't say what it was. Maybe it was a voice, maybe it was the sound of steps. The detail didn't matter, the cogent fact was it was an artificial sound. Sue and Brahimi were still inside the pod, the other four were all in sight.

"Pack it up, pack it up now!" Alice snapped as she scrabbled up the side of the pod and into the hatch. Inside, Sue had the pod's inventory laid out on the floor.

"Well we've hit pay-dirt, boss," Sue commented. The pod was designed for twelve and the supplies were extensive.

"Get it into a pack. You have one minute!"

"What?"

"We're in trouble!"

From outside there was a scream.

Alice reached for her pistol.

"Get back," she muttered as she chambered a round. "Both of you."

There were raised voices.

"I know you're in there," a human voice said. "Come out please."

There was a pause.

"We won't harm you."

Alice glanced at the others and pressed her finger to her lips.

"Please don't hurt us! We're not armed!" she called out, before slipping over beside the hatch.

She could just make out voices below, then after a moment came the sound of someone scrambling up to the hatch. A man pulled himself through, head first – then froze as Alice pressed her pistol to his temple.

"I'm not much of a shot," she carefully advised him, "but at this range, I fancy my chances."

"Easy now," he said with equal care. "We're not here to harm you."

"That's super. Who are you?"

"Lieutenant Martoma, Third Battalion, Battle Fleet Marines. We didn't come here for you. We didn't expect to meet you, in fact where did you come from?"

"I'm asking the questions," Alice snapped back.

"Alright, can I come in, this is uncomfortable," Martoma asked after a moment.

"Nice and easy."

He glanced back outside.

"Corporal, it's under control. Let's keep this cool."

Martoma levered himself up. Alice kept the pistol pressed to his head as they both stepped into the pod. He wasn't wearing the reactive armour of a marine but the uniform, webbing and the rest of his equipment were the real deal.

"Brahimi, watch the hatch," she said not taking her eyes off Martoma. "Sue, his gun."

The Lieutenant lifted his hand as Sue took his pistol.

"Boss, there's more of them, they've got guns!"

Alice glanced toward Brahimi. When she looked back, the Lieutenant was looking at her sleeve.

"You mind explaining to me, Corporal, why you are brandishing a weapon at a superior officer."

Sue and Brahimi exchanged nervous looks.

"You can't be marines, none got out of Douglas," she said.

"We never got in," he replied. "We thought everyone was evacuated to the shelters."

"They were. Douglas Base fell and we got out," Alice replied as she nervously adjusted her grip on the gun. "I was a corporal in the auxiliaries."

"You obviously saw the pod come down and, like us, you

investigated," he replied. "This can't be all of you though."

"We've got…"

"Brahimi *shut it!*" Alice snapped.

"Okay, okay. I can see you don't trust me, but let's keep this calm. Maybe we're not on the same side, but we're certainly not on opposite sides," Martoma said calmly. "And we can't stay in here forever." Glancing at the laid out supplies, he added: "Although we could clearly stay for a while."

He wasn't wrong. Whatever forces he had outside held four of hers and, the Lieutenant at gunpoint aside, she wasn't in any kind of position of strength.

"Okay, here's my offer. Tell your men to unload their weapons. We'll share out the supplies and then go our separate ways. Agreed?"

Martoma's eyes flicked from Alice to the other two.

"I think we have trust issues here."

"No, I'm okay with not trusting you," Alice bluntly replied.

"That leaves you with the only loaded gun."

"Yes, but I don't intend to start a fight. Do you?"

"All right, terms accepted."

"Just as well you didn't revive the two in the pods. Chemical Hibernation is a hell of an assault on the body and they'll need serious medical attention when they come out. Better they stay in there for the time being," Martoma said, making small talk as they divided the supplies. "Look, I don't have the manpower or the orders to stop you if you're determined to bug out."

There had been only four marines including Martoma. They didn't have the reactive armour the marines in the trenches of Douglas had used and their uniforms were worn but reasonably clean, all of which suggested to Alice that at the very least the unit's discipline was holding steady.

"But we've been out here for a long time, fighting an insurgency where we can. At the very least my commander will want answers. If we're it as far as humans on this planet are concerned, then we need to stick together."

"No we don't," Alice replied. "Look Lieutenant, I appreciate this might be exciting for you, but we don't need or want soldiers around. I've seen what happens when we try to stand and fight. We get flattened. Don't think that just because I'm still wearing these," she tapped the stripes on her sleeve, "that your orders carry any weight.

The only military order I'll follow is the last one I was given at Douglas — get my people out and keep them alive. Now, Lieutenant, it looks like everything is packed up. Those two in the pods are Battle Fleet personnel, so you can take responsibility for them. You can leave first."

"So we can't follow you."

"That's correct."

Without a further word he walked away, shaking his head.

"Well, nice at least that we're not the only ones left," Sue said as they set out half an hour later.

"If that's the last we see of them," Alice replied, "I'll eat my gun."

She wasn't wrong.

7th May 2068

"Corporal Peats, I presume," a voice said unexpectedly from behind her as she weeded a row of banana patata.

Alice scrambled for her pistol as she spun round.

"I'm not armed, I am not armed!"

The man in a marine uniform had his hands raised. The holster at his hip was open and empty. He looked to be in his early forties. His blond hair and beard appeared to have been cut by an enthusiastic but unskilled barber, but other than that he was relatively neat. His accent suggested German or perhaps one of the Nordic countries and while his clothes were ragged, she could see he wore the standard battledress uniform of the fleet marines. And his insignia was that of a colonel.

"What part of your training suggested that was the best way to approach someone?" Alice said, heart hammering in her chest and her hand still on the pistol butt.

"A demonstration of good faith and perhaps a slightly misplaced sense of humour," he replied. "I am Colonel Ernst Dautsch, Battle Fleet."

"You found us."

"Never lost you. One of Lieutenant Martoma's men tracked you, then reported back to me."

"Well, I was quite clear with him so you'll know we're not interested, unless you're here to simply take what you want by force," she replied. "Will I find the camp overrun?"

"The Lieutenant didn't exaggerate when he said you have a negative view of us."

"Not negative Colonel, pragmatic. When resources are tight, a man with a gun can simply take anything or anyone he wants. So what is it you want here, Colonel?"

"To link up with you."

"Still not interested." Reluctantly her hand dropped from the pistol butt. "But how are you out here?"

"We were among the troops that were to be dropped on Douglas Base as part of the Kite String convoy to Landfall. Unfortunately my shuttle was one of three that took hits on the way down. The pilot did well to get us down in one piece, but we overshot Douglas by a good one hundred and fifty kilometres. With all the confusion caused by the drop, it took the Nameless some time to realise some of us were out here – enough time for us to get clear of the crash sites."

"I'm guessing you must have used Douglas's back door to get you out. However, we didn't have its exact position and if we were even spotted moving towards Douglas, it would have been a giveaway that some other way in existed. So we stayed out here to contribute in whatever way we could. When we stopped hearing radio transmissions from Douglas, we feared the worst. With you out here, it seems we were right."

He paused for a moment before asking: "So how about it, Corporal? What's your story?"

Reluctantly she ran through the siege and fall of Douglas, while Dautsch listened with a thoughtful expression.

"So, there are perhaps thousands of people out there. We'd assumed that the base was overrun and that few if any got out."

"And most of them may have been subsequently hunted down in the open. I don't know," Alice replied with a shrug.

"And you decided to stop here and start farming?" he asked, looking around.

"We couldn't keep getting by on hunter gathering. Too much of Landfall's natural fauna has nothing in it the human digestive system will recognise as food." Alice gestured to the field around them. "Banana patata might not taste very exciting, but it is nutritious. Of course, whether we'll get a chance to harvest them is now open to doubt."

When Dautsch raised an eyebrow, she continued.

"If you're here then the Nameless will probably come and we'll have to run."

"Is that your plan? Run? Where do you see yourself in a year? In two years? In five? Ten? How long do you think you can survive by scavenging and trying to farm in the wilds, while avoiding the Nameless?"

"And what's the alternative? Fight? I was at Douglas I saw how that went! As far as I know, we're it. We are the human race."

She brushed angrily at her eyes. He was silent for a moment then smiled slightly.

"It never crossed my mind," Dautsch said finally, "that you've been out here with no contact with anyone else."

"What do you mean?"

In her chest she could feel her heart begin to accelerate again.

"We're not it. We are definitely not it. The Americans broke out from their shelter, although with how many we don't know. But more importantly we've received transmissions from space. Courier ships have been making periodic passes through the system. We've received their transmissions but haven't been able to respond – yet. Earth was attacked and they threw back the assault. Earth still stands. The rest of the human race is still out there."

Alice felt her legs fold as she flopped down. The colonel stepped forward and she felt a water bottle being pressed into her hand. That Earth, and everyone and everything she loved was gone, was the faceless dread she'd lived with all these months. With those few casual words, the emotions she'd bottled up for so long just overflowed.

"I'm sorry, it never occurred to me that you didn't... couldn't know the wider situation," he said, as she composed herself.

"It doesn't change anything," she said through gritted teeth.

"It changes everything," he replied as he sat down beside her. "It means there's light at the end of the tunnel. A small, weak light certainly, but it's there. You've kept your people alive and I've done the same for mine. And I've done it by not throwing their lives away on pointless military actions."

"So what's your plan, Colonel?"

"First and foremost, we stay on the board – hurt the Nameless where we can and keep our heads down where we can't. There will be a liberation and I want us to live to see it."

Chapter Eleven

Hell's Mouth

My name is Mateusz Bielski. I am... rather I was, a citizen of the independent colony of Junction Station. I remember it started with a birthday...

Junction Station 27th July 2066

"Happy birthday to you! Happy birthday to you! Happy birthday dear Brand! Happy birthday to you!"

On the control deck of Junction Station, everyone cheered as Brand managed to blow out all twenty-one candles out in one try. Bielski even saw a smile on the face of Approach Controller Caple, as he put away the fire extinguisher he'd been holding. He'd disapproved of having naked flames on the Control Deck,

"Thank you everyone," Brand said. "Consider this the warm-up for the main event. My place, twenty hundred hours, we'll rattle this tin can!"

There was another cheer from the younger individuals and grimaces from a few of the older ones. Brand's parties could get famously wild, which had got him up in front of the disciplinary board a couple of times. Brand winked at Caple.

"Alright," Bielski called out, brandishing a knife, "everyone come and get their piece of birthday cake. Then I think Controller Caple would like his deck back."

The little celebration had been arranged at the change of the shift so that the most possible people could be present. Brand had the evening off, but the rest of his watch would be back on duty during the party. Not that Bielski minded. He was getting a bit old for that kind of thing. As he walked back towards his cabins, two children chasing a third galloped past, shouting at each other.

"Be careful!" he called after them.

Caught up in their own game they probably didn't even hear him. Children definitely livened up the place and always depressed Bielski a little.

The cabin was silent when he entered. He checked the small kitchen area and found a note on the screen there reading: '*problem in dock – back soon.*' Their monthly supply ship had arrived yesterday and he could remember Nastya saying at dinner that they were having real problems getting everything aboard. Bielski put together a plate of salad and sat down in the living area.

In its fifteen years of existence, Junction Station had grown at an amazing rate. It had prospered and grown – perhaps too much so – despite all the predictions that it would be yet another failed independent space colony. With the discovery and settlement of Landfall, Junction Station offered the cheapest place for commercial and government ships to refuel en route to and from the colony. The charges for fuel and the traffic, both of supplies and people, had allowed them to continue to expand. But there were limits to the underlying infrastructure and either Junction would have to expand the colony at vast expense or stop accepting new applicants to join.

The Council was still debating the matter, but the question had split the population of Junction into two camps: those who saw it as a commercial enterprise and those who saw it as a new society. The debate had remained good-humoured, which was a relief to Bielski. He and Nastya had been in the first wave. They'd put everything they owned into it and left Earth with warnings ringing in their ears from friends and family that they'd be back with little more than the clothes they were standing in.

The two of them had wanted to be a part of a new and better society. But somehow Bielski felt it hadn't lived up to their hopes. Junction Station wasn't bad, but the high ideals had been compromised by day-to-day needs. Which made him wonder whether without those, it was really worth staying on what amounted to a floating tin can? He'd have to talk to Nastya again. They could cash in their stake here and use it to buy into a colony on Landfall. It would be odd to live with nothing but the sky over their heads again, with nothing but... Bielski drifted off to sleep without completing the thought.

He woke with a start when the alarm on his watch bleeped.

There was a blanket over him and the bedroom door was closed – Nastya had obviously come back in. Glancing at his watch, Bielski swore and wrestled the blanket out of the way.

As he made his way back up to the control deck, he could hear music coming from the direction of Brand's cabins, where the party was clearly getting underway. By comparison, the control deck was a temple of serenity and would probably stay that way. Nothing was scheduled to arrive at the station, so the only flight control tasks due during the watch were from the station's two hydrogen skimmers.

"Hey Mateusz, I think we have a tech issue."

Bielski looked up from the book he'd been reading at his assistant Michelle.

"Oh?" he replied.

Looking past her towards the display, he saw a collection of blips.

"Where did they come from?"

"That's the problem," she replied, as he got up and went over to the main plotting table. "They appeared on the plot about five minutes ago."

The blips indicated several ships in close formation. With Junction Station positioned within the planet's rings, they had no direct line of sight and instead relied on a series of satellites to bounce the signal through the rings to the station. Mostly it worked but not this time. The contacts were well inside the Red Line – the satellite's radar should have picked them up hours ago.

"No transponders either?"

"Nope," Michelle replied. "So we've either got a satellite on the blink or another software problem."

"Alright, call them up," Bielski said.

He listened as Michelle hailed the approaching ships. With the signal having to bounce through half a dozen separate satellites, there was always a lag but five minutes passed without reply. Michelle hailed a second time was again met with silence. The two of them started running system diagnostics, but the link checked out. When the original radar satellite orbited out of position to be replaced by another, they tried again but still there was silence.

Bielski looked uneasily at the plot. Battle Fleet ships were the only ones that normally travelled in groups. Junction's civilian grade radar usually didn't pick their warships up until after they'd crossed the

Red Line, but as arrogant as the fleet could be, it was also a stickler for proper approach procedures.

"Launch a camera drone, Michelle," he ordered.

"You sure? From here it won't have the reaction mass to get back."

"Yes. I want to see them properly."

It took the drone three quarters of an hour to navigate directly up and out of the rings.

"Michelle," Bielski said very quietly as the feed from the drone came up on the screen, "better get the Boss up here."

With the entire Council gathered on the command deck, space was tight. A couple of them had been at the party, a few were asleep and the rest had been pulled away from various other duties. Michelle had made the excuse that it was something to do with the party getting out of control, which was good thinking – so far no one outside the room knew what was approaching.

Alex Gibbons, founder of Junction and a bear of a man, stared hard at the screen.

"No reply at all, you say?" he asked.

Bielski shook his head.

"They don't look like anything I've ever seen."

"I have," Michelle said.

She'd been searching on the computer for a few minutes and was now looking physically sick. She passed over a computer pad to Gibbons. Bielski looked over his shoulder at it and felt his blood freeze. It was a poor quality image of a starship from one of the news feeds. The headline under the image read MISSISSIPPI INCIDENT – FLEET SHIP ATTACKED. The ship in the image wasn't quite the same as the ones approaching, but the design commonality was unmistakeable.

"How long until they get here?" Gibbons asked.

"Four to six hours," Bielski replied. "Not very long."

"Two .22 pistols with twenty-four rounds each, twelve electrical stunners, twelve batons and six stab proof vests," Gibbons summed up their armoury.

"We have a few blasting charges," offered Jesse, his deputy.

"That would blow open any section of the station they were used in. So armed resistance isn't an option and it might not be necessary," Gibbons replied. "Let's not go off at half-cock. We don't know they're here for any hostile reason."

"Well, I doubt they're here for tea and biscuits," Caple said sharply.

"No, probably not," Gibbons agreed. "However, I think there are only a couple of things we can do. I'll go out there in a shuttle – try to meet them before they come into the rings and attempt to open a dialogue."

"Jesus, Alex!" Jesse exclaimed.

"Like I said, just because they shot at that fleet ship doesn't mean they're hostile. Mistakes happen. But hey, if anyone has got a better idea, I'm all ears."

"So what do the rest of us do? Sit and wait?" Caple asked.

"No you don't," Gibbons said. "Call up the harvesters and get as many people onto them as they'll support. They can't run, but they can hide in the rings. Oh, and launch message drones to Earth."

"How many?" Caple asked.

"All of 'em. We need help and we need it yesterday."

No one bothered to point out that it would take the drones' days to get to Earth.

In the early days there had been a suggestion that Battle Fleet might station a small number of ships at Junction. Gibbon had vetoed the idea. A permanent military presence would make Junction a valid target he'd said, but as Bielski observed Gibbon's shuttle climb away, he was struck by just how alone they were. The closest of the harvesters was an hour away, while the other one was on the far side of the planet Phyose. Even if it stayed out of the rings for as long as possible, it couldn't reach the station before evening and when it did, it would be a sitting duck.

"Mateusz, Mateusz, MATEUSZ!" Bielski jumped as Caple slapped the top of the console in front of him. "Wake up! Get down to the unloading dock, we'll have to load up as fast as we can."

"How do I decide who goes on?"

"Just do your best," Caple snapped, turning away but not so fast that Bielski didn't see the tears in his eyes.

As the shuttle exited the surface of the rings, Alex began transmitting his greeting. Back on Junction, Caple must have decided to put it onto the station's main intercom. At first he spoke in the most formal terms. Welcome to Junction, we are the human race. Still the alien ships came on silently. The range dropped and as it did, they all heard something none of them had ever heard in his voice before –

desperation. He asked again and again for them to respond.

"This is an unarmed facility. Please, we beg you to do us no harm!"

They were the last words anyone heard him speak. Junction's radar barely registered the missile launch – Gibbon didn't get a chance to even scream before it struck.

"Damn it Gordon! Just close the airlock. You've got to move!" Bielski demanded.

"Screw you!" Gordon shouted into Bielski's face, "I'm not going without my wife!"

"The life support is already overloaded! It can't take more... God damn it!"

Bielski grabbed Gordon's wife and shoved her forward. That got Gordon out of the way and he slammed the airlock hatch closed. Behind, the pumps started to cycle.

As he reached the centrifuge entrance, Bielski met his neighbour coming the other way, leading his wife and two children. All of them wore survival suits.

"Russell."

"Mateusz."

Russell looked almost embarrassed.

"We will hide down on the storage levels," he said. "If they board, they may not find us – the wife's idea."

Bielski smiled awkwardly and clapped him on the arm, "If the worst happens' my friend, God willing you'll see this out. Head for C Compartment – it's the fullest at the moment."

Inside the centrifuge and the accommodation decks, panic was spreading like a disease. Bielski had to push his way through people who were crying and shouting as they attempted to gather their family members. Finally he reached the command deck.

"The harvester is away," he said breathlessly.

No one heard him. All attention was on the main screen as one of the alien ships slid out of the rings and into the cleared area around the station. The harvester was still sluggishly turning away from the station. The alien ship seemed to pause for a moment, as if to consider the scene before it. Would it pursue the harvester? Bielski found himself hoping the alien would go after it in order to give them a little more time, then despised himself for his own weakness. Then the ship turned towards the station, prompting an audible groan on the command deck.

Abruptly two missiles lanced out from its flank.

"Oh God!" someone said.

The harvester had completed its turn and begun accelerating slowly away. Coming from directly astern, the missiles slammed in, ripping open the engineering section. What remained of the engines spluttered and ceased functioning. Ahead lay one of the mountains of ice and rock that made up the rings. With engines gone, the harvester's bows and mid-ship sections coasted forwards, slowly but helplessly. As they watched on the command deck, it ploughed head on into the asteroid. There was a flash of escaping atmosphere as every compartment ruptured.

"May God have mercy on their souls," Caple said quietly.

Bielski found himself desperately hoping the end would be quick, that alien ship would fire and that the explosion would be for him at least, fatal. Better that than seeing the station hull split open and being blown screaming into the void. Instead more alien ships arrived, two immediately left, heading in the direction of the second harvester, while the largest ship edged alongside the station. Bielski only became aware that Nastya had managed to get onto the command deck when she slipped her hand into his.

There was no defence against the boarders as they burned through the hull. If anyone had seriously considered armed resistance, the casual destruction of the harvester put an end to it. But that reluctance didn't save the first half dozen people the aliens encountered. A wave of humanity fled from the invaders. On the monitors, Bielski could see the space suited aliens spread out, clearly exploring the station. After the first few deaths, the aliens largely ignored those humans they happened across. Only when someone got in their way by accident or design did they fire. But when they did, they murdered without hesitation. Finally, twenty minutes after boarding, the first of them arrived on the command deck. Everyone backed away, keeping as much distance as they could until they were all crowded into a corner. The creatures, with their strange quadruped bodies and almost snake like heads, looked around. Their interest seemed focused on the technology of the station, but eventually their attention shifted to its inhabitants. One of them advanced on them.

"Please," Caple rasped, "we are peaceful."

The alien paused as if considering Caple's words. It then prodded Nastya with the muzzle of its gun, watching Caple, as if seeking a reaction.

"For God's sake, no one move, don't do anything," Caple said, keeping as still as possible. The alien stepped back and then gestured towards the hatch out of the command deck.

Bielski was herded along with the rest back towards where the alien's airlock had punched through the skin of the station. When they reached the lock, the person at the head of the column hesitated. Bielski had just time to recognise it was Brand, before the closest alien levelled its weapon and gunned him down. Then it gestured to the next person. No one dared even glance at Brand's remains as they drifted away, leaking blood. The rest meekly made their way down into the alien ship and into what was clearly a cargo bay. As the hatch closed behind them, Bielski held his wife and looked around him and saw friends and neighbours, some streaked in blood, theirs and that of others. The air was already thick with the smell of fear and urine. But many of the population of Junction were missing. The aliens couldn't have got them all. *We should have hid*, Bielski thought as he held Nastya close.

With all electronics stripped from them by force, it was impossible to determine the passage of time. Only the pull of ship's acceleration gave any sense of movement. The lights went on and off at irregular intervals, while food and water, which clearly came from Junction's stocks, was occasionally pushed in through the hatch. Just as clearly, there wasn't enough of it for all of them. The first of the fights was between two of the mothers who hadn't made it into the harvester. Each accused the other of stealing food and the nutty bar over which they fought was smashed apart before they could be separated.

How long they were in the hold was anyone's guess, several weeks at least. There was never the familiar jolt of a jump drive but even so, no one doubted that they were far removed from Junction and probably well beyond the scope of human space. Finally, from somewhere beyond their prison, Bielski heard the unmistakable echoing rings of a docking system engaging.

"Wake up," he said quietly to Nastya. When she started to speak he put a hand over her mouth. "We need to stay in the middle of the group. It will be safer there."

Her mouth tightened and she nodded. It was an animal instinct.

To be at the edge risked being cut out from the herd. Survival meant that where possible, those who had once been friends, neighbours and people, should be now looked upon as shields.

Again at gunpoint, they were herded out the stinking cargo bay that had been their home. As they reached a ladder, Bielski felt the tug of gravity for the first time since they had been driven out of Junction's centrifuge. There was obviously no centrifuge here but by the time Bielski reached the bottom, he could just as clearly feel that he was pulling about half Earth gravity. After weeks with only intermittent acceleration gravity, Bielski's legs shook under the familiar strain but there was no time to acclimatise. All he could do was hold Nastya close as the guards, now armed with some kind of electrical baton, forced them on through several separate airlocks and into a sterile set of chambers. From behind, Bielski heard shouting and screaming. Caple and several others were forced through before the hatch closed and locked behind them. One of the women threw herself at the lock, screaming and clawing at it until the metal was streaked with her blood.

"What happened?" Bielski asked.

Caple shook his head, "They took Chris, Maria, Lana... and one of the children."

Shortly afterwards the lights all went out. In the dark Bielski held his wife tight as he closed his eyes and desperately tried to block out the sobs and cries of those around him. After who knows how long, an exhausted sleep claimed him.

Bielski was woken by the rough shake of Caple's hand. While he'd been asleep, a single light had come on, which offered just enough illumination to move around.

"We need to talk," he said quietly.

Bielski nodded and carefully disengaged from Nastya. He followed Caple as they both picked their way through the sleeping bodies to a corner of the room. There were two objects protruding from the wall. One seemed to be a tap and sink, the other a toilet of some kind. As they waited for the others to make their way over, he noticed for the first time Cable that was injured. There was a burn through his jacket at about kidney height and he was holding himself rigid. The flesh below already looked inflamed.

The group mostly consisted of what was left of the Council, along with a few other senior members of the colony. Most of them already looked like mere shadows of their former selves.

"We shouldn't do this," said Abigail Petra, "we could attract their attention."

"We're here to get attention. Nothing we can do will make us of less interest," Caple said bluntly. "We need to discuss what to do."

"Do! There's nothing we can do! They're armed, we're locked in a box!" Petra's voice rose. Around them some of the sleepers stirred. Caple clamped a hand over her mouth and scowled.

"What are you suggesting? An attack?" Bielski asked, feeling both a weak stirring of hope and a terrible fear.

"If we time it right we might catch them by surprise," said Mario Villeneuve. "Depends how many there are and whether we can get weapons."

"If we get that kind of opportunity, we'll take it," Caple said without conviction. "But we won't get that chance. We've been brought here for a reason. We're lab rats now. We're to be used for experiments."

It was a thought that no one had dared speak before now. The idea of being taken by aliens was the subject of years of overblown films and books. But for them it was a frightening reality.

"No, no!" Petra replied. "No civilised people..."

"Civilised people? Civilised people wouldn't have gunned poor Brand down! These are not people. They're monsters and we're in their power!" Villeneuve hissed before turning back to Caple. "Go on."

"The way I see it we have a responsibility to save some of us, the only way we can."

Bielski followed the other man's gaze and felt his stomach twist. There weren't many children left. Most had been lost with the harvester but eleven had made it this far, ranging from infants to early teens.

"Oh God!" murmured Bielski.

"No, we... we can't do that! It's monstrous!" Petra choked.

"They can go out easy at our hands... or slow at theirs."

Caple turned away and leaned his head against the wall.

"No. we can't even think such a thing," Villeneuve objected. "Someone will come, someone will rescue us. The Battle Fleet..."

"The Fleet!"

Caple spun round and for a moment Bielski thought he would attack Villeneuve. He placed a restraining hand on Caple's chest. The other man shook it off, but made no move towards Villeneuve.

"Where was the fleet when they came? Where was the feet when those of us who were not murdered, were taken from our homes? No, there is no one coming for us. No one knows where we are. *We* don't know where we are."

"We cannot ask mothers to kill their own children." Villeneuve persisted as others nodded or murmured their agreement.

Caple looked at them, his expression grim. "We'll wish we had," he said.

A few hours later they came and took Villeneuve.

Supposedly a man needed two thousand five hundred calories per day to maintain weight, a woman two thousand. Someone had worked out that while the human food from Junction provided that on average, they were now getting about fifteen hundred. No one on Junction had been fat. The station had been a working colony that kept people lean and as the weeks crept by, Bielski watched as what little fat anyone had wasted away. Faces became thinner and slowly people went from thin to looking starved. When the human food ran out, their captors began serving alien food. The stuff was fairly tasteless but the portion sizes went up, which raised morale for a few days. Then people started getting the runs. The alien food probably contained little a human digestive tract could recognise as nutrition. Although the portion sizes continued to increase, people began to realise that merely meant starving to death in the slowest way possible. The children were the worst to watch, lively little misses and mischievous small boys faded to ghosts of themselves.

Every few days, the aliens would come to inspect them. Most were dressed in blue sealed environmental suits, armed with shock batons that formed a perimeter around two or three individuals in yellow suits that Bielski assumed were some kind of officers or high ranking officials. On the third such visit, one of the younger men experienced a rush of blood to the head and attempted to attack one of the yellow suits. A strike from a shock baton floored him. The yellow suit issued some kind verbal instruction in a voice that sounded like a broken bellows. In response, six of the guards switched off their batons and methodically beat the young man to death.

That night Caple came to Bielski.

"The last of the mothers have agreed," he said quietly.

Nastya had been sitting beside Bielski, now she got up and moved to the other side of the room. Caple watched her for a moment before turning back to Bielski.

"What do you need from me?" Bielski asked.

"They'll probably try to stop us. I'm getting together a few people to block the hatch for as long as they can. Give us time to get this done. You understand you could get hurt or killed."

Despite the warning, Bielski felt relief. He was afraid of what Caple might ask him to do. The other man must have seen it in his eyes because he clapped him awkwardly on the shoulder.

"I wouldn't ask that of you. You are a good man Mateusz."

Maybe he didn't mean it or maybe he did, but the way Caple said *good*, sounded more like *weak*.

"The mothers then..."

"No," Caple shook his head. "No child's last sight in this world should be their mother hurting them."

With half a dozen others, Bielski stood ready at the door and listened to eleven pitiful little sounds.

If they noticed, the aliens made no attempt to interrupt. Only hours later did one of the yellow suits enter. Caple stood, defiant in the centre of their room. Before him lay the bodies of the children. The alien looked at the bodies and then at Caple. Was it puzzled, angry or merely confused? It motioned forward several guards to remove the bodies, then after a few minutes the alien turned and left.

The days, weeks, months all trailed into one another. The deaths of the children marked the final end of any kind of community. Even if the aliens took the deaths of the children calmly, they weren't prepared to see their lab animals all kill themselves. Shortly afterwards they were stripped of all remains of their clothing and fitted with a metallic bracelet. At a single press of a button, their mag-lock would pin them to the wall. They learned to either hold it until the guards released them to eat, or soil themselves then sit in their squalor all day. Some simply gave up and as they sickened the aliens took them. Finally they came for Bielski and Nastya, who along with four others were dragged out.

The chamber was both a medical room and horror show. The bodies of two of those who had gone before them lay on medical slabs, their chests opened up for study. A pair of aliens, this time dressed in green, awaited them. One of the men with them struggled and screamed as he was forced into one of six glass boxes, still determined to cling to life.

Bielski wasn't sure whether to envy or pity him. But when it was his turn, he fought too. Not to delay the inevitable but to reach out to touch his wife, before the blue suited aliens pushed him in and closed the hatch. He could only watch and wait, as the others were each in turn forced in. From piping in the ceiling came the hiss of gas. This is it, he thought as he closed his eyes and breathed deep. But although his eyes began to water and his throat went raw, it was nothing beyond discomfort. From outside he heard a muffled scream. It was Nastya, her box was filling with a greenish gas and she was fighting for breath. Beyond her, in the end two boxes, the men in each one were already slumped to the floor and motionless. His own discomfort forgotten, Bielski screamed Nastya's name again and again as he beat his fists against the sides of the box. She slowly sank to the floor, fighting for breath, and finally stopped moving. When they were all obviously dead, the alien took out the bodies. As Bielski and man in the final box were dragged out, his last sight of his wife was of her being cut open for examination.

"What happened?" Caple asked.

Bielski and other the man were the first to ever return to the holding room. Bielski had no memory of arriving back there. He'd probably been catatonic for days, only slowly regaining his reason.

"You were right," Bielski whispered to him. "We were just lab rats to them. They want to know how to kill us."

"Then I think they've found it," Caple said quietly after a while. "They've come and examined you several times but they have taken no one. They have learned all that they can learn from us and, God willing, we have reached the end of our usefulness to them."

But as with so many other hopes, that wish remained unfulfilled. Apart from guards bringing food, they saw nothing of the aliens for weeks. Then once again they came for Bielski. He allowed himself to be dragged out and hoped that this time he would die. But instead of the medical lab in which Nastya perished, this time he was taken to a smaller compartment. Once secured to the wall, he was left alone. After a while he noticed the room was filled with things – human objects. Displayed on the far wall was an oil painting that had belonged to Alex Gibbons. It was hanging upside down. It wasn't the only picture. Others were dotted about the room. They'd been taken from the cabins at Junction. Bielski let out a tortured groan as he saw one he'd known well, a picture that had decorated his own home, the one of him and Nastya on their wedding day. There were also dozens of old paper books, tools and children's toys, scattered around the room in no discernable pattern, fragments of destroyed lives. Weeping, he didn't hear the hatch open or the alien enter. It was only as the creature settled itself on a floor cushion that he caught sight of it. Sorrow turned to rage and with a wordless snarl of raw loathing, Bielski attempted to hurl himself at it. For all that he'd longed for death, in that moment he more than anything wanted to kill the alien. The manacle brought him up short.

"Damn you! What do you want! What is there left to take?" he screamed at it, before collapsing. Not even his seething hatred could sustain his starved body.

The alien quirked its head as it looked at him, then started to emit an odd wheezy rasp.

"Slower... of... speech," said a computerised voice from the ceiling.

Bielski froze in place before exclaiming: "You can understand!"

"Slower... of... speech," the computer repeated.

Bielski repeated himself, forcing himself to slowly enunciate the words.

From the sealing came alien speech. The alien listened carefully, then replied.

"Yes... with... you... speak... will... now..."

"Why have you done this to us?" It was the question that had burned them all these long months.

"To... learn..." it replied. "Young... ended... why... you... did...that?"

The alien waited patiently as Bielski worked out what it had said. Once he did his expression tightened.

"To save them from you!" he spat.

"Will... more... ending... of.... young...?"

"I do not understand."

"Conflict... wasteful... progresses... continues..."

"A war is still being fought!"

"Correct..."

"You haven't been able to beat us."

"Yet..."

The brief elation he had felt was chilled by the single word. The alien took that as its cue to continue.

"Conflict... wasteful... seek... end..."

"Yes! We seek an end."

"Positive... Require... that... to... end... bring... all... young... Produce... young... no... further... allow... we... shall... end... race... yours... without... conflict"

Kill your children! Have no more and the human race will be allowed to go extinct in peace. That was the alien's peace proposal. He wanted to vomit.

"Why? Why do you want to destroy us? Why do you hate us?"

The alien quirked its head again, as if puzzled by the question.

"No. Hate..." it said. "Hate... wasteful... Conflict... wasteful... Galactic resources... finite... Your... resource... consumption... allowed... cannot... No hate... we... wish... to... survive... Your... existence... limits... our... time."

The alien gestured around the room.

"Culture... history... that... is... yours... we... will... preserve... You... we... must... without... hate... destroy."

It paused again to enter a series of commands into the computer beside it and a holo display lit up. It selected a computer file and a star map came up.

"Here... we... are," it said pointing at one circle before moving its finger to point at a second. "You... origin... here. Speak... now... locations... of... human... worlds."

"I will give you nothing!"

The alien pressed another control and two of the blue suited guards came in. Both carried shock batons, the nodes of each crackling menacingly.

"Resistance... wasteful," said the first alien. The computer could give no emphasis to the words but the alien angled its head as if genuinely regretful. "Answers... must... give. False... answers... punished."

Bielski lay on the floor. He could feel his mind working only sluggishly now. In the distance he heard an alarm sound and stirred. Caple was the only other one to move. He was now little more than a skeleton, covered by paper-thin skin. There were electrical burns all over his body where he had resisted the interrogator and his breath was raw and wheezy. There were only a dozen of them now, none more than a few days from death. The aliens continued to dole out food, but no one now had the strength to eat and the stuff simply rotted on the floor. The alarm continued to sound and he twisted to look at the hatch. Then beneath him he felt the deck give a faint shudder and the lights flickered. As Bielski raised himself up on one elbow, the deck gave a violent jolt. At the same moment there was a distant but distinct explosion. The lights flickered and this time blacked out completely, to be replaced with the dim green glow of some kind of emergency illumination. Bielski grunted. His arm had been pinned to the bulkhead by his mag-lock manacle and now, without warning, it fell away.

"What's happening?" he whispered.

Caple shook his head in mute confusion.

Bielski lifted his hand curiously. The gravity seemed to be slowly but definitely weakening. Time passed, then in the distance they felt and heard more explosions, followed by the unmistakeable clatter of gunfire.

"It's a rescue!" someone said in a tone of desperate hope.

The gravity was almost gone now and Caple dragged himself over the hatch to slap at it weakly.

"Help us! We're in here! Please help us!" he called as loudly as his ravaged body could manage. Outside the sounds of gunfire continued, interspersed with the occasional bang of an explosion. Sometimes the sound of fighting seemed to diminish and they despaired, then it began to come their way.

Abruptly the hatch opened and one of the blue suited aliens loomed over Caple. In its hand it held not a shock baton but a gun, which it brought to bear. As it did so, however, there was a deafening rattle of gunfire and the alien shuddered as bullets ripped through it and blood splashed across the bulkheads. Its body drifted inwards through the hatch, beyond which Bielski caught a brief sight of a hand. A human hand – just before it threw a grenade into the chamber.

Chapter Twelve

Reconnaissance by Fire

1st April 2068

Willis stepped out of her cabin and was nearly flattened by a pair of dockyard workers trying to negotiate an environmental recycler down the passageway.

"Watch out!" one of them warned her in no uncertain terms.

Willis resisted the urge to bite back. They'd been waiting weeks to get *Black Prince* into dock for badly needed and extensive repairs. While not that many ships had been damaged, *Black Prince* was in the battered minority. Before the Siege of Earth began, most civilian personnel had been evacuated back to the surface and it had taken time to return them into orbit. Of course, once they did get the ship into docks, it was suddenly swarming with civilians.

They'd need to remove at least some of the ship's crew, but Willis needed to be careful about that. Crewmen who were even only temporarily without a ship, would look very available to other captains. Transfer requests fly into Fleet Personnel and before she knew it, all of her crew's most experienced hands would be stripped away. So at least a portion of them would have to stay on board. Hopefully the dockyard workers would remember to check the cruiser's compartments before they started opening up its hull. That last thought crossed her mind only half jokingly and she absently tapped the canister at her leg to ensure her survival suit was in place.

Making her way out of the centrifuge, Willis headed for engineering. *Black Prince* hadn't taken a direct hit from a cap ship missile; she doubted the ship could have survived that, but there were plenty of signs that she had taken a lot of hits from smaller projectiles. Mostly the evidence was in the form of patches of sealing foam, which was the only reason half the ship's compartments could hold pressure and loops of cable where repairs had been spliced in to cross breakages.

She found Guinness in the port side engine room, talking to an older, heavyset man with dock manager's stripes on his sleeves.

"Flooding on a starship," the manager muttered as he looked around. "That's a bloody new one on me."

"It did in a number on our electrics," Guinness replied sourly. "We been trying to run two generators – one of them bandaged back together I might add – on one control grid."

"So I see," the manager grunted examining his notes.

"There are still bits of radiator fluid in here – hard stuff to catch in micro gravity," Willis said as she approached.

Guinness saluted as sharply as was possible without gravity. The foreman gave her a perfunctory nod.

"How long do you think this will take?" she asked.

The man gave a weary sigh.

"Y'know we've only been on this tin can for less than a full watch. We're still doing a damage analysis and reviewing the paperwork your officers handed over."

"Yes, but I have to forward your estimate to Fleet Headquarters," Willis replied. "They'll want to know when they can have their ship back."

"Yeah, yeah," he replied sourly. "Don't tell me – there's a war on."

He sighed and looked around again.

"Okay, we have to remove and replace most of the armour anyway, so that makes access into the ship easier. The main turrets are all intact, which is good. Within the main citadel we're mostly talking about splinter damage. That's not so good. The problem with splinters is that you have to start pulling things open just to make sure nothing took a ricochet and clouted something without anyone noticing. And as for your liquid problem in here..."

He paused to wave his stylus around the engine room.

"We'll have to be really sure we've got that sorted. We'll likely have to over-pressurise the deck, then pop a hatch and blow it out. We'll need a tug on station though, to keep the platform stable. My guesstimate is four months, assuming we don't come across any surprises."

Willis nodded. She'd be surprised if *Black Prince* was combat worthy in fewer than six months. But better the dockyard did it properly than rush them back out only for something to crap out. Still, four months was a long time for the crew to be kept active and still part of her command.

"This would all be easier if we could put the crew off," the manager suggested.

"It would be even easier if we hadn't been shot at so much in the first place," Guinness grunted.

"True. But we'll move people around to make sure we can work without someone ending up breathing vacuum."

Willis's intercom beeped and she flicked it on.

"Willis here."

"Captain, this is officer of the day. A communication has come through from Headquarters for you – high priority."

"Alright, I'm on my way up. Chief, there's a few things I need to discuss with you," before turning to the manager and adding: "Thank you. I'm sure we'll be seeing a lot of each other over the next few months."

"No dockyard type ever likes to be told that by a skipper," Guinness said as they pulled their way back towards the centrifuge.

Willis smiled.

"I know, Chief. It's just a question of mithering them enough to get the job done fast, without being so much that they throw a sulk."

"That's an art," Guinness replied as he guided himself around a ladder. "My last skipper, Crowe, he was an expert at it. He could talk a dock manager into doing something he didn't want to do and have him convince he'd received a favour."

There weren't many crew on the bridge. With *Black Prince* in dock, there wasn't much for the duty watch to do, other than be ready for any kind of an emergency.

"I've forwarded it to your screen at your chair, Ma'am," the duty officer said as Willis entered the bridge.

She sat down and entered her authorisation code to access the message. Guinness was talking about some technical detail but as Willis read and reread, his voice became just a background drone.

"So I'll need a decision on that one, Skipper," Guinness finished.

But Willis just stared into the middle distance, her finger drumming lightly on her chair armrest.

"Skipper?" he asked carefully.

Willis had been a prickly individual when they'd first met but over the last year and a half, she'd mellowed a lot. Still, the after effects of combat could take people unexpectedly. Willis gave a long sigh and her eyes unglazed.

"I'm afraid that's not for me to decide Chief, not any more," she said. "I'm being relieved of command."

When the captain of a ship was on the bridge, every one always had at least half an ear tuned to whatever they said. All extraneous noise abruptly stopped.

"A Commander Berg will be taking charge at eleven hundred hours tomorrow," Willis continued in a slightly hollow voice. "I'm to present myself at the *Starforge* Platform for reassignment."

"Berg? I served with her on the old *Mississippi*," Guinness said before sticking out his hand. "It will be a promotion," he said firmly. "Congratulations. And by the way, I wish to request reassignment to your new command."

The Chief was probably right. Willis thought to herself as she packed her kit for transport. Aside from the latest versions of certain gadgets, she didn't own much. She'd never been one for physical possessions and of what she'd had, quite a bit had been lost on the old *Hood*. She didn't even have her own home dirtside, just a storage locker. When she did land for leave, she generally stayed with either her parents or in a hotel. But now, after packing everything she had on board in less than ten minutes, Willis couldn't help but wonder whether it was time to try to put down some kind of permanent roots and have a home that wouldn't be taken away from her at any moment.

There was no sense in getting paranoid. She'd been a very visible part of the operation that had saved Earth. She'd made her part work, so logically, at the very least, this had to be a sideways move. But just before the war her career had been about to go off the rails. Perversely, the conflict had salvaged her prospects, although the memory of seeing her career hopes crumble had left scars every bit as deep as combat. When she read that message, her initial assumption was that it represented something bad. In some respects it was. She might be leaving her successor with a banged up ship but equally this Commander Berg was inheriting a good crew. To his disappointment, she'd had to decline Guinness's request. She could hardly take him without knowing where *she* was going.

"I relieve you," Commander Berg said crisply.

"I stand relieved, Ma'am," Willis replied before saluting sharply and stepping back as the Berg turned and sat carefully down on the captain's chair. The really important parts of command handover – transfer of computer codes and the ship's formal papers – had happened shortly after the Commander boarded. Willis took her successor through key points she needed to be aware of, the kind of personnel issues that didn't show up in the formal documents and all the other details a new captain needed to have. Across the ship, all work ceased while the new captain gave a short speech across the intercom. It was a fairly standard address of the sort that ticked its way through the checklist: proud to join you, thank you to the former incumbent, big shoes to fill, glorious (though in *Black Prince*'s case short) history, a hopefully glorious future.... blah, blah, blah.

It wasn't fair to take her ill humour out on Berg. Although she'd never been good at reading people, Willis guessed her replacement had been just as surprised to be transferred as she was. From a combat worthy destroyer to a banged up Austerity probably didn't feel like much of a promotion to Berg. The question for Willis was: what awaited her? Berg's speech ended and the ensuing round of polite applause caught Willis by surprise, leaving her to join in belatedly.

With formalities over, it was time to leave and although Berg showed all appropriate respect, Willis could tell she was eager to see her on her way. There could only be one queen-bee in the hive.

"Good luck with your next posting, Captain," Berg said, offering a hand as they paused at the personnel access hatch."

"And you, Commander," Willis replied shaking it. "Sorry I couldn't hand her over in better condition, but at least with a new skipper, they are less likely to try to strip personnel off you as well."

She took one final looked around before leaning in and quietly adding: "Look after them Commander."

Built during the Contact War, *Starforge* Platform had originally been a construction dockyard. Growth in ship size had long since rendered it obsolete for that purpose and instead it had been repurposed as the fleet's orbital administrative personnel centre. When Willis stepped off the shuttle, the place was a riot of activity. A staff officer found her about an hour after arrival and hustled her in to see Admiral Clarence, the fleet's head of personnel.

All large organisations had a few characters in them and Admiral Clarence was one of the fleet's. With a huge ginger moustache and an upper class English accent, he looked and sounded like he'd escaped from the early half of the previous century.

"Ah, Captain," he said as she was shown in. "Please sit down. You look like you could do with a good cup of tea. Unfortunately I've never come across a good cup in orbit, so you'll have to settle for a mediocre one. Milk? Sugar?"

"Just milk, thank you, sir."

Once she was settled, the Admiral resumed his seat.

"I owe you an apology, Captain. One of these days I will at least *try* to give you a posting with some decent notice." Clarence sat back in his seat. "I would imagine that your focus over the last few weeks has probably been inwards. However, I'm sure you're aware that a significant number of ships have been deployed to perform reconnaissance beyond the Junction Line, even some to find out what's left of Landfall, which unfortunately, I'm sure won't be much."

Willis nodded. The first deployments had started within a fortnight of the end of the Siege of Earth. Most ships were moving forward to re-establish the former Junction Line, but if the grapevine was to be believed, some were going much further.

"Well, in its infinite wisdom and mercy, Headquarters has decided that three small task-forces are to be sent out, not just past our former borders, but past the Centaur planet, to directly find the Nameless themselves."

Now Willis's interest was really peaked. After the Mississippi Incident but before Baden, she'd been part of the original expedition to find the Nameless. They hadn't found them but they had come across their handiwork.

"Well, as you can appreciate Captain, this is real deep space work so suitable ship classes at our disposal are fairly limited. In addition, what with the war and everything, we've been struggling to manage the usual circulation of postings. There are quite a few officers who've been in post for too long already. I needed to make some redeployments before ships get sent out on missions that will take months.

"Which is where we get to you," Clarence continued. "*Black Prince* will be out of commission for months, but between Gauntlet and Dryad, you've turned a few heads and Headquarters isn't willing to have you sitting around twiddling your thumbs while your ship is being duct-taped back together."

He picked up a computer pad and handed it to her.

"I am therefore giving you command of the scout cruiser *Spectre*."

Willis caught her breath at that. *Spectre* wasn't a broken-down relic or something bodged together from of spare parts. A dedicated raiding cruiser, she was fast, discrete and just the sort of ship Willis had dreamed of commanding from the day she joined the fleet.

"Thank you, sir," she said.

"She is currently under the command of Captain Weixian. He's a fine officer but has been skippering her for five continuous years now. He was already due for a spell in a ground posting when the balloon went up. There hasn't been a suitable opportunity before now in which to slot in a replacement. If we're to be honest, right now still isn't the best time for a new CO, but you have a track record for hitting the ground running, which makes you eminently suitable."

"Thank you, sir."

Clarence smiled.

"You won't have much time to warm up. As I said I do promise one of these days to give you a posting with more than forty-eight hours' notice."

Guinness had been right after all. This was a step up. *Spectre* was a larger, more prestigious ship. However as the shuttle took her out to her new command, Willis couldn't help but reflect that for all their modernity, *Spectre* and her sister ship *Phantom* were fighting a war they were ill equipped for.

Although *Spectre* was bigger than a Myth class cruiser, she carried less armament than the much smaller *Black Prince*. Designed as a long-range raider against the Aèllr, she was heavily stealthed and gave over more of her internal volume to fuel and stores. What she didn't have though was suitable hard points on the hull to mount flak guns, so instead, the fleet's engineers had built racks onto the cruisers' wings to carry Starfox anti-fighter missiles. These offered *Spectre* some degree of active defence against Nameless cap ship missiles and could, she felt, be taken as a testament to the human ability to improvise from what was to hand. It was probably no wonder though, Willis thought to herself as she read through the briefing documents, that *Spectre* and *Phantom* had between them wracked up a higher than average officer burnout rate. When the shit hit the fan, even flak guns could feel like a pretty insubstantial defence, so a few retrofitted missiles would seem like even more of a fig leaf.

When she reached *Spectre*, she discovered that if Commander Berg had both been startled by and possibly not entirely pleased by her transfer, by contrast Captain Weixian was a man who knew it was time to leave and was profoundly grateful to do so. So six hours after handing over *Black Prince*, Willis was on the opposite side of the ceremony.

"How are you settling in Captain?" Admiral Nisman asked as Willis circulated around the small briefing room in the fleet's groundside Headquarters. The staff officers were still setting up for the meeting and Admiral Wingate had yet to arrive, so the various officers present were free to socialise. As well as fleet officers there was a pair of marines. With the defeat at Landfall, Fleet Marines were now a rare breed, with those that remained fully engaged in training and rebuilding the Corps.

"Well sir," she replied. "Captain Weixian had his ship in fine order."

Unquestionably true. After being launched into two successive commands where everyone on board was new to the ship, it was slightly intimidating to be the only new arrival. But only slightly. It hadn't taken the ship's crew long to familiarise themselves with her combat record and work out she was far from an unproven commander. A week of manoeuvres out beyond Mars' orbit was going a long way toward acclimatising her to the ship and vice-versa.

"Good," Nisman replied. "As the scout cruiser, you'll be the one out in front so I'll need you to be sharp. How are you settling with your new officers?"

Willis kept the smile on her face but inwardly winced. Interpersonal relations were important for deep space work... and there were things in her formal history that would suggest that was something she could have problems with.

"No problems sir," she replied. "I've had a lot of experience since the *Harbinger* mission – a lot of time to learn from past mistakes."

Nisman nodded, apparently satisfied.

"Deep space work is hard going," he said. "I commanded the *Rhine* on a pure exploration voyage back in the fifties. They were great days, no question about it, but a lonely job for a skipper. At least this time you'll have fellow captains around."

"That leaves you out again, sir."

"That's what I get paid the big money for, Captain. But I am looking forward to finding out where we're going."

"Into the black, Amiz."

Willis turned towards the speaker and came sharply to attention.

"Well I sort of assumed as much, sir." Nisman replied mildly. "But I hope you will at least point us in at least the general direction you want us to go."

"And cramp your creativity?" Wingate said with a smile. "Don't worry, we'll at least find an interesting star to point you at." Glancing at Willis, he added: "Well, let's get on with it, Captain."

With Wingate's arrival, the other officers present started to take their seats. Once everyone was settled, Wingate took his place at the head of the room.

"Gentlemen," he began. "I would like to first offer you an overview of the war situation as it stands. While the Battle for Earth was a great victory, the greatest in fact Battle Fleet has ever won, it has not given us everything we had hoped for. While the Nameless were routed from this solar system, it would appear that their surviving units recovered fleet cohesion much faster than we expected. In essence their retreat became orderly very quickly. Very few of their transport ships were lost in the fighting. In the immediate aftermath, those ships, both gate jumpers and those with their own drives, were shepherded clear of the fighting. The small number of combat units that we retained in Rosa and Hydra Stations attempted to cut off the enemy's salient through the Junction Line, but the Nameless's remaining combat strength held them off long enough for the salient to collapse in on itself."

Wingate paused, his expression grim.

"The Nameless did something that in many respects was very impressive. They recognised as a result of their losses, they were in not position to hold the gains they made as a result of their breakthrough of the Junction Line and made no attempt to do so. Instead throwing good after bad, they ruthlessly cut their losses. They had built a network of over a hundred space gates leading to Earth and facing the Junction Line. Now our scout ships have confirmed that they have not just abandoned these gates, they've destroyed them.

"When it came to it, The Nameless did not hesitate to write off the fruits of over a year's worth of fighting at a single stroke and fall back along their supply lines. By doing so, they have freed up ships that were committed to the defence of those gates and denied us targets. Our ships on the Junction Line report there has been some skirmishing, but nothing beyond a handful of ships committed at any one time. During these skirmishes, they've made our support ships their prime targets. They have traded space for time in which to rebuild their fleet and seek action only to impair our strategic mobility. This indicates exactly what we feared – the Nameless are not beaten. They intend to return and finish what they started.

That, Ladies and Gentlemen, gets us up to date. If this war is to be brought to a satisfactory conclusion, we need to find a way of landing a crushing blow. Your task group, composed of the cruisers *De Gaulle* and *Spectre*, the strike boat carrier *Pankhurst*, plus three support ships, all under the command of Admiral Nisman, will proceed first to the Centaur planet, then beyond. Your objective will be simple: find where we can hurt the Nameless."

Wingate nodded towards the two marine officers as he continued.

"We have no way of knowing what if anything you will find out there, so you will be assigned a larger than usual marine complement – a full company under the command of Major Kerr. That is the overview, you will now be taken through the mission in more detail..."

3rd July 2068

As the metaphorical crow flew, the journey to the Centaur planet should have taken in the region of four weeks, three, if *Spectre* had been on her own. But between the slower speed of the support ships and the need to use isolated systems when they made real space re-entry to cool down the engines, the trip took closer to nine. They didn't stop for long or even enter the system. Instead, the *Pankhurst* deployed a scout to quietly check it. A year and a half earlier, when Willis landed on the planet, it had been scoured of all intelligent life, with just the mouldering ruins of cities to declare their previous existence. Now there was a Nameless space gate on the planet's Blue Line and a handful of their transports loading or unloading from a small space station, all protected by a few warships. As a target it was well inside the task force's weight class but the Admiral shook his head. This wasn't what they were here for and there was no point tipping the Nameless off that they were there for the sake of such a paltry prize. So they turned their back on known space and headed out into the unmapped void. After all, they could always attack on the way back.

"There's one thing I just don't get," Lieutenant Yoro, *Spectre*'s communications officer said. For the first time since leaving Earth,

Spectre was alone, in jump space en route to another star system whose name was just a computer-assigned string of letters and numbers. The *Pankhurst* and *De Gaulle* were waiting behind in the previous system. There were several possible routes forward. Admiral Nisman had decided to stop his force at the edge of a small and unremarkable solar system and deploy the two scout ships carried by *Pankhurst* forward along with *Spectre*. For the first time since Dryad, Willis was out on her own, without a senior officer looking over her shoulder.

"Just one thing, Coms?" Willis replied mildly. "I'm impressed."

The young man blushed and started to stutter a reply.

"Just a joke, Lieutenant," she interrupted with a smile. "What is it?"

"We've been picking up Nameless transmissions for weeks. Mostly faint but always behind us. If we're heading towards Nameless territory, why aren't we hearing anything from in front?"

"I've been wondering that for weeks," said Commander Yaya.

As the ship's second-in-command, she'd been on watch when Willis came up to the bridge. With the ship in jump space there weren't many personnel on the bridge. The small Chinese-American officer had worked hard to ensure Willis's smooth integration with the rest of the ship. Willis's transfer in had likely delayed Yaya's promotion to a ship of her own, but she seemed to take developments calmly.

Beyond Yaya, the main holo was set to navigation mode. Before they'd left Earth, modifications had been made to the software. It now displayed lines to indicate systems that were thought to be close enough for the Nameless to jump. This far beyond explored space, the charts were based on astronomical observations from Earth and as a result, the estimated distances between stars were a bit sketchy.

With the Nameless limited to individual jumps of four point seven light years, gauging the distance between systems was important. If the gap was too wide, it could be eliminated as a route forward.

They'd expected to be able to follow the Nameless space gates like breadcrumbs, but unlike the ones closer to the combat zone, out here they were deployed in interplanetary space. So unless they were active, they were devilishly hard to spot. In fact, by now they hadn't seen one in over a week. Whether that was because they weren't spotting them, or because they simply weren't there, was the big question.

"Well, the most obvious reason is that there is nothing ahead of us to hear," Willis replied as she leaned against a support column.

Groundsiders never really understood how bloody big a galaxy was. Too many people seemed to think that a line could be drawn on a chart from Earth, through the Centaur world and onwards to the Nameless world or worlds. One of the three task groups was indeed following that path. Problem was a degree or two 'off' that line, rapidly equated to scores of light years. In fact, the course they were on was not particularly promising. They were moving slowly toward the edge of the galactic arm Earth resided in. The average gap between stars was opening and soon those gaps might be wider than the Nameless ships could jump.

"Even so, I figured we'd be picking up their FTL transmissions by now," Yoro said, "even if they were too faint to get a fix on."

"Their FTL transmitters are better than ours," Yaya added, "but they're still pretty narrow band transmissions. Outside the combat zone they might be mostly using couriers like we do. If they're making only the occasional transmission, then we could be in jump space when it happens and not have heard."

"The longer we're out here, the longer the odds we're simply missing them ma'am," Yoro politely pointed out.

"Could be a point of security," Yaya suggested. "They must know the importance of protecting their core worlds and the best way to do that is not allow us to find them in the first place."

"Or there aren't worlds to find."

Yaya rolled her eyes.

"Have you been reading science fiction again, Lieutenant?"

The theory of an entirely space-based civilisation had been suggested in the early days of the war, although mostly by people who no one took seriously.

"All possible," Willis said. "But as I said, most likely we're on the wrong track. We haven't sighted a space gate in over a week, although our route might have something to do with that. We'll make the usual quiet insertion. See what there is to see."

The first system composed of lots and lots of nothing interesting but within the second, roughly within the Goldilocks zone, a space gate floated. They wouldn't have spotted it except that a convoy of gate jumpers came through at just the right moment. Willis dispatched a message drone back to Nisman while *Spectre* held position at the very edge of the system, watching.

"There wasn't much activity," Willis said, nodding towards the display, "but what there was, was informative. A convoy of fifty gate-jumper transports came through as we were sweeping the system. By comparing their engine output to acceleration curve, we established that they must have been running near empty."

"So transports returning to base to refill," the Admiral mused.

"Yes, sir," Willis replied across the laser link.

"That was a big convoy to have only one escort to protect them," Captain Pincuc of the *De Gaulle* observed.

"Why waste armed ships back here when they've never seen us out this far?" asked Captain Beecher, commander of the *Pankhurst* and the last participant in their electronic meeting.

"Big convoys would make sense," Willis said. "While we were waiting for you, we did observe the gate re-orientate to receive the convoy, then turn again to launch them off."

"And you got a fix on that heading?" Pincuc asked.

"Yes, but that probably means the gate can only receive ships from one direction at a time. So presumably having two convoys coming in at the same time from different locations is a problem. A smaller number of big convoys are more efficient."

"So we could wait here for an inbound convoy and really clean up!" Beecher said enthusiastically.

"And give away that we're here," Nisman replied more soberly.

"I would imagine, sir, that the only reason the escort is even along is for its FTL transmitter," Willis said. "I doubt we could take it out before it got a signal off."

"Wouldn't matter if we did," Nisman replied. "The loss of even a complete convoy of those crappy gate jumpers might sting but it isn't a war-winner. No, what I want to know is where these ships are coming from. Having seen them jump, at least we don't have to guess which way to go. Where these ships come from, that's what I'd give my pension pot to know. No gentlemen, onwards and outwards."

For another five days they followed the breadcrumbs through three systems. *Spectre* led the way, charting each in turn and identifying the space gates. By now the density of solar systems was dropping significantly. The convoy outpaced them, which considering *Spectre* was the fastest cruiser in the fleet, was a bit galling. But when they found it, there was no doubt it was what they sought.

"It's big, whatever else," said Yaya as she studied the readouts. "Computer is estimating five hundred metres across and nine hundred tall."

At first they'd thought the system had just another space gate. Then Sensors reported it wasn't the standard gate design they'd become familiar with. Instead it was the more sophisticated double-gate arrangement linked by a small space station, which had been seen only a few times at major Nameless supply dumps. Then they observed a ship moving close to one of the system's planets. *Spectre* had made a quiet insertion behind a gas giant and deployed several drones to look around the planet. It was hard to know yet whether this counted as the jackpot but certainly it was, as the Admiral put it, a discovery of interest. The space station was shaped like a giant lollypop, a spherical body with a long thin structure below, terminating in a second much smaller sphere.

"Passives are reading significant heat being radiated off the lower sphere, Captain," the sensor officer said, "so that's likely to be the station reactor."

"Which puts it well away from the rest of the station," Willis replied absently. "It also makes the station very vulnerable to having its main power knocked out."

"So, not a starfort then," Yaya said. "Which begs the question, what is it?"

That was the million-dollar question all right, Willis thought to herself. But she doubted they would be able to answer that from their current position.

"What kind of defences are we seeing?" she asked.

"Not much," Yaya replied. "We can see a cruiser here, plus two escorts or scouts, here and here."

"Which is a pretty limp defence."

"Doesn't mean there aren't armed satellites as well — we wouldn't spot them at this range. That station could easily hold a squadron of fighters as well."

"Given how crude their fighters are, that wouldn't worry me much."

Willis flicked the display to visual. Nameless stellar architecture definitely had a distinct look to it. A gate jumper transport ship was little more than a shipping container with an engine and a cockpit bolted on. The space gates had an equally crude look to them. Even the space stations with their double gates had a certain 'pile 'em high, sell 'em cheap' look to them. But that big station, that definitely reminded her of the first time she'd seen *Black Prince* alongside a Myth class cruiser. Her ship had been a wartime expedience, lashed together. By contrast, the Myth had been built with the expectation of long service. Despite its obvious alien lines, there was something about the station that suggested it had been designed for many decades of service. Her gut told her there was something important within that hull, while her head wondered how to peel it open to get at whatever *it* was.

"Y'know, it might just be a freight handling centre," Captain Pincuc suggested.

"And I don't see that as a bad thing," Willis replied firmly.

Once *Spectre* had made an equally discrete retreat from the system, the Admiral ordered the task group to fall back and join their support ships at a relatively close but isolated system six light years away from the alien station. Safely hidden from any prowling Nameless warships, Nisman then summoned them to a high-level conference on board the *De Gaulle*.

"I have no doubt that we could destroy the station and every other construct in the system," Nisman said. "In fact I think we could do it with ease. But to take a hostile habitat..."

He turned towards the most junior officer present, the commander of their marine contingent.

"Major Kerr, what are your thoughts?"

With his Fleet Marine uniform and as the most junior officer present, there was no doubt Kerr was the odd man out.

"Sir," he carefully replied. "There are a lot of potential problems with any attempt to board that station. We have flat-out no idea about its layout – the corridors could be twelve inches high for all we know. It could be chock full of troops or have substantial internal defences. The delivery ship or ships would have to slow to a near halt for my men to be delivered onto target, leaving it and us very vulnerable."

"So that would be a no then?"

"Sir, we've drilled for this, and we have the equipment to breach and board, but that's against a human installation where we could be sure of the design. An op against this station would more or less be a step into the unknown."

"The Major's right to say we don't know anything," Willis cut in. "In fact, even after all this time we know next to nothing about the Nameless. Even if that station is just a floating warehouse, its' intelligence value would be incalculable."

"And we are only two weeks from our bingo point," said

Beecher. "Another fourteen days and we'll *have* to go back for resupply."

"Maybe then go back now," Pincuc replied. "Report in and come back better prepared."

"That's seven weeks to get back to Earth – bare minimum. Another seven to get back here, plus whatever turn around time. Call it four months," Beecher pointed out.

"And with respect to the Major, because frankly I know everything he says is correct, but how much better prepared can we be?" Willis added. "There's no way we can learn about the layout without going in. Right now that station is poorly defended, probably because they have lost so many ships and secondly because they've never seen us out this far. If they glimpse even one of our ships – and the odds are sooner or later they will – then we'll lose the element of surprise and this opportunity will disappear. Right now, unlike any kind of a ship, that station can't run away."

"It could blow itself up though and leave us with nothing but a lot of crispy marines," Pincuc said dourly. "No offence, Major."

"None taken."

"My gunner believes he can severe the connector between the main station body and the reactor section," Willis said. "That would cramp their ability to self-destruct."

"We could use the strike boats to take out the space gate and draw away the station's defenders," Beecher said enthusiastically.

Nisman held up his hand for silence.

"Gentlemen, it is plainly within our remit and abilities to destroy this installation. In fact, we can do it with such little risk that we would not even need our marines to do so. However, attempting to capture a hostile alien space station is something that has never been attempted before, making it a much more difficult mission by several orders of magnitude. The marines will be subject to the greatest risk, so the question must be directed to them – yes or no?"

All eyes turned to the marine officer.

The Major had given no immediate answer. Instead he went back to his own people to examine the problem. A week ticked by as the marines attempted to work the problem, while *Spectre* returned to keep an eye on the station. While they waited, another large convoy, this time on route Earthward, came through. Sitting on the bridge of a ship designed and built to hunt down enemy transports, it was maddening to see such a prize pass unmolested. Several small courier type ships, never seen before, came and went. Finally, after three days of observation, *Spectre* once again slipped away to rejoin the task group.

"It's on," Nisman confirmed as the hatch closed behind him.

Once again they were gathered on board *De Gaulle*. The Major still looked stoic, while Captain Pincuc appeared unenthusiastic.

"Or to be more precise, we're on to make the attempt. There are a number of cut-outs, which mean this will be either a smash and grab or just a smash."

"*Spectre* is ready sir," Willis said.

"Just as well, Captain," Nisman replied, "because *Spectre* will shoulder the highest level of risk."

There was little warning for the small space station and its attached gate. The eight missile strike boats and their two supporting gunboats dropped into real space right on the Red Line and powered in. The planet it was orbiting was small, roughly in the same class as Mercury, with such a shallow mass shadow that it took the strike boats only fourteen minutes to close to firing range. The cruiser and the two escorts orbiting the planet were only starting to react when the strike boats each launched a missile at the space gate. It was overkill. With no defences of its own, the first missile ripped the gate station open, the second and third blew it apart, leaving the balance to simply spread the wreckage wide. The strike boats altered course towards the approaching defender and continued to close the range. Unnoticed, a single scout ship dropped into real space a light minute out from the planet and watched.

Another sixteen minutes passed and the two groups of warships closed on each other. On the human side, the two gunboats moved to the front of the pack, ready to protect their missile-armed brethren. The three Nameless warships shifted into a triangular formation, the two escorts ready to defend and let their big brother be the one to strike back.

As one, the eight strike boats belched out the rest of their missiles, then turned their formation to make their escape. As the missiles approached, the alien escorts began to fire their own, targeting the approaching projectiles. Only one human missile got through, grazing one of the escorts. As the Nameless continued to accelerate, the strike boats attempted to reverse course. With the range dropping fast, missiles started arcing out from the Nameless ships and now it was the humans' turn to defend. The gunboats at the rear of the formation blazed away at the approaching missiles and deployed chaff. The gunboats and strike boats were too small to target precisely with cap ship missiles, but it hardly mattered, the smaller dual purpose weapons were equal to the task. One of them found its way through and a strike boat took a direct hit. Its engineering section was blown apart, leaving the gutted remains of the command deck to coast forward.

A light minute away, the scout ship quietly jumped away.

"Sensors, Bridge. The scout ship is back."

"Captain," Yoro said, "we're getting an information download from the scout."

"My screen please," Willis ordered.

The Nameless were in hot pursuit, being drawn away from the large station and towards the Red Line. They'd known almost immediately when the attack had gone in after detecting a sudden flurry of Nameless FTL transmissions.

"Captain, signal from flag: Proceed as instructed."

"Bridge, Navigation, start spin up for jump. All hands prepare for high acceleration."

Willis looked around at Kerr. The marine officer was standing in his combat gear, his suit and armour making him substantially bulkier than everyone else on the bridge. The task group's entire marine complement, a whole company, was now squeezed aboard *Spectre* and the chief engineer was muttering darkly about over taxing the life support systems.

"Ready, Major?" she asked.

"Raring to go," came his sardonic reply.

If Willis was any judge, Kerr was a conflicted man. The marines had suffered a higher proportion of casualties than any other branch of the fleet so they were keen for payback but just as eager to avoid getting killed doing it. From astern came the faint rumble of the engines as *Spectre* started to slide round the large asteroid they'd been using to break the line of sight to the Nameless. Forty kilometres off to Port, the *De Gaulle* also accelerated on a slightly different course. Along with their support ships, *Pankhurst* waited out beyond the edge of the system.

"Coms, send to *De Gaulle*: Good hunting."

"They've signalled back, Captain: You too."

Spectre cleared the asteroid. Eight light minutes ahead was the planet and the Nameless station.

"Go full burn on engines," she ordered.

The rumble from astern became a throaty roar. Willis felt herself being pushed back hard into her chair. Kerr grunted as he started to slide before his safety line brought him to a halt.

"Navigation, Bridge, we are now at safe jump speed."

Willis glanced at *De Gaulle*'s icon. The heavier ship had a shallower acceleration curve. She was still two minutes away from the velocity at which she could jump without the portal closing on her stern. That was close enough. Without conscious thought, Willis tightened her seat restrains.

"All hands brace for jump. Helm, execute jump!"

Across such a relatively short distance, the time in jump space was only a few seconds before *Spectre* jolted back into real space. The main holo blanked out and then started to fill up again as the first radar returns began to come in. Off to port was the planet, the station behind it, beyond it the Nameless ships and beyond them the strike boat. Willis winced as she counted only seven human ships.

"Helm, come to two, nine, three dash zero, zero, four – engines full burn."

On the far side of the mass shadow, the three Nameless warships had detected *Spectre* as she turned in towards the planet and were breaking off their pursuit. They were inside the Red Line but beyond the Blue. Once they'd slowed enough to jump, the Nameless ships could cross the distance between them in seconds. *Spectre*'s course couldn't have made her objective more obvious. Three to one, especially at close range, would be a fatal encounter. Had they calculated accurately enough or had they tried to pull off too ambitious a plan with too little planning? On the holo the strike boat formation opened and scattered, each on its own course, just as *De Gaulle* jumped in right on the Red Line.

"Yes!" Willis hissed.

The Nameless ships were caught facing the wrong way, with little velocity and within gun range of the Red Line. The *De Gaulle*'s first salvo blew the Nameless cruiser's engines apart. As it tumbled away in a crippled state, Pincuc's ship quickly shifted target to the first of the escorts.

"That's the first milestone, Major," she said over her shoulder.

Ahead the Nameless station orbited into view. As the fastest ship in the task group, *Spectre* was the one that could close the range most quickly. They still didn't know what, if anything, the station was armed with. If it turned out they were charging a Star Fort, then things could be about to get excessively interesting.

"Bridge, Coms, the target is transmitting again on FTL frequency."

"Understood. Inform me if we hear any replies."

Twenty minutes passed as *Spectre* thundered in and the Nameless station continued to squawk with its FTL transmitter. No missiles arched out towards *Spectre*, while, on the other side of the mass shadow, *De Gaulle* accelerated in past the wreckage of her victims. On the bridge holo, the green circle indicating the range of *Spectre's* guns got closer and finally overlapped with the station.

"Helm, cut engines. Fire Control, engage the target," Willis ordered.

As the engines stopped, the tremble she could feel in the deck disappeared. *Spectre* continued to coast along but now as a perfectly steady gun platform. The cruiser's two turrets came slowly to bear as the gunner made fine adjustments. Then the first plasma bolt belched out. A hundred thousand kilometres down range, the bolt missed the station's connecting structure by only a dozen metres, perhaps prompting it alien inhabitants to realise that mere destruction was not the invaders' objective. By then the gunner had already corrected his aim. The second shot missed by less than two metres, while the third slammed in, all but severing the connection. The FTL transmissions from the station ceased in mid-flow.

"Well that's shut them up," Willis muttered.

She signalled to Helm and the engines once again began to rumble.

"How long until we're alongside?" Kerr asked.

Willis glanced towards navigation.

"Seventeen minutes to the turnover, Major, plus another thirty-five minutes of braking to bring us to a relative halt alongside the station."

A lot of time for the occupants of the now crippled station to react. *Spectre* could pull a braking manoeuvre and keep her bows and guns facing the enemy, but she couldn't brake as hard that way. For best performance she needed to about face, which would leave the cruiser attempting to see through her own engine plume. They could, and would, deploy sensor drones to cover the blind spot, but if the Nameless retained or managed to cobble together any kind of anti-ship capability, then *Spectre* would be a sitting duck.

"I'll move aft to join my men at the turnover," Kerr replied.

Another forty minutes passed, during which the station remained inert. As the engines overcame the acceleration they'd built up, the rate at which they were closing became increasingly slow. That had always been the plan – to come to a halt within a hundred metres of the station. Unless they matched velocities perfectly, the marines would be incapable of spacewalking the last part without becoming small organic projectiles. With the most critical part of the attack now imminent Willis remained perfectly silent, keeping a close eye on the holo for any activity on the station. If it gave any sign of attack, she might have only seconds in which to swing *Spectre* around in defence. As they crossed through the hundred-kilometre mark, the cruiser's point defence guns stabbed out, knocking away aerials and sensor domes, to further blind and render the target impotent.

With a final burst of her engines, *Spectre* slotted into a parallel orbit only ninety metres away from the station. Through one of the internal cameras, Willis could see the marines lined up at the main airlock. With the ship decompressed, both airlock hatches were open and she could see her chief petty officer leaning out with a tether gun in his hands. As *Spectre* came to a relative halt, he fired, propelling a rocket-assisted line. Normally it would have been tipped with a magnetic grapple, but on this occasion it was fitted with a hull-piercing head bodged together in *Pankhurst's* machine shop.

A small puff of venting gas confirmed that the shot was good and had bitten into the hull. Inside, the head would be releasing sealant foam, which would stop the air loss and make it impossible to quickly knock out the head.

The Chief swung out of the lock and hung onto the outside of the hull as the marine breaching team snapped onto the line and pulled themselves hand over hand. The success of the mission was now out of her hands and Willis could only wait and watch. If the Nameless sent troops outside to engage the marines, then *Spectre* would offer support, but once the marines got in they'd be on their own.

Within twenty seconds the marines were on the hull. A few clamped their boots on and formed a perimeter while the rest started to stick thin hoops of explosives onto sections of the hull identified as likely areas to blast inwards. With the explosives in place, they quickly clamped on temporary airlocks. The hatches were left open to allow the explosive shockwave to travel outwards. The sergeant in charge gave a quick thumb's up back to *Spectre*. Across the command channel, Willis could hear Kerr shouting just as the blasting charges fired.

"First team, go, go, GO!" he roared.

Across the hull there were five circular flashes. Then the pressure behind blew five metal discs of hull plating outwards and the airlocks slammed shut. The first of the breaching teams reached the locks and started to work their way through, one at a time. Willis could see confusion at one of the locks and marines floundering there. But at the other four there were rhythmic flashes of escaping gas as each lock dumped atmosphere each time the outer hatch opened for the next marine. Across the radio link Willis started to hear the sound of combat within.

De Gaulle and *Spectre* lay on either side of the station. The surviving strike boats had rearmed, returned and were now patrolling at the edge of the mass shadow. Four hours after the first marines had stormed aboard, the last of the fighting was petering out. There were still a few pockets of resistance where the marines couldn't get in, but the defenders couldn't get out.

Beyond that the situation was far from clear.

"Lieutenant Kinberg here, Admiral," a marine reported from the temporary command post they had established close to one of the airlocks.

"I'm not sure how many people we've lost — the Major and most of his command section was taken out. At a guess, I reckon we've lost about a third of our fighting strength in dead or wounded."

Nisman's expression tightened. That was a lot of marines.

"Who's in charge over there now, Lieutenant?" he asked.

"Right now, sir, I think that would be me," Kinberg replied. "I'm pretty sure I'm now the only officer still standing. The enemy has retreated towards the core of the station. There isn't really room to bring everyone to bear on them so I have teams sweeping the rest of the station, but it's a bloody maze over here."

"Thank you Lieutenant," Nisman replied. "And well done. I'll be in touch shortly."

"Sir."

Kinberg disappeared from the screen.

That left Willis, the Admiral and Captain Pincuc still on the link-up. They'd picked up distant Nameless FTL transmissions an hour earlier. They were short and identical. They couldn't read them of course, but the pattern suggested some kind of status request.

"So, do your respective coms sections have any thoughts on how far off those transmissions came from?" Nisman asked, "Or more importantly, how long before the ship that sent them could get here?"

"Going by our records of past incidents and signal strength, twenty-four to thirty-six hours," Willis replied. "And that's on the optimistic side."

"We have to make best use of the time then. Captain Willis, we need to do something deeply irregular. I need a senior officer over there to take command of the intelligence gathering. I know this is more appropriate a task for a commander, but this time, we need someone with greater seniority directly on the scene. If Nameless reinforcements arrive, we may have to withdraw with haste and *De Gaulle* will have to cover that retreat."

"I understand, sir," Willis replied as she felt her heart start to hammer.

Nameless, faceless, voiceless – ever since the Mississippi Incident two years previously, they had been nothing but raw and unexplained belligerence. Humanity had fought a war of survival without knowing who or what it was even fighting. Now there was a possibility that mask was about to be lifted. As she stood still to allow a rating to fit an extended support pack onto her survival suit, Willis realised she was one part scared to one part excited.

"I still think we should send you over in a shuttle," Commander Yaya said as the two of them peered through the open airlock.

"There's barely room between us to deploy a shuttle, Commander. Besides, there's still no airlock we could lock onto. Don't worry though, I'm rated for space walks."

"Still, the Admiral should be sending me."

"You just worry about your job, Commander."

Willis tried to remove any sting from her words by adding with an awkward smile: "Besides this is a win-win scenario. If you went over and got shot, I'd have to fill in tons of paperwork. But if I go over there and do something stupid, you might get that promotion you deserve."

"Yes, Captain, but then I'll have to do the paperwork."

"True, but I'll be dead so I won't care," Willis grinned.

"So win-win for you and win-win-lose for me! I can live with that. Just the same, Captain – be careful."

Lieutenant Kinberg met Willis at the airlock as she pulled herself through.

"Welcome aboard, ma'am," he with a salute, as a pair of ratings assigned as her assistants followed behind.

Willis barely heard him, instead focusing her attention on her first look at enemy territory. At first glance, it was all very mundane. But then there were only so many ways to build a space station. There were scorch marks from the explosives and several weapon strikes. With her experienced eye, a second glance revealed details that were just wrong – like the covering on the he bulkhead behind Kinberg, which showed signs of wear like those that might be seen on a floor.

"Yeah," he said glancing, over his shoulder. "This place is like an onion – it's like layers of decks going inward. One of my sergeants was the first one in. She claims she could feel a gravity effect pulling towards the centre. Not much, a fraction of a G – at least that's what she thinks."

Humanity could simulate gravity by either spin or acceleration. There were true artificial gravity methods she'd read about in the technical journals. Some worked under laboratory conditions, others purely on paper. Either way, they were far from practical systems. It seemed the Nameless had developed some kind of system that worked. The next question was – could they find and identify it?

"With respect, ma'am, this isn't really somewhere we want a ship officer running around. We lost the Major because one of those bastards popped out of a section we thought we'd cleared, so I'm assigning you Marines Jahmene and Keys for your security."

"That's all right, Lieutenant," Willis replied. "I won't try to tell you how to do your job, but we'll have to rip as much out of this place as we can."

"Well then, follow me. We haven't had a chance to ID much so far, but you might as well get to meet the enemy."

It was hard to know what she'd expected, hard to know what even to expect from a race that had acted with such automatic hostility – certainly something more impressive. It wasn't big and probably massed less than she did. It had four limbs and, even twisted in death, its posture made clear that the normal axis of its body was horizontal like a dog or a horse rather than vertical like a human. Its limbs were much longer in proportion to a human and had four points of articulation. The back pair – dedicated legs – ended in something like a hoof. The front pair seemed to be dual-purpose. There was a hardened area at the wrist, which could presumably be used to walk on, but beyond that there was definitely a hand – very definitely by the way it still gripped the weapon it had been using when the marines cut it down.

She took a grip of its long neck and pulled the head round. Like a snake, or maybe worm, was the closest Terran comparison. The head wasn't much wider than the neck and tapered to a blunt point. It only had one eye, or at least it only had one now. The shot that killed it had blown open one side of its head, spilling a turquoise fluid. The surviving eye was forward facing, which was to be expected – every known sentient race had evolved from hunting species. The mouth was a lipless line that went back towards the neck and opened left and right. The overall effect was a cross between a horse and a giant worm.

"Ugly," muttered one of the ratings.

"Eye of the beholder," Willis said absently as she prised open the jaws with a pencil. Its teeth at the front were sharp meat cutters and the broad grinding teeth at the back those of an omnivore. A proper biologist would probably observe more. Such knowledge was unlikely to have any military relevance, but her curiosity demanded satisfaction. Looking around the chamber, that satisfaction soon disappeared. Although poorly equipped compared to the marines, the Nameless soldiers had shown no reluctance to fight and, defending familiar ground, had exacted a terrible toll on the invaders. There was a splash of human blood on the bulkhead opposite where they had nailed the first marine through the hatch.

As Willis considered all this, something moved in her peripheral vision. Turning, she caught sight of something like a rat scuttling along a cable. One of the ratings swore and took a swipe at it. The creature easily dodged the blow and continued along.

"Yeah, we've seen a few of them," one of her escorts told her. "Not hostile, but I don't know what they are. Food? Pets?"

As he spoke Willis saw the creature reach a point where the cable had been severed by a bullet strike. The gap was tiny, but the creature stopped and twitched its nose as it examined the break. Then it sat up, its rear leg gripping the cable. Willis felt her mouth drop as she saw the creature had a small bag or pouch hanging from its belly, from which it pulled out what appeared to be a small length of cable and began to splice it into place to repair the break.

"Oh my god," she murmured as she watched the tiny creature finish its work. It looked around then sprang towards another damaged cable.

"Quick, grab it!" she ordered, as the creature sailed across the chamber.

One marine's armoured gauntlet closed on it and then it did the strangest thing yet – absolutely nothing. Even the most placid domestic animal would wriggle or struggle if grabbed like that. But this thing just stopped moving. It had been a good catch by the marine, he'd avoided crushing it and wasn't holding it firmly, but the creature wasn't making any movement beyond breathing.

"Some kind of biotech?" someone asked.

"Don't know. Box it men. We'll be taking a lot of samples."

"They made their way through what were apparently accommodation areas, all of them showing signs of heavy fighting. There were bodies everywhere and in the distance there was still the occasional crackle of gunfire. They came into a large chamber with a lot of computer equipment, most of it still turned on – so some kind of command centre by the look of it.

"Bingo," Willis said to herself, as she looked around.

"Captain!"

Willis looked up from the computer panel she was examining. Even after an hour they were only scratching the surface. They'd opened up several damaged pieces and found living tissue, indicating biological computers the like of which she'd never seen or even heard of before. There were more conventional electrical computers but they appeared to be backups. With her thoughts swirling, she didn't take in what the marine said.

"I'm sorry, what was that?"

"Ma'am, Lieutenant Kinberg has asked you to join him. Ma'am we've found something."

"What is it?" she asked, still half distracted.

"Captain, you need to see this!

Finally the marine's tone penetrated her consciousness. He wasn't just rattled – he was actively shocked.

The section of the station they led her to, did not seem to have seen as much fighting as others. Several marines were there and, while it was hard to read body language through space suits and body armour, there was a definite vibe of fear and anger.

As she approached Kinberg, Willis glanced towards the marine sergeant present. Through his visor she could see his face, a strong face, but after a moment she realised that the blobs of liquid inside his helmet were tears.

"What is it? What's going on?" she demanded.

Kinberg looked sick as he waved her towards the hatch he was floating by. Willis pulled herself through – and stopped half way. The chamber looked like someone had thrown a bucket of blood around. A severed human arm drifted near the centre of the chamber. Two marine corpsmen were treating casualties – human casualties but not marines! Instead, maybe a dozen men and women were scattered around the chamber, all of them little more than skeletons, all of them naked.

"Movement was detected and Sergeant Lyons threw a grenade through the hatch," Kinberg told her as the two of them returned to the command deck. He shook his head with an expression of genuine distress. "He didn't know! No one told us there would be humans here!"

"No one knew Lieutenant," Willis said before addressing Nisman via the communications link-up they'd established with the squadron.

"To be honest, sir, I think some poor brave bastard wrapped him or herself round the grenade. Otherwise it would likely have killed everyone in the chamber."

She instantly regretted saying it within Kinberg's hearing. It wasn't the fault of the man who threw the grenade or any other marine. Based on the information available, the sergeant's decision had been correct. Even so, the emotional part of her still wondered how he could have done such a thing.

"Any idea where the hell they came from, Captain?"

"They're civilians sir, that much I'm sure of. Between Junction and Landfall, the bastards have had plenty of opportunities to capture civvies."

Nisman's expression was grim.

"The marines found a lab in a neighbouring compartment. The civilians were clearly being used for research and experimentation... vivisection and various other..." Willis had to swallow to force down the bile threatening to rise inside her. She'd taken a glance in the hatch and that had been enough. Given time, she'd process it mentally but for the moment, she had to force herself not to think about it.

"Various other procedures. I don't know why they weren't killed before we boarded, but it would appear the section of the station the prisoners were being kept in, was cut off from the rest by the first assault."

She wondered whether this could in some way account for the dogged defence the Nameless had mounted. Had they known there was no way they could hide or destroy the evidence of what they had done? Had they guessed that this act would place them beyond any reconciliation or forgiveness?

"Have they said anything?"

"Not yet, sir," she replied shaking her head. "Admiral, these people are in a bad way. Have you ever seen pictures of concentration camp survivors from the twentieth century?"

"Dear God, that bad?"

She nodded.

Nisman took a deep breath, clearly composing himself.

"Then we have a difficult decision to make. If those people have been experimented on, then they may have become biological weapons. We may not be able to take them with us."

Beside her, Willis sensed Kinberg stiffen angrily. Outside the camera's pick-up, she laid a restraining hand on his arm.

"Sir, we have a number of wounded marines with compromised suits. Unless we're prepared to leave behind some of our own, that line has already been crossed. The other thing is, sir, I could spend six months in here and not find anything we can actually use. Those people offer the best chance of getting serious intel, but that will mean professional medical treatment on Earth."

"Well, we don't have six months," Nisman replied. "We picked up another set of FTL transmissions. These didn't come from the same direction we did. They came the other way and were definitely closer than the last lot. I don't want the Nameless to know in what strength we are here or that we boarded their station. So in six hours we will evacuate and destroy it. In the meantime, get as much as you can."

"Water, water, everywhere but not a drop to drink," Willis muttered to herself as she surveyed the command area.

With the last of the Nameless eliminated, most of the marines were now actively assisting with the recovery effort, along with several more members of *Spectre*'s crew sent over to lend a hand. *Pankhurst* and the support ships had been called in, while a message drone had been dispatched in the opposite direction, back along the trail of satellites they'd left in their wake, to inform Earth of their discovery.

The *Lennox*, smallest of the support ships had been detailed to accommodate the survivors. Cargos were being hastily reassigned because once the civilian survivors boarded, the whole ship would be under quarantine. They also loaded up a dozen of the least damaged Nameless bodies. Two of them were dressed in outfits that seemed more high quality than the rest. Maybe they were officers? No way to know. The true prize should have been the computer, however. She'd examined the screen, but beyond establishing it was definitely writing, there wasn't much more that could be determined. For all she knew the screen could be displaying the Nameless's complete war plans – or someone's shopping list.

"I wonder if those brain boxes are part of a security system?" Kinberg asked, gesturing toward *De Gaulle*'s doctor as he examined one of the bio computers. With their biotech construction, Kinberg – like the rest of marines – had quickly taken to referring to the Nameless computers as brain boxes.

"I mean as soon as we unplug them, the tissue inside starts to die."

Examples of Nameless electronic computers had already being shipped out. But the bio computers could not be so easily moved however, plugged as they were not only into the electrical systems but some kind of nutrient feed that simply could not be replicated at such short notice. They could, and certainly would, take examples but it would be dead meat long, long before they reached Earth.

"That might just be an occasionally useful side effect," Willis replied. "Biotech has a hell of a lot of disadvantages on the whole. But then brain tissue is gram for gram still the best computer the universe has ever seen."

One of the marines approached and saluted.

"Captain, Lieutenant," he began, "one of the civilian survivors has requested to speak to you."

"Those people are supposed to be getting evacuated to the *Lennox*," Willis replied.

"I know, ma'am, and he is in the last group to go over. He says it's important."

"Alright, escort him here."

"Try to keep it quick though, Captain. These people are frail."

The man gently guided into the control room was beyond frail. Skeletal would be closer and Willis doubted he could have even stood in anything approaching Earth gravity. He clutched a blanket but in zero gravity it floated around him, revealing pale and papery skin. All activity within the chamber came to a halt, as everyone else, dressed in space suits and combat armour, turned to look at the almost naked man. The corpsman gently guided him over to Willis.

"Hello," she said uncertainly, "my name is Captain Faith Willis of the Battle Fleet ship *Spectre*."

"Mateusz Bielski," he whispered, "Junction Station."

"What can I do for you, Mister Bielski?" she asked after deciding a firm tone was likely to serve best.

"You're looking for information. I can help."

"And you will, sir, when you're debriefed, but I need you on the *Lennox*. We..."

"No!"

The force of his exclamation was enough to set Bielski off coughing. Doubled over, his frail body convulsed. Willis nodded to the marine.

"Get him out."

Bielski's claw like hand shot out and latched onto her arm. Beneath the suit she could feel her flesh crawl.

"No," this time his voice was calmer, "I've been here."

"Here? In this room?"

Bielski nodded.

"I've seen them use their computers. They brought me here to be examined and to interrogate me."

"Did you see what controls they used?"

Willis's voice was urgent now. He nodded and pointed to one of the freestanding computer terminals. Carefully, as if he were made of glass, she guided him over. Bielski studied the terminal for several seconds and then with a shaking hand he reached out and pressed several different buttons. A holo display at the centre of the terminal came to life.

"I don't know if this is a password or just a command line," he rasped, "but I saw it often enough to memorise. They wanted to know where our planets are."

"Did you tell them?" she asked quietly.

"Yes," he sobbed. "We tried not to but they..."

Tears floated from his face.

"It's all right, it's all right," she tried to assure him.

The burns and bruises on Bielski's wreck of a body told their own story.

Bielski steadied himself and worked the controls to bring up what looked like a list of files. He scrolled down and activated one particular file. The list disappeared and an image, not much more than a series of blips with writing beside, them appeared.

"What's that supposed to tell us?"

Kinberg said what Willis was thinking.

"It's a map," Bielski whispered, pointing an unsteady finger into the holo. "We are here and here is Junction and here – here are their home worlds."

Suddenly, like an optical illusion, Willis found she could see it.

"Oh my God," she said breathlessly.

She moved slightly to the left and allowed her eyes to track downwards. The layout of the blips started to match standard two-dimensional representations of human space. There was Landfall, below was Junction Station and the rest of the Junction Line, and below that, highlighted in purple, the position of Earth. Her gaze went upwards. There, not as far above as Earth was below, lay a cluster of large yellow blips representing planets – Nameless planets.

Bielski's hand closed around her arm.

"Captain, promise me one thing. Just one thing," he said as he stared at her, his eyes burning with a ferocity that sent a shiver down her spine. Wordlessly she nodded.

"Promise me you will make them *pay!*"

Chapter Thirteen

Search for the Grail

20th July 2068

"Council members. Our analysis of the information provided by the *De Gaulle* task force is as yet incomplete," Commodore Tsukioka told the gathering in the briefing room. "Examination of the data recovered and, more significantly, the interviews with the Junction survivors are at this time ongoing. In particular, the latter's medical condition means that the interview process is slow. Therefore, I must qualify this briefing by saying that both revisions and corrections, are not just possible, but likely."

He paused for any replies. But there was only a grunt from President Clifton that implied he should get on with it.

"The recovery of the Junction Survivors has finally lifted the veil from our opponent, giving us an insight into the history and mindset of the Nameless that we had never expected to receive and fills key gaps in the information provided by the Aèllr," Tsukioka continued. "The majority of the information comes from the testimony of the survivor, Mateusz Bielski."

"Obviously a strong-willed man and one we owe a great debt to," Clifton observed. "But I am surprised that the Nameless interrogator was willing to hand out so much information."

"Perhaps Madam President, their interrogator simply wasn't very good," Wingate said. "But it's more likely that, in so far as they knew, there was no way any intelligence would get back to us, so handing out information in return for information cost them nothing. The fact that the Nameless attempted to murder them just before they were rescued might indicate that they realised the danger. But that is conjecture."

"Before we get to the meat of the matter, Commodore, can you answer a nagging question? Do we now know what the Nameless call themselves?" Clifton asked.

"We believe so," Tsukioka replied. "However, as it appears most of their vocal range is at frequencies too low for us to hear, we can't use it. Besides which, it appears to roughly translate as 'people', so Nameless they remain. Most pertinently, one of the first things we have learned is that neither we nor the Centaurs were the first sentient beings the Nameless have attacked. We are in fact the fourth race to have been subject to their aggression.

"Their first act of genocide dates from the Nameless Diaspora period. As we know, the Nameless race depleted the resources of their home solar system, one located at the very tip of their arm of the galaxy. This latter point is important because as we now know, the distance they can jump from one system to another is limited. This meant that their jump drives – which were at this time newly developed – were operating at the ragged edge of their capabilities. The Nameless launched colony ships, most of which were lost, but at least one though which found a planet on which they could settle. The population that landed on this new world numbered only a few tens of thousands. With such small numbers their attention was, not unreasonably, fixed upon the surface. As a result they failed to observe an approaching alien vessel in real space until it was only a few weeks away from the planet.

"In contrast to their first encounter with us, the Nameless dispatched one of their ships to approach and open a dialogue with the alien vessel. It opened fire without warning, destroying the Nameless ship. It also launched projectiles towards the site of the only major settlement the Nameless had managed to build on the planet. However, while the Nameless ships of the period were crude compared to their modern designs, they were armed and they were jump capable. As such, once the attacking aliens had spent the element of surprise, they were outmatched by the jump capable Nameless and destroyed without further loss."

"Do we know what the motivation of this other race was to mount such an attack?" the Indian Prime Minister asked.

"No," Tsukioka replied. "But if the alien ship had made a real space passage across interstellar space, only to find another race already ensconced, they may have felt they had no choice. Whatever the reason, it proved catastrophic for them. This encounter seems to have had the most profound effect on the Nameless, for it was then that they developed the ideology that other sentient races cannot be allowed to exist – that other races, regardless to whether they are hostile or even capable of being hostile, are a threat. To them, even a benign race – simply through their consumption of resources – threatens the extinction of the Nameless.

"Commodore, I must interrupt," Prime Minister Layland said. "I just don't understand how a race with jump technology can look upon the galaxy and see limited resources. I mean, I can understand when they were limited to a single system, but now?"

"It would appear the fundamental nature of their jump drive technology is in part responsible, Mister Prime Minister," Tsukioka replied. "From the Siege of Earth, we know that the Nameless cannot jump to interstellar space. They must jump from one solar system to another and those individual jumps cannot be too far. Which means the vast starless void between galaxies is a barrier they cannot cross. When this galaxy dies, they will have no means of escape."

When Layland opened his mouth to speak Tsukioka cut him off.

"Sir, this is an alien mindset. It is the worldview that guides them. As humans have demonstrated repeatedly, reality is a matter of opinion. Now moving on, after the attack, they rebuilt, improved their jump drive technology, tracked the aliens back to their home world and destroyed it. Since then, they have destroyed two more races. The Centaurs and a race that had achieve stone-age technology."

"I'm sorry? *Stone age*?" Clifton asked.

"Yes, Madam President, the Nameless – an interstellar capable species – discovered a stone-age culture that had merely achieved flint knapping and basic mastery of fire. Yet they classed them as a threat and eliminated them."

Lewis had been listening silently, but now he spoke up.

"So what you are saying is that the only certain way to end the threat posed by the Nameless would be to inflict genocide on them," he said in an uncompromising tone. "Which is unfortunate; mainly because we are in no position to do it."

"Well, that confirms merely what we already suspected – that the Nameless will not end the war on any terms other than their own," Clifton said. "What else did we get?"

"The jewel in the crown of our discoveries is this."

Tsukioka pressed a control and the conference table's holo came to life, displaying a star map.

"This appears to be their region of space and ours as they know it. This cluster here at the top would seem to be the Nameless core worlds, with an outer ring of settled planets."

"That looks to be a very long way from us," Layland observed.

"They are located in the next arm of the Milky Way, which means that the distance between us and them is vast," Wingate replied. "Up to now that distance has played in our favour, since it has meant that they have not been able to project against us anything even approaching their full strength. But now it means we cannot project our strength against them. Simply put, we couldn't sustain a fleet that far from Earth long enough to win a campaign."

"Raiding cruisers?" asked the Chinese premier.

"An option certainly but raiders won't win a war on their own," Wingate said.

"Alright, carry on Commodore," Clifton said after a moment.

"Several months ago, Admiral Lewis put forward a suggestion that the Nameless used clones or some other kind of manufactured crews. Based on the initial examination of the bodies brought back by the *De Gaulle* task force, this could now be described as a working theory."

Tsukioka paused to operate the holo controls and the star map was replaced by 3D images of two Nameless bodies. Both showed signs of bullet wounds.

"The *De Gaulle* group brought back over a dozen bodies, enough of a sample to identify two clear groups. The one on the left was what we refer to as the workers. The most immediately noticeable difference is here at the head – this computer socket, with wiring that goes deep into the brain. There is no sign of scarring, which suggests that this is not surgically implanted. The opinion from the medical experts so far consulted, indicates that the only way such equipment could be put into place would be by growing the brain around the wiring."

"All examples of such Nameless were dressed in Blue. The specimen on the right was dressed in yellow. Other examples were found in various clothing of various colours and style, but never in Blue. The colour they were in, appeared to pertain to role or rank. None of these Nameless had the computer jack. Further examination indicated there were other more physiological differences."

The image changed. This time they showed each body partly dissected. A few people in the room grimaced.

"The senior doctor with the *De Gaulle* group opened up two of the bodies to perform a basic analysis. She immediately noticed that compared to those Nameless without the computer port, those with it were missing a number of internal organs. Since one of the un-ported bodies was pregnant, she was able to establish the ported Nameless lack any reproductive organs."

"So, is it an artificial life form?" Layland asked.

"Yes, sir," Tsukioka replied.

"A stripped down Nameless," Lewis interjected, "more or less a biological robot, fitted with nothing beyond the equipment it requires to do the job it was bred for."

"But to what end such... modifications?" asked the Indian prime minister.

Tsukioka glanced toward Lewis.

"There is no real evidence at this point to support a genuine theory sir," he said. "But Admiral Lewis had put forward the idea that the Nameless manufacture the ported drones, to use them as a workforce and as the bulk of their military force. It is suggested that these can be grown to a mature state much faster than a 'natural' Nameless. The computer port allows the drones to be 'educated' while they are grown, so when they are decanted, they are ready to serve as workers – soldiers – whatever Nameless society requires. The ones without the ports are the real Nameless. It offers a plausible explanation as to why the Nameless have always taken such a casual attitude to losses. If only the ship's officers are classed as real people, then the drones are treated as lost equipment. Given that the Nameless have been seen to use modified animals from the Centaur planet as foot soldiers, with brain tissue used for computers, it seems they have thoroughly mastered bio manipulation technology."

"Raising the veil seems to raise as many questions as it answers. To create such... abominations..." Clifton trailed off shaking her head.

"Abomination is a human concept," Lewis said. "If you have the technology and the willingness, then potentially you can replace a lost soldier within a few years. Whereas when we lose a man or woman, it takes us at least twenty years to nurture, raise and train their replacement. So, they have a huge advantage."

"It may be that after their original Diaspora, and particularly after the alien attack, the Nameless needed to 'make up the numbers' and from there, the practice took root," Tsukioka said. "But now we are guessing."

"If they are clones, is there any prospect of using biological warfare against them?"

Heads turned sharply. The speaker was the Chinese premier. He looked unperturbed.

"That question has been raised." Tsukioka's eyes flicked towards Lewis. "The answer appears to be no, or at least not in any timeframe available to us. With a completely new species, it will probably take ten years just to achieve enough understanding of their biology to even start work on a biological weapon. And that would still leave open the question of how to deliver such a weapon."

"Regardless of ethics, for practical reasons biological warfare is not the answer," Wingate added. "Anything too lethal will simply burn itself out before it can affect more than a small number of individuals. Anything slow enough to affect a multi-system species, would take longer to destroy such a species than we have. Even if we had such a compound, it would be a last strike revenge weapon at best."

"Alright Admiral. I appreciate that we have not achieved a magic bullet, not yet anyway. What can you tell us of the situation on the front?" Clifton asked.

"It remains as it has since we broke the siege. The Nameless continue to avoid large-scale encounters or indeed any encounters likely to result in casualties. Principally, they are targeting our support ships, while we in turn engage in search and destroy operations against their gate network and supply dumps."

"Is this the time to attempt to liberate Landfall?" the Indian prime minister asked. "Would this not force the Nameless to stand and fight?"

"It would also place a substantial part of our fleet a long way from Earth and make a large number of ground troops vulnerable to being cut off if the fleet were forced to retreat again," Wingate replied.

"Furthermore, such a move would commit a lot of resources to an operation that could not hope to land a knockout blow," Lewis said bluntly. "And a knockout blow is what we need, not a humanitarian mission."

"Admiral Lewis, I appreciate your view that we must win the war with our next blow, but we cannot wait forever," Clifton said. "As you yourself made clear, the window of opportunity is closing. Waiting for the perfect moment is likely to leave us hesitating until the moment is lost."

Lewis nodded.

"We acknowledge that Madam President," Wingate replied, "and our time resources are not being wasted. The fleet has gone a long way towards restoring its strength. When we next commit to action, it will be with a stronger and better prepared fleet than anything the Nameless have ever faced before."

———————————

A cynic would say that most military officers are promoted at least one step beyond their competence. Commodore Tsukioka was not such an officer. When he'd been assigned to head the fleet's intelligence and analysis section, he'd known this was the role his entire career, perhaps even life, had been preparing him for. He'd done his time in line postings but let others command ships and fleets, let them win success and glory in action. He would play his part here in the role nature had equipped him for.

That was generally his view but here and now, if some kind spirit had made him an offer to transport him through time and space to the Nameless space station in return for ten years of his life, he would gladly have taken it. Captain Willis had done well, very well in fact, hoovering up everything she could, but so much remained un-gathered.

The footage from the helmet cameras of every marine involved in the assault had been analysed virtually frame-by-frame. In every shot there were computer panels, storage lockers and bits of equipment that had gone un-investigated. How he yearned to know what they were. But the very last image of the station was the one of it coming apart as plasma bolts tore through it.

"I suppose the big question is how much the Nameless know or think we got," said Tsukioka's deputy, Lieutenant Commander Zindzi.

"If we have been very fortunate the station's last signal will only have warned they were under attack," Tsukioka replied absently. "However, Admiral Nisman is probably correct when he reported the task force's approach made its intent fairly obvious well before they could silence the station. Not that I believe there was any way we could have avoided that. So it seems more reasonable to believe that the Nameless will consider all information on the station potentially compromised."

"The history is interesting. You can sort of see where they've come from since then. Their First Contact nearly ended in extermination, so why ever take that chance again? I just wonder when they made their offer to allow us to quietly die out? Was it before or after the siege?"

"Hmm. The Junction survivors lost all concept of time while in captivity. Most of them thought they'd been prisoners for no more than six months," the Commodore murmured before lapsing into silence and beginning to drum his fingers against his collarbone. Zindzi knew how to read that unconscious action. *Go away, I'm thinking*, it said.

The starmap had indeed been the most vital piece of intelligence they had found. There had been no way to download the information electronically, so instead Captain Willis had used a number of cameras plus several of the marine's recorders to save it in image form. She'd then managed to identify several parts of human space, which had enabled them to marry it to human starmaps. Good work that – he'd have to see if she could be poached for the intelligence section. At the top of the map, clustered like fruit, were the Nameless, tantalisingly close but out of reach. If there was an answer, then Tsukioka felt it had to be there.

He was still standing on the same spot an hour later when Zindzi once more approached him.

"Sir, a courier has just arrived from the front with an intelligence download. *Spectre* reached the front two days ago."

After destroying the enemy station, Nisman's force had retreated back toward Earth with its precious intelligence cargo. But he'd also detached the *Spectre* to confirm several points on the Nameless map beyond the station.

"Anything of relevance?"

"Yes, sir," Zindzi replied, offering a computer pad. "We're incorporating it into the map now, but this is the raw data. Captain Willis discovered it. She doesn't believe she was spotted."

The image quality wasn't especially good. Clearly it had been taken from vast distance using optical sensors. But what could be made out was a gate station, an unusual one. Those they'd seen before had been one or two space gates tethered to a space station, usually at Nameless supply dumps. But this one was on a different scale, six gates formed into a wide circular formation with the station at the centre. At the moment the image was taken, four of the gates had been operational and ships could be seen both entering and exiting.

"Captain Willis reports they also picked up an FTL transmission from the station. It was low powered but steady and she believes it was being used as a homing beacon," Zindzi continued.

"What is its position?" Tsukioka asked.

"Coming up on the map now, sir."

On the screen the icon changed and shifted position slightly, moving further away from the Nameless worlds.

"Captain Willis got a better fix on relative position than we've previously achieved through distant observation," Zindzi explained.

Willis and *Spectre* had been further from the world of their mutual birth than humanity ever had before – a fact that would normally have been worthy of comment but not now. Tsukioka stared at the map and frowned, deep in thought.

"Please overlay a complete starmap with positions of all known stars within scope of the map," he called over his shoulder.

That set off a burst of activity behind him. There were so many solar systems in the galaxy, most were neither in useful positions or contained anything of interest or value, so were mostly stripped out of maps for the sake of clarity. But now all those blips appeared on the map. Except near the top where Willis had found the station. There few stars were visible and those that were, were widely space.

"Where one galactic arm becomes another," Tsukioka said quietly.

The system that station was based in was remarkably isolated, a single star forming a spur out towards the Nameless worlds.

"Without that system, can they reach our region of space?"

Zindzi had seen it as well. She was already hurrying away, shouting at her subordinates to pull out all available starmaps of the edges of the galactic arms.

Chapter Fourteen

The Forgotten Army

23rd July 2068

There was silence within the small hollow as they waited for the Lieutenant to return. As she waited, Alice fiddled nervously with the computer pad. Somewhere out there was a roadway, leading from some kind of Nameless processing centre in the west to croplands they had established in the east. As soon as they had discovered that the Nameless were growing food crops, they'd become an objective. As the head of the small mortar detachment, the faded corporal's chevrons on her sleeve meant something again. When the Colonel persuaded them to join his small command, she had been expecting to return to her former role as a medic and stretcher-bearer. He'd smiled and described her as overqualified for that.

He was a clever man, the Colonel. Grudgingly, she had to give him that. He had ways of getting people to do what he wanted them to do, yet left them feeling he had done them some kind of favour. In the weeks since they'd first made contact with the marines, more groups of survivors had been discovered. Some wanted nothing to do with the marines and were bypassed, but they were in the minority. Most were desperately glad to regain contact, even if only tenuously, with the rest of the human race.

"Movement!" hissed one of the marines.

"We're coming in," someone else called out quietly from beyond view. Lieutenant Byatt crawled down and in, binoculars dangling from his neck, rifle strapped across his back. He was wearing his helmet and chest plate but the rest of his reactive armour was back at base. The power cells the armour required were too difficult to keep charged for regular use.

"Okay, forward party has signalled target is on the move, so we're on," he said. "We hit them as they slow to take the bend." Then turning to Alice, he added: "Mortar section – put down four rounds rapid high explosive along the disengaged side of the road, then move to second position and be ready to drop smoke. Clear?"

"Got it," she replied.

There was a definite nervousness among the pros about having their heavy support manned by what were, at best, enthusiastic amateurs. But there were only so many marines to go round and they lacked the means to really train the amateurs.

"Alright, get moving."

Alice nodded and motioned her seven-man detachment to follow. They quickly made their way through the woods to an area that would barely justify the use of the word clearing. Still, there was an opening through the branches, which they'd widened a few hours earlier to give the mortar a clear view of the sky.

Even after all of this time around the military, it had come as a surprise to Alice to learn how simple a piece of equipment even a modern mortar was. Little more than a tube with a nail at the bottom, all the clever bits were in the support stand. Once hooked up to her computer pad, she could set the mortar to run through a pre-programmed firing pattern, within which it would make the necessary adjustments. Not quite idiot proof, but certainly close. Landfall's GPS satellites had long since been blown from the skies but the pad had an inertial tracking system. All they had to do was to periodically re-zero it and it would do the rest.

Alice supervised her team as they deployed the mortar on the very spot Byatt had selected. They were all young burly lads, selected for strong backs able to lug the mortar and its ammunition. They might have been eager but as raw recruits, her role was, as much as anything, to act as a steadying influence and to make sure they ran when they needed to.

"All set?" she asked.

"Ready to rock and roll," one of them answered brashly.

She did a visual double check and plugged in the pad. As it ran its own diagnostics, she checked the fuses on the four bombs laid out in readiness to fire. Without the luxury of spare ammunition for live fire practice, they'd had to rely on computer simulations. But no one ever claimed sims were enough.

"Alright," she muttered to herself before glancing up at the rest of them. "Sit down, we have a few minutes."

The wait was torturous. It might have been easier if they could have seen or heard something – anything, but they were a good kilometre and a half back from the roadway.

"Shit! Something's got to have happened," muttered a member of the detachment.

"No, it hasn't," Alice replied as she intently studied her pad.

Another five minutes crept past and they all fidgeted uncomfortably. Although she said nothing, Alice was starting to wonder at what point it would become prudent to retreat. For all they knew, the marines might have been blocked, intercepted or the target might have stopped. Then the pad beeped.

"First round into position," she snapped, as the loader leapt forward.

As he raised the bomb over the muzzle he nearly lost his grip and let it slip. Alice intervened just in time to arrest its fall and glared at him. On the pad, a countdown started from five.

"Go!" she said as the count reached zero.

The concussion of the bomb launch propellant took them all by surprise. That hadn't been in the simulation! But the mortar was already adjusting its aim and the pad beeped again.

"Number two! Number two!" Alice barked.

As the second projectile went skyward the crew was already lifting the third into position. As the fourth bomb coughed forth, in the distance there could hear a series of booms at they landed.

"Should we wait to see if..." one man began to say.

"Pack it up and move!" Alice cut him off as she yanked the pad out of its housing and stuffed it into her pack.

The ammunition bearers were already off and running while two other members of the team wrestled out the tube. The last three tried to remove the base plate, but due to concussion it had been forced into the ground and they couldn't get purchase. Swearing savagely, Alice snatched the crowbar they'd brought for that very purpose. Ramming it under the lip of the plate, she levered it up.

"Go! Go! Go!" she shouted as they got it out and the four of them set off after the others.

In the distance she could hear the report of small arms fire interspersed by the heavier rattle of the machinegun. By the time they reached the number two point, over a kilometre distant from the first, there was a stitch in her side and Alice was wheezing like a broken bellows. But they got the mortar set up and gathered their breath as they waited.

In the distance, the shooting petered out and Alice glanced at her watch. If the ambush had gone to plan the marines would be starting to fall back by now. Then Alice caught the sound of something she had not heard since Douglas Base and had hoped never to hear again – incoming missiles.

"Get down!" she roared as she dived for the ground.

Explosions ripped through the forest in and around their former position. The next salvo to land was further away. As she hugged the earth, the radio briefly crackled to life in her ear.

"All units fall back to the rally point."

Incoming missiles were still tearing up the forest. Given time, the whole area was likely to be blanketed in explosives. But for the moment they were clear.

"Everyone up!" Alice called out as she scrambled to her feet. "We're bugging out!"

A series of images clicked up on the screen. In the first, a convoy of bulk cargo movers burned. The cab area of each machine was riddled with bullet holes. In the next image, fires burned across acres of what had been ripening crops, while the foreground harvester exploded. As the last of the images disappeared, Colonel Dautsch rose from his seat.

"A complete success," he said as he slapped the table enthusiastically. "Everyone did very well. Four bulk movers destroyed and several harvester and irrigation machines knocked out. There's no doubt that we've completely neutralised food production efforts in this region. This was our first big operation and it has been a success. Well done to you all."

Alice slipped out of the command tent a short while later and into the night. Unlike most of those who had taken part in the attack, she didn't much feel like celebrating.

The marine camp was at the north edge of a roughly fifty kilometre wide circle that they semi-jokingly referred to as Camp Dautsch.

"You look perturbed," the man himself observed as he approached Alice.

She was lying on the ground, staring up through the branches of the forest canopy at the stars. Behind them she could hear the celebration still going on. It had taken a week to make it back to base after the raid, but sore feet weren't the only reason she didn't feel much like partying.

"Anyone else would just say worried," she replied without looking round.

"So you are worried?"

"For about two years and counting," she said. "I wonder whether we've woken the sleeping giant."

Dautsch settled himself beside her.

"They were never really sleeping," he replied. "But yes, we have definitely made them aware that we are out here. An unavoidable side effect I'm afraid."

"Is it really worth it, Colonel? I mean, how will the loss of a few trucks affect a war?"

"On its own, it's not. Then again, there is pretty much nothing that does," he replied calmly. "But we are forcing them to consume resources protecting both their farm lands and supply lines. That's often how war is waged as a resources game where it's about how much you have and how efficiently you use it. We don't know why they were growing those crops. They could be to support settlers they intend to bring in or it could be to feed their military. Either way, at least we put a small spanner in their works."

The next few months passed mostly quietly with periodic spasms of activity. There were several more attacks. Dautsch was careful to ensure that their operations did not centre on the region of the farms and camps. Instead, he chose a blank spot on the map and made sure any activities, which the Nameless were likely to be aware of, circled this point.

A couple of months after the first attack, the Nameless finally put two and two together. They carpet bombed the area and then repeatedly hit it from orbit. By that time however, the marines had expended most of their ammunition and Dautsch was content to allow the Nameless to think that their problem had been solved. So that, Alice assumed, was that.

"We need to make contact," Dautsch opened the weekly meeting.

Most of the group had dispersed across the whole region in preparation for the harvest season, when every strong back would be needed to get the crops in.

"With who?" asked William.

Dautsch pointed directly upwards.

"Those scout ships are coming through weekly now," he said. "I know that we've all found it a comfort to hear those transmissions, but we need something more substantial than comfort."

"A supply drop, sir? Into enemy held territory?" Martoma asked.

"Well, those who don't ask, don't get," Dautsch replied glibly, before assuming a more serious expression. "There are a number of good reasons to contact the fleet. Firstly and if possible, a supply drop would improve our position. Secondly, at the moment we know that they're there, but they don't know we're here. If they know for certain that people still remain, then that might encourage them to get a move on and liberate the planet. However, the challenge isn't to find a reason to communicate with the scouts – it's to find a means that doesn't immediately invite an orbital strike on our position."

"Well, broadly you have two options," said Stephan Host, a pre-war communications technician, "radio or laser. Laser requires a tracking system to aim it..."

"Which we don't have anymore," Alice interrupted.

"Correct," Host agreed. "That leaves us with option number two – a radio transmission."

"Which the Nameless will hear and respond to," Martoma said.

"Yup," Host nodded.

"Is a big transmitter needed?" Alice asked.

"No." This time Dautsch was the one to reply. "Those scouts have very sensitive communications packages and they are coming pretty close to Landfall."

"Well, there are still a lot of radio transmitters around. Every human settlements should have one," Martoma said.

"Yeah," Host added enthusiastically. "In fact, we can use a lot of old hardware. There are hard lines connecting various settlements. It wouldn't be hard to rig a set-up that will allow us to send a transmission while staying a nice comfortable distance from the transmitter."

"Pity we'll get some settlement blown off the map for the sake of one message," Alice remarked.

"Hopefully they'll do that," Dautsch said.

When they looked at him he added: "I'm perfectly happy for them to keep thinking they can solve problems by bombing them instead of putting boots on the ground."

Three weeks later Alice waited patiently as Host fussed with the connection where they'd spliced into the fibre optic cable. With the harvest of the banana patata crops under way, only a small detachment with a couple of marines for protection could be spared. It had been a nerve-wracking week, creeping into the small town that had once been a part of the Italian colony on Landfall. Aside from a number of wind turbines spinning on one of the hills that surrounded the settlement, nothing had been moving. There were signs of a hurried evacuation and the flora of Landfall was already beginning to reclaim this small abandoned outpost of humankind. There had been no way to know whether the Nameless were watching. To Alice, it would have made a lot of sense for them to do so. There were substantial amounts of useful supplies lying around – in many respects the town could easily have been a tethered goat. But the Nameless failed to put in an appearance before they reactivated the small radio transmitter they'd found in the town hall.

"Okaaayyy..." Host muttered to himself.

"Are we ready?" she asked.

"We are indeed."

Alice looked upwards.

"Now we just need them to turn up."

They were waiting for over a day, with each ten-man detachment taking its turn listening to the radio. During her time off, Alice attempted to teach herself Italian using one of the old paper books she'd picked up in the settlement. Finally the radio chirped into life.

"Landfall, this is Battle Fleet scout ship K7, signalling in the blind."

Alice closed her eyes. She hadn't listened, hadn't wanted to listen, to any of the previous transmissions. It had just been too painful.

"Landfall, this is Battle Fleet scout ship K7, signalling in the blind," the radio repeated.

"All right, Host," she said, her throat unaccountably dry.

"We are live and on air," he said as he activated their pre-recorded signal.

"Landfall, this is Battle Fleet scout ship K7..."

Then they cut in with their message, which had been recorded by the Colonel. There was no way to know how much of human communication the Nameless understood, so it was baldly factual but with the fewest details he had judged necessary. Alice looked to the north and the distant hills between them and the settlement, expecting at any moment to see a kinetic strike projectile spear down from the clouds.

The radio went silent as Dautsch's message finished.

"Come on, come on," Host whispered.

"Landfall, this is Battle Fleet scout ship K7 to Colonel Dautsch. Message received."

There was a pause – long enough for Alice to conclude that was all they were getting. Then it crackled into life again.

"Hang on in there, Landfall. We're coming."

"Alright," Alice said in a choked voice, "let's get packed up. I want to be ten kilometres away from here by nightfall."

An hour later they were making good time directly away from the settlement when the marine out front shouted out.

"Aircraft! Cover!"

Everyone went to ground.

From the ditch into which she rolled, Alice waited and listened. Something thundered directly over them and she braced for the shock of bombs, but nothing came. Sitting up she caught sight of one of the Nameless's big airship-like gunboats moving away, on course for the Italian settlement.

Chapter Fifteen

Drumbeat

31st August 2068

The small conference room darkened as the projector came on.

"Four point seven light years is the largest gap between solar systems that we have ever observed the Nameless traverse. If a jump from one system to another involves a greater distance than that, then the Nameless find a route that involves smaller steps, even if that entails a substantial detour. Certain very isolated solar systems appear to be beyond their reach, something we have used in the past and continue to use to establish secure bases."

"Yes, this is all very established but what is it that the intelligence section thinks gives us a strategic opportunity?" Wingate asked.

"This, sir," Tsukioka replied. "This map is derived from one seized by the *De Gaulle* task force. Of course, much of the military information on it will most likely be out of date as the Nameless shift supply dumps and gates to prevent us targeting them. But there are things they cannot change."

"Yes, their home worlds," Admiral Fengzi interrupted, "but we cannot project a fleet that far for long enough to win a campaign. The logistics are simply beyond us."

"I wasn't referring to the home worlds, sir," Tsukioka said. "I'm talking about this system here – one we which in Intelligence refer to as The Spur. It is in effect the first stepping stone from their arm of the galaxy to ours."

"What distance is it from the first system in the Nameless arm?" Lewis asked as he studied the map.

"Four point nine three light years."

"That's..."

"Yes sir, further than any other jump we have seen."

"So it disproves the four point seven limit theory?" Fengzi asked.

"Perhaps not sir. It is the only gate installation that we have ever seen transmit a beacon. We in intelligence believe those two points to be related. We think that this distance of four point nine three is... the ragged edge of their jump capability. Even with a gate station, they can only make the jump with a beacon to home in on. Without that beacon, the jump becomes impossible. So if this system is taken from them, then the Nameless cannot reach us."

"And simply going towards the galactic core, where the arms converge – why isn't that an option?" Wingate asked.

Tsukioka flicked a control and the computer ran through multiple navigation permutations until it settled on one.

"According to our star charts and distant observations, without the Spur and making no individual jumps further than four point nine three light years, this is the next shortest route from the Nameless worlds to Earth. As you say, they would have to travel inwards towards the galactic core, where the arms converge and star density is higher, then cross through the Aèllr Confederacy or dogleg round it. The distance between them and us would at least triple. We believe the distance they are already fighting across is near the limit of their capabilities. Even if they could manage it, the fleet they already have in our arm will have starved before they can re-establish a supply channel. Without the Spur, the war is over."

Lights came back on, but the room remained silent.

"Paul, what do you think?" Wingate asked.

"Interesting," Lewis said thoughtfully. "It is a possible target but we need to know more. A few optical images aren't enough to base an attack on. How long to get ships out there again and make repeated reconnaissance passes?"

"It's a long way. The turn around time for even our fastest couriers would be six weeks," Tsukioka replied. "That's once we get a relay of supply ships into position."

"Which is a hell of a long way," Wingate commented.

"The solution to our problems would hardly be next door," Fengzi said.

"Sadly not, but it means we will have to commit to an attack based on information that will be months out of date by the time any combat units can arrive in the area," Lewis replied.

"Follow up missions are a given," Wingate said. "We need to

work out where to place and route vessels to allow a continuous loop of reconnaissance ships.

"Some of these more isolated systems, which the Nameless can't reach, offer us secure locations," Lewis said, pointing to a number of possibilities. "In fact, we must start putting together some kind of logistical chain now. Otherwise it will be impossible keep a fleet in the field at such distance if we have to heave everything from Earth."

"Get forward supply dumps in place at the least," Fengzi replied. "We can start that now. If we can, find gas giants we can use for fuel supply."

"Which means the reconnaissance ships will have to perform a more generalised survey of the entire region," Wingate added, as he began to take notes.

The Commodore was forgotten as the three officers began to brainstorm.

"One of the problems we'll have to face is that we'll be pressing them back on their own supply lines for the first time," Lewis said during a pause.

The meeting had been going on for several hours. Staff officers had been called in and sent out for information while Wingate had departed to drum up information, leaving the commanders of the Home and Second Fleets to continue. Cold, forgotten mugs of tea and coffee were scattered across the table. They were making steady progress in identifying potential problems. Solutions would take longer.

"What are you thinking?" Fengzi asked.

"That we'll be a lot closer to their worlds than ours," Lewis replied, "and closer to whatever units they retain there."

"A home fleet?"

"Or fleets. We only have one really critical world to defend and in peacetime at least a third of our fleet is based here. They have a dozen. Based on the historical information, I can't see the Nameless leaving their worlds undefended."

Lewis paused to consider the map again.

"With the losses they took during the siege, I think they've had to feed forward at least some units to maintain a presence on the front."

"Definitely," Fengzi agreed. "There were at least six heavy units that weren't I.D'd before the siege, but have been seen since. You think there are more?"

"I'd bet my pension, and yours, on it," Lewis replied. "The problem with an assault on the Spur is that it is close enough for the Nameless to commit their home fleet to the fighting without heavy logistical support."

"So, those ships have to be given a reason, a good reason, to remain close to their home worlds."

Lewis drummed the edge of the table with his fingers.

"We have a number of un-answerables here. The beacon, if that's what it is, is there for a reason. But do they need just an initial fix to jump, or do they need it to be active for the entire transit to home in on?"

"Well, the beacon was on for the entire period *Spectre* had it under observation, so I would guess the latter," Fengzi said.

"Unfortunately, that's a guess."

"Yes, but a logical one."

"It makes a big difference, though," Lewis replied. "If they need only a single pulse, then any Nameless warship on this side of the rift can supply it. While the loss of the gate will cut off most of their supply ships, warships would still be able to make the jump from their side of the rift and into the fighting at the Spur."

"But if they need a continuous signal, then the Nameless are in a more serious position," Fengzi said thoughtfully. "If we had warships in system, then any FTL beacon would give our ships the real time position of whatever ship was providing it. Our ships would reach the signaller before those jumping from the far side of the rift. If they need a continuous transmission, then it follows that to lose the transmission mid jump might be too dangerous to risk. In effect, they would have to force our ships out of the system before they dared activate a beacon."

"They crossed it once so I'd be inclined to say they could do it again, especially since they have so many assets already in this arm of the galaxy," Lewis said

"Yes, but at what price?" Fengzi countered. "It could have been a slow-boat passage or it needed specialist ships. It might even be that several or many ships attempted the passage until one succeeded and provided a beacon to those that followed. It's not as if they are afraid of casualties."

"True," Lewis grunted. "Or they simply mounted an expedition in towards the galactic core, then worked their way back up to the Spur and built the gate station."

"That's probably the most likely," Fengzi conceded. "Their

method isn't important though."

The two men paused, both of them staring at the map, both searching for some kind of enlightenment.

"So, we're already up to a multi-part operation," Lewis said eventually. "One: assault and destroy the gate. Two: contest the system long enough for the Nameless fleet to be starved of supplies. Three: find a way to pin down the Nameless home fleets so that even if they can make the passage, they cannot leave their home worlds exposed."

"There is another point I would add to that," Fengzi said. "If the Spur really is the holy grail, then the Nameless will throw in everything to hold or regain it. Before we go in against it, we need to force them to commit their resources elsewhere. We need multiple contact points spread across multiple systems."

"Continuous assault?"

"In effect," Fengzi nodded. "Anywhere that we can make contact with the enemy, we engage them. If or when they fall back, we follow for as long as we can. Force them to burn the candle at both ends."

Lewis nodded slowly as he considered the point, then finally sat back in his seat.

"One thing for sure," he said. "While this might be our big chance, we'll only have the strength to try once."

17th November 2068

"As much as I dislike clichés," Alanna said over her shoulder, "but were we ever that young?"

"No Skip, we were always profoundly more mature and experienced," Schurenhofer replied as she leaned on the back of Alanna's seat to view the holo. "Probably better looking as well."

Not that you were around, Alanna thought to herself. Schurenhofer hadn't been there for the first days of the war – at least not in fighters. She'd done advanced fighter training, but before the war there had only been a need for so many new crews each year, with the result that only the best of them that made the cut. Now crews were being rushed through training as fast as the fleet dared – maybe slightly faster.

A dozen blips signifying the fighters of the training squadron swirled around one another as they fought for position. The trainees themselves were in simulator pods, which spun and jolted to recreate the G-forces of real flight. The effect for the outside observer was that of twelve huge and epileptic gyroscopes. It was no wonder the hall was nicknamed the Funfair. With the end of the siege and *Dauntless* heading for the repair docks, they'd been put off the ship. Schurenhofer was overdue and Alanna wildly overdue a rest period, so after they'd been dispatched for few weeks leave, the fleet posted them both to the advanced fighter training base on the moon. Alanna had expected the trainees to be the kind of people she remembered – young, cocky and kinda stupid. But those being raced through the programme were of a different breed – not least because they were aware of previous fighter crew losses. Most were eager to absorb the experience their predecessors had paid for so dearly.

Alanna was glad she and Schurenhofer had both been assigned. After so long and so much together, it would be hard to get used to a new weapons operator. She'd even managed to keep hold of *D for Dubious*, which had been given a thorough overhaul before being returned. Alanna doubted the huge, faceless and generally uncaring administration was showing any favouritism. Things were just going her way, for a while at least.

"Do you reckon these guys will be ready for the push?" Schurenhofer asked.

"It will be tough for them if they aren't."

As she watched, four of the pods had gone stationary as the main computer registered them as destroyed. The scenario was a basic six on six engagement, not the most educational but every so often it was good to let pilots have a little play with the toys.

The Big Push: it now seemed to be the only bloody thing anyone talked about. There was still fighting going on out in the region of the Junction Line but that wasn't getting attention from anyone not actively involved. Some ships were in dock for modifications no one was allowed to talk about, while others were heading out past the front line. Everyone knew that the big one was coming, everyone had heard tales of experimental super weapons but officialdom was saying nothing – very, very loudly!

"True," Schurenhofer replied, "once more unto the bloody breach; any idea where we're going?"

"Officially I haven't heard anything. Unofficially, probably back to *Dauntless*. Now where the hell will *Dauntless* be? That's the million dollar question."

As she spoke another two pods shuddered to a halt.

"It sounds like everyone with enough training to fly a fighter and find the fire button after no more than two attempts will be out there."

On the screen, one side had been whittled down to a single fighter that now dodged and weaved desperately. On the opposing side, three others attempted to box it in.

"The only people who'll be left around here are the ones who haven't even completed basic," she finished.

"The grapevine reckons this will be the last throw," Schurenhofer replied. "End game and all that jazz."

"Makes sense," Alanna agreed.

The last pilot was doing well to be holding off three opponents. He winged one of his tormentors but the computer was registering that this had come at the price of a strained spaceframe and engines that were close to overheating.

"Have you ever thought about what you'll do after the war?"

"No."

"What, just 'no'?"

"Just no. No point thinking about the future if you won't even make it through the next moment."

"I'm thinking about leaving the fleet, after the war of course. Probably won't have enough years to get full pension rights, but I'd be close enough," Schurenhofer said.

Alanna glanced over her shoulder. Funny how you could spend so much time with someone and not really know them – they'd been flying together for over a year and they'd never really talked about anything outside of the fleet.

"Any idea what you'll do?"

"There are a fair number of jobs I could go for. I'd also like to have a family and, well... there's a guy."

Schurenhofer paused and looked slightly embarrassed.

"I knew him in school," she said, "we've been talking by email. I'd like to get to know him better."

"Talking? Is that what you kids are calling it these days?"

"Hur, Hur. Seriously though, what about you?"

Alanna stared into the middle distance for a moment.

"Mars."

"Mars? It's a dump."

"Right now, maybe. I might shoot for a piloting or even management position in the terraforming project. At the very least I'll cash in on a promise to be given the full tour." Alanna paused and shrugged. "But no point in worrying about it until I know whether I'll get there."

Another pod shut down. The 'battle' was over.

"Okay," Alanna said standing up, "let's tell them what they did wrong."

7th December 2068

"Well, that was predictable," Lewis said as he straightened up. "We hit a location within three systems of the Spur, then it was inevitable that the Nameless would fortify."

"Maybe, maybe not."

Fengzi was still leaning over the table. The image was the first to arrive from the Spur since the *Spectre* made the original discovery. It was an ultra high-resolution optical picture with an astonishing level of detail, but what it revealed was heartbreaking. The super gate station was located above a Mars-like planet, locked in position at the Lagrange point between the planet and its attendant moon. The orbit of the planet bristled with defensive satellites and the moon's surface showed even more fixed defences. Finally, dozens of Nameless warships floated around. A few showed signs of battle damage, but most were fully ready to offer defence.

"The surface defences would be the product of years of work," Fengzi continued, "and clearly it's still being expanded. That certainly tells me that this is critical ground for the Worms."

"It tells me things too," Lewis said with less enthusiasm. "It tells me they don't intend to lose it and that a conventional assault will incur such unacceptably high losses in the opening stages that we won't be able to fight the second stage."

"Then an *unconventional* assault," Fengzi snapped.

"Yes," said Lewis thoughtfully as he motioned forwards his chief of staff.

15th December 2068

Wingate sat alone with his thoughts in the small waiting room. Unconsciously he ran his good hand over the nubs of his missing fingers.

Time was slipping away from them and this was more appropriately the role of Secretary Callahan, but it was no great surprise that she had chosen to bypass him. The door opened and a White House aide slipped in.

"Admiral Wingate sir," he said respectfully. "The President will see you now."

"Thank you," he replied as he tucked his cap under his arm.

President Clifton rose from behind the famous desk.

"Ah, Admiral, thank you for coming. Please be seated."

The President quickly cut to the chase.

"Admiral Wingate, I know this is irregular and apologise for dragging you all the way from Dublin, but I feel we must discuss the fleet's proposed assault."

"Which aspect, Madam President?"

"I think you know which part, Admiral. I have received the Pentagon's report regarding their ability to make the arrangements requested by the fleet. They have stated that the necessary changes can be made to these weapons. The Joint Chiefs of Staff have examined the fleet's proposal and agree with it. Yet, I am troubled.

"Admiral Wingate, the fleet proposes to use enhanced fallout nuclear weapons against civilian targets. I do wonder whether the fleet has considered the ethics of its proposal?"

"In part, yes," Wingate replied. "But we have mostly considered the practical considerations."

"Practical considerations!" Clifton exclaimed. "Practicality and military necessity have been used to justify a great deal. An orbital bombardment using kinetic strike weapons could level a city with one or two hits. Dear God, Admiral, how can this be justified?"

"Because we know the Nameless are driven by their motivation to acquire resources and above all living space. The reason we seek authorisation to deploy Cobalt Sixty enhanced fallout nuclear bombs, is that these are the only weapons we possess that will render a planet lifeless – permanently lifeless."

"And a regular nuclear bomb isn't good enough! The design for such weapons was a product of sheer wrong thinking during the Cold War period," Clifton objected.

She stood up and began pacing back and forth across the Oval Office.

"We are talking about weapons that will cause such devastating radioactive fallout that those vaporised in the first blast will be considered the lucky ones! In effect Wingate, you are asking for permission to commit something which in my view could be judged a war crime!"

"Without question it's a very big ask and one that I accept is extremely difficult for you to grant," Wingate replied with a determined calm. "I do not doubt that there will be those that will say that this was a line that should not have been crossed. But those people are not here. Most of them have never put themselves forward to be the ones to make the hard decisions."

Clifton was about to reply but Wingate raised a finger.

"With all respect, Madam President, I'm not finished."

She nodded for him to continue.

"We *need* to pin the Nameless home fleet in place. And I emphasise it's not a matter of wanting, but needing to. To the best of our knowledge, the only means by which we can do so is to attack one of their planets. Even if that attack is not completely successful, as long as we continue to possess any means by which to repeat the feat, the Nameless will have to retain a disproportionate force at each of their planets to be absolutely certain it is protected. As for the ethical considerations... well ethics are easy when consequences are limited. The question has to be, if this is an ethical red line, are we prepared to pay the price for *not* crossing it?"

"The fleet's proposed offensive represents our last and probably only real hope of beating back the Nameless. This in turn is our only hope for peace. Given our opponent's war aims – namely our eradication as a species, then the price of failure will be extinction. Are we then prepared to reduce our own chances, rather than use these weapons?"

Clifton walked over to the Oval Office windows and stared out.

"One of the great causes I have embraced since my very first day in politics is nuclear disarmament. Did you know that?" she asked over her shoulder.

"Yes, Madam President," he replied.

"Now you are asking me to authorise the use of weapons that are the very epitome of salting the ground and poisoning the wells. If I'd known that the plans and research for these weapons still existed when I came into office, I would have had them destroyed. But now, now I have the military telling me this is the only way we can survive and the only arguments the dissenters can offer are ethical."

Wingate made no reply.

"I will give the order for these weapons to be prepared and transferred because I believe I have no choice. But I am certain of one thing, Admiral, posterity will not thank us for this."

"I know, Madam President, but we have been forced down this road. With the benefit of hindsight, future generations may say it was wrong and that there were other routes we might have taken. But based on the information we have, staying our hand is a luxury we cannot afford."

"And in doing so, commit an unforgivable act," she said. "But we will do what we must and hope that future generations will at least understand why."

Wingate maintained his poise until out of the White House and on his way to DC Airport. Only then did he let out a long sigh of relief and tell his chief of staff.

"We have them."

23rd December 2068

"Jeff?"

Jeff Harlow looked up guiltily from his screen. There was a whole pile of things he really should be doing. But he was working on his book on company time – naughty, naughty. Not that Jen cared. She was just the messenger.

"Rich wants to see you in his office?"

"What about?"

"Not a clue," she replied as she turned away. Jeff shook his head. How someone could work for a news network and be so determinedly uncurious was one of life's little mysteries.

"Thanks Jen," he said getting up, "as informative as ever."

Richard was eating a sandwich when Jeff came in.

"Hi Jeff, what do you know about the Big Push?" he said without any preamble.

"That nine out of ten cats prefer it to other brands," Jeff replied as he sat down.

"Well it's about to get even pushier. This assault, offensive or whatever the military insist on calling it, is starting soon. The fleet is showing its usual fondness for embedded journalists but it looks like they'll be forced to take a few of us along. Management really wants you to be our guy. You are a known face and, frankly, your reports have generally been favourable enough for the fleet to regard you as friendly."

"Hey!" Jeff objected, "I'm not a military toady!"

"I know, I know. It's just that you've been around enough to cover good news stuff. We can work with that," Richard said soothingly. "There's no guarantee you'll be going any damn place, but we do need to know right now if you're in."

Jeff leaned back in his chair as he considered the offer. The last time he'd been an embedded journalist he'd found himself in action several times – and it had always scared the shit out of him. As soon as the network offered him a posting back on Earth he'd grabbed it with both hands. But then the siege had come and he realised he'd probably got out at the wrong time. There'd been a newbie for CNN, Rebecca something-or-other, who'd managed to get herself on board the *Illustrious*. Her reports had made her a household name. Okay, she'd lost half an arm to a flying missile fragment but the lucky bitch was *made*. Then that guy from Reuters, who'd somehow managed to get the first pictures of the Nameless bodies brought back and coined the name Worms for them. That lucky, lucky bastard! He'd been stuck in London for the siege, taken off air by the power failures and forgotten by the public as the grand ballet was danced above their heads. Okay, Mom wouldn't be happy about him going up again but if he simply didn't mention it over Christmas, problem solved.

"Where would I be?"

"Don't know yet. The Fleet is being awkward. Their Governing Council will probably force them into it but for the moment they aren't even prepared to say how many they'll take. So, we need to be able to put someone forward without knowing where. Hell, they might just dump everyone on a transport somewhere and apologise afterwards."

"No exclusivity?"

"I think some network – FOX or BBC I think... maybe Reuters – demanded they be given the exclusive on the coverage of the whole shebang."

Jeff raised an eyebrow.

"What was the fleet's response to that?"

"Let's just say if we were to repeat it word for word in our next bulletin, the regulator would slap us very hard for indecency."

"Hah! Okay Rich, I'm in."

3rd January 2069

Wingate turned to watch as the last of the ratings were hustled out of the Council Chamber and staff officers checked no other unauthorised personnel were present. The collection of operations was the most ambitious Battle Fleet had every seriously considered. K.I.S.S. – Keep It Simple Stupid – had always been the cornerstone of the fleet's military planning. But this, this whole plan, was a series of precisely planned manoeuvres – a virtual house of cards in which one misstep could leave them open and vulnerable. But it was what they had. He'd allowed Lewis and Fengzi to take the driving seat in the planning, while he looked for a simpler way to achieve the same ends. If there was such a way it wasn't too be found. Preparations were well under way, ships were being modified and they were sourcing nuclear weapons that the fleet didn't normally have access to.

Secretary Callahan was talking quietly to both Admirals Lewis and Fengzi. His role within the fleet had somewhat diminished during wartime, as world leaders sought to deal directly with those in uniform, rather than go through a middleman. Callahan seemed to have taken this effective demotion calmly, which was probably inevitable given he was dealing with a military that didn't answer to a single government.

So much of what needed to be done had to be started while plans were still being made. Unavoidably, some effort had been wasted as projects were started, then abandoned as plans changed. In peacetime that would have castigated as gross project mismanagement, but here and now it was a painful necessity and Callahan had been successful in heading off criticism. As the late arrivals made their way in, the holos of the Council members started to flicker into life and they all stood. Wingate waited patiently as the last of them came online. The heads of governments not currently on rotation on the Council would also be listening in, albeit without an avatar through which to interact.

"Admiral Wingate," President Clifton said as she looked up and down the fleet's side of the table. "Please everyone, sit. I hope everyone enjoyed the New Year I hope it marks an improvement in our circumstances. Now I believe we have a lot of ground to cover. Admiral, please begin."

"Thank you, Madam President," Wingate replied as he stood. "Council Members, you are all already aware of the broad details of the proposed operation, but I intend to start with a brief summary before moving onto the fine detail. This will be a series of interconnected operations with the primary operation aimed at seizing and holding the solar system we have designated The Spur, which by cutting off the Nameless forces in this arm of the galaxy, will result in either their destruction or retreat. The secondary operations will be aimed at distracting and diverting enemy resources from the Spur. There will be four sub-operations – Rage, Fury, Retribution and Vindictive.

"The first two, Rage and Fury, will be diversionary operations aimed at pulling Nameless units forward. Fury will be a fast convoy through to Landfall. We have become aware from our reconnaissance ships that a small number of combat units from both Douglas and Endeavour Base remain active. The blockade-runners will drop small arms to those groups, with instructions to mount attacks on ground-based Nameless facilities. Rage will be a drive towards Landfall by the Second Fleet under Admiral Fengzi. Their role is to draw Nameless units in and force them to consume resources from their forward supply dumps. In doing so, we will weaken the Nameless forces in theatre, before the start of the next pair of operations.

"These operations are codenamed Retribution and Vindictive. Retribution, under Commodore Tneba, will be the third and most important of the three diversionary operations. A small force of cruisers and a bombard will travel from our galactic arm, across the rift and into that of the Nameless. The purpose of this force will be to launch an orbital strike against the principal planet of the first enemy system on their side of the Rift. This system has been codenamed Kingdom. The purpose of this strike is to tie down their reserves in a defensive posture and so deprive them of assets to counter the final operation. Codenamed Vindictive, its aim is to cut the link between the Nameless worlds and our own by destroying the gate station that gives them access across the Rift. Then we hold the system, thereby starving their fleet of resources. The overall name for these operations will be Drumbeat."

"Admiral Wingate," Prime Minister Layland said, "before we go any further I must ask – would it not make more sense to reduce or abandon Fury and Rage and instead concentrate our efforts on the two most important operations?"

"Regrettably, it is not an option to do so, sir," Wingate replied. "The fleet assaulting the Spur is the largest we can sustain at such a distance."

"Even if we took the ships that are to be used to drop supplies on Landfall?" Layland persisted.

"Once the drop is complete, they will operate in support of the Second Fleet. Being smaller and faster transports they are better suited to supplying mobile operations."

"Admiral, I am... I wonder whether a drop on Landfall is sensible. Whatever survivors of the colonies remain, they have suffered much already. Are we not risking drawing more suffering down on their heads?"

Ah, Wingate thought. "Sir, these groups have requested military supplies. As for making them targets, given the war aims of the Nameless... This will change little other than give them a means to fight back."

Layland relented, although obviously still unhappy.

Wingate looked around before continuing.

"Moving on then to the fine detail..."

"Thank you for seeing me, sir," Crowe said as he came to attention.

"Make it brief, Commodore," Lewis said glancing up from a report sheet.

"I understand the *Mississippi* has been reactivated, I am here to request information as to what is being done with her."

Lewis looked up sharply, his eyes narrowing.

"I was never taken off the books, sir. I am officially still her captain and it is my right to request information on any work being carried out on my ship."

Rumours regarding the Big Push had been doing the rounds since the *De Gaulle* task force had returned. As an officer Crowe wasn't supposed to heed the grapevine, but you couldn't legislate for human nature. Amidst all of the conflicting rumours, there was one detail that stood out like a beacon for Crowe.

After that first shattering encounter, *Mississippi* had been pushed into a lunar orbit to await the attention of the breaker's yard. When war came, she'd been out of harm's way, the formalities of official decommissioning forgotten. As soon as he found out she'd gone into dock, Crowe knew he had to find out why.

"She's being modified, Commodore, to give me another option when we reach the Spur," Lewis replied as he brought up a document on his pad and passed it over. "When the Home Fleet leaves Earth, the most recent information we have from the Spur will be weeks out of date. So fine detail planning is impossible. Instead, we have a number of broad outlines. *Mississippi* has a place in one of them.

Crowe worked to prevent surprise from showing on his face. A right to request information was far removed from a right to receive it. As he read down the pad though, he felt his heart sink.

"Lieutenant Commander Huso is slated to command should *Mississippi* go in," Lewis informed him.

"I know her, sir. She's a good officer," Crowe replied slowly as he read, "but she hasn't served in a River class in over ten years."

"Given that the class is borderline obsolete, very few top-flight officers with the necessary seniority have recent experience," Lewis replied.

"I do, sir," Crowe said as he returned the pad.

"You also have a ship, an important one."

"Yes, sir," Crowe replied, "but if we have to use her like this, then we'll only have one shot. I believe I stand a better chance of putting her in than any officer alive."

"She's been subject to extensive modifications – past experience may not be as useful as you imagine," Lewis pointed out.

"I stand by my previous comment, sir."

Lewis stared at Crowe thoughtfully.

"Sentimentality, Commodore?"

"In part sir, yes," Crowe replied without hesitation. "But better this than the breaker's yard."

Lewis stared at Crowe for several seconds. Crowe had to force himself not to fidget under the older man's gaze. He could feel the judgement in those cold blue eyes.

"Very well, Commodore. If it comes to it, you will command.

Lewis tapped a message into his computer pad.

"I've now authorised you to be briefed on the modifications. You're dismissed."

Lewis's chief of staff Captain Sheehan entered just as Crowe left. He eyed the departing commodore curiously before speaking.

"I didn't think you would tell him, sir."

"Sometimes, Captain, it's better to let a man's demons drive him," Lewis replied as he returned to his reading. "But if he'd lied to me or himself, I'd have taken both ships off him."

Two days later

"Well we've had to make a lot of modifications sir, on top of the repairs she required," said the staff officer as they pulled themselves through the airlock. "That has meant a lot of work on a very tight schedule."

"We originally thought we'd be using the *Nile*," she continued, "but on closer examination she proved to have major fractures in two of her longitudinal beams and a long period under full thrust would likely break her back. So it had to be the *Mississippi*. Now there is buckling to the number three longitudinal beam, which is likely to cause vibration in Number Three Engine, so I recommend you only use that engine for full thrust situations. As you saw on the approach, B and D turrets have been pulled out and replaced with flak guns. Obviously we had to plate over the gap and more or less put in a barbette within a barbette. We've filled in the gap between the two, and several other cavities, with composite foam. That also improves the stiffening. We are also expanding the ready to use magazines for the point defence guns..."

The young woman's voice faded into the background as Crowe looked around the *Mississippi* personnel reception area. The last time he'd been here had been three years previously, after *Mississippi* limped home from that first fateful encounter. So much was so familiar, which made the differences so painfully obvious. New hatches had been crudely cut to allow access in or out for equipment. The paintwork was battered and blistered and there were none of the human touches that made a ship a living thing.

"This way please, sir."

Crowe followed without comment. Was it a mistake to be here? He'd asked for this.

"The modifications have added quite a lot of mass, so to compensate we've pulled out most of the crew facilities. Even though the transit crew will comprise of only ten individuals, they will still be roughing it," she continued.

As they detoured into the centrifuge there wasn't much left to see.

"You weren't kidding about lack of facilities," Crowe muttered, as he looked around.

If the main hull still contained familiar elements, the centrifuge was like a corpse. Previously, partition walls had divided it, but now everything except for the airtight bulkheads had been cut out. That meant that for the first time, he could view far enough to port and starboard to see the floor curve up and out of sight.

"If we had the time and facilities we'd have cut and shut the hull to get rid of it completely," the staff officer replied with a shrug. "We've put in spaces for beams to lock the centrifuge in place for the final run. That will help to structurally reinforce the hull. As it was, there was debate on whether to retain the centrifuge bridge, but then we'd have to leave a counterweight on the other side."

"The radar tower bridge remains?" Crowe asked.

"Sort of, sir. As you say the original layout had the bridge in the radar tower – an antiquated layout that made it too vulnerable. Fortunately there was nothing essential below it, so we've dropped the whole compartment two decks down into the main hull. That involved a lot of rewiring of command runs and we've added extra splinter protection – for what that's worth."

"Not much," Crowe murmured. "Anything left to do?"

"A few last bits sir. We still have to put in the flak-packs. They're a new feature. Basically each one is a box of recoilless rifles loaded with canister shot. You'll only have a dozen of them, enough for a pretty robust terminal defence against the first few missiles to get through, but no more. Plus, we have to put in your escape route up and down to the shuttles in the radar towers. That's probably important."

"Yeah, not having them might make volunteers a bit leery," Crowe agreed as they reached the bridge.

Back in his exploration days, Crowe hadn't used this space much and instead preferred to run *Mississippi* from the centrifuge bridge. Still there were a lot of good memories here. Looking up, he stared into the space the bridge had formerly occupied and could see the back of the shuttle bay.

"Since there will be so few crew on board, we've had to move some things around to allow the ship to be worked with the minimum of personnel."

"I see," Crowe replied as he steadied himself against the command chair and looked around. "Ah, my poor old girl, what have the bastards done to you?"

"Pardon, sir?"

"Nothing, nothing – just having a brief trip down memory lane," he replied with a brief smile.

They hurt you, he thought to himself as he patted the back of the seat, *hurt you when all we wanted to do was explore. Got you reduced to this... hollowed out husk. But don't you worry girl. They hurt you and now, we'll go and hurt them back!*

"To Operation Drumbeat," Wingate said as he raised his glass.

"And God bless all who fight in it," Fengzi replied as they clinked glasses.

The Council had formally signed off on the operation. For better or worse, it was now totally in the hands of the fleet. With a transit time of nearly two months, the Home Fleet would leave within days. If they had missed anything, then there was little time left in which to right it.

Wingate eyed Lewis over the top of his glass. There was no room for sentimentality, not when the stakes were so high. He'd given serious thought to removing Lewis from command. He could see the man was tired but then they all were. Operation Vindictive would be where the heaviest command load would fall. Destruction of the Spur gate station would be hard enough, yet that would be merely the start. After that, the battle of attrition would begin. In such a battle, as the fleet bled it would need a commander who could hold their nerve, an officer willing and able to look the Nameless in the eye and bleed as long as it took. For that task, the fleet had only one choice.

"And confusion to our enemies," Lewis added.

Chapter Sixteen

The Fury

10th March 2069

Guinness paused as a shudder ran through *Black Prince*.

"Everything all right, Chief?" Berg asked.

"Oh yeah, Skipper," Guinness replied after a moment. "It's just that you have to keep an ear open for problems. This girl wasn't exactly crafted, more duct-taped together. Not like old *Mississippi*."

"Yes, Chief, she's a different kind of a ship," Berg replied as she looked around, "built for a different universe. But this one, she's built for the one we're living in now."

Guinness grimaced but didn't disagree. The two of them had been serving together under Captain Crowe when the Mississippi Incident changed everything. Berg had been shocked when she first took command to find a former shipmate aboard. She knew for a fact he'd retired out of the fleet after their previous service together, but her predecessor on *Black Prince* had, off the record, advised her not to say anything. It was solid if unnecessary advice. The Chief had always been good at his job and with the random mix of outdated components inherited by the austerities – she was a job for an older engineer.

"It was strange watching the old *Mississippi* head off without us," Guinness reflected. "If I'd known she was going, I might have put in for a transfer. No offence, Skipper."

"None taken," she replied. "Of course I would have refused the request, no offence, Chief."

"None taken."

It had required months in dock to repair the damage to *Black Prince*. Despite Berg's best efforts, that time had also seen a significant number of the ship's petty officers transferred to other ships, with the result the cruiser had required even more time to work up once released from docks. A brief tour on the Junction Line hadn't resulted in any significant combat, so this operation would be the first serious action since *Black Prince* came under 'new management.'

"Any engineering problems I need to know about?" Berg asked as she pulled herself along the passageway.

"Nothing new," Guinness replied as he followed. "We're still finding blobs of escaped coolant and probably will be until the day this tin can goes to the breakers."

Berg nodded as she looked around the portside engine room. The tour of the ship was both a chance for the crew to see and be seen by their commander and a time killer for the captain herself. Beyond *Black Prince*'s hull plating, out in the jump conduit, were their squadron mates *Saladin* and Fu Hao, the heavy cruiser *Horus*, a section of destroyers, the barrage ship *Schumann* and six fighters. All were there to provide an escort for four fast pod-droppers and the drop-carriers *Long March* and HMSS *Courageous*. The *Schumann* and a couple of the pod-droppers were new constructions, the rest veterans to a greater or lesser extent. Repair teams had only just finished replacing those pieces of the Chinese carrier that had been shot away the last time she was out.

Berg didn't want to think about that but of course that meant her brain would fixate on it. The last time Battle Fleet had gone to Landfall had been for Operation Kite String, during which she'd been stationed on the Junction Line. On paper it was a successful operation in the face of significant opposition, but she could still remember the horror she'd felt when the losses were reported. The fact that the fleet never even attempted another resupply before the shelters fell was telling – they simply couldn't afford another 'victory' like that. Now however, Intelligence thought the enemy deployment around Landfall was severely reduced and was largely composed of orbiting weapons platforms, primarily there to fire on the surface of the planet.

"It will be an interesting few hours, Skipper," Guinness said with a sigh.

"Followed by an interesting few weeks," Berg replied before glancing at her watch. Jump in was now an hour away. "Well, let's get on with it Chief."

Space rippled and burst open as the jump portal formed right on the Landfall Red Line. The convoy filed back into real space. On the bridge, Berg watched intently as the first radar returns came in.

"Bridge, torpedoes away. They will be on station in eight

minutes," came the report from fire control.

"Understood," she replied as she watched the holo.

There was no pause to settle the convoy into formation. Instead, every ship began to power towards the distant planet.

"Coms, Bridge. Signal from *Saladin* – they're transmitting our arrival. No response from any of the planet drop sites."

"There wouldn't be, Coms, not yet," Berg replied. "They'd be asking for an orbital strike if they were. They need us to clear the skies first."

Blips appeared on the holo showing the torpedoes as they curved round to get astern of the station, ready to attack anything that tried to jump in behind them. Then further away, red blips and, beyond them, the planet Landfall.

"Tactical, Bridge. We are picking up multiple enemy contacts. Provisional count on mobile units is one cap ship, three cruisers and seven escorts. We also have readings on eight orbital weapons platforms and two cargo platforms. The Breaker's Rock starfort is currently behind the planet."

"Understood Tactical, keep an eye out for it," she replied.

Berg had to wonder at the wisdom of this entire mission. The risk to ships and crews was easy to understand, but the cargo – small arms, munitions and light artillery – provided everything needed to fight the Nameless on the ground. It was not enough to win but enough to draw attention.

In fact, this entire convoy was first and foremost a provocation, designed to pull back Nameless units from the Junction Line and draw forward their more distant reserves. At roughly this moment, Second fleet was breaking Earth orbit and heading for the Junction Line. Safeguarding Earth was being left in the hands of Planetary Defence and a handful of ships that couldn't be made ready in time. Five days from now, Second Fleet would start noisily smashing its way towards Landfall, hitting the various Nameless space gates and supply dumps identified by reconnaissance ships.

The Nameless might choose to yield ground, but intelligence believed they would contest Landfall – their only true prize so far, if only to bleed the Second Fleet. But even there, they would find their strength being drained.

Six modified support ships had already infiltrated forwards and would at this moment be launching space mines and torpedoes into the orbits of gas giant planets that could or had served as fuelling points for the Nameless. The wells were being poisoned so now their fuel would have to be moved forward from more distant sources.

"Coms, Bridge. Enemy cruiser is transmitting on FTL Band A."

"They know we're here now," Berg said quietly. "Helm, tighten us up on *Saladin*. Guns, stand by."

Alice glanced up at the sky for the umpteenth time and for the umpteenth time cursed herself as an idiot. What the hell was she expecting to see? Holding at the edge of the forest, ahead of them lay the weed-choked farmlands of the former Italian colony. The beacon they'd brought with them from the main camp was set up about a kilometre from their position. She couldn't help but cast her mind back to the last time she'd worked a drop. Then she'd had hundreds of soldiers standing between her and the Nameless. This time, they would just have to hope for the best. It really made her wish the Colonel had chosen someone else or that she'd had the sense to sit this one out. Behind her was a fifty strong group of volunteers, cream of the crop since their drop was further from the settlement than any other. She'd been surprised there had been that many. Surely any sensible person would have sat this one out. But she was there, so she could hardly judge. These were strong people. To make it this far, they'd had to be, and maybe they just wanted it all to be over, one way or another. There was some murmured conversation but most of them waited silently.

"Why can we not say: we've done our bit, good luck and let us know how it turns out?" Alice asked the Colonel in the privacy of the command tent.

"We're still stakeholders in this," he replied, "in fact more so than most people. This, this lifestyle..." he waved a hand vaguely, "it's not sustainable. Not in the truly long run. If we don't get the Nameless off this planet, well, none of us will die of old age."

Alice made no reply. She knew what he was gesturing towards – the hidden farms, the dispersed settlements, the three thousand people they'd so far managed to gather, feed and protect. But it was slowly falling... no, drifting apart. People, good people, were dying of illnesses that should have been treatable. Their farming was little better than subsistence level. Just one pest infestation or blight could leave them without enough calories to go round. Finally, you could smell the fear every time a Nameless gunboat went over.

"It will be volunteers only, of course. No point trying to draft people that don't want to be there, but I'd like you to lead one of the collection groups," the Colonel had continued. "What marine resources I have are best deployed on decoy raids. The drops are just so damn vulnerable, we have to give the bastards something else to worry about – unless you want to pick up a rifle and start shooting."

"You keep putting undue influence on this scrap of material," she replied, tapping the threadbare corporal's stripes on her sleeve as she looked at the map.

"And you don't put enough emphasis on them. I know you prefer to think of yourself as an academic but you aren't, not any more. You've kept people alive under the most difficult of circumstances and that puts you well ahead of some of military history's leading lights. I just need you to keep doing that."

"And you think a few rifles and bombs will make us meaningful? I mean a couple of hundred marines against..."

"Nothing we do, even if we were fully equipped and up to strength, would win the war on its own," he replied. "Wars aren't won by single great deeds – I doubt they ever were. No, instead we try to nibble each other to death. A few rifles and bombs will allow us to nibble that little bit harder."

Alice jumped as the small radio at her hip started to click sharply and looked down the line of people.

"Everyone listen up! We've just got the first signal," she alerted them. "The convoy is entering orbit. Get ready." She glanced up at the sky again. "We'll have to move fast."

"Yeah, at bloody light speed," someone muttered.

"Just keep a look out," she replied sharply as her radio continued to click.

The frequency was increasing as the starships above closed. He wasn't wrong though. Descending drop pods would be a giant signal to the Nameless that 'Humans Are Here' and that was if they were lucky. If unlucky, that sign would read 'Bombard Us From Orbit Now.' Two pods were supposed to come down and they would have to move fast once they left the protection of the woods to covered the open ground, retrieve the cargo and get it and themselves back to the trees. If they were caught in the open, they'd be massacred – and all for the sake of a few bloody guns.

The click cut out and was replaced by a long squeal. She flipped it onto another channel and transmitted. A moment later it began to ping as their beacon went active.

"We're on."

The last of the weapon satellites blew as a volley of plasma bolts crashed through it. The Nameless ships had broken orbit as soon as they sighted the convoy and were firing from long range, but their small number of ships couldn't put out enough fire to break through the escort's counter fire. Once an asteroid destined to be harvested for metal and now a Nameless starfort, Breaker's Rock might have made a difference. Taking account of its position locked at the Lagrange point between Landfall and the planet's moon, they'd timed their jump in to deprive their foe the opportunity to fire for as long as possible. As it orbited into sight it unleashed its first volley.

Even though she had been expecting it, the sheer volume of fire still made Berg gasp. The Nameless had clearly upgraded the fort since Kite String and ten Nameless cap ships couldn't have matched the weight of missiles it unleashed.

But this was what the barrage ship *Schumann* and the Myth Class cruiser *Horus* had come for. As the storm of missiles bore down on them, *Schumann* began to work up to her maximum rate of fire, her flanks rippling as she fired dozens of explosive charges. The aliens' missile salvo smashed headlong into a wall of overlapping explosions and nothing but fragments got through.

As *Schumann* absorbed everything the fort could throw, *Horus* gave it back. The range was long but Breakers had no capacity to manoeuvre. Against one of the few ships to retain her heavy calibre railguns, the starfort was a sitting duck. There was no way to know whether its garrison even saw the small high velocity projectiles before they began to slam home. Little more than space cannon balls, the metal heavy asteroid was sturdy enough to absorb the first few strikes. But as successive projectiles continued to hammer the target, cracks appeared across the surface. Then fragments began to detach from the fringes of the asteroid and the stream of missiles suddenly spluttered out as Breakers Rock abruptly shattered, spilling wrecked equipment and stricken Nameless soldiers into space.

"That's the route open," Berg said with satisfaction as the large red blip showing the fort was replaced by a smear of much smaller contacts.

"Coms, Bridge. *Saladin* is transmitting the all clear. We're getting... a dozen beacon signals from the ground."

"Tactical, give me a display of the signals on the holo."

The main holo's tactical display of the space around *Black Prince* was replaced with one of the planet. Most of the visible contacts seemed to be forming a large open circle around the lost shelter of Douglas. There was a single contact a few hundred kilometres from the Chinese shelter. The American shelter was still hidden on the far side of the planet. Before the war, Landfall had a seven-figure population and Berg wondered how many people those twelve blips represented.

"Navigation, crunch the numbers and give me the most efficient course to make drops on those contacts," she ordered.

The same calculations would be made on *Saladin*, but as the second ship they had to be ready in case something happened.

"*Saladin* is uploading manoeuvring instructions. We're also receiving a data upload from one of the fighters. They've achieved line of sight on the American base. We have another fifteen beacons."

"Understood," Berg replied. "Helm, upload instructions from *Saladin*."

The escort hovered over the top of the carriers and pod-droppers as they did their work. They mostly delivered arms and ammunition, but two carriers dropped a few hundred brave soldiers, joining a fight from which there would be no retreat. As the *Schumann* held off the small squadron of Nameless ships, the convoy manoeuvred in turn over each of the beacons below. As pods dropped down and away, *Horus* completed her second duty and remorselessly pounded any major enemy surface targets they could identify from orbit. Job done, the convoy broke away, climbing up and over the Red Line.

As her radio started to ping again, Alice hesitated at the edge of the woods as she stared up at the sky. The clouds were so low the drop pod would only become visible a few hundred metres up. Under the best of circumstances the pods were usually only accurate to within fifty metres of their beacons and that was under peacetime conditions. Lashed together from scavenged parts, their beacon was likely to be even less effective. If someone got under the pod, that would permanently solve all their problems but they needed to empty it fast. No, they couldn't afford to wait until they saw it.

"Alright, let's move," she ordered, "spread out and watch the sky!"

No one needed to be told to stay low. Everyone ran half crouched, their heads turned uncomfortably to keep an eye on the clouds. Out in the open Alice, could feel her flesh crawl with the sense of exposure. Her radio still pinged as the beacon continued to transmit.

"There's one!" someone shouted.

"There's the other one," came a second cry.

Alice spun round and, after a moment, spotted them. Like giant onions with a spinning propeller on top, there was no danger of either of them landing on anyone. One was coming down right on target, but the other one – the damn thing was well off course, angling in towards them, but about to miss its beacon by at least a kilometre.

She hesitated in a moment of indecision.

"Franks, take number two and get the closest one. Number one group, with me!" she bawled out as she began to run. "Now everyone move!"

From behind she heard the thump of the first pod hitting the ground. Ahead, the second was still coming in. It bounced as it hit the ground then dug in and tipped over, its' spinning rotors shattering as they hit the ground. The fastest runners reached it before Alice and were struggling with the access hatch when she arrived wheezing. The sides of the pod were still hot from its passage through the atmosphere and the hatch frame seemed to have buckled from the impact.

"Pry bar! Where's the pry bar?"

The biggest man in the group was bringing up the rear, puffing like a steam engine. He barged through the clustering crowd and sank the pointed end of the two-metre bar into the frame like a spear. He, Alice and another man leaned into it and with a sudden bang the hatch gave way. They began unloading immediately, dragging the packing cases out.

"Two to a case, grab on and get moving!" Alice ordered as she glanced back towards the woods from which they'd come from. They'd ended up more than two kilometres from where they needed to be, with no cover. She anxiously began to search the skies again, this time for Nameless aircraft.

Twenty minutes later they abandoned the now empty pod and spread out across the grasslands in two lines. At the back of her line, Alice still scoured the skies. Then in the distance, over her own heavy breathing, she heard what she had most feared – the sound of an aircraft engine.

"Oh God," she murmured before shouting down the line. "Pick up the pace!"

As they lurched across the open ground, she fumbled off her backpack. Inside it was their only real defence against whatever that aircraft might be about to drop — one of the few precious thermite grenades left to them. Hidden by the clouds above, the aircraft passed over them.

Trust me, we're not important enough to bomb, Alice thought.

Then she heard it turn.

Her end of the packing case thumped to the ground as she dropped it. Jolted to a sudden halt, her partner swore loudly. Alice ignored him as she twisted the priming cap and threw the heavy device as far as she could.

"Go! Go!" she shouted as she seized her end of the packing case.

"One, two three..." she counted beneath her breath as she ran.

From high above, she heard the distinctive pop of a missile launch, while from behind her came the whoosh of the thermite going off. Even at a distance she felt a flush of heat on the back of her neck. Lungs straining, legs burning, she forced herself to run faster to put precious distance between them and the burning grenade that would be suckering in the heat seeker missile. Hopefully.

A sound like a rising whine reached her ears.

"Get down!"

Hitting the ground, she lay as flat as she could, nose in the dirt. Then behind there was an explosion that went beyond mere noise, emitting a shockwave that knocked the breath out of her. She felt rather than heard metal fragments spin through the air above her.

Staggering to her feet, Alice looked back at where the grenade had been. It was now a circle of small fires where the thermite had been scattered. Five hundred metres ahead she could see smoke rising. The first of the group back to the wood had started the bonfire they'd laid down. Even with an emergency flare and a dozen marine firelighters, it would take time to get going.

Moving again, they caught up with the next pair ahead. A young woman, Alice couldn't remember her name, cradled an equally young man, screaming incoherently as his blood soaked into her clothes. Alice glanced at him. After the trenches of Douglas, a glance was enough to tell her that if he wasn't already dead, then he was certainly beyond saving. He hadn't ducked fast enough. She could still hear the aircraft.

There wasn't time to be gentle and Alice dragged the woman to her feet by her hair, kicking and slapping her until she was moving again. The body was left where it lay. As they ran, Alice saw at least three cases abandoned in the grass. She didn't have the breath to curse about it.

With her laboured breathing blotting out the sound of the aircraft, they were now under the first of the trees. Her partner paused at one trunk, gasping, but she didn't have the breath to urge him on. The blood soaked young woman slumped to the ground, too exhausted to cry. Hands on her knees, Alice looked around just in time to see the small Nameless jet dip below cloud cover and turn towards them. Its engines howled as it accelerated towards them. Close to its nose there was a glimmer of light.

"Down!" Alice shouted as she dived behind a tree. As she huddled and threw her arms over her head, she could hear the thud of bullets hitting the ground and the ping of flying fragments all around them. The tree behind which she hid shuddered from the impact of the rounds and shredded leaves and branches rained down. Some distance away, she heard a brief, cut-off scream and knew she'd lost another one. Above them, the jet's engine roared as it passed directly overhead. As her adrenalin kicked in, Alice leapt to her feet, grabbed the box and sprinted with three others further into the trees. Alice briefly registered the body of another man, torn open by gunfire. But they were now going deep into the woods and the worst was over.

It had taken them five days to walk from their hiding ground to the drop zone. It took them nearly seven to get back. Repeatedly, they were forced to go to ground as Nameless aircraft buzzed overhead. Several times the aliens must have got some kind of read and dropped bombs. Most missed by wide margins but one stick of four straddled their column. It was a miracle no one was hurt.

Seven days after the drop they were intercepted.

The forest was silent but for the steady tramp of their boots. At the head of the column, Alice paused and crouched down. Those behind immediately followed suit and within seconds no one was moving.

Up ahead the sound came again – a whistle. Alice pulled out hers, blew twice and then waited, hand resting lightly on the butt of her pistol. The figure of a marine stepped out of the undergrowth ahead.

"Lieutenant Byatt, what are you doing out here?" she said in recognition.

"Looking for you," he replied, "was starting to think they'd got you."

"We came under air attack and it slowed... What's happened," Alice said as she registered his grim expression. Behind him two more marines appeared. Byatt motioned her away from the rest.

"Shit's hit the fan," he said grimly. "Don't know how, but the bastards got some kind of idea of our position."

"Oh God, have they..."

"Not yet. Fleet's bombardment must have taken out most of their air and orbital assets or we'd have been carpet-bombed by now. Or if they wanted to be really sure, they'd have nuked us from orbit. They're coming in from the west with infantry and armour. They've got a few gunboats but after we tagged one of those with a SAM, the rest are keeping back."

"Can you stop them?"

"If we couldn't stop them at Douglas Base with all of it fixed defences, we sure as hell ain't gonna stop them here. All we can do is slow them a bit."

"Then what will we do?" she asked. "What's the Colonel ordered?"

"Retreat and scatter. I've been ordered to find you and then get the military supplies to the fighting. The Colonel wants you at the farmland to organise an evacuation."

She would be running again. Alice hadn't realised she'd allowed herself to hope, but now she could feel that hope dying. Byatt snapped his fingers in front of her face.

"Hey, wake up! This shit is happening and we need to deal with it."

Alice shook herself.

"Arms and munitions are in the first ten crates, food and medical supplies in the ones after that. No point taking those in. If we're running, those emergency rations might be what stands' between us and starvation."

Byatt nodded as he pulled out his computer pad and brought up a map.

"What we need is a rallying point," he muttered.

Before she reached the outer perimeter Alice could hear the horribly familiar sound of Nameless missiles coming in. Byatt had detached his two marines to escort her and all three of them had to fight the urge to run, either away or towards the fighting. When they reached the first of the farms the evacuation was well underway and Alice met her old deputy William.

"Hi, Boss," he said as her saw her approach. "Looks like the uniforms have fucked up again."

There wasn't any real anger in his voice. He sounded too tired and too defeated for that.

"Yeah," she replied as the two marines, aware of the air of hostility around them, shifted uncomfortably. "What have you heard?"

"Only what the first group of people to come through told me. The bastards came during the night. Anyone that could get out ran for their lives – no food, no supplies, no nothing, just the clothes on their backs."

William nodded towards the closest group of people. Now that she looked properly, Alice realised they were mostly packing ripe banana patata into backpacks woven from vegetation. In the distance there were three deep crumps as Nameless missiles landed.

"We can't carry the whole harvest," William said. "We'll take what we can. The rest we'll leave and hope we can come back for at least some of it."

That last part sounded over-optimistic and looking up at William, she could tell he knew it too. In fact, as she looked around the camp, Alice saw her own errand was probably futile. Any central control was already breaking down. Those who would survive were the ones already reacting. Any of the farming settlement simply awaiting instructions, would not get out.

"You might as well come with us, Boss," William said.

She wanted to, she wanted to finally rip off those cursed stripes on her sleeve. But people still needed her and there was still a chance she could get at least some of them out.

It took another four hours to reach Camp Dautsch and Alice was in no doubt she was walking toward a battle. The landscape rocked and echoed to the sound of artillery fire. When they did finally reach the camp, her two escorts were immediately commandeered and ordered towards the sound of distant small arms fire. Alone, Alice continued towards the Colonel's command post. The camp, orderly when she'd left nearly two weeks ago, was now a shambles. Holes had been torn in the forest canopy with trees either felled completely or severed mid-trunk. Packing cases like the ones she'd recovered lay around in piles, emptied and abandoned.

"Corporal, you're not dead," Dautsch observed as she walked into the command post. Only a single marine was in attendance, his arm strapped across his chest in a grubby sling.

"We got twenty-one out of twenty-five cases at the cost of two dead and three walking wounded," Alice began to report before petering out.

Dautsch smiled bitterly.

"I think as you can gather, things have moved on a bit," he replied as he gestured her forward.

The map in front of them gave a rough layout of the camp and the surrounding farms. Projecting in from the northwest was a red line that pushed in through the outer farms and up to the camp. Somehow that simple line on the map, through locations she had come to know and associate with people, made it even more real than the sounds of battle.

"It's a delaying action," Dautsch said in a tired voice. "That is all we can hope to do. I think that by the way they're coming straight at us rather than attempting to work around our flanks, means they don't know how widely spread we are. They located this camp but didn't realise that the farms were there. That gives us a chance of getting people clear."

"What do you want me to do?"

"Head south. Rejoin your own farm group and get yourselves away."

"What will you do?" she asked quietly.

"Engage them for as long as we can, then break off."

There was no need to point out how difficult that would be.

"You'd better go while there are still a few hours of light left," Dautsch finished.

"Good luck," she said, for want of anything better to say.

As she turned to leave, he spoke again.

"I shouldn't have asked for the drop," he said. "It was over-ambitious and I've brought this down on us all. I should have kept our heads down, waited it out."

"We couldn't wait forever. Remember?"

"We got a briefing download when they made the drop. No details, but the fleet is coming. We only needed to hold on for a few more weeks."

Looking at him, Alice realised with shock that the confident man she'd known all these months was gone. In his own mind, Dautsch had made a terrible mistake and now his troops and those he'd come to protect were paying the price. He turned his back to her before she could say anymore.

No other civilians remained in the camp and she charted a lonely course back towards what had been her own settlement before they'd met the marines. When it became too dark to see where she was going, Alice settled in to wait for dawn. She could still hear the fighting in the distance and several times caught sight of missiles arcing down onto the site of the camp. After a day of hard walking, and almost in spite of herself, Alice slipped into a restless slumber.

She woke at first light, as rain began to fall. To the north there was an ominous silence. Resuming her trek, a thought occurred to her, one that should have come before. What would she do if she found no one at the farm? What if they'd already evacuated, leaving her alone? Once that thought arrived, it tormented her. In her mind's eye, she could see herself blundering around the uncharted wilderness until starvation or illness felled her. When she heard the sound of voices, Alice threw caution aside and ran towards them.

Two of her old group looked up from the banana patata crop, startled, as Alice came crashing out of the undergrowth.

"Boss," one of them said, "what are you doing here?"

"Thank God, you're still here," she exclaimed. "Why are you still here?"

"What?"

"What do you mean 'what?'" she demanded. Then looking at their baffled expressions, she realised they didn't know of the attack. Shielded by the hills between them and the main camp, they'd seen and heard nothing.

"We have to get out of here!"

Alice waited impatiently, occasionally glancing to the north. Around her pandemonium reigned. People were attempting to pack up everything they could. The sky above them was a monotone grey and the rain was falling hard now, drowning out any other sounds. Instinct told her to shout at them to drop everything and move, but her intellect said that was exactly what they couldn't afford to do. A few weeks until the fleet arrived Dautsch had said. No, she couldn't believe that. That promise had been made and broken too many times now. Even if it was true, a few weeks were more than enough to starve.

Badie approached.

"Another half hour," he said forestalling her question. "We had people out on the fields that haven't even got back in yet."

"We can't wait much longer."

"We have to. We have wives and husbands that won't leave without their spouses," he replied, before hurrying away again.

There was no warning. The big Nameless gunboat dropped from cloud cover, its engines howling to full power. The muzzles of it guns flashed and rockets raced out, terminating in explosions that shook the ground and cut down men and women only beginning to react. Hovering in the air, lines dropped from its belly and Nameless soldiers came abseiling down.

"Run!" Alice screamed as she reached for her pistol. "Everyone, run!"

Then she was on the ground with no memory of how she got there. She could see people, people she had known, running, screaming, falling and dying. The sounds were muted, as if they were from another world. Turning her head, she saw the gunboat moving forward slowly, guns still flashing. Below the Nameless infantry squad unhitched their lines and reached for their guns.

Dazed, Alice raised her hand to her face, but it wasn't there. Her arm ended just above her wrist and blood oozed through torn flesh over white bone. A Nameless soldier saw her move and raised its gun. Alice watched helplessly, knowing she should move and knowing she could not. From behind the Nameless, something flashed and there was no warning for the gunboat as a missile speared out of the forest and knifed into it. The ensuing explosion tore open the fuselage, rupturing gas cells. The engines howled now, battling but failing to keep the mortally wounded craft airborne. Then the gunboat's munitions detonated as it ploughed into the forest. Seconds later, the Nameless soldiers began dropping as gunfire ripped into them and Alice lost consciousness.

"We can't make the problem any worse, we operate or she dies."

"What are her chances?"

"At best... Fifty-fifty. She really needs a blood transfusion but we don't have the means to give one."

Alice opened her eyes and attempted to speak. All she could manage was a dry croak. It was dark but there was enough light to make out Badie's silhouette leaning over her. Even that effort was enough for her nearly to pass out, but she fought to stay conscious. She was tightly wrapped in blankets and lying in a crudely built shelter.

"Boss, can you hear me?" he said. "Don't worry, you're safe now."

"Where am I?" she asked.

"Twenty kilometres from camp," he replied. "We're laid up for the day."

Over his shoulder a tired and bloodstained marine looked down at her.

"A few of the marines got away and came our way. They used up their last missile saving us," Badie explained.

"They owed us," she whispered. "How many got away?"

"The Colonel led a counter attack to buy..."

"No. How many of my people?"

"We lost eleven boss," Badie replied. "Boss, I'm so sorry but we're going to have to amputate your arm at the elbow. We have no choice."

Alice could feel the blackness rising again and this time couldn't fight it.

"Badie, in my pocket, a map," she whispered.

As her voice dropped he leaned in.

"That's where I sent the supplies. Take my stripes. You're in charge now."

Chapter Seventeen

Day of Retribution

10th April 2069

Positioned on the very shores of intergalactic space, the gulf between the arms of the Milky Way was not a place for humanity. The holograms, which usually showed views of outside the ship to prevent the crew from going mad with claustrophobia, had mostly been turned off, as even the steadiest individuals felt the chill of the unimaginable emptiness beyond the hull. But in this war, if not a place of comfort, this was a place of safety, a place where the Worms couldn't reach them and final preparations could be made. *Spectre*, her sister ship *Phantom*, the strike boat carrier *Pankhurst*, three support ships and, bringing up the rear, the lumbering presence of the former bulk carrier *Sherlock*, now converted to a very different purpose, all drifted while within their hulls, their crews prepared.

Willis steadied herself on one of the deckhead grab bars and looked over the shoulder of the Russian army officer as he worked through his checklist. Finally a green tick icon appeared on his screen and he looked up at her.

"That is all of the warheads done, Captain," he said. "I will have to check again before the attack, but I can certify these warheads as cleared for operation. The missile propulsion systems are your responsibility."

"Thank you, Major," Willis replied as he straightened up. "I should be able to confirm the time of the assault to you within the next few hours, so that you can plan your check. On an unrelated matter the wardroom extends its hospitality to you this evening."

The grim-faced Russian smiled slightly.

"A last supper before we go forth. I will be happy to accept," he replied. He rubbed at his eyes. "I am still waking up, so I will have to beg to be excused if I fall asleep into my plate."

"You might not be the only one, Major," she replied with a smile.

After leaving Earth, the squadron had made its way across the front line and back towards the worlds of the Nameless. To avoid detection, most of their cool down jump in points had been to interstellar space, while most of the crew had been in Deep Sleep hibernation for the journey to save on supplies. The weeks of travel had been close to the sleep system's safety limits and several of the crew were still shaking off the effects.

"I'd imagine the fleet doesn't often entertain national military officers. At least not outside of space dock," the Major said.

"True enough."

Willis looked around *Spectre*'s magazine. Missiles lay waiting in their racks, mostly standard anti-ship, but six of were for a very different purpose. Painted yellow and black so that there would be no mistaking them, they were five-megaton thermonuclear devices, each fitted with ablative nose cones to allow atmospheric re-entry and, worst of all – Cobalt Sixty tampers.

Willis had never heard of them before they were brought on board her ship. God knows, she considered herself to be a hard-nosed officer who'd seen too much to get sentimental. But what she'd subsequently read about these enhanced weapons in public and military sources had been enough to send a shiver down her spine.

The governments of the Council had never been comfortable with the fleet – an essentially stateless military – possessing nuclear weapons, while for its part, the fleet was equally content not to have them. In the vacuum of space, such weapons were far less effective than in atmosphere, which combined with other practical problems meant they offered too few advantages for too many practical, political and ethical complications.

But for this mission, no other weapon would do.

Leaving the magazine and the Russian major, Willis made her way up to the bridge.

"Captain," said the officer of the watch as she entered, "I was about to call you."

"What is it?" Willis replied as she glanced around the bridge displays, making sure everything was in place.

"The reconnaissance ship has just jumped in," he nodded towards the holo, set to wide view. "They're three hours out but their transmission has just reached the flagship. The scout is making the approach in real space."

Willis nodded. Without a star or planetary bodies to get a fix on, jumps were pretty inaccurate out here and the scout's commander had clearly decided to traverse the gap between them in real space rather than risk a jump that might end up even more off target.

"Did we get the data upload as well?"

"Yes. Captain. Flag forwarded it onto all ships."

He nodded to a rating and the scout's reading appeared on the main holo.

The information they'd gained from the captured data had been sketchy, navigation data but not much more. There hadn't been time for scouts to be dispatched from and return to Earth with the detailed information needed to plan an attack. Instead *Pankhurst* had to give up three of her strike boats to carry scouts and, along with the rest of the squadron, had set off from Earth knowing that they'd have to work out the fine detail when they got there.

Headquarters had designated the system KINGDOM and the star at its centre was slightly larger than Earth's sun. It was perhaps a little older but still in its middle years, so stable. Orbiting it were seven major planets – two frozen rocky planets in the outer orbits, three gas giants with their attendant moons dominating the middle orbits and two more rocky planets occupying the inner orbits. Of these last two, one was smack in the middle of the star's Goldilocks zone and reading at about two percent more massive than Earth. Atmosphere readings indicated oxygen, carbon dioxide and nitrogen in ratios compatible with life, as they knew it.

There were three large space docks in orbit along with one major station of a type Willis immediately recognised

"That's a space elevator," she murmured to herself.

It was no surprise the Nameless race could have such technology. Earth had one after all but Earth's was at the centre of the human universe and was only used for the bulkiest of cargo. If they applied human criteria, this planet had a population that likely only ran to tens of millions. The elevator's tether traced downwards to the edge of the only major city in the entire system. Planetary defences seemed to consist of several small starforts, an unknown number of weapons satellites and a small squadron of warships based around two capital ships. There was no sign of any carriers but there were various small transports moving around. Out on the edge of the Blue Line was a space gate with what looked like another two starforts as protection. Out in the wider system, there appeared to be a fuel industry hard at work around the second largest of the gas giants.

"Call up Tactical," Willis said. "I know flag is working on it but I want us to look into it just in case we spot something they don't. First figure out which direction that tether will fall if we take out the station and if it will land on anything expensive."

"Would that be important ma'am? I mean if we..."

Willis glanced towards him.

"Yes, you are likely right but worth considering anyway."

"I just wonder whether this is the right thing to do."

The question wasn't put to the table at large. It was said during a gap in the discussions but and was heard by all. Conversation ceased as all eyes focused on the source of the question. It was the ship's doctor and he had been talking to the purser.

"We're obeying our orders," Commander Yaya said flatly.

The Doctor briefly looked awkward at finding himself at the centre of attention, then his expression became defiant.

"When you strip away the military language and political niceties, those orders are to burn a world to the ground," he said. "We aren't just targeting a civilian population; we intend to render even the land they stand on dead. We are planning to turn their world into a sterile, lifeless planet and we don't even know that will work!"

"It's not as if they haven't done the same to others," the ship's navigator dismissively retorted. "So sauce for the goose as far as I'm concerned."

"So we lower ourselves to their level?" the Doctor responded heatedly.

Two officers started to reply with equal force but were cut off by the sound of a glass being tapped with increasing force. Everyone looked to the head of the table as Willis lowered her glass.

"Calmly everyone," she said, looking around the table.

Spectre's wardroom was a microcosm of a fleet at war, with pre-war officers holding the senior positions. By peacetime standards, most were young for their rank as they filled dead men's boots. Next came the fleet's reservists and, after them, those who had been transferred into the fleet from the national militaries – men and women from different traditions but still professional soldiers. Finally there were those who had volunteered and come directly from the civilian world. That last group in particular, came to the fleet with a different mindset, not necessarily worse, but different.

"First and foremost, doctor, we are doing this because we have been ordered to," she told him.

"Some terrible things have been done by soldiers who then said 'I was obeying orders'," the Doctor replied sullenly.

Yaya started to speak but stopped when Willis raised her hand.

"That, Doctor, is unfortunately very true, but some even worse things have been done by men and women in uniform, who decided to pick and choose which orders they would obey. *I'm not finished, Doctor.* No one knows whether we can even successfully put in this attack. What we do know is that with their drone soldiers, in the war to date the Nameless have only suffered at most a few thousand 'real' casualties. This will be our first and probably only real chance to bring the true cost of war home to them."

"We do not know what effect a successful attack will have. Will it be shock and awe or something that they will ever after seek to avenge? No one knows. But we have been given an order by Council, a gathering of the governments of the majority of the human race and, as such, the most legitimate body that any military force in the history of the human race has ever answered to. We as individuals have the right to have private reservations, but as officers of Battle Fleet, our duty is to carry out our orders."

"You certainly slapped the Doctor down pretty hard," Yaya observed as Willis poured a drink.

With the conclusion of the meal she had invited Yaya to her cabin to cover a few last points before she retired for the night.

"I would have said that was fairly gentle," Willis replied as she slid over a glass. "Saying a soldier should disobey an immoral order is nice in theory, but when people say that, they always consider themselves to be on the right side of the moral argument. It never seems to occur to them that someone might take the same factors and get a different answer, which they to consider to be the moral choice."

"May I ask, Captain, whether you think this will work?"

"Depends on what your definition of work is," Willis replied as she swirled the drink round her glass.

"I would say that preventing them from wiping us from the universe would be the pertinent one," Yaya replied.

Willis smiled slightly as she glanced at her second-in-command.

They'd got along well since she first arrived on *Spectre*, principally because Willis had recognised Yaya as being very much a younger version of herself – although the Commander seemed to have avoided the worst of the career missteps Willis had made.

"Well, if that is your definition, I think it's already failed," she said after a pause.

"Captain?" Yaya said sharply.

"If our definition of success is to pin down the Nameless reserves in defensive positions while the Home Fleet attacks, then I think we can succeed in that. But that's a short term objective."

Willis smiled bleakly.

"In the long term... The Nameless believes us to be a threat to their continued survival," she continued. "If we succeed with this mission or even get close enough for them to know what we tried, we'll confirm as fact what up to now they have merely believed."

Willis leaned back in her chair and sighed.

"In some respects it's a tragedy for the Nameless and everyone they have encountered. They believe so profoundly that we are threats, that it becomes a self-fulfilling prophecy and now we have to *become* threats just to survive. Personally, I believe this will reinforce their attitude towards us – that we are a threat that must be destroyed. I don't think this will be the last shots of this war but it will be the first of the next."

"But we'll do it?"

"Yep. I don't have any better ideas on what we could do – and as I said, we have our orders."

"In six days time the Home Fleet begins its attack," Commodore Tneba said as the holo displayed the system. "Given the distance between us, the exact moment is unknown and unknowable. But our attack has to go in first since the element of surprise is essential for us. So it will have to be the old bait and switch."

The commanding officers of the small squadron had been gathered on board the *Phantom* to hash out the details of the attack.

"While the system defences aren't that impressive, they are enough to fend off any direct assault we could make. Fortunately, the *Sherlock* doesn't have to get particularly close to the planet to do her thing, but she does need time to establish her position and work out the firing solution. That is something that cannot be done if she's taking hits."

"For best effect," added Commander Bronsman of the *Sherlock*, "we need to strike at the side of the planet with the city and space elevator."

"As I understand it," Willis said, "with these weapons, it hardly matters which part of the planet we hit."

"That's assuming the Nameless aren't as casual about the lives of their civilians as they are with their military."

Tneba paused and shrugged.

"There's simply no way to know, yet," he resumed. "If we hit towns on the far side of the planet, the city won't be affected by the initial bombardment but the fallout cloud will reach them within two or three weeks. Just a few hours of exposure from Cobalt Sixty will be fatal and the radiation levels will remain so too long for anyone to wait it out in a shelter. No, if the Nameless place any value on their civilian population, they'll attempt to evacuate and that's when we'll know. But right now, we need to land our strike on or near the city."

There were grim expressions around the table but no one objected.

"So we need to draw the mobile units away and pull the orbital defences over to the far side of the planet," Tneba continued. "That requires splitting our forces."

He pressed a control and the holographic solar system twirled and spun.

"There are two targets in the system that the Nameless will defend if threatened – the fuel industry around the gas giant and the space gate over the inhabited planet."

He pressed the controls again and the holo froze.

"This position occurs roughly every seventeen hours. The space gate is on the opposite side of the planet from the space elevator. I plan to dispatch *Pankhurst*'s strike boats against the gate during one of these orbital periods. Irrespective of whether they destroy it, the very act of it being attacked should compel them to start moving most or all of their mobile units up and out of the planet's mass shadow. Simultaneously with our strike boats pulling away, I will then take *Phantom* in against the gas giant's fuel industry, thus forcing them to pursue into that planet's mass shadow. Once they've cleared, *Spectre* will escort and protect the *Sherlock* as she attacks."

"That will put you a very long way into the gas giant's mass shadow, sir," Willis commented.

"And in danger of being cut off," Bronsman added.

"True, true," Tneba said, "but if we are to get any action, we'll have to show a little leg."

"Would the *Spectre* be a better choice than the flag ship, sir?" Willis carefully asked.

Tneba shook his head.

"The ship covering the *Sherlock* will have to get into position well ahead of time and once there will have to stay silent. I need to remain in control and *Phantom*'s engines are in slightly better condition than *Spectre*'s, no offence. *Spectre* simply has more kilometres on the clock and for this purpose, speed is more important than armour. I could shift my flag to *Spectre* but I believe the critical tactical decision will be when *Phantom* makes her move. The big decision at this point is finding somewhere to put *Spectre* and *Sherlock* so that they can see developments around the planet, without being so far back that time lag becomes a problem."

"My own tactical team, sir, believes we have found such a spot," Willis said as she pointed into the holo. "The readings from the reconnaissance ships picked up a comet, a big one about four light minutes out from the objective. Its current position means nothing around any of the planets with activity have line of sight behind it."

"That's a pretty tight jump in," Tneba said, slightly dubious.

"Ideally, sir, we'd want to be jumping to make our attack as the mobile units chase you across the Blue Line into the gas giant's mass shadow. The closer in we are, the better we can make that judgement call," she continued. "It is achievable. We'd have to make a couple of jumps in quick succession but the first will allow us to get a good enough fix to make the second. If we can take one of the reconnaissance ships with us, then we can use its towed array to watch and stay completely behind the comet."

"Alright, but I'll want my own staff to check the maths on that,"

"Of course."

Because God knows, Willis thought to herself, *if we've screwed up the navigation calculations, I'd rather find out now.*

The following few days managed to be both intensely busy and interminably drawn out. Even at this late stage, there was always a chance that an abort order could be issued. Each time Communications reported an FTL transmission, Willis found herself going tense but every time it was identified as Nameless. In the engine rooms and weapons bays, systems were checked then double-checked. In the personnel section, all unnecessary fittings and personal effects were stripped out and sent over to the support ships. Every gram removed was mass that wouldn't have to be accelerated when the time came and that tiny difference might be vital. As captain, Willis was the only person on board without enough to occupy the days and eventually she found herself alone in her cabin with an old fashioned pen and a sheet of paper.

She'd got as far as *Dear Mum and Dad*, before stalling.

She had written them a goodbye letter years ago, back when she was a junior lieutenant, before the war, when death was more likely to be the product of an accident than anything else.

Since the start of the war she'd periodically thought about updating it, but the thought had only occurred when combat was imminent and time too short. Before they left Earth would have been the time but she hadn't got to it, probably as much a mental defence as anything else. A goodbye letter was an acknowledgement of the possibility of a future you wouldn't have a place in, a line of thought not many people would wish to pursue.

Also, thinking about the future meant thinking about the past. There would be only one letter. Aside from her parents, there wasn't really anyone else to write to. On her desk was a picture, something that should already have been sent over to the transport but she couldn't bring herself to part with it. The photograph was of her and Vincent Espey on their graduation day. If he were still alive to read it, he would have got a letter.

She'd always put career ahead of people and now, looking back, she couldn't help but feel a twinge of regret. *Hey! I've done stuff*, she mentally reprimanded herself. *I'm good at what I do and what I do is important. Maybe there aren't many people who'll miss me but right now, it's hard to see that being a bad thing. If I do make it, then I've got time to change that.* The internal demons didn't have an answer for that. Willis nodded to herself and picked up the pen again.

Dear Mum and Dad,
If you are reading this, then the worst has happened. Given the nature of these things, odds are it was quick for me. I know you never really wanted me to join the forces and this is probably the day you've feared, but you always supported me and I thank you for that. I suppose, if I do die, the only really irritating thing will be that I won't know how it all turned out...

As *Spectre* lurched back into real space the collision detection siren screamed. Across the command channel, Willis heard the helmsman swear as he flipped to manual and went all-astern on the engines. The cruiser shuddered and jolted violently and Willis felt the harness straps bite into her shoulders.

"Navigation!" she demanded.

"We're off target! We've come out... inside the comet's tail!"

On the visual display she could see the reconnaissance ship being thrown about by the comet's boiling gasses. Bigger and heavier, the *Sherlock* was weathering the unexpected conditions better than her smaller comrades.

"Got positional lock! We came out a hundred K closer to the comet than we should. *Jesus Christ*! I think we only just missed its mass shadow!"

Willis could see the navigator's face had gone pale.

No time to think about that, at the rear of their formation, *Sherlock* had gone all back on her engines and was now slip-sliding out of the comet's tail.

"Helm, eighty percent back on Engines Two and Four, starboard side thrusters to full!" she snapped as *Spectre* continued to pitch.

"Got it," the helmsman shouted back as he worked the controls.

As they slid clear the pitching faded away.

"I'm sorry, Captain," the navigator started to say, "I must have..."

"No time for that now," she cut him off before flicking her intercom to the main command channel. "This is Bridge to all department heads. Commander Yaya, I need a full damage control check of the forward compartments. Engineering, Coms, Sensors and Fire Control, I want full systems checks. Report in ten minutes!"

Her orders prompted a collection of affirmatives across the channel. That done, Willis turned to the navigation display. The difference between where they had intended to come out and where they'd actually emerged was tiny, barely a few hundred kilometres. Compared to the multiple astronomical units they'd jumped, the difference was merely fractions of one percent. Yet it had nearly killed them and might do so yet.

The emergence point was outside the blind spot they'd been aiming for. Could the Nameless have spotted them through the comet's plume material? If they had, this offensive could be about to end very badly. Minutes crawled past as around her the crew worked. Willis paid particular attention the coms section. If the Nameless had seen something, then communications chatter would be the likely giveaway. But the solar system remained peaceful. On the bridge though, reports started to filter through from both inside and outside the ship.

"Bridge, Sensors. We've gone blind on the forward ventral passive array."

"Bridge, Coms. Laser signal from reconnaissance ship. They report they've sustained micro-asteroid strikes. They've taken casualties and their towed array has been ripped away. Report from *Sherlock*, they've taken several small hull breaches and scoring to the forward abrasion plates but report as fully functional."

Willis listened impassively as her subordinates reported in.

"Any chance of a work around?" she asked as Yaya finished.

"We'll try but I'm not optimistic, ma'am," the Commander reported. "The passive array took a direct hit. About a third of it just isn't there anymore and the Lazarus systems can't seem to find a working power connection."

"Keep hands working on it for the moment," Willis instructed, "we'll just have to manage."

To have sustained damage to her ship at this early stage wasn't good, but the damage to the recon ship was a more immediate problem. The whole point of the small ship was to spool out its towed array to allow them to see past the comet without revealing anything that might be spotted in return. It was gone but they still had to be able to see the Nameless planet to judge when to move.

"Helm, shut down the dorsal wing's manoeuvring engine and programme thrusters to move us just far enough to show the dorsal tower. We'll move up in an hour, when the engine has cooled down."

She glanced up at the bridge clock. *Phantom* and the strike boats would still be getting into position. It was now seventy minutes to kick off.

Willis found herself holding her breath as *Spectre* slid slowly upwards. How closely were the Worms observing the space surrounding the planet? Was there a screen on the planet or on one of the orbiting starforts, registering that the comet's profile had just changed? As the cruiser's dorsal tower crested the top of the comet, a quick burst from the thrusters arrested their drift. As they did, the surviving passive arrays started to get their first reading and Willis felt herself calm a little.

For the past hour she'd been forcing herself not to fidget as they waited. But in that time, not much seemed to have changed compared to the previous reading received from the reconnaissance ship before they jumped in. There was traffic near the space gate and several of the Nameless warships were visible in orbit. But there was no sign of any alarm. The engines of the warships were still cold, while transports continued to go about their business.

"Bridge, Sensors. Captain, one of the enemy ships moving towards the gate is not a transport. Engine profile is consistent with a cruiser, moving at low acceleration."

"Damn," Willis said quietly.

The strike boats would probably run into more opposition than they expected. There was nothing she could do about it and in any case, what they were seeing was already four minutes out of date.

"Captain, it is now zero hour," the Navigator said quietly.

Willis nodded without replying. Out past the heliopause, seven strike boats and two gunboats would be spinning up their jump drives. Between spin up, time in transit and distance induced lag, *Spectre* wouldn't see them for another ten long minutes.

Although she'd been expecting it Willis jumped when the sensor operator eventually announced it.

"Bridge, Sensors. Nine new contacts, confirmed as friendlies!"

On the holo, nine blips appeared next to the Red Line and immediately vectored towards the orbiting gate. Around them appeared a circle to indicate the effective range of their missiles. Even on full burn they were a good twenty minutes from achieving firing range on the gate. The transports moving to and from the gate scattered like startled pigeons, each trying to put distance between themselves and the strike boats' obvious target.

"Coms?" Willis said quietly.

"Confirmed, Captain, the enemy has commenced FTL transmissions," the communications officer replied.

"Enemy starships are powering up engines."

Willis gritted her teeth as the holo showed the first missiles beginning to fly from the starforts on either side of the gate. Further back, the alien cruiser was also firing but the strike boats continued to push in. One of the blips winked out and another started flashing damage codes. The circle for their missile range still wasn't overlapping the gate and their formation was getting ragged as each boat desperately tried to find a way through the defensive fire. Another blip disappeared from the scope, while a second started to fall behind.

With painful slowness the strike boats crossed into firing range but still closed.

"Oh come on!" Willis said to herself. "Fire and get out of there!"

The distance was too great for *Spectre*'s passives to make out individual missiles but a haze of small signals appeared as the strike boats all sharply turned and made for the Red Line. The straggler didn't make it but the space gate and one of the starforts also disappeared from the plot, to be replaced by the indistinct signals of wreckage.

"Captain, enemy mobile units are on the move."

"All of them?"

"Negative. We can see one escort still in orbit and the visible ship count is missing a second escort and a cruiser. Estimate they are currently located behind the planet."

And if we're really lucky, Willis thought to herself as she followed the blips gathering speed away from the planet, *they're all down for maintenance*. But for now all she could do was continue to wait.

The blip for the surviving strike boats crossed the Red Line and disappeared as they jumped away. Now might be the moment it all unravelled. If the alien ships returned to the planet, then *Spectre* would be faced with too strong a defence. They would have to fall back and head deeper into Nameless space, losing time along with the element of surprise. Worse, the Worms wouldn't be trying to absorb a strategic hammer blow just as the Home Fleet went in.

But then there came a second flurry of FTL transmissions, this time from the gas giant. The readings from the passives were minutes out of date but *Spectre* could hear the FTL transmissions in real time. Willis shifted in her seat as she waited to see what decision the Nameless command would make. Had they successfully made them an offer they couldn't refuse?

On the holo, the blips continued towards the Blue Line. As they crossed, the passives could see them braking hard to jump. Then as they came to a near halt they disappeared from the plot. Willis exhaled a long shuddering breath and switched the intercom to ship wide.

"All hands, stand ready, we are about to jump."

Now all Willis had to do was judge the precise moment the Nameless ships would be deep into the gas giant's mass shadow, but before they could hunt down and destroy *Phantom*.

She decided on twenty minutes. That would be long enough.

As the minutes passed, they listened to the Nameless FTL transmissions, going back and forth from between the two planets. If they'd stopped that might have been an indication *Phantom* had been destroyed. *Spectre*'s sensors could see the gas giant but it was over twenty light minutes away. There was just no way to know. But Willis couldn't worry because their turn was about to come. As the countdown approached zero, she put her intercom to ship wide.

Willis had never been one for last minute pep talks. People knew what they were there for and that should be enough. But it wasn't always and it wasn't fair to expect it to be. Most of the crew were in sealed compartments – each in a small metal box with no way of knowing what was going on beyond its walls. But all of them would know they were about to make a frontal assault in a ship ill equipped for such a task. The right words could make that load a little easier to bear.

"All hands, this is your captain. In a few minutes our wait will be over. *Phantom* has succeeded in diverting most of the enemy's mobile units to give us a clear run at our objective. There's no doubt this will still be a rough ride for us all but this is also where we start to fight back. This is when the Nameless will learn the real meaning of the phrase 'reap the whirlwind'. Remember our comrades at the Spur and the entire human race are counting on us. Let's not disappoint them. Good luck everyone and let's get this done!"

Flicking off ship wide and returning to the command channel, Willis spoke again.

"Tactical, let's make sure everyone is awake. Sound Red Alert!" she said, stretching as much as her harness would allow.

As the alarm sounded across all channels, Willis surveyed her bridge.

"Bridge, Coms. The reconnaissance ship is requesting instructions."

They were to have waited and observed the results of the attack but with badly damaged sensor systems there was no point now.

"Order them to jump to the gas giant and, if they can, inform *Phantom* that we've started our run," she instructed. "Then tell them to get the hell back to their carrier!"

A tactical upload from the *Sherlock* showed she was fully operational. All that remained was for *Spectre*'s jump drive to spin up. A moment later, even that was done.

"Helm, take us in."

Spectre emerged from jump space less than a hundred

kilometres from the Red Line. Astern, *Sherlock* followed them back into real space. The bridge holo blanked out then started to fill in as the first returns came in. One of the Nameless ships was just orbiting into view. None of the starforts were on their side of the planet and the only other visible asset was the space elevator and the space docks.

"*Sherlock*'s going full burn, Captain."

"Helm," she ordered, "match her acceleration."

"Understood, engines going to sixty percent."

On her visual display, Willis could see the *Sherlock*'s cargo hatches slide open. That's when the converted merchantman showed her teeth – eight massive racks of missiles with enough firepower to sterilise a world, jacked out into firing position. They just needed time to put it on target.

Against a planet, with its predictable orbit, the firing solution for any projectile could potentially be worked out on a blackboard with chalk. But they wanted to hit particular parts of the planet and that required more time to establish their location.

"Bridge, Sensors. Enemy ship has just lit up her drive. She's moving to intercept. Contact separation, we have incoming."

"Point Defence batteries," Willis said calmly, "Counter Measures, stand ready."

The range was too long for the small Nameless general-purpose missiles, which would have overwhelmed *Spectre*'s slender defences. By contrast, their big long-range cap ship missiles were already starting to arc out. Two of their ships accelerated around the planet and brought their first salvo to bear. *Spectre*'s plasma cannons stabbed out but hit only a few. As they closed, the first of their Starfox missiles sped away. The space in front of *Spectre* erupted in fire as missile met missile and *Spectre*'s point defence guns rattled into action.

"Captain, the first of the starforts has orbited from behind the planet, it's launching... Captain! It's launching fighters."

"Shit!" Willis muttered to herself as she mentally ran through the possibilities.

At this range the fighters would struggle to get to them before *Sherlock* was ready to fire. But they had another possibility – move forward to intercept and destroy the missiles launched by *Sherlock*. The Nameless had never used their fighters like that before but they'd seen humans do it often enough. Given the nature of *Sherlock*'s payload, the alien fighters had to be kept close to the planet. That meant distracting them. *Spectre*'s own nukes were part of the planned bombardment and in any case there weren't enough of them to use as a sacrifice to get the others through.

Then there were their anti-ship missiles. While those could be sacrificed, they weren't capable of making atmospheric re-entry. They needed to be directed at something the Nameless *would* defend.

"Fire Control, clear the nukes from the forward tubes and reload with standard anti-ship missiles. Then target the enemy space elevator!"

There was a pause on the line. When he did speak, the gunner sounded confused.

"Captain, at this range on full burn our missiles will be ballistic for over ten minutes before they reach the target."

"Understood."

"Captain, even if tethered a lot of our missiles are going..."

"Understood! Just put those missiles in the air!" Willis virtually snarled across the connection.

The ship rattled as the result of a near miss. On the holo Willis could see the Nameless fighters surging forward. Another starfort and a second starship were now also coming into view. Both started to throw missiles but didn't co-ordinate, each platform firing separately. With only their big cap ship missiles available to them, they weren't putting out enough fire to guarantee saturation of *Spectre*'s defence. Then on the holo two of the Nameless missiles that had made it past the Starfoxes disappeared, to be replaced by much smaller but faster moving projectiles. Mass driver missiles!

"Helm! Evasive manoeuvres! Coms! Signal *Sherlock*!"

The collision detection alarm sounded as *Spectre* jolted to port. On the holo Willis saw projectiles flash past them, missing by only a few hundred metres. She turned to the visual display just in time to see *Sherlock*'s communications tower disintegrate as a projectile punched straight through it.

"We've lost all coms from *Sherlock*."

They'd been crunching the numbers. Had the evasive action thrown out the calculations? With the *Sherlock*'s coms gone there was no way to know. They just had to hang in and hope.

"Bridge, Fire Control. Commencing missile fire."

The first of *Spectre*'s missiles accelerated away. Thirty-five seconds later a second pair followed as the system went to rapid fire. On the holo the Nameless fighters continued in, then hesitated. As *Spectre* fired more missiles, at least half started to drop back.

"Bridge, Fire Control. We are down to our last five Starfox missiles."

"Understood Fire Control," Willis replied.

Sherlock was still holding straight, steady and mute. How long did the bombard need? By now, she should have fired in accordance with their plan, but there was no way to tell how bad the delay was. On the display, *Spectre's* missiles were starting to disappear. Unaccountably, one got through and slammed into the space elevator's hub but the Nameless fighters picked the rest of them off. Diversion over, the alien fighters that had held back now surged forward.

"How long until the first fighters reach us?" Willis asked without looking away from the holo.

"Six minutes, Captain."

"Fire Control, do you have firing solutions for the nukes?" she asked.

"Affirmative. The first of the nukes are in the tubes."

"Fire as planned."

There was no comment across the intercom, just the thump of the first pair of missiles clearing the tubes. Perhaps a moment like this should have been marked with deeper words. Then again, the six nuclear missiles probably wouldn't get through the Nameless counter fire.

"Captain! *Sherlock's* firing!"

As she spun round to the visual display, Willis just caught sight of the last of the first rack of munitions being volleyed off. Even at that they presented an awe-inspiring sight as dozens of missiles sped forward. It might have looked fearsome, but the first volley would still only be in its boost phase when they reached the leading Nameless fighters.

Most of the projectiles weren't nukes. They were kinetic strike penetrators, little more than solid lumps of metal. Once clear of the boost phase, there would be little the fighters' guns or missiles could do to break them up or even knock them off course. Even a direct hit from a Nameless cap ship missile might achieve little more than the obliteration of the missile.

But if the Nameless managed to hit their volleys while they were still in their boost phase, then all of *Sherlock's* calculations would count for nothing. Suddenly, whether through ammunition exhaustion or holding back for the close assault they perhaps expected *Spectre* to make, the Nameless starships and starforts thinned their fire. Whatever the reason, Willis saw a window in which to deal with the fighters that were now the main threat to the mission.

"Helm, engines all ahead full!" she roared. "Fire Control, concentrate point defence on those fighters. We must break them up!"

Willis felt herself being pressed into her seat as *Spectre* stretched her legs. The Nameless fighters were taken by surprise as the cruiser suddenly lunged forward. As they scattered, astern *Sherlock* fired the last of her payload. Delivery completed, the big ship began to lumber round, away from the planet. By contrast, *Spectre* continued in. Around her, space erupted as the Nameless fighters swarmed in, their guns stabbing out.

"Bridge, Damage Control! We've just lost the Number Five engine!" came Yaya's voice across the intercom. "Hell's teeth! They're picking off out point defence guns!"

On the holo, the first of *Sherlock*'s projectiles abruptly transformed into hundreds of separate contacts and Willis knew immediately what it meant. The projectiles had reached the end of their boost. A small backward facing rocket had popped the warheads and penetrators away from the expended motors and released a puff of chaff. Now the scores of contacts that mattered – the warheads and penetrators – were concealed within a cloud comprising thousands of fragments of chaff and burnt out rocket motors. By now the Nameless ships and starforts had resumed their fire. Large and small missiles alike headed into the fast approaching mass but with so many to intercept and no time to differentiate, whether they struck anything of importance was now no more than a matter of chance.

The planet behind them, the one the Nameless sought to defend, was already doomed.

"Helm, come to starboard sixty degrees and get us out of here," Willis ordered.

Around them, Nameless fighters swirled and space burned as point defence blazed and chaff rockets discharged as fast as their crews could reload them. With their missiles expended, the fighters attempted to nibble *Spectre* to death. On the bridge, damage reports poured in – the starboard wing was shot to pieces, the upper radar kept blinking out as power runs were severed and the Lazarus system found alternatives. Willis didn't have time for any of that. The Red Line was coming up and they only had to survive another few minutes. Ahead, a few fighters had reached the *Sherlock*, the big lumbering transport turned destroyer of their world, now flailing desperately with its few small guns at those that would have revenge.

"Navigation, are we ready to jump?"

"Drive spun up, we're ready."

Even as the Navigator called out another explosion shook the ship. The fighters were trying to get round in front to strike at their jump drive, but *Spectre* kept twisting.

On the engineering display one engine blinked out while another started to stutter. Willis felt *Spectre*'s acceleration drop sharply. *We won't make it!* Another engine went down. The fighters were overhauling them.

"Bridge, Damage Control!" Yaya shouted. "We've lost Point Defence One and Five! We're wide open to the front!"

Ahead, *Sherlock* crossed the Red Line and disappeared. The pursuing fighters braked hard and came back at them. To port and starboard, fighters overtook *Spectre*, boxing her in, all of them attempting to target the jump drive.

"Roll to port, try to protect the drive!" Willis ordered.

The dorsal radar tower took another hit and half the holo blinked out.

"Keep rolling!" she shouted as she desperately sacrificed bits of her ship.

"Bridge, Sensors. New contacts!"

Two contacts appeared on the holo, right on the Red Line. Flashing the ID codes of *Pankhurst*'s two gunboats, they appeared behind the fighters that had been pursuing *Sherlock*. Taken by surprise, the fighters were torn apart as the two gunboats accelerated towards *Spectre*.

"Helm, turn towards them!" she shouted. "Get us onto a reciprocal course!"

The two gunboats flew in, engines at full burn and guns blazing as they blasted a path through the Nameless fighters, now scattering to left and right.

"Bridge, Coms. Signal from gunboats – road clear."

Their rescuers sped away and left the *Spectre* behind, getting clear before the fighters could rally and mob them. But they had done enough. The aliens had lost momentum. Some attempted to chase the gunboats now curving back towards the Red Line. Others tried to get back to *Spectre* but they'd lost vital time and ground. Minutes later, Willis's ship limped across the line and disappeared into the safety of jump space.

Out beyond the heliopause, nearly twelve light hours from the system's star, the human squadron gathered to lick its wounds – and count the cost. *Phantom* had not reached them. And never would.

"What happened?" Yaya asked as Willis washed her face.

The ship had re-pressurised, at least she had in those compartments that could still hold pressure. The air retained that metallic whiff it always seemed to pick up and everything was frigid.

"There was a small starfort close to the largest of the hydrogen facilities," Willis answered. "Neither reconnaissance nor tactical identified it. It must have held its fire until *Phantom* got close. They didn't get any warning and it managed to knock out most of her engines."

Willis shrugged helplessly as she rubbed her face with a towel. Commodore Tneba had taken his near crippled ship far deeper into the mass shadow than planned, deep enough to use the facilities he was targeting as cover from the mobile units. Whether it was a vain attempt to save his ship or a deliberate effort to exact the highest possible price for her destruction, they would probably never know. The reconnaissance ship Willis had sent to him arrived just in time witness to *Phantom* succumbing to a hail of missiles.

"So that puts you in command then, ma'am," Yaya said heavily.

"Technically the captain of the *Pankhurst* has more time in grade than me, but I've spoken to him and he isn't contesting it." Willis said with a slightly bitter smile before adding: "This isn't what any of us joined up for."

The Worms' fighters hadn't inflicted any real structural damage but they'd pecked away at everything on the outer surface. Three engines were down and the ship's engineer had already reported that at least one was beyond any field repair. The passive sensor arrays were mostly shot to pieces and the point defence grid was severely compromised. The crew had also suffered seventeen casualties, five of them fatal, while the Doctor had warned that two more were likely to follow. *Sherlock* had got off lightly – the two personnel in the coms tower were dead and engineers were trying to jury rig something, but other than that, the bombard had sustained little more than a few punctures in the outer hull.

With initial repairs done or at least underway, the support ships were moving up to resupply the survivors. But what Willis was really waiting for, were those first light speed signals.

"Bridge to Captain," crackled the intercom dangling from her waist.

"I'm here," she replied, putting her earpiece in place.

"Ma'am, it's time."

"Alright, I'm on my way up," she replied before turning to Yaya. "You might as well join me, Commander. The odds are that from here on in, this is the first thing anyone will ever want to ask us about."

There were more people on the bridge than there should have been. With the ship opened up from action stations, only the duty shift should have been present. But most of the senior officers were already there. Willis made no comment as she pulled herself into her seat.

The main holo was set for visual mode and showed the planet. For the first time, Willis was struck by how pleasant it looked. Green of land, blue of oceans and white of wispy clouds, the landmasses were different from Earth's, but otherwise it could pass as a twin. The starforts and Nameless ships were also just visible as they broke the illusion of serenity, lashing out with their missiles in sheer desperation.

"There's the first one," someone at the back of the bridge said only to be immediately hushed by others.

No one could have missed the line of fire that cut across the sky. It disappeared, then a moment later there was a sharp flash. Even at such a distance, it was enough to trigger *Spectre*'s computer to dim the display for a second.

It was a nuke, probably one of *Spectre*'s, targeted at a small population centre seventy kilometres outside the main city. The device was set to detonate at two thousand metres to maximise devastation against civilian targets. Another line traced across the sky and seconds later another settlement was erased by a spreading brown cloud.

In orbit, the defending forts and ships redoubled their effort. Abruptly one of the forts blew apart, its orbit intersecting with a kinetic penetrator. Off to the left of the display, the space elevator also shook as a projectile cored it, shearing the station away from its tether and sending it tumbling away into space.

It was a breathtaking sight, but no one on the bridge commented because dozens of projectiles were now entering the atmosphere. Penetrators impacted with duller flashes and irregularly shaped clouds began to overlap and merge. Nukes were still going in but now almost nothing of the surface was still visible. The second wave of projectiles spread out in all directions from the Nameless city, landing strikes all over the visible side of the planet.

A little over fifteen minutes after that first flash, it was all over. The last projectile had landed and now all that remained were the consequences.

Little remained of the green, the blue and the wispy white, which could now only be seen around the edges and it was diminishing fast as material thrown into the atmosphere spread rapidly. Light boiled up from the below the clouds – uncontrollable firestorms Willis guessed. The fallout would already be spreading. Within weeks, few parts of the planet wouldn't be intensely irradiated. With the space elevator and probably any launch fields gone, it would take Herculean efforts to save the populations of the small towns on the far side of the planet. If the Nameless couldn't, or didn't try, the inhabitants would have only enough time to see their doom coming.

"Well that learned 'em," someone said from the back of the bridge.

Several people, including Willis, turned to frown at the speaker – one of the younger officers – who visibly wilted under their glares. As she turned back to the holo, she wondered whether the planet had been naturally life bearing or terra-formed. She hoped it was the latter. Better that than to have snuffed out millions of years of development. Mentally she forced herself to set such thoughts side. Now that they knew the results of their attack they had work to do.

"Coms, prepare a message drone for dispatch to the Home Fleet's position."

She paused as she looked again at the holo and a world in its death throes.

"Attach our logs with a message: Stage One Retribution successfully complete. Moving to second positions. Get that away within the hour."

Soon, the depleted squadron would be moving deeper into Nameless territory. They'd take position in the void between stars and deployed scouts to observe the next three closest Nameless worlds. This time though their approach would not be discrete. They'd let the Nameless see them. They'd let the Nameless know that the ships, which had turned a living world into a dead rock, were still there. The Worms would then know that if they were given an opening or space, Willis and her squadron would do it again.

Chapter Eighteen

Barring the Gate

15th April 2069

The scout ship *K23* hung in geo-stationary orbit over the dwarf planet situated seventy-two astronomical units from the system's star. The dwarf was too far out for the Nameless to reach. Otherwise it would have had observation satellites ringing it like the system's true planets, ready to alert the defenders. Nonetheless, discretion was required.

K23's nose cone pointed directly at the planetoid. Astern, her towed passive sensor array spooled out just far enough to peek over the horizon and in towards the depths of the system. On the bridge, Lieutenant Rey frowned as she studied the readings. Their computer didn't have sufficient processing power to interpret all the data the array was soaking up, but what it could determine was frightening.

"Those are serious defences, Skipper," said Petty Officer Allen as he studied his screen.

"Yes," Rey reluctantly agreed. "Observation satellites, weapons platforms, ground bases, minefields and mobile units."

She paused. There in the centre of that layered defence was the jewel – the Nameless space gate, access point into this arm of the galaxy and their objective.

"If there's a route in that won't see us bleed every metre of the way, I can't see it."

"Let's hope better paid heads can spot something."

"We can but... hang on... New contacts!"

Rey tensed for a moment but whatever had caught Allen's attention was around the gate, light hours from *K23*.

"We have ships making jump in through the gate station, at least a dozen."

"Type?"

Allen made a few adjustments before shaking his head.

"Can't tell at this range."

Rey studied her screen for a minute. The newly arrived ships seemed to be manoeuvring round the gate. They looked like they were lining up for jump out, which likely made them support ships en route to the front line, carrying the munitions and supplies that were the very lifeblood of conquest. Another few minutes and the new arrivals had disappeared again.

"They don't hang about," Allen observed.

"Doesn't look like they use this system for supply dumps," Rey said. "Might be too far back or putting too many eggs in one basket." Then a thought occurred. "Is the gate station's FTL beacon still online?"

"No, Skipper. It's just cut out."

"Now that is interesting. Those are the first ships we've seen coming through. What's the estimated time for them to jump the rift?"

"Intel reckons..." Allen checked a database, "...six to seven hours."

"And we've been on station for four hours and it was on when we arrived. Make a note in the log to check if or when the ship ahead of us saw the beacon come on."

"What we can now confirm is that, as with the Siege of Earth, the enemy is operating on a nineteen hour cycle," Sheehan reported. "In the past twenty-four hours we have observed one convoy of what we assume were transports jumping out across the Rift, in the direction of the Nameless core worlds, and one jumping in. In the case of the convoy arriving, the gate station's beacon transmitted for the ten hours preceding their arrival. In the case of the departing convoy, our scouts detected another beacon on the Nameless side of the rift. Again the transmission was continuous for ten hours."

"So, they need the beacon to be continuous to make the jump across the rift," observed Admiral Sekhar. "Do we know why?"

"Well, sir, there has been..."

"The why is not particularly important, Captain Sheehan," Lewis cut him off. "Nor do these readings definitively prove anything."

"Sir, we have witnessed three convoys arrive across the Rift," Sheehan replied. "We know that these are coming from the Nameless home worlds because the gate station lines up to receive them. When ships arrive or depart from our side of the rift, the alignment of the gate station is different. Every time ships are in transit across the rift, the beacons, whether on this side or the other, are active. So by extension, we must assume the beacons are necessary. As far as we know, their space gates and ship-mounted jump drives fundamentally work the same way. If the gate jumpers need the beacon, then so do their jump-capable ships."

As he followed the exchange, Crowe wondered whether he was the only one in the conference room expecting to see the Admiral's patience snap at being corrected, but Lewis took it calmly. It had surprised Crowe to be summoned to the decision meeting. Several more senior divisional commanders were not in attendance. As a mere commodore, he was somewhat out of his pay grade. Still, he wouldn't just sit there like a lemon.

"Sir, I think our scout ships have made out one detail that is very telling," he said.

Lewis's cold eyes turned towards him.

"It's the level of defence, sir. We knocked out a lot of gates when we fought on the Junction Line last year. Most were completely unprotected and the Nameless seemed to follow a policy of rapid replacement rather than attempting to defend them, which is in absolute contrast to what we see here."

"That's true sir," Sekhar said. "We never saw anything even close to this kind of defence, even around their biggest supply dumps. If they are defending it, then it must be for a reason."

"Not to mention that compared to the reading *Spectre* took when she first discovered the system, the defences have been substantially beefed up," said Admiral Paahlisson."

"Given that we hit an important position within a few systems of here, that was as sure as sunrise," Admiral Conrad Kanter responded, "which reinforces the supposition that this is critical ground for them."

"A reasonable line of thinking," Lewis replied after a pause. "So if we assume that the gate, and more importantly the beacon, is the key to the system, how do we proceed?"

"Go in hard and fast," Kanter said firmly. "That gate can't get out of the way, so we roll in and take it out."

"And that will take us straight into the teeth of their defence," Sekhar objected. "With the gate positioned at the Lagrange point between the planet and its moon, the Home Fleet would also have to get between the two. Once there, we'd be fired upon by the orbital installations around the planet, the ground installations on the moon and the mobile units – in short, from every damn direction. I know the new barrage ships are impressive, but that kind of crossfire will overwhelm them."

"But won't overwhelm the fleet as a whole," Kanter replied.

"We would take damage and therein lies the problem, Conrad," Lewis said before Sekhar could reply. "If it was simply a question of destroying the gate, then a frontal assault would be the simplest and most reliable route. Unfortunately, destroying the gate is merely step one. After that, we will have to hold this ground for as long as it takes for the Nameless to be starved of supplies. That will be a question of endurance, so the more we lose in the first phase, the harder that will be to endure."

"Long range fire perhaps?" Sekhar hazarded.

"By the time we're close enough to use even heavy plasma cannons, we'll be taking fire from the defences," Kanter said shaking his head. "We don't have enough ships with heavy calibre railguns anymore and just because that station is at the Lagrange point now, doesn't mean it can't be shifted to get out of the way of a long range shot."

The discussion broke down into several overlapping conversations as various ideas were thrashed out. Lewis spoke only occasionally, mostly to point out why each suggestion would come up short.

"Sir," Crowe said finally, "I think we have to go back to the plan proposed back on Earth and use the *Mississippi*."

"That plan was proposed by someone who needed to get out more!" Sekhar said sharply. "You're talking about charging three ships – only three ships – into the very teeth of those defences!"

"Yet, sir," Crowe replied, "if it cost us only those three ships it would be a good exchange, they are..." the word caught in his throat, "... they are expendable."

"Those ships would be better deployed as decoys," Sekhar countered. "We should use fighters to attack the gate."

"That would bleed the fighter squadrons white, even if it succeeded," Kanter replied.

"Using *Mississippi* does have one other virtue, sir," Crowe said as he turned back to Lewis. "If it fails, it doesn't block an attempt by the rest of the fleet."

Lewis made no reply and instead sat staring at the grainy image of their objective on the screen. Finally he stood up.

"Gentlemen, I need to consider the data further. You're

dismissed."

Crowe was waiting for his shuttle back to *Deimos* when Lewis's chief-of-staff appeared at his elbow.

"Commodore Crowe, the Admiral is asking to speak to you privately."

"Of course. On what matter?"

"He didn't say, sir," the Sheehan replied.

Lewis was sitting down when Crowe stepped into the cabin, with his jacket cast carelessly onto the cabin's bunk and his collar loosened. He looked far less forbidding than usual.

"Commodore, please take a seat," he said.

"Thank you, sir."

"Commodore, you appear to be the leading proponent of the *Mississippi* attack."

"Yes, sir, I guess I am. I know the points raised against it are valid and that it must have looked like a good idea from a desk on Earth..."

"Actually, Commodore, the basic idea was mine," Lewis interrupted.

"Err..."

"Others developed it further, but I still do not regard it with much favour. But this was always going to be an offensive based on intelligence information that was weeks out of date. We needed to bring with us the means to have as many options as possible."

"Sir, as you said, we need to destroy the gate station without the fleet itself getting knocked about. If we can pull their defences out of position, then I believe at least one of the three will make it through," Crowe replied.

"Hmm," Lewis said. "Are you still set on commanding *Mississippi* again?"

"Yes sir," Crowe replied.

There was a catch in his voice. Lewis misinterpreted it.

"Are you afraid of death, Commodore?"

The Admiral raised his hand before Crowe could reply.

"No slur is intended. The Mississippi Incident, the Junction Line, Kite String and the Siege of Earth, your record in combat is second to none, but no man is without limits. This plan, the principal reason I do not like it, is because it hinges on courage. It hinges on the courage and willingness of the officer in command to, if necessary, lay down his life to make it work."

"Sir, I believe I am that officer."

"Very well, Commodore. You may make preparations to transfer to *Mississippi*."

19th April 2069

Journalism was definitely not a profession for those with a thin skin, even more so when you were an embedded journalist in a military unit. Oh, when the camera or microphone was on, they were all polite professionalism but once off, then a journalist was regarded with, at best, a level of enthusiasm usually associated with an imminent dental examination. The most junior officers and ratings were usually less guarded, but the more senior an individual, the more they seemed to look upon journalists with pained resignation.

When Jeff first arrived on board the Myth class heavy cruiser *Freyia*, Captain Hicks seemed to be particularly despondent. Just before Jeff went into the Deep Sleep capsule for the long journey to The Spur, he found out from a friendly NCO why. When the captains of Sixth Cruiser Squadron discovered that they would be hosting an embedded journalist, they'd played poker to decide which ship would get Jeff. Apparently, Hicks was blown out of the water by a royal flush.

Still, there was no point crying. Jeff had signed on for this and at least the accommodation wasn't bad. He'd expected to be bunked with the ship's NCOs or officers. Instead he'd been assigned his own cabin. All right, cabin was probably overstating it – it was a partly cleared out storage locker in which he had to sleep slightly curled up since it wasn't deep enough to straighten out in it without leaving the hatch open. But it was a nice private little spot, which on a warship counted as luxury.

When he heard he'd got one of the precious Home Fleet assignments, Jeff had performed a little dance of joy in the office. This could be the assignment that sealed his career and made him a household name across the States. Then one of the office girls, one he'd been sort of seeing, wished him luck with a sick look on her face. On a starship, a journalist took damn near all the same chances the crew did. There was no way to do the job and not take them. Still, no guts no glory.

Once all the soon to be embedded journalists were in orbit they'd been given a detailed briefing on the coming operation. They'd then been allowed to each record a report to be released by the fleet once the operation was underway. With that done they were ferried up to their assigned ships. Any communication out was extremely limited and closely monitored. There was a lot of grumbling about that, but this was a case of either play ball or go home.

Once out of Deep Sleep he'd expected the attack to get underway pretty much straight away, but no, days passed quietly. On board, *Freyia* preparations were made with quiet earnestness.

"I know they say no plan survives first contact with the enemy," Lieutenant Grambel, the gunnery officer, commented when Jeff remarked on it, "but frankly we still prefer to have one. It beats frantically 'winging it'."

So Jeff spent the time doing interviews with the crew. He didn't think their officers had briefed them but it was funny how people automatically reached for a lot of the same terms. Again and again, he heard men and women tell him with nervous earnestness how they didn't want to let down their shipmates or their families. It was time to bring their A game, this was the big one, the one that would win the war. The network would likely only ever use short excerpts from interviews with the younger or more photogenic members of the crew, but some of film archives companies might be interested as well.

There was a ping outside and Jeff pulled himself up from his bunk and stepped out into the passageway so he could hear the address system properly.

"All hands, this is the Captain. A few minutes ago we received notification from the flagship that Operation Vindictive is now officially a go. We will move out at oh seven hundred hours tomorrow. *Freyia* will be on the left flank of the fleet."

There was a pause that made Jeff think it was over, so turned to go back into his cabin. Then the Captain's voice came through again.

"I won't ask you to get ready because I know you are. You are the best crew on the best ship in the best fleet and we will do what needs to be done. For this evening's meal, the galley has assured me that they will pull out all the stops. Until tomorrow morning I'm putting everyone on light duties. Finish what you are doing and then get as much rest as you can. This is the Captain, out."

Jeff leaned against the bulkhead. This was it! He'd almost managed to convince himself that nothing would happen but it really was. Shit really was about to hit the fan, with malice aforethought. He noticed that he had the camera in his hand. He must have picked it up automatically. He switched it on and turned it to face him.

"Ladies and Gentlemen, this is your ace reporter Jeff Harlow, all set to have his ass shot off in the name of news and entertainment."

Turning, he saw one of the crew watching him, an engineering rating going by her uniform. She smiled nervously and it struck him that she was kinda pretty.

"I've just gone off duty. Are you still doing interviews?" she asked.

"Sure, step into my office," he said waving her in.

"Well, Commander," Crowe said as he put his signature to the document formally transferring command, "you are now formally the skipper of the good ship *Deimos* and all who sail upon her."

"Temporarily, sir," Commander, now brevet Captain, Bhudraja replied unruffled. "And I look forward to signing the document that returns her to your command."

"Thank you, Captain. It's good to know she's in safe hands," Crowe replied, as he offered his hand and Bhudraja shook it firmly.

All but the duty shift had lined up in the crew receiving area. Crowe moved slowly down the line, pausing to speak a few words to a man or woman here or there. When he had arrived on board *Deimos*, it had been as an officer no longer trusted by his superiors or subordinates. Now, as he paused to look back on so many familiar faces, he realised that this ship had become home.

"God willing, we will see each other in a day or two and have stories to share. All of you, do me proud."

As the hatch closed behind him, he heard someone call three cheers for the Commodore.

Crowe took the co-pilot's seat for the journey from *Deimos*. Their destination was in the middle of the Home Fleet's formation. In amongst the support ships, the *Mississippi* awaited him, floating alongside two converted transports that would join her for this, her final mission. In his mind's eye, Crowe could remember her, as she had once been, an elegant lady, aging gracefully. Now she showed too many signs of harsh surgery to ever again be called graceful. The point defence grid had been completely overhauled, two of the plasma cannon turrets replaced with flak guns and chemical booster rockets strapped to the sides of the hull. Overshadowing all of those however, were the scars, the ones from the first shots in this war. But better this than a lingering death in the breaker's yard. When he pulled himself through the airlock, only one person waited to meet him, Lieutenant Craven, his new second-in-command.

"Welcome aboard sir," Craven said saluting. There was no need here for the niceties of a formal command transfer. He'd never been taken off her books as captain.

"Thank you, Lieutenant, where are we up to?"

"The commander of the transfer crew is waiting on the bridge to complete handover. The munitions ship has signalled that the nukes are on their way over. I've got everyone doing final checks now."

Crowe nodded. Almost everything was in place, not long now.

"Cold start assembly."

"Check," Schurenhofer replied.

"Magnetic constrictors," Alanna continued down the checklist.

"Check."

During the journey to the Spur, *D for Dubious* had been comprehensively overhauled. The deck chief had actually been a bit sour on that point. Before leaving Earth, Alanna had been offered a factory fresh machine. While *D for Dubious* was probably no different from any other Raven class space fighter – in fact she now had a lot of miles on the clock – Alanna was used to her and her quirks. Better a reliable warhorse that maybe wasn't quite as quick on her feet any more, than an unproven mount that might do something unexpected at an awkward moment.

It had been an unexpectedly difficult moment watching the class of trainees, whom she'd done her best to guide, disperse towards their war stations. She was well aware some of them just weren't ready but there was nothing more she could do for them. For her part, it was a return to *Dauntless*. Apparently, once his ship re-emerged from the repair docks, Captain Philippe had pulled every available string to recover her as the carrier squadron's second-in-command. There weren't many familiar faces among the flight crews from their Siege of Earth days, but a few familiar faces remained.

"You know it's not too late to swap this bird out for another unit," Squadron Commander Len Deighton said as he pulled himself up to *Dubious's* access hatch.

"Hello, sir," Alanna looked up from her checklist. "Has the Chief got you doing his dirty work?"

"He did come to speak to me quite extensively on the dangers of aged spaceframes, that much is true."

"I'd be touched if I wasn't convinced he's more concerned about his own workload than my personal safety. *Dubious* has had a complete strip down. All components are well inside their operating lifespan. I have the documents and signatures to prove it."

Deighton let out a faint snort. No pilot ever quite entirely trusted the documentation from the deck crews. If something did go wrong, it wouldn't be their immediate problem, which was why Alanna and Schurenhofer had spent an hour personally working through the checklist.

Deighton certainly had the authority to order *Dubious* put into stores, but like Alanna, he knew that a pilot needed to trust their machine.

"Well, you've got forty minutes to wrap it up in here," he said. "Pilots briefing – orders have finally arrived from Flag."

"Do I get any spoilers?"

"Yeah, *Akagi* and *Huáscar*'s fighters will clear the way for the *Mississippi* group by striking at the lunar weapons batteries. We'll provide their top cover and act as the flying reserve."

"So ground fire and enemy fighters then?"

"That's about the size of it. Going by the list of objectives Flag sent over, I'd say it is damn near certain we'll have to attack ground targets."

"Glad to hear it sir," Alanna replied with a nod. "The old *Dauntless* stopped them from winning this war and the new *Dauntless* will help us win it. Just as it should be."

"Alright, get this wrapped up," Deighton replied. "And Lieutenant, if this bird doesn't check out *perfectly*, I want it struck down and a replacement delivered from stores."

"Of course sir, no room for sentimentality," she said as Deighton pushed himself off from the hatch, back towards the hangar airlock.

"No room for sentimentality?" Schurenhofer said. "Skipper, I get nervous every time you mention the old *Dauntless*."

"Just a turn of phrase. I'm just glad I'm here Kristen, here for the death."

Schurenhofer gave her a cautious look.

"Just as long as it isn't *our* death, Skip. The only way I really want to see the Spur is behind us as we leave."

Alanna glanced over at her weapons controller, ready to offer some kind of joke, but Schurenhofer's expression was deadly serious.

"I haven't come here to die," Alanna said, "and if I've got this far without cracking, then I think we're safe from that at least."

"And you just go ahead and keep saying that, Skipper. Just remember we're not here as some bit of universal balance or some such new age happy horseshit."

"You don't believe things happen for a reason?"

"Nope, a lot of shit happens randomly. You aren't getting God are you?"

"No, no I'm not. Just..." Alanna trailed off, her fingers rubbing her dog tags. "Once this is all over," she said after a moment, "there'll be stories to tell. In the case of the old *Dauntless*, I'm the only one left to tell theirs."

She looked sadly at her weapons controller and added: "I don't have a duty to join them; I have a duty to stay alive."

At oh six hundred hours the next morning, the Home Fleet would make the jump across the few light days that separated their staging area from the Spur system. Unlike their first battle of the war, there was no need for a mad dash to the Spur. On board *Warspite*, Lewis sat in his cabin, lost in thought, although for the first time in weeks they weren't about military matters. Instead his mind went back to goodbyes.

The small coffee shop located in the city's outer suburbs was experiencing the usual post-lunchtime lull. A single patron was sitting in a corner, his feet up on a chair, reading a book. As the bell over the door jingled, the young woman behind the counter glanced up from where she was slowly cleaning a glass – and then did a double take as two fleet Admirals walked in.

"Two teas," Lewis said curtly as his wife selected a table.

"And four portions of cake," Laura Lewis called around him before addressing her husband. "And don't snap at the girl, Paul!"

Lewis smiled slightly and nodded to the young woman.

They talked about minor matters, both of them studiously avoiding work. All the while, Laura kept an eye on the door.

"There's Brian now," she said as a man entered with a small child hanging off each hand.

Their son walked in and looked around for a moment before

spotting Laura's wave.

"There's granny and granddad," he said, letting go of the children.

A while later Laura was still playing with the children. Their young faces were smeared with chocolate cake and crumbs were spread across the table. Both of them were telling her a story with the desperate earnestness of small children.

"Dad, when do you leave?" Brian asked quietly.

"Within the next two days. Your Mother is to be the divisional commander of the Eighth Cruiser Squadron. She doesn't ship out for another fortnight. But she'll be heading for orbit within the week and won't be coming back..."

Lewis stopped.

"She won't be coming back until this is done," he corrected himself.

His son's grim expression made clear the slip hadn't been missed.

"Dad, what are the chances? I'm not asking for details but don't give me the party line."

Lewis made no immediate reply. He half turned to look at his grandchildren. He'd known early that his son wasn't cut out for a military career. Frankly, he had been relieved when, as a boy, Brian had shown no interest in one. Too much of a dreamer for military life, he was doing well in his chosen career in architecture though. But Brian had grown up in a military household, so he knew the language and understood far better than most what they faced.

"Attack," Lewis said quietly, "everywhere we are in contact with the enemy we will attack and keep attacking until we've won or been destroyed."

"Can that work?"

"Distance means the intelligence details are incomplete. A lot of the planning will be done on the fly. If some of the assumptions we have made are wrong, then we could be heading into a battle of attrition, with no prospect of a big payoff. If we're right, then the Nameless will come at us with all the strength of desperation. This will be a slogging match, a battle of attrition where the winner will be the one who can bleed hardest and longest."

Brian didn't ask for more and the two men returned to the children. An hour later, Brian called time on the visit.

"Come on. Your Mum will be wondering where we've got to," he *said into the face of combined complaints. "Not to mention," he added to the two Admirals, "they'll be bouncing off the walls after so much sugar." Nodding to fragments of cake and discarded biscuit wrappers, he added: "Dinner is certainly a write-off anyway."*

With coats gathered and chocolaty faces wiped, Brian paused to look at his parent awkwardly.

"Bit of a déjà vu thing," he said. "Spent most of my childhood watching one or other of you head off. This is the first time it's been both of you."

"Brian..."

"I know. It's necessary. God knows, that's been proven. Look... just come back with your shields, not on them – both of you."

He left without waiting for a reply.

"Hmm?" Lewis asked as he emerged from his thoughts.

"I just asked, sir, whether you want anything?" Sheehan asked from the cabin hatch.

"A great many things, Captain, none of which are within your power to supply," he replied. "Thank you, but that will be all for this evening."

"Yes, sir, I'll see you in the morning."

Lewis returned to his thoughts before the hatch closed behind his chief of staff. The cabin's holo projector was showing the feed from one of the ship's external cameras. Battleships, carriers, cruisers, destroyers, missile boats, bulk transports, forward repair ships, fuel carriers and several thousand men and women – The Home Fleet, the most powerful armada of starships that had ever set forth from Earth. Would they be enough? There was simply no way to know. Now all he could do was hope.

Over a light day from the edge of the Spur system, the Home Fleet separated into its component parts. The support ships spread into a loose arc, while the fighting ships formed up by division. *Mississippi*, the small, militarised transports *San Demetrio* and *Nolan*, plus six small gunboats, had moved to one side, accentuating their place as members of neither group. On every ship, final preparations were being made, including many that weren't strictly necessary but provided a welcome alternative to having to sit and think.

Crowe listened as the other two ships of his squadron checked in. They wouldn't be jumping with the rest of the fleet. Their time would come when every Nameless ship and installation was too pre-occupied to wonder about a cluster of contacts jumping in, a few light minutes away from the Nameless gate station.

"Do we have word on the fighters?" Crowe asked.

"We have confirmation from *Akagi*. Once they've neutralised ground targets, any fighters with remaining ordnance will move to cover us."

Turning, Crowe looked towards the three officers who were not in Battle Fleet uniforms sitting at the back of the bridge. One was American, one Chinese and one Russian, each one a key-holder for the three thermonuclear devices now on board *Mississippi*. Simply aiming to ram into the gate station had been computer-modelled back on Earth. Against the lightweight gate structure, there was too much of a chance that if they merely clipped it, they would only sweep away a small portion, leaving the rest fundamentally intact. The three bombs, which the crew had predictably named Hope, Faith and Charity, would ensure it didn't survive. But only if *Mississippi* could hand deliver them, so to speak. The other two ships, *San Demetrio* and *Nolan*, would provide cover for as long as they could or ram with their own bombs. Only one of them had to make it.

"All set gentlemen?" Crowe asked.

The American gave a thumbs-up while the other two nodded.

"Bridge, Coms. Signal from flagship, they've ordered us to put this to ship wide."

"Looks like the Admiral wants to give us all a last pep talk," Crowe grunted as he nodded his assent.

There was silence for a moment. When Lewis's voice came through, it was hesitant at first, but became firmer.

"Officers and crews of the Home Fleet, this is Admiral Lewis. In a few moments I will give the order to jump to the Spur system. In doing so, today we will begin the final step in a journey that we all embarked upon almost four years ago.

"The attack upon the *Mississippi* was both a foretaste and warning of what was to come, one that we could not understand. Since we first reached for the stars, both as a fleet and as a species, we have made our share of mistakes but not this time. Because what we could not understand was that, from the first moment they became aware of us, the Nameless have desired only one thing – our destruction as a species.

"We now know that there was no mean by which we might have avoided this ordeal. Had we gone down upon bended knee and begged them to allow us to live in peace, they would have showed us not one shred of mercy.

"We did not beg. We fought, we bled and we sacrificed. In our journey to this time and place, we have known victories and many defeats. We have left behind both friends and comrades. However, their sacrifice was not in vain. They have bought us this last great chance to uphold our oaths – to stand between Earth and all that would threaten it, and to say to them: not while we draw breath.

"In a few minutes we will begin our last great charge and I wish you all to understand one final thing. Once this begins, there will be no retreat and no surrender. We will not take one step back. If we are to return to our families and loved ones, it can only be as victors. This is Admiral Lewis. Good luck to you all."

The connection clicked off.

The sensor operator tried to report but his voice was choked, Crowe waited for him.

"The Home Fleet is jumping, sir."

"I see it," Crowe acknowledged as he saw the icon for *Deimos* disappear.

Ten light seconds from the planet's Red Line and behind the orbital track of the small moon, the Home Fleet dropped back into real space. Lines of battleships, carriers, cruisers, barrage ships and other smaller vessels filed out of the jump portal and re-established their formations. Torpedoes were launched and moved onto their programmed positions on the flanks and rear.

Strapped into his command chair, Lewis waited while his fleet assumed formation. The sluggish barrage ships were still lumbering out onto the flanks, while fighters accelerated out in front, ready to thin the waves of the missiles that would soon be coming their way. On the holo he could see the Nameless fleet beginning to move. They'd already been active before the Home Fleet had arrived and, clearly, news of Operation Retribution had reached them.

As he watched, they began to split their formation into sub-groups and advanced to envelop the approaching human ships. They wouldn't attempt to go head to head – their fixed defences would do that, while their warships bled the Home Fleet from the flanks. They probably expected to lose the gate station, and, just as probably, they most likely had replacements ready to activate once the system was clear. Most of the orbital defences were autonomous missile packs. Worthless once expended, they needed the Nameless to expend as many as possible.

"Admiral, our defensive fighters are now on station."

"Good," Lewis replied, "any sign of enemy fighters?"

"Yes, sir. They appear to be sticking close to the starships for the moment. Tactical's current count indicates they have a numerical advantage of two to one."

Lewis nodded without replying. That wasn't enough to offset his fighters' qualitative advantage. Those from *Illustrious* and his cruisers would be enough to hold off their Nameless counterparts, should his opposite number choose to commit them at this stage.

Lewis attempted to get into his opposite number's mind. What could the Nameless commander see? Hopefully, he would be fooled by the illusion of an apparently cautious advance by a fleet that needed to get deep into the planetary mass shadow. Nothing appeared out of place for that. The gate station was still hidden behind the moon but as Lewis watched, it appeared on the holo as one of their reconnaissance ships jumped to a position to achieve line of sight. The Worms' transports and other non-combat types were all turning for the gate station, using it to jump away. Jump-capable transports would likely reach the edge of the system, out of harm's way, while gateships would move to the next gate in the system. There was no hint of panic. The Nameless ships were withdrawing in good order. The Home Fleet continued to move in.

With the figurative starter's pistol fired, launch was a relief. The Admiral's words had brought back too many memories for Alanna. It had returned her to the speech given by the late Admiral Brian on board the Old *Dauntless*, just before that last fateful attack. For an hour after jump in, she waited impatiently in the pilots' ready room. Some of her comrades tried to sleep. A few had even succeeded but she was too keyed up. Finally, they were sent to their fighters.

First off the rail, *Dubious* coasted down the line of warships. Astern, her section formed up and, with a touch on the controls, Alanna turned them towards the fighter rally point. The rest of the strike was also gathering, as were, more ominously, the search and rescue shuttles.

They mustered five full fighter squadrons, sixty fighters gathered along with the reconnaissance ship serving as strike leader, who finally ordered them to move off. Around *Dubious*, space lit up with engine flares as the fighters accelerated away from the Home Fleet. Alanna looked back over her shoulder at the fast shrinking fleet and could just make out the first bursts of gunfire as Nameless missiles probed the fleet's defences.

"Mind on the job, Skipper," Schurenhofer muttered as she hunched over her instrumentation.

At eighty percent thrust it took nearly an hour to cover the distance between the fleet and the moon. While the Nameless would have seen them approaching, any fighters on the aliens' mobile units had been pulled away from the moon when the enemy fleet deployed. That left whatever was based on the moon itself as their only direct opposition.

"Strike leader to all units," the radio crackled. "We are detecting enemy fighters launching from the lunar surface. Launch positions have been marked and added to target list. Dauntless Wings One and Three break formation and engage."

"Roger that, Strike Leader," Alanna heard Deighton reply before they opened their throttles and began to accelerate away.

She watched them go, wishing their strike leader had ordered her section in as well. Ahead, the moon was beginning to loom large and she could begin to make out details. On her display she saw a mass of enemy fighters rise up and out of the moon's radar clutter. Wings One and Three vectored towards them, eight blips against upwards of fifty.

"Squadron leader to Wing Three," Alanna heard across the radio, "you take the thirty on the right and we'll take the thirty on the left. Go get 'em!"

Blips showing the Nameless fighters began to disappear as the fighter's missiles clawed them out of space. Then the two groups met and became an overlapping mass of signals as the rest of the strike doglegged around the melee.

The moon had no atmosphere so there was nothing to obscure the view. *Dubious*'s computer started to highlight targets.

"All wings, this is Strike Leader. Dauntless Section Two, form top cover – all other units, move to engage primary targets."

"Roger that," Alanna replied as she flipped *Dubious* over and went full burn on the engines for orbital insertion.

Schurenhofer's console beeped.

"Fresh contacts," she said, "missiles!"

A dozen installations across the moon commenced missile fire at the approaching fighters. The strike was opening up as individual wings headed for their targets. The strike groups went low but Alanna's wing had to stay seventy kilometres above the surface where they could respond quickly, albeit at the cost of making them targets for several separate installations. Alanna gently jinked *Dubious* left and right, just to keep things moving. She switched her radio to sweep across the channels and listened as the other squadrons went in.

"I can't identify the target. Wait, I've got it."

"I have the target locked..."

"Just lost my port engine!"

"Watch the right. Watch the right!"

"Target destroyed."

"Ejecting!"

"Strike Leader to all wings, enemy is fielding new missiles and fighters, both improvements on previous versions. *Dauntless* number Two Wing, we have identified a secondary fighter launch facility. Move and engage."

"Understood, Strike Leader Wing, follow me, Second Section hold up here," Alanna replied as she pointed the nose down.

Dubious's radar was designed for open space, not to deal with the clutter of ground returns. Beside her, Schurenhofer swore softly as she tried to sort through the conflicting signals.

"Fresh contacts, dead ahead!"

"Engaging with missiles!"

Half a dozen contacts appeared and Alanna rolled *Dubious* as missiles accelerated off their rails. The threat detection system whooped loudly as enemy missiles burned towards them and their turret guns stabbed to the left and right. Explosions erupted ahead of them as *Dubious*'s missiles went in.

"Have you got a fix on the launch point?" Alanna demanded as she dropped *Dubious* below the hill line to avoid incoming ground fire.

"No, Strike Leader didn't get a good fix – must be buried," Schurenhofer replied. "We'll need them to launch more."

It wasn't just missiles. Plasma bolts were burning past them now.

"Well it's around here somewhere," Alanna said as she released chaff rockets.

"Hang on, fighters... Christ, they're coming out underneath us!"

There was a bang and a jolt as a plasma bolt punched up through the starboard wing. Alanna swore savagely as she threw *Dubious* into a spiral that put her nose straight down. In front, half a dozen Nameless fighters accelerated in. Behind them a camouflaged hangar door was closing.

"Wing," she shouted into the radio, "target the launcher! I've got the fighters!"

As they spiralled through a hail of fire, *Dubious* shuddered as she was hit again. The status board was still green and Nameless fighters flashed past to their left and right as Alanna yanked the nose back around and rammed the throttle to plus ten override. The spaceframe let out a groan of complaint at the abuse and Alanna gasped as the G-forces pressed her back into her seat. *Dubious* came to a virtual halt in the sky, nose pointed up at the tails of the Nameless fighters. Alanna put a long burst into one, while Schurenhofer picked off two more with the turret guns. They clipped a fourth and watched as its engines cut out and it started to tumble as gravity claimed it.

"Missile away!" a voice on the radio announced.

Second later, they saw an anti-ship missile plunge downward and into the concealed hangar. A flash of light from behind lit up the cockpit.

"Target destroyed!"

"Strike Leader, target destroyed! We are returning..."

The sight of her wingman taking a direct hit suddenly interrupted her. She watched, transfixed, as the cockpit ejected seconds before the shattered Raven disintegrated and fell away.

"Shit," she hissed. "Strike Leader, I'm returning to my holding position."

Lewis winced inwardly as the blip representing a cap ship missile merged with that of the *Loki* and a moment later, the heavy cruiser started flashing multiple damage codes. So far their losses hadn't been as bad as he'd feared. One destroyer had been destroyed and the cruiser *Charles Martel* so badly damaged she could do little more than shelter inside the perimeter.

The Nameless had learned from past experience. Thanks to the presence of the barrage ships, their mass salvoes – so characteristic of their tactics in the past – now merely represented a waste of ammunition. Instead, they were spreading out their ships and directing in steady streams of missiles from multiple bearings, searching for chinks in the barrage ships' protective walls of fire, always picking on one target.

At this range it should have been just cap ship missiles, but here too the Nameless revealed another change. Their smaller dual-purpose missiles now made a brief burn after launch, then powered down and went ballistic until within a thousand kilometres of the Home Fleet, at which point they reactivated and accelerated in for final attack. It was a tactic that gave them most of the advantages of close range fire while staying well out of harm's way. Within the Home Fleet's formation, squadrons manoeuvred to offer as much mutual protection as possible.

"What have you got for me, Captain?" Lewis asked as he sensed Sheehan approach.

"The fighters report they have suppressed or destroyed sixty-five percent of the lunar targets but they've expended ninety percent of their ordnance."

"Have they got the critical ones?"

"All but one, sir. The installation codenamed the Rose is still operational."

Lewis considered his options. The *Mississippi* group was at best a glass hammer and if it failed, he would have no choice but to take his ships into the meat grinder he so desperately wanted to avoid.

"Bridge, Admiral," Captain Holfe's voice came across the intercom. "Enemy fighters are leaving their holding positions."

Lewis turned back towards the holo. The Nameless fighters weren't approaching the Home Fleet. They were instead on a course to cross over the top, towards the moon.

"Damn it," Lewis cursed.

"Sir?"

"Captain, they've realised they we aren't attacking those installations just to clear our own path."

Like the Rose, there were installations on the far side of the moon, which although not in a position to threaten the Home Fleet, would be perfectly placed to fire on *Mississippi*. The Nameless commander or its staff had worked out that the Home Fleet was a decoy, one that had already sucked their fleet away from the moon.

"Coms, instruct our escort fighters to block the enemy fighters,"

Lewis ordered.

"Which ones?"

"All of them!" Lewis snapped back.

On the holo, a quarter of the Nameless fleet had turned away and was now going full burn for the Blue Line. Lewis wracked his brain, searching for a way to block or slow them down. Once over the Blue Line, the Nameless would be free to jump and, if he were right, that jump would place them on the far side of the moon, ready to intercept the *Mississippi* group.

"Captain, order Strike Leader to put all remaining assets onto the Rose. We must neutralise it at all costs and we must do it quickly. Send a message drone to our strike boat carriers. Order them to launch a maximum effort strike against the enemy units heading for the Blue Line. They must stop them or at the very least slow them down. And turn the fleet through ninety degrees towards the enemy's mobile units. There's no point getting any closer to the planet now."

Sheehan took a quick glance at the holo.

"Those enemy ships still have fighters escorting them, sir," he said. "The strike boats will take serious losses."

Lewis didn't hesitate for a second with his reply.

"That's unavoidable, Captain."

Seated at the back of *Freyia*'s bridge, where his presence was just about tolerated, Jeff followed events intently. The atmosphere was one of near silent and intense concentration. He'd been allowed to set his suit intercom to listen to the command channel, while he panned his camera across the bridge. This was his first proper space battle and it was certainly different from what he'd even half expected.

Captain Hicks gave orders in short terse bursts and then waited to see the consequences of those orders as he stared at the bridge holo. With the bridge decompressed, there was no other sound except from the intercom. Jeff could feel the deck plating trembling from the force of the engines and small jolts each time the plasma cannons fired. But there was no sound and that struck him as profoundly... well, it was just wrong! So he attempted to fill the silence with his own commentary.

"As you can see from the holo," he said to his future audience, "there are no clever computer graphics here. Those are neither needed nor wanted. Instead, everything is kept as simple as possible. Yet, it still takes years for the officers and crew to learn how to read what they are shown. With scores of ships and hundreds of other contacts like missiles and fighters, it isn't hard to be simply overwhelmed by the amount of data received."

That was certainly truth in journalism. After his time on reconnaissance ships, Jeff had thought he could read a display holo, but this? There was no doubt stuff was happening, but he could understand none of it.

On the intercom, an alarm briefly sounded and the holo flashed red before zooming in. A mass of detail disappeared as the focus switched to just the *Freyia*, her squadron and the immediate area of space around them... *and the streams of red blips coming right at them!*

"Bridge, Tactical. Contacts crossing inner perimeter, time to impact forty seconds!"

"Coms, signal *Valkyrie* we are taking evasive action," Hicks shouted. "Helm, turn us towards them. Point Defence batteries, commence, commence, commence! Countermeasures on my mark, full spread. All hands, brace for impact!"

"Ladies and Gentlemen, we are being targeted by multiple enemy ships firing from several different directions. Even combined with those of other two ships in the squadron, *Freyia*'s flak guns can't target all the missiles in the time available. So Captain Hicks has turned his ship into the oncoming fire to present the smallest possible target,"

That was what Jeff wanted to say in his best and calmest professional voice, but if he said anything at all, it was an incoherent mumble as every muscle in his body attempted to clench simultaneously and *Freyia* turned into the storm. In their sponsons, her flak guns rattled away knocking down incoming missiles, while in the ventral and dorsal turrets, plasma cannons speared at targets more elusive than they were designed to deal with. Around the cruiser, space erupted in explosions and in flame.

"Countermeasures!" Hicks roared, thumping the armrest of his command chair.

From across *Freyia*'s hull, small rockets lifted from their silos, bursting between the cruiser and the onrushing missiles, scattering a curtain of radar-disrupting chaff. Some missiles lost their lock and detonated and others veered away. As they plunged through the chaff, most of those left could not adjust in time to steer in. But a few held their course and charged in with murder in mind. In his seat Jeff could only hang on as the cruiser bucked like a horse gone wild.

"Cap ship missiles! One to port! Two to starboard!" someone

called out.

On the holo, Jeff could see the three big ship killers and with them another half dozen of the smaller dual-purpose missiles.

"Helm! Port five degrees, engines emergency power! Fire control, concentrate fire to port!" Hicks bellowed.

The red blips converged with the big green blip at the centre of the holo, the one symbolising *Freyia*.

"Oh God! We'll be kill…"

Jeff didn't get a chance to finish.

There was no noise or flash, just an almighty concussion. The side of Jeff's helmet smashed against the nearest wall. Lights flashed inside his head, his teeth snapped down on his tongue and he heard someone scream. For several seconds he was as dazed as a punch-drunk boxer. Then, as voices resumed across the command channel, Jeff gathered his wits.

"Jesus Christ!" he muttered.

Droplets of blood were stuck to the inside of his visor.

"We're still alive, but I think we've been hit bad," he mumbled around his already swelling tongue.

"Damage Control, report," the Captain was demanding.

"Bridge, Damage Control. We've lost the port wing, looks like that cap missile took it, and the upper port passive array has been torn away. Point defence gun P1 primary command line has been severed. We've got some splinter damage in Frames Five to Eight. We took two hits from dual-purpose missiles but the armour kept them out. Confirmed, we are still combat worthy."

Hicks grunted an acknowledgement.

"Helm, get us back into formation before the bastards have another go."

On the holo, the next stream of missiles was on its way, another ship was about the meet the storm. God willing – if there was such a being Jeff thought – they'd be as good, or lucky, as *Freyia*.

"This is Strike Leader to all wings, sound off anyone who still has anti-ship ordnance."

"Strike Leader," Alanna replied as she flew down a shallow valley, "this is *D for Dubious*, confirming I have ordnance."

The old Nameless dual-purpose missiles, with which they started the war, had always been a bit of a jack-of-all-trades but master of none. A bit sluggish for anti-fighter work but too small for taking on ships but their new missiles seemed to be dedicated anti-fighter weapons. As a result, flying at an altitude of several kilometres above the surface had proved too dangerous. Perversely it was safer to fly low, where *Dubious* could shelter in the valleys that criss-crossed the surface. Safer but not completely safe – for pilots used to the emptiness of deep space, flying mere tens of metres away from the sides or bottom of a valley was something of which they had no experience. Too many weren't flying low enough to avoid the fire of point defence type guns abruptly opening fire from the surface. Alanna heard too many pilots' last exclamation or scream.

"*Dubious*, this is Strike Leader. Make for the Rose and report in once you are on station."

"Roger that," Alanna replied as she glanced at the navigation screen for the best route to the target.

"I thought one of *Akagi*'s squadrons was tasked with that," Schurenhofer said as she rotated the ventral turret in case another enemy battery might be lurking the end of valley.

"Wing, get the hell back onto position," Alanna shouted across the radio.

Astern, her new wingman kept drifting upwards, toward the false safety of clear space.

"A whole squadron went in," she replied to Schurenhofer. "Let's hope they have at least softened things up a bit."

Ten minutes later they cleared the valleys and entered a broad flat open area. As she saw the carnage Schurenhofer let out a sigh.

"Oh, this will be worth a whole chapter in the handbook on coping with disappointment," she said.

The Rose was sited in the crater of a volcano, with a dozen cap ship missile launchers protected on all sides by stone walls. More batteries and dozens of point defence guns studded the lip of the crater. Unlike much of the rest of the moon, the area surrounding the Rose was a flat and almost featureless plain stretching at least thirty kilometres in every direction. It was the crown jewel of the Nameless defences and *Akagi*'s pilots had beaten themselves bloody trying to get through. As she skirted the edge of the plain, Alanna could see the wrecks of their fighters scattered below.

On the radio, she heard Strike Leader mustering what remained of their assets.

"Sounds like we've got about four anti-ship missiles left

between us," Schurenhofer said as she listened. "We must have given them a kicking everywhere else."

"Which probably will count for f– all if we don't get this," Alanna replied as she surveyed the battlefield.

"Strike Leader to *D for Dubious*," came across the radio. "We have identified the command bunker, we're sending imagery now."

A picture appeared on her communication screen. With the cap ship missile silos taking up so much of the available space, the inside of the crater was crowded. And because the volcanic rock was so difficult to excavate, they weren't dug in deep. In fact, they stood densely packed protruding from the surface.

"They mustn't have had time to dig in," Alanna called.

"One missile in and we'll get a mighty bang," Schurenhofer replied.

The area around the Rose lit up as the installation's point defence batteries erupted. Lines of plasma bolts pulsed out, sweeping the space around and above their target.

"Crap on a stick. How the hell will we get through that?" Schurenhofer said, awestruck.

"*Dubious*," Strike Leader ordered. "Hold at the southern edge for my command."

"Understood," Alanna replied.

As she spoke half a dozen Ravens broke cover and made for the Rose. Four ran interference and one laid down covering fire, while the last Raven – the one with the missile – charged in astern.

"Get lower you stupid bastards, get lower!" Alanna urged through gritted teeth.

But they weren't. They were space fighter pilots – not trained, equipped or experienced at nap of earth flying. They weren't like her. They hadn't flown and fought among the asteroids of Junction Station.

If the fire from the Rose had seemed ferocious before, now it was like nothing Alanna had ever seen before. The point defence guns switched to rapid fire as the Nameless sought to leave the Ravens with nowhere to go. A dozen anti-fighter missiles raced towards them. Alanna flinched as first one, and then another Raven was blown out of the sky. Then a burst of gunfire intersected with the fighter carrying the precious missile and tore its wing off at the root. One engine exploded and the stricken craft plunged downward. At the last moment the pilot managed to spin his plane round and use the remaining engine to kill most of the velocity. The Raven bellied in, throwing up dust and rock as it bounced across the plain, breaking up as it went.

"Strike Leader to *D for Dubious*."

The strike leader's voice had the monotone of someone who knew he was ordering another person to their death.

"You're up. Stand by for me to get planes into position to run interference."

Madness, Alanna thought to herself. One of its definitions was to try the same thing but expect different results. To simply throw herself at the Rose in the same old way would simply see her brought down in the same old way. Guiding *Dubious* round the edge of the plain, she searched with her eyes – the old Mark One eyeball offered more than any of *Dubious's* hi-tech toys. They needed something new. The only visible feature was a small hill roughly to the west of the Rose, but it was thirty kilometres away, in space terms a barely mentionable distance but here, a killing zone without...?

"What's that?" Alanna asked.

"What's what?" Schurenhofer replied.

"That," Alanna said pointing.

Leading from close to the foot of the hill to within a kilometre or two of the Rose was a faint shadow. Pulling back the stick she angled *Dubious* upwards and Schurenhofer turned the ventral turret towards the shadow. On the screen Alanna, could make out the barest dip in the ground, forming a channel from the hill to the Rose's doorstep.

It was their way in.

"You aren't?" Schurenhofer said.

"I am," Alanna replied firmly.

"Strike Leader to *Dubious*, are you ready to make your run?"

"Confirmed Strike Leader, I'm ready. I'll be making my run from the west."

"Confirmed *Dubious*, from the west. All units stand by to run interference. This is damn near our last shot people. Make it work."

"So no pressure then," Schurenhofer muttered as Alanna turned off *Dubious's* collision warning alarm. "Skipper, how low do we plan to go?"

"Scarily low," Alanna replied. "*E for Envy*, join the interference groups, I'm going solo for this one."

Alanna worked her way round to behind the hill, flying a wide circle to get lined up.

"Tally Ho," she said quietly to herself before speaking into radio. "*Dubious* to all units, commencing run."

She pushed the throttle forward and the hill loomed large. Alanna flipped *Dubious* onto its back and dropped lower. Schurenhofer gave her a frightened glance and hunched over her console. The lunar surface flashed past as they gained speed and dropped still lower. The ground rose up to meet them as they reached the edge of the hill and Alanna pushed the stick forward.

Still upside down, they skimmed up the side of the hill with the ground just metres from their heads, the surface just a grey blur now as they sped on. Between the ground and the Raven's nosecone, Alanna had only a tiny slit of visibility to their front. Cresting the hill, Schurenhofer popped the last of their chaff, just as Nameless targeting radars locked on and their threat detection system wailed. Alanna yanked the stick back and slammed the throttle to full. *Dubious* charged down the hill, the canopy now only centimetres above the unforgiving rocks. The threat detection system cut out as the Nameless radar lost them in a flurry of confusing ground returns.

Missiles erupted from their launchers on the crater lip and flashed across the intervening space in seconds, only to miss wildly as their highly sensitive guidance systems were overwhelmed by the sheer mass of returns. Under Schurenhofer's control, their ventral turret gun picked off one or two missiles that only through chance ended up heading in their direction.

Alanna search desperately for the depression. Had it been a trick of the light? No, it was there, off to the left. With the lightest touch she pointed *Dubious* toward it. As they slotted in she heard a brief ping from astern as some part of *Dubious* clipped the surface and was ripped away. Alanna didn't dare glance away as she pulled back on the throttle. The engines were barely at half power. Height, or lack of it, was now their protection, not speed. This was seat of the pants flying no pilot was trained for. They were safe from the point defence fire cutting across the sky above, but as *Dubious* hurtled down the shallow ravine, the fighter was lower than any of them could bear.

"Put the missile to manual," Alanna grimly ordered as the ground began to rise ahead of them again.

Pushing the stick forward, she rammed the engines to all astern. Beside her, Schurenhofer cried with pain as she was thrown with bruising force against her restraints. Their velocity plummeted just as the fighter reached top of the crater. With their speed suddenly down to only a few metres per second, *Dubious* virtually floated over the Rose. The threat detection system began to scream again as the enemy radar abruptly found the elusive contact right above them, and missile batteries and guns slewed round to engage the enemy in their midst. As Alanna twisted the fighter's nose downward, Schurenhofer opened up with their turret guns, indiscriminately spraying fire around the crater, shredding radar towers and guns.

Below, at the very bottom of the crater, the missile silos drifted across Alanna's sights and her forefinger squeezed the trigger. The fighter's anti-ship missile lanced downwards towards the silos. As it cleared the launcher, Alanna pointed *Dubious*'s nose towards a random edge of the crater and rammed the throttle all the way forward. The fighter leapt forwards like a stung horse. As they plunged over the crater edge, a massive flash from astern lit up the cockpit. Schurenhofer let out a celebratory whoop – and then something swatted them.

The control stick was knocked out of Alanna's hand as *Dubious* was thrown into a tumble. The entire control board went dead and she lost all sense of up and down.

"Reactor off line!" Schurenhofer screamed as she flailed for the eject handle and missed.

As Alanna struggled with half dead controls, she felt no fear. In fact, she felt only peace. It would be quick, no lingering in a dead fighter, waiting for the air to run out.

But there was no follow up strike. As *Dubious* tumbled, Alanna caught sight of the horizon and wrestled the fighter's half dead controls until they were at least pointed in the direction of travel.

"Restart the reactor," she snapped.

"What d'ya fucking think I'm trying to do!" Schurenhofer snarled back, before shaking her head. "No response, we've had a full reactor scram. Engines... Christ, they must be hit. We're not even getting status readings! We're down to the backup batteries."

Alanna only half heard. She twisted round in her seat and looked back the way they'd come. The Rose was now an inferno as the crater erupted in a succession of massive explosions. Several of the Nameless guns maintained fire, but they weren't tracking anything. Locked on whatever had been their last command, they continued to send lines of burning plasma bolts into the sky. Alanna could see other fighters nosing in, checking to see if a follow up strike was required, but she doubted it would be. Nothing inside the crater could still be functional... or alive.

"Skipper, *the ground*," Schurenhofer said with alarm.

Returning to the matter at hand, Alanna checked her controls.

They were still on a ballistic curve from when the engines cut out.

"What have we got in propulsion?"

"Docking thrusters."

Alanna waited for more.

"Just docking thrusters," Schurenhofer emphasised.

In the moon's low gravity it was enough to keep *Dubious* up, at least until the thrusters burned through their propellant. Another Raven, her wingman formed up alongside them.

"*Dubious*, are you receiving me!" the radio crackled.

"Confirmed, receiving you."

"*Dubious*, your engines are gone! Sweet Jesus Christ, I can see your reactor casing! How the fuck are you still alive?"

Alanna closed her eyes for a moment.

"*Envy*, if I could reach you, I would hurt you!" she replied before tightening her grip on the column. "*Envy*, inform search and rescue they have another customer inbound."

As she spoke she could hear Strike Leader making the call. Their primary targets were either destroyed or suppressed – the way was open.

––––––––––––––––

"This is Strike Leader to *Mississippi*: the road is clear, repeat the road is clear!"

The wait had been agonising. On his bridge, Crowe had listened to the radio chatter of the Home Fleet. Every now and then he would catch an occasional transmission from *Deimos* – and felt a sense of relief each time he did. But that was all they'd been able to do as they waited for their turn.

"Tactical, bring us on line. Navigation, make the calculations."

As he gave the orders, Crowe turned to the trio of national military officers who had been a part of their vigil. They were already pulling themselves towards the bomb control board. The American nodded and the three turned their keys together. The board went active.

"Sir," the American reported. "The weapon board is green. All three devices are now active and tied into the control grid."

"Thank you, Gentlemen. You may take your posts.

Before they left Earth, documentation had been signed authorising that each man would receive a temporary fleet commission once the weapons were armed. All three left the bridge, heading for their assigned positions. On board *San Demetrio* and *Nolan*, other groups of officers were going through the same steps.

"Sir, the Squadron report is in," the communications officer confirmed. "All ships are standing by."

"Coms, signal *San Demetrio* that she is to lead. Gunboats are to bring up the rear. Jump when ready."

Across such a short distance their time in jump space was no more than a few seconds. Then the squadron erupted back into real space.

"Navigator, report," Crowe demanded.

"Heading's good. Position is... good. Right on target sir," the navigator reported. "We're in the pipe."

"Good. Order *San Demetrio* and *Nolan* to engage boosters."

Crowe watched the holo fill back up as *Mississippi* began to receive radar returns. Ahead loomed the moon – if the fighters had missed any of the fixed defences, they'd find out any second now. The lunar mass shadow represented a killing ground they needed to cross as quickly as possible. Their solution was crude and old school: chemical booster rockets to give that initial push, fitted to the outside of each ship's hull.

Usually used to launch bare hulls from the shipyards on Earth's moon, no one was quite sure if they had ever been used to move a complete ship before. So when those on *San Demetrio* erupted into life, Crowe wasn't the only one to let out a gasp of surprise. The lines of fire from each of the four boosters were as long as the transport herself and, even though *Mississippi* was on full burn, *San Demetrio* actually began to pull away from them.

Then it was their turn. From astern, Crowe felt the hull groan, the deck tremble, and the ship's structure compress under the G load as their boosters fired.

"Engineering, watch out for resonance build-up on Number Three Engine's pylon," Crowe warned through clenched teeth as the acceleration pressed him back.

The Squadron strung out as the three ships zoomed in, their gunboats bringing up the rear. As the boosters reached the end of their endurance they jettisoned.

"Bridge, Sensors. Contact separation, we have incoming. Launch point is the moon," the intercom alerted them.

"I see them," Crowe replied as he felt the tension rise.

As the three ships resumed formation, the huge bay doors in the flanks of *San Demetrio* and *Nolan* opened and armatures telescoped out, each one with a box on the end. This was their part in the plan: as each arm reached full extension, the front and rear of its box exploded. Little more than a rack of recoilless rifles, they unleashed a wall of ball bearings. These took several minutes to reach the incoming missiles but when they did, every single Nameless missile disappeared from the plot.

"Keep it up guys," Crowe muttered to himself as the arms jettisoned the expended packs and retracted for rearming.

There hadn't been time to convert the two vessels into barrage ships. Following the introduction by the Nameless of recoilless rifle missiles as battlefield weapon however, humanity had done what it did so well – make do and adapt. Thanks to their spacious cargo bays, *Nolan* and *San Demetrio* could store more than enough rifle packs to simply fill space with heavy counter fire – so long as they held out.

For thirty minutes the three ships continued to accelerate in. Missiles sporadically erupted from the lunar surface but the fighters had done their work well and *Mississippi*'s flak guns remained silent.

"Contact, fresh contact!"

The suddenness of the report made Crowe jump and when he regained his composure, the cluster of red contacts on the holo made him grimace. They were on the squadron's right flank, with the moon on the left. No matter what he did now, they would take fire from both sides.

"Tactical?" Crowe asked.

"Estimating one cap ship, six cruisers and ten escorts – they came in right on the Blue Line."

"Navigation, how long to orbit?"

"Nine minutes to orbital insertion, we cannot, repeat cannot take evasive action," came the tense reply.

"Understood. Guns, stand by to engage."

A swarm of new contacts appeared on the holo as the Nameless flanking force opened fire. *Nolan* responded by deploying rifle packs to fire into the broadside, but this time the missiles were curving in on long separate tracks. And it wasn't just missiles.

"Bridge, Tactical. Force composition alteration! The cap ship is launching fighters."

"Shit," Crowe muttered to himself.

The Nameless fighters sped away from their carrier and, unlike the missiles, didn't head directly for the squadron. Instead they spread out, some looking to pursue from astern and others working their way round to their front. The carrier must have been a new type. It was smaller but had put out its birds faster than any they'd seen before.

"Tactical, give me an analysis. Can those fighters achieve firing range before we reach our objective?"

"Confirmed, sir."

Crowe's mind raced through the possibilities. *San Demetrio* and *Nolan* were carrying nukes just in case, but there had never been any serious expectation that they'd make it to the gate. They were there to absorb Nameless fire, any way they could. With her armoured hull, *Mississippi* would be the one to make the last charge in. But aside from four point defence guns, she was vulnerable to assault from behind.

"Coms, signal *Nolan* we're taking number two position. Navigation, adjust our heading and give Helm the new settings."

Crowe heard the navigator let out an alarmed hiss before crouching over her terminal, her fingers dancing over the keyboard. Astern, the tone dropped as their engines dialled back to make the critical insertion.

"Uploading!" shouted the navigator.

The engines surged powerfully and they slid past *Nolan*. *Mississippi* jolted violently as she made orbital insertion at a velocity that under any other circumstances would have bought its captain a permanent ground posting. The ship bucked as she powered in. At this velocity, they wanted to slingshot out, but the helm's direction was forcing *Mississippi* in, gathering speed as she went. Crowe could only hang on as they powered round the curve of the moon. More missiles accelerated up from a surface that was now less than fifty kilometres below them. The gunboats raced forward to engage, guns rattling and picking off missiles. *Mississippi*'s joined in with her guns, while point defence stabbed out lines of plasma pulses terminating in a hail of explosions.

Some missiles made it through. One gunboat took a direct hit and vaporised as it raced down the squadron's flank laying down chaff. It was all Crowe could do to cling to his chair when a missile punched through the ventral wing and the cruiser lurched violently. Seconds later, the first of the Nameless fighters caught them and gunfire flashed back and forth as *Nolan* and the gunboats fought a frantic rearguard action. *Mississippi* continued to accelerate as the transport and gunboats began to fall behind in their battle with the fighters. Crowe could offer them nothing more than prayers as one gunboat after another was picked off. *Nolan* took a toll of her tormentors, her rifle packs allowing her to fire indiscriminately astern. But Nameless gunfire and missiles savaged her unarmoured hull.

"Coming up on slingshot!" shouted the navigator. "Thirty seconds!"

Ahead the gate was coming into view.

"Bridge, Coms. Transmission from *Nolan!*"

"*Mississippi*, this is *Nolan*. We've taken heavy engine damage! We're…"

The sound of an explosion interrupted the speaker. Crowe could see with a sinking heart she wouldn't just fail to keep up. Her port side engine smashed, the transport was angling inwards towards the moon – its gravity had her.

"We're out of control," the speaker on *Nolan* shouted again. "All hands, abandon ship! Abandon ship!"

Escape pods started to eject as the ship plunged downward. Crowe tore his eyes away from the battle astern as ahead and still locked in the Lagrange point, the gate station came into view. *Mississippi* and *San Demetrio* launched themselves up and out of orbit, just as the universe ahead of them erupted in flame.

Literally hundreds of missiles big and small launched from scores of weapons satellites. They met a wall of counter fire from *San Demetrio*'s flak packs. Most, almost all, died, by the sheer law of averages a few leaked through. The flak guns on *Mississippi* and the transport tried to catch the leakers, but there were now so many contacts, automatic systems were being overwhelmed. Missiles were still coming from the starships astern and the two human ships looked like comets as fire blazed around them.

Mississippi's port wing was sheared away, too fast for Crowe to even register what had hit them. *San Demetrio* took it far worse, though. The front quarter of the ship simply dissolved under multiple strikes. Fragments of her hull and centrifuge tumbled back, forcing *Mississippi*'s helm to take frantic evasive action. But most of the mid-ships, with its rifle packs, survived and the transport ploughed forward into the deluge of fire, firing as fast as her crew could reload.

"Tactical, have we got lock on the target?" Crowe shouted.

Mississippi jerked as a missile got through. A glance at the damage control repeater panel confirmed her armour had kept it out.

"Confirmed! We have lock!"

"Helm! Prepare to lock on course. All hands, prepare to evacuate!" Crowe ordered just as a big cap ship missile found its way through from astern. Its terminal guidance locked onto the strongest signal and powered into *San Demetrio*'s starboard rear quarter. The explosion shattered the engineering spaces and must have killed most of the crew. With a last dying splutter of her engines, *San Demetrio* tumbled end over end, one of her flak guns still firing on automatic. Crowe could see what was about to happen, but there was no time to react in the split second before the flak gun stitched a line across his ship.

The armour on *Mississippi*'s bows wasn't proof against a kinetic strike of that size. One flak round crashed through and burst half way down the length of the hollowed out centrifuge.

On the bridge, sparks flew and equipment shattered as shrapnel flashed past even faster than thought. Crowe just had time to register the helmsman at his station suffer a direct hit and virtually explode in a crimson spray. The holo flickered as the mess of blood and tissue blocked half its emitters.

"Auto pilot offline!" Crowe heard the Navigator scream as he savagely brushed blood off his visor.

On what remained of the holo display, a green line showed their intended course and a yellow line the course they were actually on, and the two lines were diverging. As she powered past the shattered remains of *San Demetrio*, *Mississippi* was already drifting off course. They were about to miss!

Slapping the release on his harness Crowe forced himself up and out of his seat. On full burn it was hard to pull forward toward helm. A sensor operator got there first and snatched at the helm's manual control. Crowe grabbed the man by the shoulder and pushed him gently to one side.

"I have this," he said and caught a brief look of gratitude from the other man as he elbowed what was left of the helmsman out of the seat.

"Damage Control," Crowe called as he got them back onto course, "report."

"Navigation sub-system has lost power and the Lazarus systems are looking for another link. Just give it a minute!" Craven shouted back.

Minute? Might as well ask for an hour, Crowe thought as he directed the ship back on course. On the helm display, the green and yellow lines converged and merged, then jolted apart as another impact shook the ship.

"Bridge, Damage Control. We've lost Engine Four!"

San Demetrio, *Nolan* and all but two of the gunboats were now gone, leaving *Mississippi* and her last two escorts to charge into the maelstrom of fire. Crowe could hear the cruiser's own flak packs starting to crack off in desperate defence. The tactical display showed the gate station was attempting to break out of the Lagrange point, but the thrusters along its flank were struggling to overcome the inertia of the station's mass.

I'm going to die. The thought went through his mind as clear as a bell. Without navigation, with the engine damage they'd sustained, there was no way *Mississippi* would fly straight. She could no longer hold a steady course. Not without navigation. Or hand at the controls.

The *Nolan* had gutted those Nameless fighters coming from astern but now those that had taken the long route were reaching *Mississippi*. The last two gunboats were picked off as the Nameless fighters swarmed in, through the fire of the gate station's defences. But they weren't the only fighters closing in.

Hoped for but not expected came human Raven fighters, arriving fast. As survivors of the lunar assault, there were no complete squadrons, just flights and remnants of flights. They launched themselves in, ripping at the Nameless. The alien formation fragmented as individual fighters tried to force their way through. Their guns and missiles stabbed out, gouging out fragments of armour and hull.

"We're crossing the bail out point!"

"Navigation?" Crowe rasped.

"It's not getting a feed from radar! We can't get a lock!"

He glanced back at the bloodstained men and women of his crew. He couldn't make out many faces. They weren't looking at him or back towards the escape tubes. Every single one of them was bent over their stations. Only the dead had abandoned their posts. God, what a crew! Crowe opened his mouth to speak, to issue the order to abandon ship, knowing he wouldn't be going with them.

"Coms, Bridge! Enemy beacon is still transmitting! We have a lock on!"

It took Crowe a moment to understand what that meant. They'd timed the assault to fall into the beacon's active period but everyone always assumed the Worms would shut down the moment the assault began. How could a race that so willingly wrote off lives and material be expected to do otherwise? But no, the beacon was still there, guiding in all that could hear it.

"Tie into helm control!" he roared.

A moment later he felt the control yoke shift under his hand as the autopilot took over.

"Ninety seconds to impact!" the navigator screamed.

"Guns to auto, everybody out!" Crowe shouted as he kicked out and away from the helm. "All hands abandon ship! All hands abandon ship!"

In an explosion of movement everyone was out of their seat and scrambling for the exit. As he reached the escape tube, before swinging himself down to the escape shuttles, Crowe glanced back at the scarred bridge of the *Mississippi* for the very last time. He saw the displays flicker as they updated readouts that no one remained to study. On the holo, the blip for *Mississippi* continued down the green line toward her destiny.

Goodbye Girl.

The hatches for the shuttle bays flew away as controlled explosions blew them off at the hinges. The shuttles blasted clear, accelerating down and away, their engines going full burn as the weapons computer opened clear channels in the defensive barrage. The Nameless ignored the fleeing craft, understanding that the crew of *Mississippi* had become irrelevant now.

Alone and deserted, the cruiser continued to accelerate well beyond any velocity ever attained during her long life. The Nameless missiles now struggled to track the projectile hurtling toward them with the result that one after the other overshot, not turning in time to impact. Within her hull, *Mississippi*'s nuclear cargo awaited its moment.

Most of the Nameless missile platforms with a clear line of fire had exhausted their ammunition. For those that remained, *Mississippi* was now too close and too fast for them to track. Other missiles launched from Nameless warships far astern would not reach her in time. Instead it fell to the last few Nameless fighters to stop her.

They threw themselves forwards. In response, *Mississippi* fired the last of her flak packs and those of her guns that remained, blazing away. Her bows were ripped open as a fighter, itself riddle by gunfire, swerved in and smashed the bomb they'd named Faith, pitching its broken remains out into space. A missile slammed in amidships, through a weakened armour plate, speared in deep and killed the one called Hope. The last Nameless fighter impacted astern, all but tearing Engine

Number One from its mounting.

D for Dubious lay broken at the end of the short furrow she'd dug in the lunar surface with her belly-landing. As she bounced awkwardly towards the rescue ship, Alanna looked back at her fallen mount and caught sight of a line of fire cutting across the sky beyond.

"Look!" she called out, prompting Schurenhofer to turn and see.

"It's the *Mississippi*!" she breathed.

"Go on! Go on you beauty!" Schurenhofer shouted as she bounced up and down.

On the bridge of *Mississippi*, where only the dead remained, the computer fought to control a ship on which shattered systems now outnumbered the functioning. With one engine gone and two more stuttering through their death throes, *Mississippi*'s stern began to fishtail. All down the flanks, her remaining thrusters fought to keep her on course.

They failed.

Mississippi swung broadside onto her direction of travel. In another split second and her own engines would have pushed her off course, wasting her sacrifice but it had been enough. Side on, breaking up at she went, *Mississippi*, the ship that first encountered the Nameless, impacted the gate station.

And deep within her hull, nestled between the two fusion reactors, the last thermonuclear weapon, the one named Charity, detonated.

For the briefest moment, her hull bulged outward as the structure resisted the monumental pressures within. Then the cruiser's reactors breached and in a flash *Mississippi* transformed into a vast white sphere of expanding plasma, obliterating the gate station, which added to the fireball as its reactors ruptured. Following the course of the dead cruiser, the expanding and deforming sphere consumed everything that got in its way until finally, its force spent, it dissipated. In its wake, it left nothing more than vaporised metal.

On *Warspite*'s bridge holo, two blips merged and disappeared.

"Sensors confirms, the gate station is destroyed, sir," Sheehan said after a moment. "We got it sir, we got it!"

Lewis nodded slowly.

"That was the easy bit, Captain," he said quietly. "Now the real work begins."

Chapter Nineteen

Taken at a Run

22nd April 2069

In the engine room of *Black Prince*, Guinness braced himself as the ship lurched violently back into real space. Even as they exited the jump portal, the cruiser was making a hard turn to avoid any missiles that might already be inbound. On the bridge, the Skipper would be calling for a full sweep. If the order came through for a crash spin up of the jump drive, then he'd know they'd found something or something had found them.

The austerities really weren't suitable for this kind of sneak and peek work, but most of the fleet's dedicated scout cruisers had gone with the Home Fleet. The little cruiser had one virtue for this sort of thing – expendability, although it was hard for Guinness to regard that line of reasoning with any kind of enthusiasm. Seconds ticked by but the main alarm failed to sound. After a minute the tone of the engines dropped as they throttled back and the atmosphere in the engine room lightened.

"All quiet on the Western Front," remarked one of the petty officers.

On the bridge, Berg frowned as the first sensor returns came in, revealing – well, bugger all really. Consisting of an elderly star and three profoundly uninteresting planets, the system had never warranted a name. In short, it was normally only worth going through to get somewhere more useful. Eight months previously, a deep space reconnaissance ship had spotted a Nameless space gate there. It could have been destroyed then, but the Nameless would simply have rebuilt it in a different location. Instead, along with the rest of the Nameless gate system, the gas giants they used for fuel and their forward supply bases, its location had been charted.

When the Second Fleet opened its grand offensive, they knew exactly where to strike. The supply bases were destroyed within forty-eight hours of the Second Fleet crossing the Junction Line, while the upper orbits of those gas giants usable for fuel were seeded with mines and torpedoes. Further up the space gate line, strike boats tore out entire stretches of the network, isolating chunks of the front line.

The fighting in that first seventy-two hours had been savage. As a result, fully a quarter of the Second Fleet's combat strength was either lost or limping back to Earth, their war over. But if it had been bad for Battle Fleet, it had been worse for the Nameless. With their forward positions cut off and overwhelmed, they began to fall back.

Eight months ago the gate had been orbiting the second planet of the system, right on the Blue Line. Now there was a noticeable lack of anything resembling a gate. The Nameless could and did move gates within a system, so it might now be somewhere in the outer reaches.

"Engines to standby," Berg said, "let's give the passives the best chance of spotting something. Navigator, give me a location in system that will cover our current blind spots."

"Aye, Captain."

Berg waited patiently as the sensor operators sorted through the readings from the passives. It was uncomfortable sitting out here alone, to be confronted by nothing. It really was the worst of both worlds. If they'd met too much opposition defending the gate, then she could have ordered an immediate retreat. If their enemy had been in *Black Prince*'s weight class, then they would have piled forward to take out the gate before jumping away. Instead they had to stooge around, painfully aware that if there were Nameless ships somewhere in the system, they were being given ample time to detect and attack them. But if they were attacked – well, then they'd be doing their job.

There was no way to know how the Home Fleet's attack on the Spur had gone – too much distance and not enough time. But assuming it had been successful, the Nameless would now be cut off from their home bases expending munitions they couldn't replace. What would the effects be? Well, that was anyone's guess.

"Contacts! Contacts bearing three, four, three dash zero, two, two, range, seven light minutes. Contacts appear to be one vessel and a space gate. It's inside the mass shadow of the innermost planet."

"Well done," Berg said.

At such range the contact was faint and indistinct. The sensor operator had done well to tease as much out of his equipment.

"Navigator, make calculations for immediate jump, go to combat alert," she continued as she buckled herself back into her command chair.

Black Prince came out shooting as she dropped back into real space but met nothing coming the other way. Berg waited eagerly for the first radar returns. The planet was small, roughly half way between the size of Mars and Earth's moon. The distance between the planet's Red and Blue Lines was only marginally wider than plasma cannon range. Which made it a vulnerable position for the fragile Nameless ships.

"It's a scout, ma'am," Sensors reported as the blips appeared on the main holo, "and a space gate."

The scout was at rest close to the gate, clearly there to provide protection.

"Something bigger would be nice," she said "but beggars can't be choosers. Point Defence, batteries to standby. Fire control, prepare to receive fire."

As *Black Prince* moved in, Berg studied the holo intently. Any moment now, she thought to herself. Tactical I.D'd the scout as one of the newer versions that had sacrificed two of its general-purpose launchers for a second cap ship missile launcher. But they still didn't carry many of the large ship killers. Its best chance of getting one past *Black Prince*'s flak guns would be to put out those it had, as fast as possible. With such a shallow mass shadow, *Black Prince* would need only seven minutes to reach maximum plasma cannon range.

The scout's engines came online – that was a fast reaction – and immediately it began to perform unexpectedly. Rather than stand fast directly in their path, Berg expected it to begin to angle out and away from the gate, trying to build up velocity to run for it and also pull them away from the objective. Instead it turned sharply and headed directly for the gate, which turned to face the oncoming ship and came online. Stranger still, the scout's missile ports, which had opened as soon as *Black Prince* arrived, now closed again.

"Bridge, Coms. Enemy ship is transmitting on an FTL frequency. Transmission has ceased."

"*Scheiße!*" Berg swore, "It's an ambush! Helm, come to starboard, forty degrees. Navigator, give me jump out calculations!"

The momentum they'd already built up continued to propel

them towards the planet. Even with their engines at full power, they'd need another twelve minutes to get out of the mass shadow. Any second now, Nameless ships could start dropping in around them.

"Communications, prepare to launch message drone!" Berg ordered.

That was all she could do until she knew where the Nameless were coming from. The scout was still moving towards the gate, around which a blue vortex had completely formed. Without hesitation, the scout passed through and disappeared. Then abruptly the gate exploded.

"What the...?" Berg exclaimed. "Sensors, was that deliberate?"

That was probably the wrong question to ask. The sensor operators should have been searching for signs of Nameless jump ins, but an answer came immediately.

"Captain, detonation was consistent with a deliberate fusion reactor self-destruct."

Berg remained on the edge of her seat as she waited for the ambush that her instinct insisted would come, but as the ship neared and passed the Red Line, nothing happened. Why the hell destroy their own gate without making any attempt to defend it? Against her instinct Berg delayed jumping out. For an hour *Black Prince* accelerated away from the planet in real space, waiting for any other sign of the Worms. But there was nothing. With the gate gone their mission was complete, but in a deeply unsatisfying way. As they spun up for their jump out, the navigator turned to her.

"Do we count this one as a win, Skipper?"

For the ships that had been dispatched on independent missions, the rendezvous point was beyond the heliopause of a system seventy light years from the Junction Line. Most of the Second Fleet was already there when *Black Prince* jumped in. Berg was surprised to be summoned to the drop carrier *Overlord*. They were safe here in interstellar space, where the Nameless couldn't reach them. Nonetheless, it was unusual for the Admiral to order a gathering for a face-to-face meeting or briefing.

Overlord was one of the fleet's two big drop-carriers, designed to carry the fleet's marines into action, although after the defeat at Landfall, she could comfortably have accommodated every surviving soldier on her own – with room to spare. She also had many spare shuttle docking points. The shuttle from *Saladin*, Berg's divisional flagship, was docking in one of them as she arrived. Commodore Dandolo was waiting for her beyond the airlock.

"Sir," she said, saluting him.

"Captain, glad to see you back," he said offering a hand.

"Thank you, sir," she replied, "although I'm at a loss to know what's going on."

"You aren't the only one," Dandolo said as they made their way toward the centrifuge. "I'm a low man on the totem pole but I have heard that you aren't the only one to have come across spontaneously exploding gates."

"Oh?"

"Oh, indeed," Dandolo agreed. "It appears the mighty wish to have a confab."

Overlord was probably the only ship in the fleet with a compartment large enough for the Second Fleet's senior officers. They weren't all there. Several ships were still out on missions and no one below the rank of captain was present but even so, the compartment was crowded and stuffy.

"Your attention please," Admiral Fengzi said from the head of the room, thumping the podium. "Alright, let's get this going."

"Time is short," he continued once the room had quietened down. "First off, over the last few hours those ships that were dispatched to strike at targets in the enemy's rear areas have been returning. Their reports have painted an unexpected picture. Some of you will be aware that in the last few days, the enemy has apparently changed their strategic and tactical priorities. Reconnaissance boats from the strike carriers have detected wreckage at locations that we know were previously sites of enemy space gates, but had not yet been attacked. Furthermore, the cruisers *Herald* and *Black Prince* have directly observed Nameless warships retreat from combat without firing."

Fengzi paused and activated the holo beside him.

"This is the gate network as we knew it when this offensive began."

The display showed a starmap with red dots indicating those systems known to have gates.

"This is the network as we know it right now."

A massive swathe of red dots disappeared.

"Jesus, that must be about twenty percent," Berg murmured to

Dandolo.

"Those are just the ones we've checked in the last five days," Fengzi continued. "Additionally, the supply dump at this system, which was listed as a priority target, was being evacuated when the cruiser *Ganges* passed through. Vice Admiral Gordon decided to mount an attack without waiting for the rest of the fleet, a decision I agree with, but by the time his squadron arrived ten hours later, there was nothing but a few empty cargo containers."

"My staff and I have analysed the information and the only reasonable conclusion we can draw is... that the enemy is in full retreat."

A congratulatory murmur went round the room, but was abruptly cut off as Fengzi loudly added: "And that is a problem. Our mission, for those of you who appear to have forgotten, was to keep up the pressure on the Nameless, to keep hitting them, to keep forcing them to hit us – something WE ARE NOT DOING if they retreat out of contact."

"Can we take it from this, sir that Admiral Lewis and the Home Fleet have successfully put in their attack?" asked another officer.

Fengzi looked like he'd bitten into something that gone off but nodded sharply.

"Yes, Admiral, it seems your husband and the First Fleet has been sufficiently successful in their attack to force a reaction from the Nameless. That would mean that, as hoped, they have been cut off from their home bases. This is obviously a good thing but what's less good is that they have reacted quickly and decisively. If the Nameless are in full retreat, then they have abandoned in a matter of days all the gains it took them two years to achieve."

"Most of those gains are just empty space, sir," observed Admiral Gordon.

"True," Fengzi agreed. "But there is the infrastructure they have built in that time – now they are destroying gates and moving back the supplies they previously made a considerable effort to move forward."

"They still have Landfall," Berg murmured.

"Yes, Captain Berg," Fengzi said, apparently hearing her, "they also still have Landfall."

Berg felt herself flush with embarrassment but the Admiral had already moved on.

"Landfall is the jewel in their conquest crown and possibly the last place before the Spur itself where they might be compelled to stand

and fight. Therefore I propose that rather than continuing to sweep forward across a broad front, we make a narrow front drive to Landfall, thereby cutting off the Nameless line of retreat."

"That, sir, runs the risk of leaving Nameless combat units in our rear areas," Laura Lewis commented.

"Given their willingness to accept casualties, we couldn't rule out them sacrificing a few smaller units to harass our supply lines," added another officer.

"And sir," Dandolo spoke up, "that assumes that they are actually retreating. The Nameless might just be clearing the area around us."

"All of those points are valid," Fengzi replied, "which in my opinion means we need to attack ground they must defend. Landfall is the only place that meets that definition."

"Is it though, sir?" Gordon persisted. "Much as we know they have committed resources to Landfall, right now it is in no way contributing to their war effort. If we take it from them, it will not be making any contribution to ours."

"But everything they have gained will be lost," Fengzi replied frowning.

"Yes, sir, but if the Home Fleet has cut them off from their home bases, then right now they are living on borrowed time. If someone comes at you with a knife, you'll willingly grab the blade and loose a couple of fingers rather than get stabbed in the chest! This might be their attempt to grab the blade."

"What would you recommend, Gordon?" Fengzi asked after moment.

"Go after the supplies sir. If they are cut off, then the battle at The Spur will become one of endurance, what they already have over on this side of the rift will be the last of their oxygen. Anything they manage to heave back up the line, gives them a little more to hurl at the First Fleet."

Fengzi drummed his fingers on the podium.

"How would you go about it?" he eventually asked.

"Take the fleet beyond Landfall. Take out an entire stretch of gates and blockade them."

"No."

"Sir..."

"No, Gordon," Fengzi said more forcefully. "We do not have the ships to impose an effective blockade. We already know from experience they can replace gates quickly. We need to force contact on the enemy and I believe a direct assault on Landfall represents the best way to do that."

Berg raised a hand and Fengzi nodded towards her.

"Sir, we could send portion of the fleet to…"

"If the whole fleet couldn't enforce a blockade then a squadron certainly won't cut it," Fengzi interrupted. "The strike boat carriers will be dispatched to go deep. They're not much use for a fleet action anyway. Now unless someone has any other point, we jump out at seventeen hundred hours."

"We're potentially leaving a lot of Nameless units along our own supply lines," said Gordon in a resigned tone.

For a moment, Fengzi looked like he would lose his temper, but instead he emitted a long sigh.

"That can't be helped – and if they do attack our supply lines, well, then we'll have stayed in contact."

"Gordon has always been a bit of a narrow focus man," Dandolo remarked as he and Berg made their way back to their respective shuttles. "From what I've ever seen, he tends lack a feel for the big picture."

"You don't think a blockade would work, sir?" Berg asked.

"With ships spread out, to my mind it would be too vulnerable to the Nameless coming through one system en masse and overwhelming whatever ships we have there, before the rest of our fleet can join them. But that's a moot point. We barely have enough supply ships to get us as far as Landfall, let alone any further."

"Let us hope Landfall is enough," she replied, while thinking that Gordon might not be the worst at not seeing the big picture.

"Indeed, Captain. I'll see you there."

24th April 2069

When the war started was a matter of definition. As second-in-command of the *Mississippi*, Berg would say that first encounter had been the beginning. The history books would be likely to record it as the destruction of Baden Base; either way, Berg had been there for both and now she was back.

The last time she'd seen Baden had been from the bridge of the destroyer *Mantis* as they desperately ran for the Red Line. She could still remember the sight of it burning as if it had happened yesterday. Any ships that couldn't run were still here and it had taken months for her nightmares to fade.

Nearly two years later the fires were gone, long since snuffed out by the vacuum of space. The debris remained, however. Given time, the weak gravity of the asteroid on which Baden had been built would pull it all back down, but for now anything that hadn't been blown completely clear still orbited the asteroid.

On the visual display she could make out an engine here, a radar tower there and the entire gutted hulk of the carrier *Yorktown*, lying broken at the mooring she'd been trapped against. Yet that was still easier to bear than the smaller contacts, those tiny drifting human shapes. As *Black Prince* nosed closer to the station, every so often her sweeping searchlight would illuminate a body. Each time that happened, the light's operator would hesitate and sigh across the command channel. Berg had spoken to him about it the first few times he'd done it but had since given up. You couldn't damn someone for having humanity. The focus wasn't tight enough to make out faces but it was enough to see that most of the dead hadn't managed to get into their survival suits. Perhaps they'd been luckier than those who had.

"Captain, do you think there might be anyone still alive?" the coms officer asked quietly.

"If someone made it to an escape pod but didn't eject, then they could have easily survived this long in hibernation." Berg shook her head before continuing. "If we take the system, then we can send people into the station and... " she hesitated for a moment, " ... and the wrecks to take a look. But that's not a question for today."

Astern of *Black Prince*, the rest of the squadron held at Baden's Red Line, ready to offer support if needed. Other ships were checking the blind spots behind the various planetary bodies before the main body of the fleet moved in. They didn't have long. Their arrival hadn't triggered any urgent FTL transmissions but in a few hours, the light speed emissions from their engines would reach Landfall, where the Nameless would definitely pick them up.

Their enemy had no doubt picked the station's bones bare after their first great victory, but nothing more. If they were about to stand and fight, it wouldn't be here. At Berg's command, *Black Prince* turned away.

The Second Fleet filed back into real space a good fifteen light seconds out from the planet's Red Line. As soon as *Black Prince* cleared the jump conduit, communications reported a mass of FTL transmissions. More ships were now assembled than when *Black Prince* had been here for the Fury convoy – a lot more, in fact.

"Tactical, what breakdown are you getting?" Berg asked as they got into position.

Fengzi had wanted his fleet formed up and ready before they entered the mass shadow. By extension, this offered the Nameless the opportunity to come forward to meet them.

"Count is still provisional at this point, Captain," came the reply, "but at the moment we are seeing three cap ships, possibly two carriers, a dozen cruisers and over twenty escorts or scouts, plus several dozen transports, all of them in orbit."

"Is that all? Could some of those transports be warships?"

"That's a negative, Captain. We're picking up their engine emissions on the passives and they are consistent with gateships... Hold on! Fresh contacts... negative those are more gateships and a second gate in lunar orbit. The second group of gateships are moving towards it. We are also seeing multiple small contacts coming up from the surface of Landfall."

"This isn't a defence," Berg said as she came to a realisation, "they're evacuating!"

"Captain, that... that appears to be correct."

On the holo, she could see the activity around Landfall become more frantic. Some gateships broke orbit and started accelerating towards the closest gate. The two presumed carriers disgorged their fighters, and then did something strange. Both turned and began to accelerate after the gateships. Bugging out? Berg wondered as she watched, her expression puzzled. The rest of the warships were also on the move, but there was a clear separation between the smaller and larger ships. The smaller ones were moving forward and around to get onto the flanks, but their larger ships were showing no inclination to close in. They weren't in full retreat like the gateships and carriers, but they were definitely being tentative. The fighters showed no reluctance, however. They were accelerating at full bore straight towards the Second Fleet.

"Bridge, Sensors. Contact separation, we have incoming."

More blips appeared to join the fighters, all converging on the Second Fleet.

The Second Fleet had only one small carrier to supplement the fighters carried by the heavy cruisers and battleships. The Ravens rushed forward to meet their Nameless counterparts, while the rest of the fleet began to accelerate towards the planet. With the human ships formed up and on the move, Berg had a moment to study the screen as the opposing fighters clashed. The focus of the holo wasn't tight enough to make out individual craft but she did see the Nameless break through.

"Sensors, give me a close-up of the fighters!" she snapped.

The holo zoomed in just in time to see two fighter blips – one human, one Nameless – converge. And disappear. The front rank of Nameless fighters had blown a hole by the simple expedient of ramming anything that got in the way! The carriers weren't hanging around because none of the fighters were coming back. As they tore open a gap in the human screen, the rest of the Nameless charged through, engines on full burn. Berg realised what they were facing just as the collision detection alarm sounded.

"Suicide ships inbound!" she warned, "Helm, stand by for instructions!"

The Nameless warships launched a combined salvo timed to reach them just as the fighters did. The human fighters had been wrong footed and were now frantically pursuing. They probably would have done better to concentrate on the salvo of missiles now accelerating through and past them. Floundering between two targets, they dealt with neither. Berg tightened her grip on her armrests as she saw five fighters turn their way.

"Engines! Stand by for full power! Point Defence, commence, commence, commence!"

Space around the fleet lit up as every gun fired. Plasma bolts burned through the approaching fighters, attempting to at least break up their formation. Several blips disappeared as fighters were vaporised. Individual ship captains realised what they were facing and the Second Fleet's formation began to loosen, as vessels looked for room to manoeuvre. On the *Black Prince*, the collision alarm sounded again as two of the approaching fighters latched onto *Black Prince* and came burning in, behind two cap ship missiles. Impact from any one of them would be devastating. Should they attempt to dodge them or stand fast and place faith in their guns to knock them down? Berg had a split second to decide.

"Engines, hard back! Helm, port ninety, bows down twenty!"

She could feel the hull groan at the abuse, as *Black Prince* lurched violently out of formation. The cap ship missiles tried to match the manoeuvre but they were too late; they were still trying to turn as they flashed through the space *Black Prince* should have occupied. The fighters were quicker to react and came in firing both guns and missiles but met a storm of counter fire. One took a burst of fire that ripped away the entire cockpit area. Without control it skimmed past, close enough to knock away an aerial. The second detonated when a round of flak ploughed through it. Fragments peppered *Black Prince*'s port wing with holes.

Reports started to come in, but immediately Berg could feel the damage was only cosmetic. On the holo, however, she could see several ships were flagging damage codes and gaps in the fleet's formation. Those Nameless fighters that had missed their targets were trying to turn but the pursuing human fighters would catch them first.

"Bridge, Coms. Signal from *Colossus*, we're to take *Saladin*'s place in the formation."

"Sensors, give me a visual on *Saladin*," Berg ordered.

When it appeared on her screen she hissed with horror. Their squadron mate's entire bows had been completely obliterated. Its forward bearings gone, the centrifuge was swinging loose.

"Coms, signal the flagship message received," she replied. "Do we still have the link to *Saladin*?"

"Confirmed, sir. We do."

"Order them to tuck in under our port wing. We'll cover them," she said, before adding, half to herself: "this isn't over yet."

The Nameless might be pulling out but they were determined to exact the highest possible price first. The Second Fleet was still moving forward but now, on the holo, she could see full extent of the gaps in its formation. The Ninth Destroyer squadron was down to just one ship, the icon for the cruiser *Ganges*, was moving in a slow circle behind the fleet, flashing multiple damage codes. Ahead, the Nameless scouts, escorts and a few of their cruisers still advanced, firing as they came.

"Bridge, Sensors. Incoming entering our area."

"Guns! Stand by to engage."

Guinness took a firm grip of the man's shoulder and hit him

hard on the side of his helmet. He followed up with two more blows before the man recovered enough of his reason to stop his panicked attempt to open his helmet visor and instead defend himself.

"Get your mouth piece in, you fucking clown!" Guinness shouted as he pressed his helmet to the other man's.

Even if the vomit inside the helmet had shorted out the helmet's internal speakers, it should be audible. Clearly it was. Guinness saw the panic in his eyes fade before they closed and the man began to reach with his lips for the emergency breathing tube. Vomit and spittle still almost filled the helmet – damn fool must have overeaten before they all sealed up and the ship depressurised.

The first casualty was already on his way to sickbay.

"Get this plonker to sickbay to empty out, then send him back here," Guinness roared at one of the damage control ratings.

"And take this," he added, as he grabbed the severed leg that was drifting down the access way. "He'll probably want his shoe back!"

Guinness turned back towards the rest of his engine crew. Blood had splashed across several of them and odds were that a few other helmets had blobs of unpleasantness floating around inside. God only knew how that missile splinter had ricocheted its way into engineering. Damned bad luck about Rating Hickey standing where he was. Still a man could get by easier without a leg than his head.

"Well don't stand there scratching yourselves! Check for damage!"

Black Prince gave another violent lurch and the display beside Guinness indicated the main guns were drawing plasma again. Reactor power had been all over the place over the last hour as the engine performed everything from emergency all back to full ahead. Right now though, they were running at forty percent maximum, from which they concluded they weren't in full retreat or full pursuit. Beyond that it was impossible to know what their situation was – and that was becoming harder and harder to bear. As a younger man he'd been able to accept it. He kept the engines going and those at the front had the easier job of everything else. But now Guinness knew he would rather know if his last moments were upon him.

The front quarter of the Nameless cruiser began to burn as it de-orbited and started to brush against Landfall's atmosphere. The last of the Nameless ships had jumped away more than an hour ago, the space gates detonating behind them as they went. The cap ships all made it out, as did most of the gateships and cruisers. The scouts and escorts sacrificed themselves to hold off the Second Fleet long enough for the more important vessels to make it clear. Left in possession of the field of battle, the Second Fleet now orbited over Landfall, once again a human world but now a soiled prize. A handful of weapons satellites remained, obviously installed after the convoy into Landfall had offered a final tenuous line of resistance, one the Second Fleet swept away as a virtual afterthought. As the satellites died, there were at least four nuclear detonations on the surface of the planet. Sensors reported the readings as consistent with fusion reactor breaches. It wasn't as bad as a fission reactor meltdown but significant sections of the planet were now being heavily irradiated. A few shuttles were on their way down, to establish contact with whoever was left but the fleet didn't have the capacity for humanitarian operations. Whatever survivors of the planet's population remained would have to manage for at least a while longer yet.

These were all wider concerns that weren't part of Berg's mental list of problems. *Black Prince* was now alongside *Saladin*. From a visual inspection of her twisted hull, Berg could already tell that if they did manage to get her home, it would only be so the dockyards could remove any parts that were still good. Commodore Dandolo had transferred across but not to command. With both his legs mangled beyond any hope of recovery and *Saladin*'s own sickbay now ruined, he'd been brought aboard to stabilise. Once the fleet's support train arrived he'd be transferred again to a hospital ship. For now, Berg was senior officer for the Twenty-third Cruiser Squadron.

"Final damage reports, Captain – ours and *Zulu*'s," Commander Chuichi said as he passed over a computer pad.

Berg skimmed down it. The Chief had made his usual careful appraisal of the engine conditions. Any other damage was little more than cosmetic. Their squadron mate *Zulu* had also got away clean.

"Send to the Flagship that we are fully combat worthy."

"I've seen reports from other ships. Looks like the fleet is now divided into two groups, the undamaged and the severely damaged, with not much in between."

"That kamikaze thing will never work again," Berg observed. "We're wise to it now."

Chuichi opened his mouth to reply just as the command channel of the intercom buzzed to life.

"Captain to the Bridge! Captain to the Bridge!"

"On my way, what is it?"

"Captain, the fleet train has just jumped in. Several ships are flagging damage codes."

How much things could change in just a few hours, Berg thought to herself as she lay in her bunk. No Nameless forces were present but the Second Fleet was about to have to retreat back to the Junction Line with its tail between its legs. Just as Admiral Gordon had feared, they had either overtaken Nameless or run into units their enemy had deliberately left behind. Whether by accident or design, they had come across the fleet's supply train. There hadn't been many Nameless ships but they had pressed in regardless of loss. Before they succumbed to the escort, they'd put missiles into two of the fleet's biggest fuel tankers. Now the fleet now didn't have enough fuel to go forward or even hold its position. News had raced around the ship before she or any of the other officers could do anything and morale aboard *Black Prince* dropped like a stone, as the crew figured out that this setback had virtually nullified all the efforts of the past few weeks. One of her communications ratings, a big tough man with a reputation as a hell raiser, had been reduced to tears after he overheard a conversation between the drop carrier *Overlord* and someone on the surface, begging for food supplies.

On her belt her intercom buzzed and Berg wearily pushed the earpiece into place.

"Captain here."

"Skipper, we're being signalled by the Flagship. The C-in-C wants to speak to you, privately, ma'am."

Odd.

"Put the connection through to my cabin," she ordered as she pulled on her jacket.

A moment later, Admiral Fengzi's face appeared on the screen.

"Captain, this will have to be brief," he said. "You know the fuel situation. If I am to get the fleet back to Junction without leaving ships drifting, then we have to leave within the next six hours."

Berg's eyes widened with shock.

"I didn't realise it was that close to the wire, sir," she said.

"It's not. But if we move now, then that leaves us with two fast tankers and their load 'spare'. Captain, you know our role here was to put pressure on the Worms. Well it's pretty obvious that they've realised that the battle around The Spur is now the only one worth fighting. If they can win that, then everything they have abandoned here can be regained in the long term."

"What do you need me to do, sir?"

"You put forward the idea of a limited blockade. Well, now we'll have to go with a version of that. I'm detaching your cruiser squadron and the First Scout Cruiser Group. The two squadrons will travel separately but your orders are to make for the Spur at your best speed and engage targets of opportunity – supply bases and other fixed facilities being the priority."

"We may not catch them, sir. They're faster than us in jump space and they have a head start."

"I know that, Captain, but you can take the direct routes to make up ground and frankly, we have to make the attempt."

"How far am I to go?"

"The Spur, Captain, or as close as your fuel will take you. My staff is drawing up formal orders now. I know you may not catch them, Captain Berg, but even if you can nip at their heels, that might be enough."

"I understand, sir. We'll do our best."

As the Second Fleet suffered the ignominy of retreat, four cruisers embarked out beyond the borders of human claimed space. To have gone from being a minor cog in a larger whole to fifty percent of the entire show took some getting used to. For days after they detached from the fleet, every time she looked at the bridge holo, Berg caught herself wondering where the other ships were. Curiously however, although morale on board *Black Prince* had nose-dived following the battle over Landfall, it had now soared. Certainly she herself felt better to be on the advance. She'd expected Admiral Fengzi to transfer in a flag officer to command the detached squadron but no such move was made before they jumped away. So even though this formation would normally have been well beyond her rank, Berg remained the commanding officer.

For days they travelled at a pace Berg judged to be the best compromise between speed and economy. The scout cruisers *Herald* and *Messenger* were to directly follow the path of Nameless space gates, while *Black Prince*, *Zulu* and their tanker the *Ohio*, took the straight line route in its attempt to get ahead of the retreating Nameless fleet. Unlike the Home Fleet when it had journeyed to The Spur, when they dropped back into real space to purge their heat sinks, it was inside solar systems. Several times they found gates and destroyed them but it took six days after departing Landfall before they found something solid.

"Bridge, Sensors. Contacts bearing zero, one, zero dash, zero, zero, one."

"Strength?" Berg asked.

"Ten to twenty, in close order, accurate count cannot be determined at this range, ma'am."

This far out from charted space, their star maps weren't entirely accurate and the squadron had come out only just inside the edge of the system. The contacts were over four light hours away, on the far side of the system, close to but outside the mass shadow of a small moon.

"Twenty ships," Commander Chuichi said quietly rubbing his chin. "That's a lot to take on with two."

"Assuming they are even still there," she replied studying the holo. "Tactical, give me a current position estimate, assuming enemy contacts hold current velocity and course."

On the holo a second cluster of blips appeared.

"They're moving slowly enough to be able to jump at any time," Chuichi observed.

Berg made no reply. At four light hours the Nameless, assuming they were even still there, couldn't yet be aware of the human ships. Their long-range real time sensors that gave them such advantages at closer quarters only seemed to be effective up to a few light seconds. So right now, *Black Prince* and *Zulu* were in a fleeting position of advantage. She could consult with Captain Ewald of *Zulu*, but he couldn't see any more than she could.

"Coms, order the tanker to jump clear, then signal *Zulu* to prepare to jump," she said before turning to Chuichi. "We'll make a jump in eighty thousand kilometres out from their port flank. We'll inflict as much damage as we can, then jump away again before they can counter, assuming anything is there."

Twenty minutes later the crew were closed up at action stations and from the bows came the rising whine of the jump drive building up. *Black Prince*'s two plasma cannon turrets were already trained out to starboard, ready to engage.

"All sections report ready. *Zulu* reports as ready," came the report.

"Very good," Berg replied as she absently tightened her restraint harness. "Navigation, jump."

The thump of the jump out was followed seconds later by that of the jump in. *Come on, come on*, Berg thought to herself as she waited for the holo. No blips appeared in the estimated position. At some point in the last four hours they'd jumped away, it was the most likely scenario, yet the bitterly disappointing...

"Contact! Multiple contacts, bearing: zero eight, seven dash zero, zero, one. Range: one hundred and thirteen kay and closing."

Three blips appeared on the holo and Berg's mind began to race as she took in what the display was presenting. They were outside of plasma cannon range, not by a lot but by enough so that they could peg at *Black Prince* without them being able to respond. It was exactly the situation she didn't want. But the three were moving slowly and towards the small moon. *Black Prince* and *Zulu* were already moving more quickly and could accelerate harder than any Nameless ship. The display indicated the three hostiles were already too deep inside the moon's small mass shadow to jump. There was still an opportunity to close to gun range and hit them before jumping away.

"Helm, turn eighty degrees to starboard, all ahead on engines!" she snapped. "Navigator, keep the jump calculations rolling."

Berg barely heard the acknowledgements as she stared at the holo. Tactical identified the three contacts as escorts, early versions. None of the three was under power. In fact their engines were cold and dark. At any moment, the Nameless ships would begin to react. Would they attempt to make a run in real space or turn and fire? Either way, their first action would likely be to transmit the alarm. Seconds seemed to drag past like minutes. She frowned and looked at the bridge clock. Time wasn't dragging, what felt like minutes actually were minutes, yet the three ships hadn't reacted.

"Sensors, confirm we are getting no reading off their engines?"

"That is... confirmed Captain, passives are reading some residual heat but that is diminishing, not increasing. Captain, there is something else odd. The contacts' current vector puts them on a collision course for that moon."

There was puzzlement in the voice of the sensor officer and Berg shared it. Military grade engines could crash start but that wasn't something any captain really wanted to do.

"Orbital insertion?" she asked.

"No Captain, unless they change course radically and soon, they will not go into orbit. They'll go straight in."

"What is the range to target?"

"One zero one, Captain."

Berg bit at her lip, it didn't feel like an ambush or if it was, it was a stupid one.

"Guns, target the nearest contact and fire."

"Captain, be advised target is four thousand kilometres beyond effective range."

"Understood, fire as instructed."

At such range the firing solution should have been difficult. It took the plasma bolts several seconds to reach the target ship, any course adjustment by which would have been enough to cause a miss. Yet the target made no move as the six bolts bore down on it. Berg watched for a reaction. The six blips converged and disappeared as they impacted the escort. The damage couldn't have been serious – at such range the plasma bolts would have lost coherency as their sustainer fields collapsed.

"Bridge, Sensors. Target heading is changing!"

"Sensors, give me a visual."

For a moment she thought it was finally turning to face them, but no. She could see atmosphere escaping where the hits had pierced the inner hull. Jets of escaping gas caused the ship to slowly tumble. Meanwhile, the other two continued to drift along serenely. Powered down and on course to crash into a moon, there was only one explanation. These ships were being scuttled!

"Navigator, could we catch those ships to board them?"

The question was automatic and unthinking. To take a ship in anything resembling working condition, would be an intelligence coup beyond measure.

"That's a negative Captain," came the reply after a moment. "They will impact the moon before we could come alongside them. Our shuttles wouldn't be able to do it either."

"Alright, make calculations to rendezvous with the tanker," she said as she watched the three doomed ships plummet to destruction.

"We'll have to move faster," Berg said across the video link, its screen was split between that of the captains of *Zulu* and *Ohio*, "because right now, we've been left behind."

The two cruisers were on either side of the tanker. Fuel lines pulsed as hydrogen was forced along them. Berg had originally planned to travel one system further up before pausing to refuel but the sight of those undamaged ships cast aside, had caused a rethink.

"Well unless you two want to give me a push, I've already been doing my best speed," *Ohio*'s captain said bluntly.

"I know. That's why I plan for us to move at *our* best speed," she replied. "Unless we get ahead or at least up to them, we're not achieving anything."

"What? That leaves me on my…"

"I know," Berg cut him off. "Make your cool down stops in interstellar space and you'll be safe. I know there's a risk but we have to take the chance. I've had a think about this. It would make sense to abandon and destroy damaged ships that couldn't fight. If ships simply couldn't match the pace then you'd leave them to follow at their best speed. But those ships were scuttled and scuttled in a way that wouldn't use resources. That says to me that they were probably stripped of fuel and munitions – yes I know I don't have proof of that, but it is the only reasonable explanation."

"Which would suggest the Worms are on right on the wire for supplies," Captain Ewald said.

"Yes, if we take out one or two gates ahead of them, then any gateships are stranded. To do that we have to get ahead of them, but we stand no chance doing that travelling at the *Ohio*'s best speed."

"Still, we need a destination and a rendezvous point for the *Ohio* to meet us."

"The next few systems we skip completely," she replied as she brought up a starmap. "But after that, star density drops and the routes the Nameless can take to the Spur narrow. See these two systems here. With full tanks, they're within our range. Reconnaissance didn't check them for fear of being spotted but the Nameless route to the Spur has to go through one or the other. I'll take one, *Zulu* will take the other and, God willing, one of us will find something."

"We'll need to let *Herald* and *Messenger* know." Ewald said. "If for no other reason than to ensure someone knows where we are."

"Agreed," Berg replied with a nod. "We have their planned route. We'll launch a message drone each to three different systems and set them to make real space re-entry at the edge of the system where the Nameless can't get them and transmit. Hopefully the two of them will be able to crack on at a bit more speed and reach us."

The days that followed were mostly spent in jump space, with their stops in real space cut as short as possible. With the decision made, Berg was left with a lot of time to second guess it. There was a sense of disquiet on board ship, especially once they separated from *Zulu*. Out here, at the very edge of the galaxy, they all felt very small and alone. Nobody said anything to her directly, not even the officers, but there were little indications. System checks on the emergency message drones and the escape pod's hibernation capsules started to feature more prominently in the engineering reports. If something did happen to the *Ohio*, they would be left without enough fuel to go either forward or back.

"So?" Berg asked as she leaned over the shoulder of the sensor operator.

The close proximity of his captain was making the rating nervous, but after days of travel and nights of restless sleep, and now that they had finally reached the system that might be the Nameless route through to the Spur, Berg no longer had the patience to wait.

"We're still getting reading from the passives, ma'am," he reported. "It is a complex system."

"It is a young star, Captain," said the duty sensor officer. "A lot of the planets haven't finished composing so there is a lot of material out there. A lot of blind spots."

"What about the gas giant? Any reading on it?" she demanded.

They had come out at the edge of the system, beyond the heliopause and it was as well they had. There were planets, twelve at least, although going by the smears of asteroids, most of them hadn't yet finished forming. In another few billion years the whole system would stabilise but for now this part of the cosmic dance was still chaotic. Amidst that chaos, something as small as a space gate would be difficult to see, even assuming it was there.

"Captain, the gas giant is approximately one eightieth larger than Saturn. Emissions indicate high levels of hydrogen in its atmosphere."

"Concentrate the passives on it. If anything is here, then it is around that."

"There may well be nothing here,"

"I know, Commander," Berg said with a shrug "but now we're here..."

After a further twenty minutes, Chuichi spoke again.

"It appears the gas giant had two or more moons that collided. They've spread a lot of debris between the planet's Red and Blue Lines."

When Berg made no reply he continued: "Putting a gate in there would be difficult."

"It isn't like we have anywhere else to look Commander," Berg replied wearily.

"Contact!" the sensor rating warned.

Berg, too keyed up to go below, but too tired to stay awake, had been dozing in her chair and woke with a snort.

"It's in a low orbit over the gas giant," the rating continued. "Contact is only just coming over the horizon."

"Are you sure it isn't natural?" Chuichi demanded as he hurried over.

"Negative, sir, we are detecting an engine burn."

Chuichi pushed the rating aside as he leaned over the display. After several seconds he turned to Berg, with something almost like a smile on his face.

"Captain, the readings are consistent with Nameless ships."

It took the contact another half hour to orbit far enough round the planet for *Black Prince* to get a clear view. It wasn't ships after all or to be exact, it wasn't just ships.

"Two cruisers, Captain. Both of which appeared to be docked and possibly under repair. Three or four escorts or scouts, seven or eight gateship transports and an orbital facility. We're still not seeing a space gate though."

"It must be here somewhere. Tell me about the facility," Berg replied.

"It's big, Captain. It's seven hundred metres long and appears to be a mixed installation. One end has at least two dockyards and the rest appears to be a hydrogen refinery. Two hydrogen skimmers are docked on the far side and there seems to be two more docking points on this side. There are also a lot of storage pods visible, at least thirty."

"Those pods would be enough for a fleet," Chuichi said.

"If they're full, then yes. Still no sign of the space gate?"

"There's just so much material in the same orbital band, we won't spot it unless it goes active."

"That is a very deep mass shadow," Berg observed.

This installation was better than anything she had even hoped for. This had to be the primary fuel source for the Nameless on this side of the Spur. If the Nameless fleet coming back from Landfall hadn't passed through yet, then they couldn't be far away. But if they got caught inside that mass shadow...

"I don't think there is a clever way to do this," she said after some thought. "With a mass shadow that deep, even if we jump out right on the Red Line, achieving firing range on the installation will take a minimum of six and a half hours, with another six to get back out."

"That's a long time in a mass shadow, especially as the first thing they'll do is signal for help," Chuichi grunted, "and we can't use the asteroids as cover. By the time we'll be close enough to engage the refinery, we'll be well clear of them."

"I am open to suggestions, Commander," Berg replied mildly

"And if I had one I'd offer it Captain," he said shaking his head. "It is a target that right now we can attack..."

"Therefore," she finished, "we have no choice but to do so."

Black Prince shook as she dropped back into real space right on the Red Line and immediately went full burn. The Commander was certainly right about the Nameless response. Almost before they'd cleared the jump portal, communications was reporting FTL signals from the defenders. An hour later Coms confirmed a reply but could offer nothing on the proximity of the signal's source. On the bridge, none of the officers made eye contact. No one wanted to be the person to suggest retreat. With a mass shadow this deep, it would be hours before either side would be close enough to fire and every hour spent going in, would mean another to get back out.

Ahead, the Nameless escorts had been accelerating towards them almost from the moment of detection. By contrast, it was nearly three hours after their jump in before the first of the enemy cruisers began to move. As it slid clear of the dock, the visual sensors could make out the front of the hull and see that it all-important cap ship missile launchers were opened up – and useless. The sensors could now make out that the second Nameless cruiser's engineering spaces were also open. It was a target, not an asset. The escorts began to manoeuvre for position, spreading out, in order to direct fire along separate channels. Berg hoped it was a sign that they knew they were on their own.

With such a long approach, once they were well clear of the Blue Line she allowed the crew to stand down from action stations. It gave everyone a chance to crack open their survival suits and get a bite to eat. She'd gone below herself when abruptly the main alarm went off.

"Report!" she responded as she shoved her earpiece back in and headed for the hatch.

"Captain, a space gate has just gone active, right on the Blue Line, at bearing one, nine, three dash zero, zero, three. New contacts arriving via the gate, we have seven, eight, nine... *oh fuck me.*"

She didn't berate the watch officer. She'd just reached the bridge and her first sight of the holo showed a nightmare.

There were contacts both emerging from and arriving around the gate. Already, over forty were visible and more were arriving. Tactical was playing catch up but from the display it was clear they were facing carriers, cap ships, cruisers and a plethora of others. It must have been every ship that had retreated away from the Second Fleet.

There was no escape route they could take that the Nameless couldn't cut off, yet against that many ships, the *Black Prince*'s two flak guns be like would pissing into the wind. She'd led them into a massacre.

"Captain, what do we do?"

"Stand by," she snapped back as her mind raced, trying to find some way out. But there was none. There was no route the Nameless couldn't close down. That realisation was strangely calming.

"Coms, prepare our message drone for launch. Give it a rolling update of our log and have it standing by to launch. If we cannot get out, then we may as well do as much damage as we can first."

Looking around her bridge, she could see a mix of emotions, on some fear, others anger and a few, resignation. In war, you might find people willing to be the first to die, but you'd find few willing to be the last – which was exactly what she might have made them.

"Captain, the four escorts ahead are closing."

"Understood," Berg replied as she carefully pulled herself over to her command chair.

Her hands were shaking and it took her a moment to get the buckles into place.

"Guns, engage with flak at maximum range. No point playing the long game, let's just make sure we make it to the station."

"Aye, Captain."

Black Prince couldn't put out that much fire but then neither could four escorts. Astern, the faster elements of the newly arrived armada were beginning to accelerate after them, likely beaters to drive them onto the guns of the rest of the fleet. The defence from the four escorts was almost a comfort.

None of them fired more than three cap ships although each should have been carrying six. Even their supply of small dual-purpose missiles seemed to run out all too quickly. But they continued in, dodging and weaving on an intercept course. If ramming was the plan they never got a chance. When they entered gun range, *Black Prince*'s plasma cannons tore them apart one at a time and Berg knew that, whatever else, their deaths would mean something. The station was important to the Nameless.

The enemy cruiser mounted the final defence, its few dual-purpose missiles contemptuously swatted aside, even as plasma bolts tore through it. Far behind, the new arrivals continued to accelerate after them, but they were too far away to be anything more than witnesses as *Black Prince*'s main turrets swung to bear on the orbital facility. Plasma bolts slammed into and through the structure and atmosphere jetted from its wounds, while fragments of metal tumbled away. On the bridge, Berg smiled as the refinery's increasingly fuzzy radar signal indicated it was beginning to break up. As fragments large and small began the long tumble into the planet's gravity well, they switched their guns to the fuel pods, successively and methodically riddling each one in turn.

"Bridge, Coms. We're picking up FTL transmissions from the enemy fleet and replies from the pursuit elements."

Berg popped her harness and pulled herself over to the communications console. The first signal had been short and sharp, the second much longer, then a third from the main fleet.

"Bridge, Sensors. The enemy pursuit elements are changing course and decelerating."

"Give me a focus on the enemy fleet," she ordered.

The holo focused on the activity around the gate. Ships were manoeuvring round into a single column. As Berg studied their movements, the first of them passed through the gate and disappeared. It took the Nameless fleet hours but eventually, their very last ship jumped away and the gate itself disappeared from the holo, leaving behind only icons for wreckage.

"They couldn't spare the fuel to hunt us down," Berg said. "We have them."

Chapter Twenty

Breaking Point

8th May 2069

"Oh come on, you stupid-bloody-malfunctioning-sack-of-made-in... ah got it!" Jeff muttered as he tried to get his camera to turn on.

The damn thing had been marketed as 'rugged construction' but had been as temperamental as hell since being bounced off a bulkhead. Something had definitely been knocked loose and he sure didn't know how to fix it.

"Right, now I've got this thing going again I guess I'd better do an update," he said to the camera as he got it hooked up and facing him. "I'm not really sure if I've lost stuff to equipment damage. Let that be a lesson to you kids, always back up your work!"

He took a deep breath and sat up a bit straighter.

"It's now been about three weeks since we destroyed the Nameless gate station – Christ only three weeks?"

As he spoke he unconsciously slumped.

"Well I suppose the first week wasn't bad, the Nameless retreated from the system. We got a message from the ships that crossed the Rift that they managed to destroy the Nameless planet on their side... Well destroy is probably the wrong word, depopulate the planet – that doesn't sound any better really.

"Anyway, it was a bad week for the Worms and, as I said, they retreated out of the system. We stayed and took the opportunity to deploy torpedoes and mines into the orbits of the system's planets. If the Worms now try to jump in using the mass shadows as cover, it will be like jumping into a running blender. With that done, all we could do was wait. While we were, we heard a lot of Faster Than Light transmissions going back and forth from the Nameless fleet and their home worlds. Guess they were trying to figure out what the hell had just happened.

"At the start of the second week, Nameless scouts began to appear in the system again, mostly well clear of the fleet and mostly they didn't attack. I guess they were waiting to see if we would retreat of our own accord, but by the start of the third week, it was getting real again. Mostly it's been small scale attacks. Jump in a couple of light seconds away from us, crack off a few salvoes and jump away before our fighters can get to them. It was every few hours at first, then up to every couple of hours, now at least once an hour, all steadily escalating. They've also attempted to build space gates in the system to re-establish their connection to their home worlds. Our recce ships have taken heavy losses and now the strike boats and fighters are having to do a lot of that work, because if the Nameless do get a gate up and running long enough to run a supply convoy through... well, then we're boned.

"Fortunately, they've had to activate a beacon for the ships crossing the Rift to lock onto and we can hear the beacon as well. But they've used some of their ships to send false signals, to try to decoy us away from the gate. So far the Home Fleet has always found the gate in time to roll in and flatten it. In the case of the second one, transports were coming through when we hit it. You've got to wonder what happens to a Nameless ship if there's no gate there to receive them. Can they turn around and go back?"

Jeff paused for a moment, lost in thought.

"It's not going all our way though. At first we could send a few ships at a time back out of the system, to rearm and let the crew get a few hours of sleep. Well, that's a thing of the past. The fleet's lost too many ships now.

"The battleship *Titan* was the first major one to go – an entire battleship and everyone on it, just gone. She took a direct hit from a mass driver missile, which probably went through a reactor. One of my media colleagues, Catherine Mead, was on board. We worked together about five years ago – couldn't stand her as a person but she's... she was good at her job. Well, *Titan* was the first but she hasn't been the last. A few ships have been lost outright and more have been damaged to the point where they can no longer fight.

"Out beyond the edge of the solar system, where our supply ships are, there's a growing fleet of ghost ships, broken warships that have been limped out there and been abandoned, their crews transferred to make up losses on those that remain. Here on *Freyia*, we had one guy transferred in. He'd had two ships shot out from under him in as many days. First time the alarm went off he hid in a corner and cried. I guess he'd just taken as much as he could. I hope the fleet is gentle with him because I don't think anyone else is far behind.

"I'm no strategist but I can tell it's now just a matter of hanging on. We're not looking for a knockout blow, not any more. Now we just have to hang in so that when the bell rings for the next round, we're able to come out of our corner still bobbing and weaving."

The main alarm began to howl.

"ALL HANDS TO BATTLESTATIONS! ALL HANDS TO BATTLESTATIONS!" the intercom screamed.

Jeff gave the camera a tired smile.

"Well folks, here we go again."

"Fuck," Crowe muttered as the main alarm sounded and he glanced up at it with an expression of personal betrayal. Wiping at the half of his face he hadn't managed to shave, Crowe sealed back up his survival suit and locked the helmet into place. Survival suits never had the most pleasant feel but his was now a week overdue for a full clean and the sensation on his skin when he closed it up was... special.

"Report!" he practically snarled as he pulled himself onto the bridge.

"Multiple contacts across our frontal arc..." Colwell began to say.

"I can see that for fuck's sake!" Crowe interrupted, gesturing towards the holo. "What the composition?"

Knocked out his rhythm, it took Colwell several seconds to mentally change gear. Crowe gritted his teeth as he physically forced himself not to snap again.

"Composition is three cap ships, seven cruisers, twenty-one escorts or scouts. We have three carriers further back launching fighters with five more escorts.

"Guns, status report."

"Sir, all weapons are at status green, standing by for firing instructions. Current flak ammunition level at sixty three percent," came the reply.

"Bridge, Sensors. Contact separation, we have incoming."

"Guns. Stand by to engage."

As Crowe spoke, the duty fighters were moving from their standby positions, down the safe lanes into blocking positions. Plasma bolts began to flash out from the battleships, seeking the larger cap ship and mass driver missiles.

"Missiles now entering range," the gunner's voice came dispassionately across the intercom.

"Fire," Crowe said flatly.

The barrage ship, which should have been on their side of the fleet formation, was away rearming, so it fell to *Deimos* to pick up the slack. On the display, blips for Nameless missiles began to disappear, some to be replaced by icons for larger pieces of wreckage, no longer under power but dangerous to anything that got in the way. Most missiles were shot down before reaching the inner perimeter but weight of numbers carried a few through, although none targeted *Deimos* directly. The cruiser's point defence guns rattled at those missiles that brushed across the outer edge of their range.

Nameless ships began to disappear as their escorts exhausted their meagre supply of cap ship missiles and jumped away. The larger ships didn't have enough launchers to put out the weight of fire to force through and they followed their smaller brethren. The Nameless carriers were the last to go and, as several human fighters closed in on them, they were forced to abandon a number of their fighters. Twenty minutes after the alarm sounded, the raid was over. On the holo several ships were flashing damage codes that hadn't been there before.

"It is becoming an issue, sir," Bhudraja said as Crowe completed his shave. "Chemicals are a poor substitute for sleep."

"And what do you want me to do, Commander?" Crowe said in an exasperated tone. "And for God's sakes, sit down."

Bhudraja sat on the cabin's spare chair, with a studiously neutral expression on his face, which was unaccountably grating on Crowe's nerves. Well not unaccountably. After more than a week of little sleep and intermittent food, almost everything was grating on his nerves now. In that time, there had been several moments when all he wanted to do was to just hit someone.

Mississippi now seemed like something out of another universe. By the end of the first week, people were actually starting to say outright that the combination of the destruction of Kingdom and the Gate station had been too much. When he'd returned to *Deimos*, he was practically killed in the rush of officers and crew coming to congratulate him – as if he'd done it all himself.

They could hear the distant signal of the FTL beacon on the far side of the Rift. Maybe the Worms were already retreating – wishful thinking at its most optimistic. Even if the Nameless had been bugging out, they would have had to enter the Spur system to make the jump across the Rift. If they could launch off from anywhere other than the Spur, then the whole premise of the offensive fell apart. But beautiful fantasy would always be preferable to a harsh reality. Now though, three weeks in, with the tempo of assaults only increasing, no one was talking about the end. No one had the energy. Crowe realised he'd tuned out from his second-in-command.

"We are losing ship efficiency, sir," Bhudraja was saying. "That last alert, it took over five minutes longer for all sections to come to full combat readiness than it did a week ago."

"It's been a long week," Crowe replied rubbing his eyes. "I thought this would be over by now – feels more like it's barely begun."

"They don't seem to be weakening," Bhudraja said.

"Stand off firing at long range means they won't be weakening until the moment they run out of ammunition. I just wish to fuck I knew when that would be."

Bhudraja didn't make any comment. There wasn't anything that could be said. If the Nameless had managed to find another supply route, then the Home Fleet might be fighting a battle it had no possibility of winning.

"Well, we'll have to leave some people to sleep through alerts," Crowe said after a moment of thought. "Work out, or get someone to work out, a schedule to have an individual or two out of each section put off duty for a few hours. They'll have to sleep in their suits…"

"I think most of the crew could sleep on a bed of nails at the moment."

"True," Crowe replied with a forced smile. "A few hours might take the edge off the tiredness."

Crowe's intercom buzzed before the Commander could say anything.

"Crowe here."

"Commodore, we've received a signal from Flag," Colwell reported. "The carrier *Dauntless* has been hit, she cannot currently recover fighters. Flag is requesting all ships with fighter recovery capability to report their status."

Crowe paused. A hit to one of their carriers positioned at the heart of the Home Fleet's formation was something he should have noticed or had reported to him, but he had no recollection of it."

"What is our status?"

"We haven't yet received any word on replacements for either of our fighters."

"Alright, report we can recover and rearm two."

"Yes, sir. Bridge out."

"Well, it looks like we're about to have visitors. With a little luck we might be able to hang on to these two. Alright, Commander, unless you have something else, I'll go for half an hour of shut eye."

As the Nameless escorts began to jump away, Alanna pushed the throttle to full. *J for Jolly* trembled as the engines went full burn and the fighter broke formation, wingman in tow, heading for the distant Nameless carriers. Those Worm fighters that had survived contact were falling back for recovery. *Jolly*'s approach was noticed and two Nameless fighters swerved towards them on an intercept. Schurenhofer registered their approach, glanced at their inventory and tasked two of their remaining anti-fighter missiles. As the computer registered lock on, she fired and the Raven shuddered as the pair of missiles came off their rails. Seconds later the two contrails terminated in two sharp explosions.

More fighters attempted to intercept, but *Jolly* now had the advantage of acceleration and Alanna wove round them, not giving them a chance to get into range. Ahead the Nameless carriers were already recovering the fighters that had been deployed as a screen around the cap ships and cruisers for the assault. Astern, other Ravens were also accelerating towards the carrier but they'd had to wait longer than *Jolly* to block the Nameless missiles, so Alanna would get there first by a wide margin.

"We have lock," said Schurenhofer sharply.

"Firing," Alanna replied as she pressed the firing stud. The anti-ship missile burst from its housing and speared towards the carrier. A second missile lanced out from her wingman. As the missiles accelerated away, *Jolly*'s threat detection system whooped an alarm and Alanna threw the fighter into a violent corkscrew.

On her display, Alanna saw Nameless fighters that had been lining up to dock having to break formation and lunge towards the two missiles, while the escorts surrounding the carriers redirected their attention.

"Wing, through and go for the engines," she snapped into the radio.

"Roger."

Alanna steadied *Jolly*, established with a glance that her wingman was still gamely clinging to her tail and continued to accelerate in. Neither of the anti-ship missiles made it to the carriers. But the need to stop them had thrown the enemy landing cycle into chaos. The Nameless fighters floundered as *Jolly* flashed through their formation, her turret guns firing left and right as she burned down the flank of the nearest carrier. The Worm fighters tried to follow, but they had shed velocity to land and now couldn't accelerate hard enough to match the Raven.

As they passed the carrier tail, Alanna dragged *Jolly*'s nose round and pushed the engines to plus ten override. In her seat, Schurenhofer groaned at the deceleration. As the guns lined up on one of the carrier's engine pods, Alanna fired and a moment later Schurenhofer directed the two turret guns onto a second pod. Both engines stuttered and expired as plasma bolts ripped at them. The threat detection system whooped again. The Nameless fighters they'd blown through were coming up fast and Alanna rolled *Jolly* away.

"The carrier's jumping," Schurenhofer called as Alanna twisted their craft to use it as cover from the approaching fighters. She raked it with fire until she saw the bolts pass straight through the now almost ghost-like ship. A few more seconds and the Nameless ships were gone. All that remained were thirty odd Worm fighters, with nowhere to land and more Ravens coming up from astern.

"Good work, everyone," said Commander Deighton across the radio as they destroyed the last of the Worm fighters. "You especially, *Jolly*. Looks like you gave that carrier a good slap before it went. Everyone back on station."

"Well surprise, surprise, that actually worked," Schurenhofer said. "I didn't think we'd get that close – I owe you a five."

"They'll be a lot more careful about how close they get the carriers," Alanna replied as she lifted her hand away from the control column and flexed her fingers.

It was probably her imagination but when she'd first taken *Jolly* from stores, the new fighter had felt lighter and more responsive to the touch, but now, like old *Dubious* before her, the Raven had the feel of a tired warhorse. But that was probably just her projecting. Taking hold of the controls again, Alanna put them on course back towards the fleet.

"Anyway, status check," she said.

"We are bingo fuel. We have one anti-fighter missile, three hundred rounds for the nose gun, two hundred for the dorsal turret and one hundred and fifty on ventral. We have fuel for seven minutes at full combat consumption. One more contact and we'll be drifting and down to harsh language."

The Nameless had been trying to use their fighters to interfere with the Home Fleet's fighter screen. The human counter had been standing orders for the fighters. As soon as the Nameless battle line started to jump away, they were to run at the carriers and knock them out if they could. If this was not possible, they were force them to jump away and abandon their fighters.

"Give *Dauntless* our status and request authorisation to land and rearm," she ordered.

"Maybe get some shut eye as well," Schurenhofer said, "or is that me getting wildly optimistic?"

"That's not optimism Kristen, that's just crazy talk," Alanna replied.

After they lost *Dubious* it had taken a few days to source a new fighter, but once it arrived and after they were assigned the letter J, Alanna decided to claim *Jolly* as their call sign. Schurenhofer seemed torn between whether this was a good sign or some new and ironic manifestation of her pilot's psychosis.

Psychosis took effort though. Combat always got the adrenalin pumping but now sitting there, without either a computer beeping at her or any instructions coming through over the radio, she could feel her eyes starting to close as the tiredness returned. It was starting to feel like the Siege of Earth. Time was becoming a nebulous concept beyond understanding. She'd stopped thinking about the future – next year, next week, tomorrow, even just an hour from now, it was just too much effort for tired brain cells. All she could do was concentrate on making it through each moment, hoping someone would tell her she could lie down and... get... a... few... hours... of...

"Shit," Schurenhofer said abruptly and Alanna's head snapped up. "Skipper, you need to hear this," Schurenhofer continued before flipping a switch.

"All fighters, flight leader." Deighton's voice was grim. "I have just received notification, *Dauntless* is negative, repeat negative, for fighter recovery operations. Stand by for instructions to redirect. Any pilots rated to land on cruisers make immediate contact with class types. Over."

"How the hell?" Schurenhofer said. "*Dauntless* is smack in the middle for the fleet. How the hell did a missile get to her?"

"The inner screen is a lot more porous than it used to be," Alanna replied before switching herself onto the radio channel. "Flight leader, this is *J for Jolly*, instructions received. Be advised I am rated to land on a Luna class cruiser."

Alanna started flipping switches to power down systems.

"Understood *Jolly*," replied Deighton, "Not sure how bad the situation is on *Dauntless*. How long until you have to refuel?"

Alanna glanced at Schurenhofer who shook her head.

"I am at bingo fuel Flight Leader."

"Understood. Stand by, *Jolly*."

Alanna waited impatiently. On her radar display she could see the duty fighters from the other carriers falling back, while others moved forward to take their position. The half dozen Ravens from *Dauntless* though were all drifting, as every pilot cut power to reduce fuel consumption to a minimum. The course they'd established to meet the fleet had been based on a longer acceleration period. Now drifting, their course convergence point was already behind the fleet and the gap was steadily opening. *Jolly*'s computer was dispassionately calculating how much fuel would be required to get back. The number was already worryingly close to that of their remaining fuel and getting closer.

"If the fleet jumps or accelerates we're boned." Schurenhofer said conversationally.

"*I know*."

Another ten minutes ticked past and the fuel warning light came on.

"Flight leader, be advised *J for Jolly* is now declaring a fuel emergency," Alanna reported.

"Understood, stand by."

Alanna's fingers drummed with increasing force on the control column. The Nameless attacks were erratic but they were now at a point where they would no longer have the fuel to either run or fight. Finally instructions came in across the radio.

"*Jolly*, you are to proceed with your wingman to the *Deimos*. Their hangars are clear and a ready to receive you."

"Understood *Dauntless*, *Jolly* over and out," Alanna replied as she powered up the engines again and searched for *Deimos* on her display.

"*H for Humble.* Form up on my wing. Do you have enough fuel to make it?"

"Just about *Jolly*, but I'll need to land on the first attempt."

Making their way down the approach lane, *Dauntless's* transponder appeared on Alanna's display. Schurenhofer focused one of their cameras on the distant carrier. There was a destroyer clearly standing by ready to assist. At such distance the detail wasn't great – a gouge in the hull where the two aft portside hangars should have been was obvious though. The next pair forward was wrecked and pair after that were clearly splinter damaged.

"Dual-purpose missile then," Schurenhofer said. "Looks like it locked onto the engineering section. It must have got really close to the Number Two Reactor."

"If it had been a cap ship missile, there wouldn't be anything left to see," Alanna said grimly as she put *Jolly* onto approach. She'd left *Deimos* more than a year ago but still thought of it as more a home than any other ship she'd served on. Although the landing approach for the flak cruiser was always a bit more awkward than a proper carrier, it immediately came back to her. From within *Jolly* there was a cough as the last of the fuel went to the fighter's reactor, just as the undercarriage touched down and the magnetic clamps got them.

Schurenhofer let out a long sigh of relief.

"How bad is it, Captain?" Lewis asked.

The expression on the face of *Dauntless's* commanding officer was grim.

"It was pretty much a fluke hit sir," he responded. "The angle the missile struck meant that the blast came through the hangars access hatch and penetrated into the main hull. The blast front went through damage control and killed everyone in there. It also severed the main fuel runs to the hangars and that's the big problem.

"Captain, can you get your ship to a state where she is capable of operations?"

"Right now we can take fighters on board in our starboard side hangars and we could arm them, but we couldn't refuel them. In a few more hours I may know more but we need more hands. My executive officer is dead and so are most of his damage control parties."

"I'll have personnel transferred over and I'll speak to you again. This is Lewis out."

The Captain of *Dauntless* had already turned away from the screen before it blanked out. Lewis stared it, lost in thought until he caught movement in his peripheral vision.

"What is it, Captain?"

"Latest availability reports sir," Sheehan replied as he handed over the computer pad.

Lewis scanned it. The list of ships reporting as fully combat worthy got shorter every day, while the list of those that were damaged but could still fight lengthened. But looming over both was that of the ships lost outright or that had been forced to limp over the system's heliopause to be abandoned – so many fine ships and fine crews gone.

"And what of enemy losses?"

"Page four, sir."

In contrast, this list was heartbreakingly short. The Nameless were expending ammunition, the Home Fleet was expending ships. The Nameless had bled fighters. By now there could barely be a human fighter pilot that hadn't made ace, but their enemy still seemed able to keep their carriers fully stocked. Lewis had expected that by now some element of desperation would be creeping into their tactics, but not so. So far the Nameless had continued to snipe from a distance, largely safe from retaliation. They seemed to have abandoned their attempts to put in another gate. Did they realise the futility of it while the Home Fleet was in system or – and this was the stuff of nightmares – were supplies making it across the Rift by some other route?

"Order the Twentieth Destroyer Squadron along with the *Io* and the Third Cruiser Squadron to escort the barrage ship *Piper* to the supply fleet. All of them are to refuel and arm. We have three dedicated reconnaissance ships left. I want them dispatched to the three closest solar systems on this side of the Rift."

Almost as soon as he spoke the order Lewis wished he had not. He could reverse it, only Sheehan would know but even that would be too little too late. He had just verbalised doubt.

Black Prince edged alongside the *Ohio* and a series of clunks echoed through the ship as the magnetic clamps locked onto the hull. The robotic arms quickly got the fuel hoses into position and Berg felt at least one source of tension melt away. She'd never seen fuel levels so low on any ship that wasn't actually in space docks. They'd been forced to shut down a reactor and actually dump mass to reduce fuel expenditure. Even at that they'd barely made it.

"Well, we found absolutely nothing," said Ewald. "Our charts proved to be inaccurate, not by a lot but enough that the system was too far from the next one for the Nameless to transit through."

"Well we struck gold," Berg replied, before briefly outlining the destruction of the Nameless fuel depot. "The Worms might have all the ships from Landfall but by the time they reach the Spur, they'll be flying on fumes."

"Congratulations! Oh and our message drones obviously found *Herald* and *Messenger*. One of their drones was here by the time the *Ohio* arrived. They haven't managed to catch up with the enemy but as soon as they were close enough, they launched a drone towards the Home Fleet to warn them what's coming. I guess we should have thought of that."

Berg opened her mouth to reply then paused.

"What did the message say?" she asked.

"Here," Ewald replied as he sent it across.

Berg read and as she did, a frown formed.

"Mutter des Gottes," she muttered, "those fools should have sent nothing at all."

Ewald looked nonplussed

"They've told the Home Fleet that over a hundred extra Nameless warships are about to arrive in theatre but there is no reference to their fuel situation. The Home Fleet won't know that the Nameless are running on empty – that what is coming towards them is a glass hammer! Do you have a message drone?"

"No, when you were late arriving here, we launched our last one towards your position to double back here with any message you sent to it. It hasn't arrived back yet. What about you?"

"We had to dump ours to make it here," she replied as she felt a stab of bitter regret.

Everyone in the fleet knew the rough details, take the Spur then hold it. The Home Fleet's exact situation was impossible to ascertain, but the message Lewis was about to receive indicated that a powerful, perhaps overwhelming, force was heading his way. How might he react to that intel? Could the war be lost for the sake of one message drone?

"Could you make a fast run to the Spur?"

"No," Ewald replied without hesitation. "To get here as fast as we did, has already damaged my machinery. *Zulu*'s in no condition to make another fast run and that's not the only factor. The fuel we have in our bunkers and *Ohio*'s tanks is enough to get us all back to the Junction Line from here. Go any further and that is no longer true."

Berg made no reply as she mentally crunched the numbers. They'd lost ground on the Nameless coming up from Landfall. While the Worms couldn't be going full burn, not if they were as short on fuel as she suspected, it was still unlikely she could get ahead. Or could she? After a long transit, any fleet would need to at least pause to reform and get the latest information on the tactical situation. That would take a minimum of a few hours, maybe even a day or more, depending on the situation. She could potentially get there before those additional units joined the fight. The message drone though would reach the Home Fleet hours before she could. Would Lewis act on the strength of that message or wait for evidence?

"Carol, we do not have proof that the Landfall force has a fuel shortage. Not absolute proof," Ewald said.

"And we won't get *absolute* proof," Berg replied. "But my ship was alone and deep inside a mass shadow. A squadron of cruisers would have been enough to hunt us down. It was an easy kill and they didn't take it. No, we have better information than *Messenger* or *Herald* and we *must* pass that information on. Captain Ewald, once *Black Prince* has finished refuelling, you are to escort the *Ohio* back to Junction and inform Admiral Fengzi of developments. I will make for the Spur at best possible speed and –and hope for the best."

––––––––––––––––––––

10th May 2069

"Jump in complete," Colwell reported, "we're on target."

"Understood," Crowe replied, "Coms, signal *Dauntless* to tuck in tight and be ready to manoeuvre."

"*Dauntless* acknowledges, sir."

The battered fighter carrier was already in closer to *Deimos* than normal safety margins would allow. Equally, their jump in was far closer to the rest of the fleet than would be acceptable under any other circumstances. Two days of repairs out beyond the heliopause, where at the very least there was no threat of attack and the carrier was ready to resume operations, just as long as they could get her back inside the fleet's perimeter before the Nameless could react. Ahead, the fleet's fighter screen distended outward to meet them, while around them debris from the Worm's most recent attack still dissipated.

"That was well timed," Crowe said, half to himself, as *Deimos* slotted back into her place in the fleet's outer formation, while *Dauntless* continued inwards to her place. One of the barrage ships and a cruiser squadron were moving clear, on their way out to the supply fleet.

"Bridge, Coms. Sir, signal from Flagship, a piece of housekeeping."

"On my screen," Crowe replied before reading down. Most of it was a tactical update, with a summary of the twenty hours *Deimos* had been out of the line. There was also a transfer order for the two fighters again currently in *Deimos*'s bays. They were to go back to the carriers. It was disappointing but not surprising. There weren't that many fighters left now. The carriers had enough berths for most of them with the balance earmarked for the most robust of the battle line ships. He'd spoken only briefly to Lieutenant Commander Shermer, enough for them to congratulate each other on their respective feats. After that, with no official position in *Deimos*'s table of organisation, she and the rest of the flight crews had disappeared into whatever bunks they could borrow and were likely now the most rested people on the ship.

"Lieutenant Colwell," he said unclipping his seat. "I'm going below. Send someone down to Lieutenant Commander Shermer to inform her she and her flight are to return to *Dauntless*. No point launching just for the transfer. We'll launch when an attack comes in or it is their turn to join the screen."

That had been one of the things that virtually every captain in the fleet had been forced to learn here at the Spur. To get off their bridges and get themselves some rest. Before the war, it had been expected that battles would be a few hours of intense action, preceded by perhaps a few days of build up. But here at the Spur, as the days became weeks, he'd had to accept he could not stay on duty twenty-four, seven. To try would mean being useless when the action really did come.

He could have chosen to eat in his own cabin but instead went to the main canteen. In gave an opportunity to see and be seen by the crew. Once he waved down any attempt to come to attention, there was a certain amount of carefully chosen questions from the junior members of his crew.

"No one knows, Mister Long," he replied between mouthfuls to one such cautious question. "There are three things the Nameless need to sustain their fleet: fuel, ammunition and enough transportation to get those to their fighting ships."

"Fuel is the easiest of the three. They can get that on this side of the Rift from many gas giants and while we have been able to mine the orbits of any such planets within several systems of here, they undoubtedly had stockpiles built up."

"Transport is the next problem. They have a lot of transport ships but most are gateships and those gates cannot be put in a combat zone. So the Nameless are being forced to base their operations outside this system, wasting time and fuel transitioning warships in and out of the combat zone."

"The final and most important factor is the ammunition. Without missiles they can't fight and to get missiles, they must re-establish a connection to their home worlds. All they have is whatever stockpiles they had on this side of the rift."

"We haven't seen them use mass driver missiles in days," remarked a sensor rating.

A few people around the table winced. Those missiles had always been a rarity but when used their potential for catastrophic damage was horrifying. No one on *Titan* had stood any kind of chance when they were hit.

"Well, you wonder what the bastards – sorry, sir – the enemy will do when they really do run out," ventured another rating.

"They will have to cut and run," Crowe replied. "Even they cannot fight without weapons."

"It's what they'll do when they've nearly run out that worries me," said another rating.

He mumbled it but everyone heard him. Crowe opened his mouth to reply just as the main alarm went off.

"Hold that thought," he said as a mass scramble began for the hatch .

"Report!" Crowe ordered as soon as he entered the bridge.

"Enemy ships jumping in, bearing three, three, four dash zero, two, seven, range *thirty thousand kay*."

"Guns stand by, get those fighters... wait! Sensors, confirm range at thirty thousand kilometres?"

"Confirmed, sir!"

Well inside plasma cannon range! The Nameless knew what kind of abuse human ships could hand out at such distance. With the ships still phasing in, the tactical count remained uncertain and composition unknown.

"Bridge, Coms. Signal from *Valkyrie*, firing instructions."

"Transfer to Fire Control. Guns, engage in line with those instructions," Crowe replied without taking his eyes off the holo, trying to figure out what the Nameless were attempting.

No, the Nameless must have made a positional mistake and jumped into the wrong location. Plasma bolts were now pouring out from the ships on the port side of the Home Fleet's formation. One of blips blinked out as it came far enough into real space to be struck by half a dozen plasma bolts. Tactical started to establish a count, a dozen escorts, six cruisers and two cap ships, all near stationary from the jump and formed into a shallow arc. Another escort vaporised under a salvo from the battleship *Yavuz Sultan Selim*. The remaining ships began to accelerate hard, but not away from them or on evasive manoeuvres. No, instead they were powering in.

"Oh shit," Crowe said quietly as he realised the *Deimos* was at the focal point of the half arc formation in which the Nameless had emerged.

The readings from the passives sensors showed every ship was red lining its engines. There was also order in the formation. Each of the larger ships had at least one escort between them and the Home Fleet, shielding the larger vessels. The smaller craft were being torn apart by a maelstrom of fire. Most never got a chance to fire but they were buying time for their larger compatriots, time to ready their weapons and obtain targeting locks. Sensors were showing infrared spikes as the larger ships prepared to fire.

While their escorts died, the larger ships swung out from behind them and, as one, simultaneously emptied every one of their launchers. Seconds later, one of their cruisers and a cap ship were destroyed, but the salvo they'd sacrificed more than a dozen ships for was off and away. On *Deimos*, the bridge holo flashed red as the computer registered that their course was set to converge with the cruiser.

Crowe's eyes widened in horror.

"Evasive manoeuvres!" he bellowed. "Fire Control, everything on those missiles! Point Defence, commence, commence, commence! Countermeasures full spread!"

But the short-range launch meant *Deimos*'s computers hadn't had enough time to track and prioritise the incoming missiles, now heading for them at full burn. Like the escort ships before them, the smaller dual-purpose missiles were out in front, sacrificing themselves to screen the cap ship missiles following behind. Other ships were now switching target from the fleeing starships onto the incoming missiles, but precious seconds had been wasted. The salvo melted away as it hit a hail of counter fire. Out ahead, one of the barrage ships belatedly opened up and consumed a few tail end Charlies, but as he watched Crowe realised it wouldn't be enough.

"All hands, BRACE FOR IMPACT!"

———————————

On *Warspite*'s holo the *Deimos* briefly flashed damage codes then all information disappeared. The surviving Nameless ships were accelerating away. Not many would make it clear but on the holo, another group of icons was appearing on the opposite side of the fleet. This time the target was obviously *Deimos*'s sister ship, *Io*.

"Fleet heading change!" Lewis snapped. "Bows down seventy degrees, maximum fleet acceleration! Navigation, calculate immediate jump to number four quadrant!"

With his orders issued, he could only look on as the fleet began to react. The barrage ship *Brahms* twisted out of formation to bring its broadside to bear and commenced firing to cover *Io*. Their intended target denied them. Twisting and losing ships as they came on, the Nameless formation threw themselves at the *Brahms*.

Forgotten by friend and foe alike, the blip showed *Deimos* astern, continuing to drift on her last course.

———————————

Alanna screamed as she slammed into the rim of the hatch. When the alarm had sounded she was sleeping and it had taken her sleep-fogged brain a moment to figure out where the hell she was. Coming out of the cabin she collided with Schurenhofer.

"To the fighter!" she'd roared as the two of them disentangled.

Climbing up and out of the centrifuge, she'd felt the ship's guns begin to fire. When *Deimos* started to take violent evasive action, the two of them were thrown back and forth as they tried to pull themselves along the passageway. Grabbing an electrical junction box, Alanna launched herself at the next hatch, just as the entire universe seemed to explode. Everything twisted violently around her. Abruptly, instead of the hatch way opening, she was going toward the rim. Flailing desperately she tried to avoid it but there was nothing to grab. Pain exploded across her shoulder and chest as she hit unyielding metal and a moment later Schurenhofer cannoned into her from behind. Then all the lights went out. A moment later the red emergency lighting came on. Alanna barely noticed as she writhed in agony.

"Jesus, Skip! Are you all right?" Schurenhofer exclaimed.

It was seconds before the pain unclenched enough for Alanna to answer. By then, Schurenhofer was performing a basic medical examination.

"I think you've broken your shoulder, Skip."

"Of course I've fucking broken it!" Alanna gasped.

Schurenhofer was already pulling a first aid kit off its wall mount.

"We need to..."

"Shut your yap," Schurenhofer muttered. "We have to immobilise this." Alanna gasped in pain as Schurenhofer got the sling into place. "We've got to get you to sickbay."

"No, get to the fighter," Alanna grunted.

"Skip, you can't fly with a broken flipper!"

"Shut up and feel it."

"What?"

"The engines, they aren't firing."

Schurenhofer laid her hand flat on the deck. There was usually the faintest of vibrations. Now it was totally still.

"Generators aren't running either. That means both the reactors are off line," Schurenhofer said in a sick voice.

"Get to *Jolly*. See if she's still operational," Alanna gasped as she pulled herself round with her good hand.

"Where are you going?"

"The bridge. Find me once you know the situation."

Signs of damage were everywhere but with her intercom not tuned to *Deimos*'s command grid, she couldn't hear anything. She passed several groups of crew, some obviously injured, others attempting to make repairs. It was obvious that confusion reigned. Finally she reached the bridge. The hatch had warped and two damage control ratings were trying to force it open with a pry bar. Alanna leaned her own mass into it and slowly the hatch gave way.

As soon as she pulled herself onto the bridge, she knew that they would find no one alive. The only light was from survival suit status displays – every one of them was red. The main holo was simply gone. Something had ploughed across the bridge, through anything or anyone that got in the way. Glancing to port, where Lieutenant Colwell and his section should have been, she could see the stars through the ragged gash in the hull.

She'd known most of the men and women that had served on the bridge when she'd been stationed on *Deimos*. Now she determinedly pulled herself past them without looking. Better to remember them as they once were. One though she had to check. The command chair was bent over but still in place, the seated figure within it, motionless. Pulling herself over with her good hand she gently pushed back the Commodore's head. There were two ragged holes in his chest and blobs of blood floated in front of him. Crowe's expression was one of surprise. When death came for him, he hadn't had a chance to feel it. As Alanna hung there in front of the corpse of a man she'd respected, but one she'd known had doubts about her. She felt her eyes begin to sting – for him, for all of them, to have got from the war's start to so close to the end... After a last look back, Alanna made her way out. There was nothing she could do here.

"The Commodore's dead?" the junior lieutenant looked young, frightened and completely out of his depth. After reaching Damage Control, she'd finally got her suit tuned to the command frequency but there was only the one officer left to report to. The ship was in a state, cables had been ripped from their mountings, metal had crumpled like tinfoil, most sections seemed to have lost pressure and what was left of the ship's systems were obviously running on the emergency batteries.

"What have we got?" Alanna asked. "Or more importantly *who* have we got? Where's Commander Bhudraja?"

"He took a smack to the head, ma'am," replied a petty officer. "He's alive but he weren't making a lot of sense. Heavy concussion I reckon. We got him down to sickbay."

"The gunner?" she asked.

"Don't know."

"Alright, so what will we do?" Alanna asked turning back to the Lieutenant. As a pair of frightened eyes stared back at her, Alanna realised she had no recollection of him, which made him a newcomer to the ship. Here and now, he'd just frozen under the weight of responsibility.

"Alright, we need to un-fuck this situation *right now*! PO, get yourself down to engineering and get the most senior person still standing up here. You," she continued, pointing at a random rating, "yes, you, sickbay, I need a report on who we've lost. You, Fire Control, tell the gunner to get down here, he's probably now the commanding officer."

When they hesitated she added: "Don't stand there staring – *fucking* MOVE!"

"There you are boss."

Turning, Alanna found Schurenhofer with the crew of *H for Humble*.

"Well?"

"Glad to see you too," Schurenhofer replied, when Alanna gave her a get-on-with-it look. "*Jolly*'s dented, but the board is still green," she continued. "She's still space worthy."

"*Humble* and the entire port side hangar are gone, though," added Lieutenant Stein, *Humble*'s pilot. "*Jolly* might be okay but we need to open the hangar doors before you can launch."

Alanna smiled slightly bitterly and wiggled the fingers of her injured arm.

"There's no we, I won't be flying out."

"Boss?" Schurenhofer said.

"You're right. I can't fly. I'm... out. If we can we get *Jolly* off the deck, then you three head for a carrier. I'll help here once we figure out who's in charge."

"Boss, I can..."

"No, Kristen, your place is still on a fighter. Report to me if or when you get the hangar door open."

As they left, the surgeon came in, blood streaked up his arms and a face shield still clipped to the top of his survival suit.

"Shermer, what the hell happened to you?"

"Lost an argument with a hatch. Not important now. Where are we with casualties?" she impatiently replied.

"Twenty wounded so far, several of them serious so I can't stay long. There are only three fatalities that I know of but damage control parties aren't bringing in any bodies..."

"The Commodore is dead, as are the rest of the bridge officers," Alanna told him. "I need to know about the other officers."

"Err... Well, I have the Commander, who has taken a head injury. He'll live, I think but he won't be in any condition to command anything. The gunner was brought in, he's dead."

"What about the Chief?"

"Still alive," the chief engineer's voice came from behind here. "Although Christ knows how."

His suit was scorched and there were cracks in his helmet visor. If he was surprised by Alanna's presence he made no comment and she rapidly brought him up to speed.

"The first thing we need to know is who's in charge," she finished.

The surgeon and engineer exchanged a look.

"Lieutenant Commander, I think that's you."

"You're not in the ship's table of organisation but aside from me and the doc," the engineer continued, "you outrank anyone still standing by a lot. I need to be in engineering and the doc..."

"Is not a ship's captain," finished the surgeon.

Alanna nodded, she'd suspected as much.

"Err... Captain... ma'am... someone," the speaker was one of the damage control ratings.

"What is it?" Alanna replied.

"Ma'am, we just got the external cameras on line and we just saw the rest of the fleet jump out!"

Alanna turned back to the Chief.

"Can we save the ship?"

"Both the reactors scrammed," he replied.

"Can they be got back online?"

"By the book start-up from a scram is at least three and a half hours."

"Three and a half hours," the surgeon exclaimed, "we're sitting ducks. You've got to be able to do it faster..."

"Hey! This is not some science fiction bullshit where I can pull a number out of my arse!" the Chief responded heatedly. "If I try to restart a reactor that turns out to have a casing crack we could blow ourselves to kingdom come!"

"Chief, can you shave anything off that?" Alanna cut in.

He opened his mouth to object but paused.

"We were hit to port so the reactor on that side took a heavier G spike," he said thoughtfully. "The starboard side is our better chance for a recovery. If I concentrate all the hands I have left on that, we might be able to take a bit off. But not much, Captain."

Alanna made no comment on the honorific. They were alone,

crippled and defenceless but someone was in command. Right now that was enough.

"Three hours is too long. I know you can only do what you can do. But right now we're a written invitation for someone to come along and finish us off. We'll retain a skeleton crew, mostly engineering, the rest will abandon ship. That might make us look like we're not worth another missile or at the very least save most of what is left of the crew. Doctor, get the injured out first, then supervise the rest of the evacuation. Turning she spotted the young lieutenant she'd spoken to before.

"You, find the two most senior gunnery crewmembers you can. Get the rest off the ship."

"I'll ask for volunteers, ma'am."

"No. Select two of them. The time for volunteers has gone," Alanna said firmly. "Chief, get back to Engineering and get started on the reactor, but if we can't save her..." She didn't finish but the Chief understood.

"Skipper?"

"What is it Kristen?"

Alanna had buckled herself into Damage Control's command chair after pushing aside the junction box that had brained Commander Bhudraja. For the moment there was little for her to do. The first escape pod was about to eject with a dozen of the most seriously injured who had been carefully loaded on board. Several of the unwounded had volunteered to stay. Whatever else, the crew of *Deimos* had retained their discipline.

"We've managed to crank the hangar doors open so we can go at any time. Lieutenant Stein is requesting instructions. We've got a full fuel tank so we can hold and offer some cover it they come back."

"No, if they see a fighter hanging around," Alanna replied, "they might jump to the right conclusion that we're trying to save the ship. Tell the Lieutenant his orders are to return to the fleet, request search and rescue pick up survivors and to inform them we'll rejoin them if we are able."

"Alright, Skipper," Schurenhofer replied reluctantly. She looked around the battered chamber. "Just promise me, Skip, you'll run for a pod if it comes to it."

"Off you go and don't worry about that," Alanna replied with a forced smile.

A short time later she watched on one of the few external cameras that still worked as *Jolly* undocked and left her behind.

At the edge of the system, there was a brief ripple in the fabric of space before the messenger drone dropped into real space. Stencilled along its flank was MESSENGER.

"The drone arrived in system about an hour ago, sir," Sheehan said offering the computer pad. "The transmission reached us ten minutes ago."

The staff officer sounded sick.

++To Commander Home Fleet from Commodore Brahimi, First Scouting Group: Advise that on 24th April enemy units in region of Landfall and Junction line commenced retreat towards the Spur. Enemy units have broken contact with advanced elements of the Second Fleet. Believed unlikely at this time that contact will be regained. Estimated one hundred plus enemy combat units are converging on your position. Estimated arrival time after the 15th May.++

Lewis put the pad down carefully. Another hundred fresh units, a hundred! Against his fleet... or rather what was left of it.

"What do we do, sir?"

"What we will do, Captain," he said wearily, "is stand our ground."

Chapter Twenty-One

To the Last

13th May 2069

Berg was in her cabin when the explosion rocked the ship. *Black Prince* swerved violently as she lunged for the hatch, throwing her against the bulkhead. Bouncing off, she grabbed the hatch handle as she staggered past. As she pulled herself through, the main alarm sounded. The ship was still swerving with enough violence to overcome the centrifuge's effect and Berg was thrown up towards the ceiling, before being launched back towards the deck. She managed to grab a hand bar and get a firm enough hold to avoid being thrown again. Mere metres from her bridge, she was trapped in the small access way, unable to even reach for her intercom as the ship violently jolted in all three axis.

"Damage Control teams to the Starboard engine room!" sounded the main intercom. "Sickbay, stand by to accept casualties!"

She began to drag herself along the bar.

"Damage Control, all hands emergency venting, brace, brace, brace!"

There was a second bang and the cruiser swerved downwards but less violently this time. Damage Control's brief warning had been enough and helm countered without over compensating. After a few more moments Berg was able to release her death grip on the handrail and get her feet under her again.

"Report," Berg called out as made her way onto the bridge.

"Captain," the duty officer replied, "we've had a failure on Engine One! The emergency pressure seals on the starboard side engine room have been blown and atmosphere has vented. We have reduced power on Engines Two and Four to compensate. Two casualties are on their way to sickbay with burns. I don't know how bad they are and I don't know whether we have secondary damage."

"Bridge, Engineering. Chief talk to me!" Berg snapped as she got her intercom earpiece into place.

"Skipper, we just had a blow in on one of the ignition chambers," Guinness replied after a moment. "Engine plasma came inboard. We've evacuated and vented the compartment. Sensors showing fires are out and we've cut plasma flow to the engine."

"Can you fix it?"

"Jesus, Skipper, I don't even know how badly it's broken yet! We won't be able to get in there for at least an hour until temperature and radiation have dropped. Skipper, we *have* to dial it back. Our engines are old and reconditioned. This is more than they can take!"

"Chief, we need to get to the Home Fleet as soon as we can."

"Skipper, you're asking for more than she has to give. If we don't slow the pace, we might not make it at all!"

Even across the intercom, Berg could tell that he sincerely meant it.

On the bridge holo, she could see *Black Prince*'s track down the jump conduit. The yellow line was stabilising again but astern, she could see where they'd avoided going into the side of the conduit by a hair's breath.

"Okay, Chief, give me your best offer."

13:40hrs 15th May 2069

"Well, this is new," said Captain Sheehan nervously as the two of them stood on the outer hull of *Warspite*.

To their left and right was a grey wall of armour plate, pitted here and there by missile impacts. Lewis grunted a reply as he observed the approaching cruiser. Two wars, a handful of skirmishes, a lifetime in uniform and as his staff captain said, this was new. Not just that the two of them were hanging from the side of his flagship, but the cold fear that gripped his heart had nothing to do with duty and everything to do with personal survival. *This is not the time to freeze up,* he admonished himself. *Get on that ship and take back command!*

Three hours earlier

"We're now in a situation where, of our original combat strength, a third has been destroyed or rendered non-functional. Of the balance, less than a third remain fully combat worthy. The rest are at varying levels of damage with some held together with little more than duct-tape and the power of prayer! On top of that, it's no surprise the crews are exhausted. Sir, we are not nearing breaking point, we have reached it!" Commodore Hooper said forcefully.

"Yet we have them on the ropes!" cut in Rear Admiral Paahlisson, "Dear God, they are trading ten ships for each one of ours that they knock out. Those are the tactics of desperation!"

"I'll grant you those are bloody tactics," Vice Admiral Sekhar replied. "But look at the ships they've taken out. In the last twenty-four hours we've lost the barrage ships *Schumann* and *Piper*, plus the flak cruiser *Deimos*. The *Brahms* is damaged to the point of borderline combat capability. Those vessels represent a disproportionate number of our best anti-missile ships. With those gone or damaged, we can expect them to achieve a better kill ratio with any further attacks they mount. Even if we assume they have only missiles in their own magazines and – and that's a fucking optimistic assumption – their ships from Landfall won't have to trade ten to one."

"It's a desperation tactic," Paahlisson insisted.

"That's worked," Sekhar replied. "Keeping the fleet in the system, is allowing the Nameless to direct their strikes accurately. We need to fall back beyond the heliopause where we..."

"No!"

The single word was enough to silence everyone in the videoconference.

"We stay in system," Lewis continued. "We leave the Nameless with no choice but to come at us. If we fall back, they will begin to run supply shipments through again. If that happens, then the balance will shift against us."

"With respect, sir," Sekhar replied, "we are at breaking point. If we fall back, then we can attempt to enforce a distant blockade. We could also strike at the next system, where the Nameless marshal their units, rather than allow them to do so in peace."

Lewis made no immediate reply and Sekhar shifted uncomfortably. Sekhar had started this battle on the *Loki* and was now on the *Fortitude*. Lewis could only wonder whether that influenced his opinions. Three weeks previously, Lewis would have scoffed at the idea of a man like Sekhar advocating giving up. But exhaustion did unpredictable things to a person. So did loss. There were gaps in the videoconference that should have been filled by men and women Lewis had known, in many cases for decades, for whom the war was already over. The lucky ones were now in the steadily filling hospital ships waiting beyond the heliopause. The rest were in body bags or part of the clouds of debris now scattered across the system.

"The strategic situation has not altered. The Spur remains the critical ground. I agree these tactics by the enemy do represent desperation. That means that, at the very least, we can now be certain that supplies are not reaching them from their home worlds."

Lewis paused and looked at them all.

"If we withdraw, then our response to their moves will become too slow," he resumed. "If we retreat from the system, then we'll have lost the battle and if we've lost the battle, then we've lost the war. I believe the next few days will be the deciding moment. We know via the courier that came from Captain Willis of the *Spectre*, that the Nameless have a small fleet of gateships and jump-capable transports waiting for their path to be cleared. If even a few of them get through, that will extend the Nameless ability to fight by days."

"But, sir..."

Lewis raised his hand and Sekhar stopped.

"Captain Willis has also made clear that her task group is close to the point where they have to retreat for supplies. Once she does, the Nameless squadrons that she has pinned down protecting their home worlds will be free to move forward to assist."

"They know they must break us," Paahlisson added, "and that they must do it soon."

"Which would be great except they have the means to do just that," Sekhar warned. "We're throwing good after bad."

―――――――――――

"Skipper?"

Alanna looked up from under the sensor panel she'd been working on. The long hours of inactivity had sat uncomfortably with her and finally, as much to pass the time as anything, she'd decided to try to repair a console that had had its power cable torn out by the concussion – difficult with only one hand but she had been making progress.

"Yes, what is it?"

The speaker was a grubby and tired looking engineering rating.

"Ma'am, the Chief reports he'll be ready to make another attempt at starting the reactor within the hour."

"Alright, tell him to give me a heads up when he's about to try."

"Yes, Skipper," the rating replied before heading aft again.

She didn't bother asking for details. The Chief's original three-hour estimate had proved laughably optimistic. While the reactor itself was apparently sound, the control systems it relied on had been severely compromised by the whiplashing of the hull when they were hit. But the Chief hadn't been willing to admit defeat and as their bit of the system seemed to have become an oasis of calm, there seemed little justification to abandon ship just yet. If they could get the vessel going at all, then they could fly her from Damage Control.

Still, as she looked around the deserted and darkened compartment, Alanna wondered for the umpteenth time whether this was a fool's errand and for the umpteenth time she answered herself: no. It was strange. She hadn't known Crowe especially well. He'd just been her senior and, strangely, had always seemed closer to his ship than his crew. But the Commodore's death had affected her more than she'd expected. Others, hundreds and thousands of others, had died but Crowe had been there since the start. It seemed... wrong that he'd fallen only now. Maybe, in an odd way, if she could save his ship, it would mean something. She was about to return to her work when she noticed a light flashing on another console. Pulling herself over, she turned on the screen and, after a moment, cursed softly to herself.

"When will we be inside their range?" the Doctor asked.

"If we can see them with the external camera, then we're already inside missile range and probably have been for a while," Alanna replied as she viewed the screen.

The image on the screen kept blinking on and off as *Deimos*'s slow tumble forced the computer to switch from one camera to another. With only the small emergency computer online, it was some kind of miracle that it had managed to spot the small group of Nameless ships. Possibly though, ignorance would have been bliss.

"Any idea how close we'll get?" the Chief asked.

"Probably inside a hundred kilometres but that's just a guesstimate."

"That sounds very close," the Doctor ventured.

"It's far too close. Since we've been powered down for hours our engines are cold so they mightn't have seen us yet," Alanna said, as she thought out loud. "Or we just look like an abandoned wreck."

"Is it time to eject then?"

"I don't think we want to climb into pods that will catch their attention as soon as we launch, especially as we won't be able to run away," the Chief warned. "There's a lot of broken spaceships floating around this system by now. We could just drift right past them."

"Only if our luck improves," the Doctor replied.

"How close are you to restart?" Alanna asked.

"Half an hour," the Chief said, then added a qualifier, "assuming it fires up. But if we do try..."

"They'll detect it, regardless of whether the reactor starts up," Alanna said wearily. "We'll be so close they might even pick up the heat from the crew. Keep working on it, Chief. If we can, we'll just keep drifting. If they make a move towards us... well, then we can try to start the reactor and make a run for it."

"Is the jump drive working?" the Doctor asked.

Alanna and the Chief exchanged looks.

"Damage Control isn't registering any damage to the unit itself but whether power supply from the reactors to it is okay – that's a different question. We won't know until we power up."

Once the other two officers had left Alanna made what little preparations she could. This certainly bore no resemblance to any tactical situation she'd ever trained for. One flak cruiser with no functioning power systems and with a crew of less than two dozen, versus an enemy force of unknown composition and strength – if that came up in the academy then you'd know your training officer hated you. If they did have to power up, then their only hope would be to hose fire at the Worms as they ran for it.

On the screen the enemy ships kept rolling into view. The emergency computer wasn't programmed for tactical purposes but Alanna had been close enough to Nameless ships to be familiar with their visual appearance. With no other preparations to make, she buckled herself in and waited.

Every time the Nameless ships came back into view after each slow tumble, they had edged a little closer. Alanna stared at the screen until her eyes hurt. Was that movement? The ships disappeared as *Deimos*'s latest roll took them out of the line of any of the surviving cameras. It would take twenty-one seconds for the ships to come back into view.

"One, one thousand and two, one thousand and three, one thousand..." she counted off slowly, "twenty-one, one thousand... Christ! Chief, fire it up! Oh no!"

The profile of that overlapping mess of ships had changed,

although only because one of them had moved slightly. It wasn't turning to face them or taking any hostile action, but her response had been that of a fighter pilot. It was too late now. They were committed. From astern came a thump and in Damage Control the main lights flickered on.

"Engineering, Damage Control, reactor online! Generators One and Two spinning up!"

Alanna didn't respond as she pulled herself over to the emergency helm station. The emergency computer had powered up the control consoles but the main computer and all the remaining systems were still booting. They were still at least twenty seconds from being able to do anything!

"Bridge to all guns, fire when you are able!" she ordered as she gripped the helm's still useless manual controls.

The ship's power board showed the generators had spun up. Electricity flowed to the flak guns and Alanna felt the deck tremble. On the visual display she saw first one, then another flak round burst among the closely grouped Nameless ships. Then the roll took the gun out of arc.

"Shit!" Alanna shouted as she uselessly rattled the control yoke. With the engines not yet online, she still couldn't arrest *Deimos*'s roll.

The radar did come back though and on it she could see the alien formation beginning to shift. Another gun came into arc and opened fire, throwing flak rounds indiscriminately at their packed ships. Then the engine display on her console lit up and Alanna rammed the throttle to full. Warning alarms buzzed as several control surfaces shattered under the temperature shock as the engines went to full power. She struggled with controls far more sluggish than anything she was used to.

"Captain! The jump drive is responding, it's getting power!" shouted the rating at navigation.

"Calculate a jump out of the system!" Alanna shouted back as she wrestled *Deimos* onto a facing to bring two of their guns to bear and give her a visual. On the screen the Nameless reappeared. The aliens were scattering as flak round burst among them. With the guns on local control, the fire was utterly indiscriminate. In the centre of their formation, Alanna got the briefest glimpse of something large, before flak rounds worked along its length and it disappeared in a fiery flash.

"What the hell was that?" exclaimed the rating at Sensors.

"Calculations complete, Jump Drive spinning up!"

Deimos accelerated away. Such was the chaos she had wrought that not a single vengeful missile pursued before she jumped away.

"Sir? Sir?"

Sheehan's voice woke Lewis from the doze he'd slipped into, his fingers tingled as he lifted his chin up and blood flow was restored.

"What is it, Captain?" he croaked.

Sheehan handed him a computer pad but his tired eyes just couldn't focus. Letters seemed to dance back and forth. *Christ, I can't read any more*, he thought before handing it back.

"Just give me the highlights," he said.

"One of the reconnaissance ships you sent out of system has reported in, Sir. They came through the next nearest system. Yesterday they observed one hundred and twenty-three Nameless ships arriving, mostly lighter types but none of them show damage, so we have to assume they are the ships from Landfall," Sheehan grimly summarised.

They'd never got a clear estimate of the number of Nameless ships in theatre, but one hundred and twenty-three! Even if they were mostly escorts, it would still double the forces available to them, especially if they were arriving with full fuel bunkers and missile magazines. The Nameless had done it again – reacted with decisiveness that under other circumstances would be something to be admired. They'd realised that this was the last battle that would matter and sacrificed everything else to win it.

"What do you want to do, sir?" Sheehan asked quietly.

"Inform our divisional commanders. Instruct them to stand ready. I expect the Nameless assault will begin within hours."

When Sheehan had gone, Lewis opened his desk draw and took out a packet of tablets. The doctors had been handing out wake up pills since the end of the second week. He'd always loathed such things. No matter what the bloody doctors and pharmacists promised, chemicals always came with a price. The main alarm started to sound. Lewis ripped open the packet, swallowed two and pulled on his survival suit helmet.

Nameless ships were detonating before they even managed to complete their jump in. There were fifty of them formed in a half circle around the front of the Home Fleet, none of them more than thirty thousand kilometres from the human ships. A dozen were little more than drifting debris inside thirty seconds. Mostly escorts and scouts, the survivors went full burn as they made it back into real space. Missiles began to fly and further back, at the edge of plasma cannon range, Nameless carriers arrived and began to launch. Space around the Home Fleet erupted as every gun on every ship opened up. This time however, none of the alien ships pulled away. As they launched, scouts, escorts, cruisers and even capital ships charged in, straight into the Home Fleet's withering fire.

On *Warspite's* bridge, Lewis felt the great ship shudder as a missile found its way through and slammed into her belt armour. The Nameless were dying in droves but even as they did, they remained lethal. Burning, exploding wrecks stayed on their ballistic courses into and through the Home Fleet's formation, which disintegrated as ships scrambled out of the path of these fiery battering rams. Lewis winced as he saw the course of one scout intersect with that of the destroyer *Knight* and both disappeared from the scope.

"Coms, fleet course change. Five degrees to port and bows down forty degrees. Acceleration, fleet's best," he ordered.

On the holo the cruisers *Churchill*, *Thor* and the battleship *Yavuz Sultan Selim* began showing damage codes. As Nameless ships or their wrecks came charging through the formation, individual ships found themselves isolated. The barrage ship *Drummer* was slow to react to the heading change as three Nameless ships zeroed in on her. Two were shredded as they attempted to charge straight through her barrage but the third swerved round the wall of explosions. *Drummer* sluggishly attempted to dodge, even as her small point defence battery savaged at the Nameless ship. It wasn't enough and the two disappeared in a flash as the alien craft slammed in and their fusion reactors breached.

On *Warspite*, an alarm sounded as the computer registered a pair of escorts powering down towards them on a collision course from above, behind several cap ship missiles on final approach. Lewis could only watch, helpless to make any useful contribution, while the battleship's crew fought to save their ship. *Warspite* rolled to reveal her broadside and place her heaviest armour between the approaching danger and her vitals. Half the ship's original heavy calibre railguns had been exchanged for flak guns, which now poured fire at the approaching missiles, while their heavier counterparts spat fire at the charging escorts.

The first railgun round performed exactly as designed. Striking the escort square on, it ploughed down the length of the alien ship, coring it. Even as the Nameless detonated, *Warspite*'s guns were already shifting to the second ship, which was attempting to both stay on its suicide run and dodge. Railguns and plasma cannon lashed at it. One railgun round grazed it, a glancing hit that was enough to tear the side off the fragile little ship. Disintegrating as it tumbled, the escort couldn't match *Warspite*'s last evasive manoeuvre. But the sacrifice of the escorts allowed two of the cap ship missiles through. As he was thrown against his restraints, the last thing Lewis saw before the main holo blinked out were serried ranks of Nameless ships dropping into real space ready to fire through the gaps their colleagues had torn out of the Home Fleet.

"Talk to me Damage Control," Captain Hicks shouted, "how bad is it?"

Jeff was only half aware of the conversation that was going on across the command channel. He was too busy trying to pin down a sensor rating, as a corpsman fought to save her. Without gravity all three of them kept floating off the deck and as the cruiser manoeuvred they were thrown about.

"Please, please, please," she begged.

Jeff could see blood squirting out of the wound in her stomach. With the bridge decompressed, the blood crystallised and froze within seconds. As Jeff physically struggled with her, he tried to erase from his memory the... sensation of missile fragments blowing through the bulkhead and cutting across the bridge faster than the eye could see or the mind comprehend.

"For fuck's sake, hold the bitch down!" the corpsman cursed as he tried to line up his sealant gun.

Jeff pushed one leg under the console now covered in the woman's blood, then twisted to place his forearm across her chest and forced her back to the deck. The corpsman was still swearing as he sealed the wound.

"Up, got to reach her back."

Jeff released his hold long enough for the corpsman to flip the woman over, then clamped her back down. It only took the man a couple of seconds but in such an awkward position that was enough to set his back muscles screaming.

"Okay, got it. Let's go!"

"I'm not crew. I'm a journalist. I've got to stay here."

All of those words sprung to mind. He said none of them. Inside her helmet the woman's head lolled and her eyes rolled back. The monitor connected to her suit flashed red.

"Got it," Jeff replied.

Making their way out of the back of the bridge, Jeff reflected he'd never realised how hard it was to carry something in zero G. Sure their patient was also weightless but he couldn't get his legs underneath. With one hand to hold her and the other trying to pull him forward, that left him at least a hand short. As the two of them struggled down the passageway a pair of Damage Control ratings, carrying lengths of cabling, shot past them like missiles. The climb down into the centrifuge was even worse as their load gained weight. By the time he reached the bottom of the ladder, Jeff's arm was nearly pulled out of its socket. The corpsman took her over his shoulder though and headed for sickbay at something close to a run, while Jeff tottered after him.

Passing through the sickbay airlock, Jeff was confronted by something he'd never before seen in the otherwise sterile world of space. Blood was splashed on the bulkheads and even though his survival suit was still sealed, he could have sworn he could smell it. As they came in, the Surgeon and one of his orderlies were pulling a sheet-covered body off the bed. On one side of the sickbay three more bodies lay neatly stacked. Seeing the three of them arrive, the Surgeon hurried over. Before the battle he'd spoken to and interviewed the man. He'd been well spoken, even witty. Jeff had marked it as one for transmission but now the man's eyes were dead.

"What have we got?" he snapped.

"High velocity abdominal penetration, through and through, major blood loss, probably spinal damage," the corpsman grunted as he gently laid her down on an empty bed.

As the man spoke the surgeon was already pulling a small x-ray machine into position.

"Cut her out of her suit," he ordered before frowning at what he saw. He glanced around the sickbay. "She's borderline. Alright, we'll have to operate, but if anyone else comes in, we'll have to abandon her."

Jeff felt sick as he realised what the Surgeon had said. It was a triage decision – if more casualties arrived, then the efforts to save the sensor rating would just simply stop.

"Are you hurt?"

"Hmm?" Jeff said when he realised he was being spoken to.

"Are you hurt!" the Surgeon demanded.

"No, no!"

Looking down at himself he realised for the first time that the chest of his suit was streaked crimson."

"Then get out of here," the Surgeon snapped as he pulled on surgical gloves, "I don't need some fucking media vulture in the way!"

Jeff made his way back to the bridge, desperately hoping that at the very least he wouldn't see another casualty en route to sickbay. By the time he'd got there order was restored, with another rating occupying the seat with a hole in its back. On the holo he couldn't see any red blips of Nameless ships in among the humans' green. But there were a lot less green than there had been. Then in the distance, off to starboard, more red blips began to appear. The Battle Fleet ships on that flank continued to fire, but for the moment, *Freyia* seemed to be on the disengaged side of the battle.

"Any instructions from the Flagship?" Captain Hicks demanded.

"Negative sir, nothing."

"Well..." Hicks started to say.

"No sir, we are getting absolutely nothing. No communications, no damage codes, we're not even getting a friend or foe response."

"Sensors, what's *Warspite*'s status?"

"I see a major plasma leak from her engines but she's still underway and firing."

"Looks like *Warspite*'s lost her coms," Hicks said, looking troubled. "Who's next in chain of command?"

"Admiral Sekhar, on board the *Fortitude*, sir. We're being instructed to shift formation and fill in the gaps."

"What have we still got in terms of good anti-missile ships?"

"Right now, sir, we have the *Yavuz Sultan Selim*, the *Fortitude* and the *Io*. I can't see any of the barrage ships – I think we've lost the last of them."

"Bridge, Coms. Orders from *Fortitude*, Captain. Fleet is to turn ninety degrees to port and make best fleet speed."

"Understood. Helm, adjust heading."

On the holo Jeff could see that the turn placed the newly arrived Nameless astern. They were launching the first of their missiles but even Jeff could see that their overtake velocity was slow.

"With the barrage ships gone, fleet speed has actually gone up a bit," someone said and Hicks nodded.

"Looks like Sekhar is in command now," Hicks said. "I wonder what he'll do. The Worms will probably jump some of their sections out onto our flanks in..."

"Bridge, Coms. Captain, we're receiving a transmission from *Warspite*, its' low powered... I think it's a suit radio." The communication officer looked up from her console with an expression of surprise. "Captain, it's an any ships request for a pick up. Admiral Lewis is transferring off!"

"Bridge, Sensors. We have ships jumping in, bearing zero, seven, six, dash, one, six, eight – range, one fifty thousand kilometres. I count thirty of them."

Jeff could barely keep pace as he swung his camera back and forth towards the different voices. The Captain though, seemed to be calmly keeping ahead of developments. He turned back to the front of his bridge.

"Looks like we've got the best position for a pick up. Helm, break formation and put us on intercept for *Warspite*. Coms, advise *Fortitude* we are making for *Warspite*. Then get back onto whoever that is and tell them we'll come down the port side and that we'll get only one try. Get someone outside and on the dorsal wing!"

Hicks turned and caught sight of Jeff.

"They don't cover this shit in training," he said with a wild grin.

"Main coms is down, as is the back up," Captain Holfe said, his expression bleak as Lewis pulled himself through the hatch into the main bridge. "We've lost everything – radio hook up to the main grid, the coms lasers, even a good chunk of internal communications."

When *Warspite*'s flag bridge had lost power, Lewis immediately abandoned it. Behind the Captain, Lewis could see that the Damage Control display and multiple sections were flashing red. The bridge holo was still online but had been stripped of almost all detail. There were greens and reds for friends and foes but nothing to indicate which ship was which.

"The fleet?"

"I can barely tell what the hell is going on out there, sir. All I can do is follow the fleet's movements."

"Captain, sir," a junior officer shot onto the bridge. "Sir, the first officer reports main communications took a direct hit. Everyone is dead and there's heavy damage to backup coms. It will be at least an hour before we can establish even basic coms systems."

"We are deaf and dumb," Holfe said grimly, before turning back to Lewis.

On the holo, the fleet re-orientated as its sub-commanders realised the flagship had dropped out of grid. With no ability to communicate, Lewis no longer held a place in the chain of command. In fact, the rest of the fleet now had to assume he was dead. That put Sekhar in command.

What to do now? As Lewis studied the holo, the fleet turned and accelerated away from the newly arrived Nameless. The aliens should have done as their colleagues and jumped in closer to force immediate contact. But after days of savage losses, perhaps some Worm had finally succumbed to the siren call of self-preservation and a desire to finish the job without further loss. Turning away was giving the Home Fleet time to re-establish formation but would Sekhar use that time to jump away? The order might already have been given. He would only know when ships began to disappear.

"Sir," Holfe replied, "my ship can move and she can fight, but she cannot serve as a command vessel. We *have* to get you off this ship."

"Have we got a shuttle?" Lewis asked.

"No," said the junior officer still awaiting orders. "We've had them all checked and even the ones that haven't been obliterated are beyond use."

"We need a shuttle to come to us," Holfe said. "But we haven't the coms to communicate with anyone."

"Put someone in an airlock and use their suit radio," Sheehan said.

"If that doesn't work, get someone to stick out their thumb," Lewis replied with grim humour. "Sheehan, you've just volunteered. Get out there."

As Sheehan dashed away, Lewis turned back to the holo. He could see small blips racing into and through the fleet's formation. Some probably missiles, others fighters, but whether they were friendly or hostile was impossible to tell.

Minutes crawled by and all Lewis could do was clench his fists and follow a battle he had no ability to influence. Was this the moment when everything slipped away?

"Admiral, sir," the junior officer said reappearing at Lewis's elbow. "We've managed to make contact. It's the heavy cruiser *Freyia* under Captain Hicks. She's already on approach for the number seven airlock."

"That will do." Lewis replied. "Captain Holfe, if the fleet jumps, then jump *Warspite* to the supply fleet. Make emergency repairs then get this ship back into the fight."

"Of course," Holfe replied simply as Lewis headed for the hatch.

"Captain Hicks says he can't stop," the junior officer explained breathlessly as the two of them shot down an access way. "This will be a drive-by."

Carefully controlled movements were what they taught for moving in micro-gravity, even more so when a ship was under power. But now Lewis threw caution aside as he raced to the airlock, collecting bruises as he went.

Sheehan awaited him at the open airlock.

"We don't have long, sir," he said as ratings clipped long-term survival packs onto their suits.

Lewis hesitated.

"You don't have to come, Captain."

"Duly noted, sir."

Stepping through the lock Lewis looked aft, along the battleship's scarred flanks. There was *Freyia*, less than a kilometre away, angling to get around *Warspite*'s wing. Below his feet, the entire universe beckoned. Step out, it said to him, leave it all behind and fall forever. Edging along the foot rail, the additional air tank clipped to his suit grated unexpectedly against the hull. The contact was enough to momentarily loosen his grip on the handrail and he snatched desperately at it. In the corner of his eye a red light in his helmet blinked on and off as the suit registered he was at the edge of hyperventilating. Pausing for a moment, Lewis forced himself to breath slower. With him and Sheehan hanging from the side, *Warspite* couldn't take any violent evasive action that might be required. They needed to get off the ship.

"Well, this is new," said Sheehan nervously as the two of them waited. Lewis grunted a reply as he watched the heavy cruiser approach. Beyond her, he could see flashes of gunfire and explosions. As *Freyia* rolled smoothly to starboard, Lewis caught sight of damage all along her side. As the cruiser approached he began to make out two small figures standing on the dorsal wing's manoeuvring engine. The cruiser was in too close now to use the main engines to brake, as the plume would fry both of them. Instead, the docking thrusters were firing continuously.

They were close enough now for Lewis to see the crewman on the wing leaning outward, one hand reaching out, the other braced by his comrade. A small dispassionate part of Lewis's mind admired the display of perfect ship handling, as the roll was arrested, bringing the manoeuvring engine down perfectly to the level of the airlock as the cruiser slid smoothly alongside of *Warspite*. The crewman of *Freyia* stretched out his arm, Lewis could see his mouth moving, urging them on. Lewis took a deep breath, and stepped out into space.

The other man's hand closed around his wrist and with a twist shoved him into the arms of the second man.

"Sheehan, are you there?" Lewis asked as the second man clipped him onto a safety line.

"Just about, sir," he replied with relief in his voice. "Can we *please* go inside now?"

As he walked down the wing towards an open hatch, Lewis felt main engines firing as the ship began to accelerate. Looking back, he caught a last sight of his flagship of three years. The hull had been speckled by impacts, one of the forward passive arrays was a twisted wreck and B turret had been opened up, while astern he could discern the haziness of leaking gas. As he watched, one of the remaining turrets turned and fired at a distant target. There was a hiss in his ears as his suit radio picked up the backwash. The great battleship looked like an old attack dog, scarred, maimed, mute, yet still ready to fight any takers.

"Welcome aboard, sir," Hicks said as Lewis was escorted onto the bridge. "Coms, make signal to all ships, *Freyia* is now flagship of the fleet!"

"Mutter des Gottes," Berg breathed as the fleet appeared on the holo. The Home Fleet had left Earth with four battleships, twenty cruisers, four carriers and forty or so various other types. Now Berg could see barely half that and of those, only half a dozen *weren't* flashing a damage code. Bleeding plasma from two engines, *Black Prince* had dropped into real space a good light minute out from the fighting. Nameless ships and missiles were throwing themselves forward in a way she wouldn't have believed if she wasn't seeing it with her own eyes.

"Bridge, Coms. Skipper, the *Freyia* is showing as fleet flagship.

Admiral Lewis is still in command."

"What the hell is he doing on *Freyia*? Never mind. Contact her now!"

"Yes, Captain."

The distance added an agonising delay. Behind her, Berg could still hear half a dozen alarms sounding from the engine display. The heat sink was close to melting, one engine dead, another dying, *Black Prince* was in no condition to fight. Nearly three minutes later Admiral Lewis's tired face appeared on her screen.

"Captain, I don't know where you came from but you'd better keep whatever it is brief," he said tersely, glancing away from the camera as he spoke.

"Admiral, I was ordered to pursue and maintain contact with the Nameless fleet as it retreated away from the front line and Landfall. Two days ago that fleet intercepted us just as we destroyed a fuel refinery. A superior force trapped us within a mass shadow, but once we destroyed the refinery they immediately retreated. Sir, it is my belief that the Nameless fleet is flying on fumes! They are running out of fuel! We are downloading our logs to you now."

Over the past few days Berg had attempted to rehearse what she would say. She had no proof, only a belief and perhaps only minutes or seconds to convey that belief in a convincing manner. As she looked at the battered remnants of the once formidable fleet, she wondered whether she was too late.

Two, three then four minutes went past. Then finally came a perfunctory reply.

"Message received."

And the screen blinked out.

Berg sat back in her seat, so many planned words unsaid.

"Captain, enemy ships are moving to intercept."

Berg shook herself. She'd delivered the word. She'd done what she could.

"Navigation, calculate a jump over the heliopause. Get us out of here."

"That's a lot of conjecture based on a very small amount of evidence," Sheehan said as he and Lewis reviewed the data download from *Black Prince*'s communication. As he quickly scrolled through it, Lewis nodded but made no reply. By the time he made it to the bridge,

Freyia was already receiving orders to jump out of the system, orders Lewis had quickly countermanded. Sekhar had yielded only reluctantly and it was plain the man was a spent force.

He wasn't completely wrong, though. The fleet couldn't sustain this battering much longer. The suicide runs had decimated what was left of their best anti-missile ships. Now with those gaps in the anti-missile screen, the cap ship missiles targeted at them from further out were getting through and their destroyer screen was suffering as they tried to protect the larger ships. The next wave of ships was coming up from astern. With the Home Fleet accelerating their overtake speed was low.

On the face of it Captain Berg's information changed nothing. Their objective remained as before: stay on the field of battle and deny the Nameless the ground they needed to command. But, with an optimism he hadn't felt in days, Lewis realised that this changed... *everything*. Missiles would only be used up if the Home Fleet stood and let the enemy throw them. Fuel was another matter, however, because fuel was being used every moment. They couldn't help but use it. Lewis spun back to the main holo. Several ships had lost their jump drives but Sekhar's orders had resulted in the fleet bunching up, ships without drives had been paired with those that still did.

"We'll jump, Captain," Lewis said, straightening up.

"Away, sir?" Sheehan asked with surprise.

"No."

Lewis pulled himself across the bridge to the navigation section.

"I want the fleet to jump to here."

He pointed to a random piece of the solar system.

"We've stood and taken it long enough. I want a schedule of jumps to random locations around the system worked out. I want to be able to send individual ships back to resupply and then for them to be able to jump back to rejoin the fleet. I also want to be able to deploy what fighters and strike boats we have left as scouts. They'll need to have the schedule, so that if they find something, they can jump back to us."

"Sir?" Sheehan said trying to keep up with Lewis's change in direction.

"We've been letting them use up missiles against us, but if Captain Berg is right, then their fuel is running out and we need to force them to burn it."

Lewis glanced at the holo. The next wave of Nameless ships was closing fast and they had only a few more minutes before the he would have to turn the fleet to present their broadsides.

"Now get on with it, Captain."

Nameless missiles, large and small, powered along in the Home Fleet's wake. The few guns that would bear stabbed out, then the space ahead of the human ships opened up as they jumped out, leaving the missiles to burn through nothingness.

Ten light minutes away the Home Fleet dropped back into real space, Lewis waited patiently as Sheehan and the small staff he'd managed to assemble from whoever Captain Hicks could immediately spare, attempted work out a series of jumps. With orders issued, Lewis could only wait. He found himself sharing space against the bridge's rear bulkhead with the embedded journalist.

"Jeff Harlow of…"

"I don't care," Lewis cut him off.

Jeff wilted, but only for a moment.

"How will this help? I mean, anywhere we jump they can follow."

"They can eventually follow," Lewis said in spite of himself. "But those FTL sensors of theirs are only good for a few light seconds and a solar system is much, much larger. Unless we jump in close to one of their ships, it takes time and fuel to regain contact with us." The space immediately around the fleet remained free of any Nameless. "Just give us enough time to work this out," Lewis murmured to himself, almost completely forgetting the presence of the journalist.

It took the Nameless nearly an hour to find them again. An hour for Lewis to reorganise what was left of his fleet and an hour to listen to Nameless FTL transmissions. The coms section on board *Freyia* lacked some of the facilities on *Warspite*, but their direction finding was enough to confirm the Nameless were spreading out. At least some ships had jumped as close to the edge of the solar system as their drives could manage, which in turn was as close to the Home Fleet's support ships as they could reach, presumably trying to see whether their enemy had retreated there.

They also heard distant signals from the Nameless home worlds. Was there an element of hope in those transmissions? If so, it was crushed when the Nameless scout jumped in two hundred thousand kilometres from the fleet and, by pure good fortune, within a few thousand kilometres of a pair of screening fighters. It got the word out but was obliterated moments later. By the time Nameless cruisers began dropping in around the Home Fleet's reported position, the humans weren't there anymore.

17th May

For two days it continued. The Home Fleet made dozens of jumps, from one side of the system to the other and all the while the Nameless flailed after them – always one step behind. The drives of some ships struggled to keep up the pace but now there was the opportunity to send them back to the support fleet for repairs. Even as they left, other ships, hastily repaired, started to trickle back. *Warspite* arrived at the end of the sixteenth followed, to everyone's surprise, by the cruiser *Deimos* with a scratch crew under the command of a fighter pilot. Others continued to join them and the fighting strength of the Home Fleet slowly grew.

The Nameless tried scattering scouts and escorts across the system to find their elusive target. These isolated and vulnerable ships were easy meat for even the small number of human fighters that remained. Ship after ship was burned down and when the Nameless did make contact with the Home Fleet, it was piecemeal, not the hammer blow they required. All the while, Lewis could feel the advantage shift as the Nameless lost momentum.

"The burning question is what will they do when they reach the point where, if they don't leave, they won't have the fuel to make it across the Rift," Lewis mused out loud. "The point where they have to commit to one course of action or the other, with no ability to change midstream."

"There's no saying that point hasn't already been reached, sir," Hicks replied. "They may well have decided to commit to forcing us out to the last. Those ships could sit dead in the water for a while if they knew tankers were inbound. If they can force us out, then they only need one ship with enough juice to run the beacon for a few hours."

In the background Lewis could hear the journalist taking notes, his presence just about tolerated.

"Fair point, Captain," Lewis replied. "The Phantom task group confirmed that Nameless ships are waiting for an opportunity to jump the Rift."

"A beacon has to stay on for six hours. That's a long window," Sheehan said. "*Deimos*'s skipper reports that they blundered into a squadron and she hit a tanker on the way out."

"I'm not sure how much confidence we can put in that report," Hicks replied. "*Deimos* is pretty beat up and the new skipper is beyond green."

"There are two reasons they would risk bring a tanker into the combat zone," Lewis said. "They had us on the ropes a couple of days ago, so it might have felt safe. Alternatively, it could be they didn't have the resources any more to play safe and send ships back out of the combat zone to resupply. We simply have no way of knowing. No gentlemen, for the moment we keep jumping the fleet and avoiding contact. However, we will deploy our reconnaissance and fighter elements wider. If we can catch a section of their fleet resupplying outside a mass shadow, then we might be able to land the knockout blow."

19th May

Alanna didn't respond at the first insistent shake. The second was a good deal less hesitant. With a groan, she returned to consciousness.

"Skipper, the officer of the watch is asking for you," said a petty officer. "Something's going down."

As she made her way back towards the Damage Control station, the signs of hurried repairs were everywhere. Here and there lumps of sealing foam dotted the bulkheads, sufficiently closing off breaches so that the ship could at least hold atmosphere. Bits of broken cables drifted like seaweed, while other pieces hastily spliced back together and duct taped out of the way were visible everywhere. The whole ship was held together by tape and hope – and she was still in command.

When they'd been out beyond the heliopause with the supply fleet, she'd been promised that a new commander would be arriving shortly. The crew they put off the ship had mostly returned. The few remaining junior officers filled dead men's boots, but no one arrived to relieve her and when *Warspite* lumbered back towards the figurative sound of gunfire, she knew *Deimos* had to follow. They'd patched the ship up enough to fly, but weapons control was a wreck. However, Coms had somehow avoided damage and they'd paired off with the badly damaged destroyer *Voulgiers*. She didn't have a working gun left in her but her weapons control was still functional and the two ships could function together in a brains and brawn arrangement.

"What is it, Lieutenant Dolezal?" she asked as she pulled herself into the command centre.

"Skipper, we're getting something odd from coms," he said.

If you have woken me for 'odd' then prepare to die. Alanna suppressed the urge to say it as she pulled herself over to the communications display. The urge to punch Dolezal disappeared the moment she saw the screen.

"Twenty-one FTL transmissions..."

"Now twenty-two," interrupted the rating at the display.

They were dotted all over the system and as Alanna watched, another two appeared.

"All hands to battle stations," she said before pushing off towards her command chair.

"It's levelling out at thirty-four signals, sir," Sheehan said as he leaned over the shoulder of the communications rating. "The signals are consistent with the navigation beacon from the gate station."

"Show me," Lewis said as he buckled himself in.

Action stations hadn't been ordered for the fleet, but crewmembers were already rushing onto *Freyia*'s bridge and struggling into survival suits. On the main holo, the blips for individual ships were lighting up as they reported as ready for action. It wasn't just him. The fleet could feel it too. The Worms were making their last move. The holo zoomed out to display the entire system. Thirty-four signals were pulsing out.

"Are all of those signals the same?" Lewis asked.

"Yes, sir," Sheehan replied after a moment. "All the same frequency, all the same strength."

"What are your orders, sir?" Hicks asked.

In his mind's eye Lewis could see the situation of his opposite number. Their fuel status had hit critical. Their salvation was only six hours of flight time away but with no mass shadows to hide in, any ship transmitting a beacon might as well paint a bull's-eye on its hull.

So the Nameless were returning to the game they had played so many times before: the numbers game. The Home Fleet would catch and destroy ship after ship but with enough alien ships transmitting together, they could maintain their signal for the required six hours. But somewhere out there, there was a point, perhaps even a powered down gate, where the relief force would arrive. If the Nameless could make jump in, then after a very short time they could jump away again. If there was a gate, then dozens of the expendable gateships could solve their supply problem.

"Start a countdown for six hours," Lewis ordered. "Instruct all fighters to land and rearm for anti-ship strikes. The central core of the fleet will remain here. Light units will be dispersed in squadrons to strike at enemy beacons. Either run them off or destroy them. Work from the outer edges of the system and move inwards."

"What if they run into heavy opposition?" Hicks asked.

"Then we follow in with the main fleet." Lewis replied.

The signal from the Nameless scout ceased abruptly as a squadron of destroyers, with *Deimos* and *Voulgiers* in support, jumped in less than seventy thousand kilometres away. The alien ship salvoed off its missiles before it turned to run.

"We have hook up to *Voulgiers*," Dolezal reported. "We're firing, Skipper!"

"So I can see, Lieutenant," Alanna said absently as she gazed at the screen.

The handful of missiles stood no chance and died as they hit the effective range of flak guns. By the time they did, the scout was already dead as a hail of plasma bolts from the destroyers ripped it open and sent the wreckage tumbling away.

"Signal from the *Cuman*, moving onto next target."

"Acknowledge it. Helm, stay on station," Alanna replied before glancing at Dolezal. "That's us two for three," she remarked as the rising whine of the jump drive spinning back up rose from the bows.

On *Freyia's* main holo, Lewis could follow the progress of the ships ranging out from the fleet, albeit not directly. With combat breaking out all over the system, the signals to radar and passive arrays were minutes and sometimes hours out of date. But each time one of the outlying beacons was snuffed out he knew that contact had been made. Those signals from the outer edges of the system were being silenced faster than they could be replaced. It was now three hours since the first beacon went active and the Nameless had lost six ships without reply.

The Home Fleet hadn't moved in hours, but in contrast to the previous weeks of bloody combat, no Nameless ship approached. The only vessels appearing on the scope now were those sent out as they reported back, before being dispatched again. But although every signal had been forced to terminate at least once, the Nameless had always managed to keep at least ten beacons active at any one time. The relief force would have a signal to home in on all the way, but the Home Fleet now had a fix on every possible location. Wherever the Nameless arrived, the humans could be there within minutes.

"Captain," Lewis murmured without looking round.

"Yes sir," Sheehan replied.

"You said all the signals were the same."

"Yes, sir."

"Watch for any signal that is different. Order all ships to converge on the fleet in two hours, forty minutes."

Sheehan paused but nothing more was forthcoming.

"Yes, sir."

Again and again, Lewis caught himself glancing at the bridge clock. With two more hours gone and over twenty additional Nameless ships destroyed, he could feel this was the moment. This entire operation had been born of the need to land a knockout blow and all the Nameless had to do was avoid it. Four years after the Mississippi Incident and everything that had followed, this was the moment that would settle it.

"Admiral! We have a transmission, it's different!" Sheehan shouted.

Lewis didn't wait for it to be passed to the holo and instead was instantly up and over to the communications section. Another twenty FTL signals had gone active but there, almost submerged beneath them, was the one exception. Lower powered, with a different rhythm of pulses, it was the signal that might have been missed if they hadn't been looking for it. It was close to one of the system's inner planet, where the fleet's torpedoes and mines had denied them the safety of the mass shadow.

"Navigation! Jump calculations to that point!" Lewis barked out. "Communications, signal all ships prepare to jump into combat!"

"How close sir?"

"Jump us directly into gun range!"

Three battered battleships, two carriers, with less than a third of their complement between them, a dozen worn cruisers and a handful of destroyers erupted back into real space. It was a far cry from the fleet that had blasted its way into the system all those weeks ago, but as the first radar returns came in, Lewis knew that victory was at his very fingertips.

There ahead, lit up and active was a Nameless gate. As he watched it, another gateship came through and phased back into real space. Around it warships were appearing. A few were being flagged as familiar but most were newcomers, fresh undamaged Nameless ships, barely moving and already inside gun range.

"Bridge, Tactical. Confirmed contacts profiles consistent with Nameless gateship tankers with heavy escort."

"Bridge, Sensors. We have contacts, enemy combatants jumping, bearing two, seven, one, dash, three, five, nine – range thirty thousand!"

"Coms," Lewis said quietly, "order, *Io* and *Deimos* onto our left flank. All battleships and heavy cruisers to engage the tankers with plasma cannons."

It was doubtful whether most of the ships had received the order before opening fire. They had targets in range and that was all they needed. Plasma bolts flashed across the intervening space, smashing through the helpless tankers. Attempted to protect them, the newly arrived Nameless warships sent missiles burning back. A human cruiser corkscrewed out of control as a cap ship missile blew off its bows, but it changed nothing. On the flank, what was left of the original Nameless fleet threw itself forward, even though few of them seemed to have missiles left to fire. For all its desperation, their charge proved futile as they ran into an unyielding wall of counter fire that burned starships like moths in a flame.

The gate was almost the last to go was. A direct hit cut it in half, its field dying as the fragments tumbled away. As the last of the tankers detonated, Lewis turned his attention to the Nameless fleet. *Is that enough you bastards*, he thought, *please let that be enough!*

He focused intently on the holo . There were few missiles flying now but the smaller alien vessels continued to throw themselves forward, forcing the human ships to engage them. Lewis's heart was beginning to sink when he saw it. Their remaining cruisers and cap ships were decelerating hard. On the holo, blips began to highlight as *Freyia's* computer registered they were going slow enough to...

"Admiral sir! They're jumping out!"

"I see it," Lewis whispered.

As the last of the larger ships disappeared, the few surviving escorts and scouts, changed course, swerving around the Home Fleet, accelerating towards the planet to use it as cover, chased as they went by plasma cannon fire. Finally the only ships on the holo were human.

21st May

As *Spectre* completed jump in, Willis found her grip on the armrests of her chair tightening until she heard the material creak. *Spectre*'s computer had a record of the Spur system but now, as the holo began to fill up with data from radar and passives, thousands of new objects that weren't there before appeared. On the holo, the computer dispassionately classed most of it as debris.

"Captain," the sensor officer reported, "we are picking up the Home Fleet, range thirty light seconds."

She could see it herself but the number of blips was wrong — there were far too few. Willis felt her throat go dry.

"Bridge, coms, we are receiving a transmission from the *Yavuz Sultan Selim*. It's Admiral Lewis."

"My screen please."

Lewis's face looked like death warmed up.

"Captain Willis," he said, "report please."

"Sir, we reached the limit of our supplies. I can confirm that on the nineteenth the beacon on their side went active. A few hours later a series of enemy ships were detected jumping into the system. Many were observed to be carrying battle damage. We believe them to be the survivors of the battle on this side of the Rift. They remained in system for a few hours before jumping away in the direction of their core worlds."

"I see," Lewis replied. "Thank you, Captain Willis."

———————————————

Lewis slumped back in his seat as the connection terminated. He let out a long shuddering breath and wiped at his eyes.

"Are you alright, sir?" Sheehan asked as he appeared at Lewis's elbow.

"Yes, Captain, I am."

Lewis restrained an impulse to respond with his customary snap, then paused and, half amused at the simple truth of the question, smiled before looking up.

"Yes, Captain, I am alright. In fact, we all are. Dispatch a courier to Earth. Send: Sir, It is my duty to report that Operation Vindictive has been successfully completed. All enemy resistance has ceased; the Nameless have been driven from this arm of the galaxy."

Epilogue

12th August 2069

"Ladies and Gentlemen, I am delighted to introduce my guest for this evening, Mister Jeff Harlow author of 'The Nameless War – A View from the Sidelines'."

Jeff adjusted his collar, put on his very best smile and stepped onto the stage. He and the show host exchanged utterly convincing and equally insincere smiles as they shook hands.

"So... A View from the Sidelines," the show host began once they were both seated. "Critics are already describing it as the first great history of the conflict. But what I think amazes so many of us, is how fast you managed to get it written."

"Hah! Well, oddly enough, the Worms themselves had a bit of a hand in that. One of the missiles that hit my ship wrecked all of our Deep Sleep capsules and, well, it's a long way back from the Spur. Had to do something to keep myself busy," Jeff replied with a modest smile.

When the dust settled and the fleet was finally prepared to admit that it had actually won, he'd realised he was the only member of the press to have made it. The rest had been either killed or been on ships that were put out of the battle early on. He was the only press witness to the entire Battle of the Spur. While the cripples headed for home, *Freyia* and the few other ships still standing remained on patrol there. With his reports dispatched, there was nothing for Jeff to do. Then he'd had an epiphany. If he could get the first eyewitness account out, well... ka-ching! He'd broken the back of it on the trip home but he'd still needed another month hot-boxing once he got back.

"There must have been some decidedly scary moments."

"More than a few I will admit, yet, I believe to have been out there was very much something worth doing," he replied.

"And heroic."

"No, no! The true heroes are the men and women of the fleet," Jeff said conscientiously – his publicist had been firm he needed to say that. "It is an often thankless job and even after being out there, I can't imagine being the one who had to make the hard decisions."

That much was true. If only he'd been able to get a proper interview out of Admiral Lewis but the man was incorrigible.

"I suppose the big question – the one you haven't answered – is the Nameless themselves: will they come back?"

"Well," Jeff replied, "that is the big question. The answer is no one really knows. Personal opinion though, I don't think they will. After the hammering we gave them, I don't think they will be in a hurry to return. We don't know what or who else is out there, but, unless we go after them, I don't think the Nameless will dare come after us again."

"Hawkings Control, this is the cruiser *Black Prince*. We are clear of docking port, request exit vector."

Berg half listened as her new communications officer worked through the formalities of clearing Hawkings Base. Looking around the bridge, there weren't many of the old faces left now. In war she'd been crewed by reserves and now that peace had returned they were all gone, replaced by veterans from ships that had either failed to return from the Spur or come back badly damaged.

"Captain, Hawkings Control has given us permission to depart. We are to take exit path Omega."

"Very well," Berg replied. "Navigator, give Helm a course."

She stayed on the bridge as the cruiser navigated around the commercial traffic and began to accelerate out of the planet's mass shadow. Ahead was a week of patrolling the systems close to Dryad, a job that really required two or more ships, but which was more than could be spared. Battle Fleet might be victorious but it was also exhausted. Looking around the bridge, Berg couldn't help but feel her ship probably summed up the fleet in general. Not an old ship but already hard used and tired. Those of them that remained would carry a heavy burden until the fleet could rebuild.

"Captain, a piece of housekeeping has just come in from Earth, which Hawkings has forwarded to us. Headquarters has announced all Battle Fleet personnel who have been awarded the Fleet Cross. Commodore Ronan Crowe is the first name on the list – posthumously."

"I served with him," she replied simply.

There was movement on the bridge to suggest that everyone was now listening to the conversation.

"May I ask Captain, what he was like?" the communications office asked carefully.

"Good explorer, a good man, a good officer and an unlikely war hero," she said.

Had he lived, Crowe would have hoped to return to the exploring he loved – and been disappointed. The days of exploration were on hold, at least for the moment. These were the days of retrenchment, drawing lines on maps and saying this far and no further. As terrible as it was to think, perhaps it was as well he hadn't lived to see that.

"Captain, the *Clover* reports the last of the torpedoes are away."

On the holo Willis could see them making their way down into the planet's mass shadow, joining the scores that had already been deployed by the Home Fleet. Any attempt by the Nameless to use the shadow, as cover to transfer through the Spur would be met by an immediate hail of torpedoes.

And that was only the beginning. Given time, the Spur would become the most heavily defended point in human space. Even now, months after the last Nameless ship had fled the system – it still had the feel of a combat zone. For a good reason – with so much wreckage and various munitions floating about, it was rare to get through two consecutive shifts without an alert. Some ships had taken hits – and casualties, but then this was the new frontier.

When most of the battered remnants of the Home Fleet set course for Earth, *Spectre* and a few others had stayed behind to protect what had been so dearly won. Not only that, but surveying nearby systems and deploying sentry satellites. Willis had seen and contributed to the first draft of plans for what was already being described as the Rift Line. When, or perhaps if, the Nameless came again, if would have to be through here.

Willis nodded. "Alright, Communications. Navigator, make the calculations for jump," she ordered.

"Well congratulations on the successful completion of your final mission Captain," Yaya said.

"Not quite, Commander," Willis replied with a smile. "I have to do the hand over to the new Third Fleet. But once that's done, we're on our way home."

"And thank God for that," Yaya agreed.

"Yes. Well, I'm going below to try and have my reports ready. I don't know about you, but I'm ready for home," Willis said with a wan smile.

Sitting down in her cabin Willis wearily rubbed at her eyes. No one could know the future, least of all if or when the Nameless would return. But she did at least know her own future. *Spectre*'s withdrawal was already overdue. Her battle damage had been only roughly patched and her machinery badly needed an overhaul. Once that was done, *Spectre* would head back out, but Willis knew that she would not be in command. A communication for her had arrived with one of the ships of the newly re-formed Third Fleet. Her next posting would back on Earth, back in Headquarters. It would be a twin posting, both as an instructor in the Advanced Tactical Training School and a planner in the Strategic Forecasting Section.

Three years ago her career had been going off the rails. Now, not only was she back to where she had expected to be, but far beyond it – very much on the fast track for senior command. But then that would mean that if the Nameless came again, she would be among those standing in their path. Willis looked around her small cabin, at the pictures she'd started to hang up – ones of home, of family, poor old *Hood*, the austerity cruiser *Black Prince*, *Spectre* – the ship that brought death to an entire world – and last but by no means least, the late Commander Vincent Espey. No. If the Nameless came, if would have to be through her. So things were as they should be.

"Good to have seen you and thanks for coming. See you again soon," Guinness said as the last of the guests wobbled their way out the door.

"Is that everyone?" his son called from the kitchen.

"Yep, that's the lot," Guinness replied.

Thanks be to a good and merciful God he thought to himself as he made his way into the living room. They'd meant well, they really had, and he'd brought it upon himself by letting them know when he was being demobbed, but really he could have done without the surprise party. In a day or two he'd have felt far more ready for it but what could you do? It was not as if he'd really even wanted to come home.

Moving a couple of plastic plates, he sat down in his easy chair with a sigh. He'd lied about his age to get back into the fleet, while it, desperate for trained personnel, looked the other way. But with peace came the inevitable sorting of paperwork and it had been 'discovered' that he was overage. So they'd given him a pat on the back, some new medals, a place in the victory parade... and a gentle shove out the door.

"You all right, Dad?"

Guinness looked up at his son – he hadn't heard him come in – and realised his mind must have drifted.

"Yeah, just tired."

"It wasn't too much for you was it?"

"No, no, it was... nice to see everyone. Although I supposed we'll be doing the same song and dance again next month."

A couple of local councillors had popped in during the afternoon and one had mentioned a formal memorial event for the following month. Guinness was one of four people from the county that had gone to war. One came back minus his legs and one didn't come back at all. Now the council wanted to hand out freedoms of the city or some such.

"If you want to head for bed I'll deal with the clean up," his son continued.

Guinness looked around. The place certainly gave the impression that it had been bombed in the middle of a burglary. Then he looked up again at his son. He was a good lad, looking out for his Da. But then his Da was a man who'd spent the last three years keeping antiques and patchwork ships going as they were shot to pieces around him. He'd walked in the door in his uniform, a chief engineer, master of the engineering spaces, but at some point during the festivities, he'd taken off his jacket and become an old man again. In a few weeks he'd probably be just some old fart to be avoided before he started banging on about the war to people who wouldn't be able to understand what it had been like.

"No, I'll help," he replied getting up, "you don't know where half the stuff goes anymore. If I let you do it, tomorrow I'll be wondering where half my plates have gone. Anyway tomorrow I've got stuff to do."

"Oh? What kind of stuff?"

"Figuring what the bloody hell I'm doing with the rest of my life."

"Congratulations Lieutenant Commander," the Admiral murmured as he pinned on the medal.

"Thank you, sir," Alanna replied as she saluted sharply and the

Admiral continued down the line of recipients.

The awards ceremony was followed by an obligatory reception, for which the fleet had put on a surprisingly good spread. But then how often would there be six freshly minted Earth Crosses, the fleet's highest award, in a single room? Given that half of the medals had been posthumously awarded, if never again then, to Alanna's way of thinking, that wouldn't be a bad thing. Her conversation with Commodore Crowe's widow had been awkward. She hadn't realised he'd even been married. Always the unspoken question – why did you come back and he didn't?

Alanna took a spot by the buffet table and a particularly good cheese platter where she could watch the room. It was vaguely amusing to observe the full range of military personnel from ratings to admirals sharing a space, each attempting to make awkward small talk, while civilians – friends and family – blithely sailed through the middle of it all. She could see Schurenhofer, her father, and her former gunner's boyfriend near the centre of the room, talking to a senior captain, which under other circumstances might have made her nervous.

"Ah, there you are. I was looking for you Lieutenant Commander."

It was Admiral Clarence. Alanna automatically started to salute but with one arm still in a sling and her other holding a wine glass, she realised she was stuck.

Clarence grinned.

"Don't worry about that. How's the arm?"

"Getting better, sir."

"I wanted to have a little word with you."

"About, sir?" she asked, although she immediately guessed what he wanted to talk about.

"I understand from my office that you've put in to resign from the fleet."

"That's correct, sir," Alanna replied. "On medical grounds. The doctors say my shoulder is mending well but I'll never regain full mobility in the joint. Ninety to ninety five percent but that's not enough for fighter operations."

"I know this might sound like heresy to a redoubtable pilot like yourself, but there is more to the fleet than fighters. You've proved in the field that you have an aptitude for other command roles. You saved *Deimos* when no one would have faulted you for punching out," Clarence said.

Maybe it had been an acknowledgment of her success in saving the ship or perhaps it was simply a reflection of how many had died, but Alanna had been left in command for the long flight home. It was only when they reached Earth, once they had solemnly carried off the coffins and *Deimos*'s battered hull was towed into dock that she finally handed over command.

When Alanna made no reply he continued.

"The thing is, the fleet is about to lose a lot of people over the next six months. The reservists are being demobilised as we speak and the national militaries will want back the various bods they transferred to us. We will face not only a shortfall in numbers but also a real skills shortage. So I'm really hoping to persuade you to stay."

Alanna looked out across the room and listened to the babble of conversation. Through the windows she could see down into Dublin city and beyond that, the rest of the world.

"I promised myself two things if I made it through. I promised that if I did, I'd find out what else is out there and I promised that I wouldn't let the *Old Dauntless* be forgotten. I'm sorry sir – I'll serve out my enlistment period of course and do whatever it is the fleet wants while it has me. But then I'm done. I'm looking into a job with the terraforming project on Mars. I'm still owed a guided tour at the very least."

Clarence sighed.

"Can't say that's unexpected. Unwelcome, but not unexpected," he said. "Take a look by all means. The fleet will wait for you – not forever mind – but it will wait for a while. Good luck, Lieutenant Commander Shermer."

"Corporal Alice Peats? Or is it Doctor Alice Peats? Is there an Alice Peats here?"

"Here!" croaked Alice as she turned her head towards the flap of the medical tent.

"You've got a visitor."

Wearily, she noticed the medical orderly duck his head back under the tent flap and then heard him speaking to someone before the flap was pushed back again and an almost forgotten face came through.

"Damien!" she whispered.

Damien Demolder, her former deputy, friend and lover. He tried to keep the shock at her appearance from his face and comprehensively failed.

"Sorry I've kinda let myself go a bit since we last met," she joked weakly. "I didn't get fat though."

"Oh Jesus," he said.

There was no disguising what had happened. She'd been lucky, that was what she kept telling herself. She'd survived the amputation and blood loss, although fever had nearly carried her off. But she clung to life as those who'd found and protected her clung to a precarious existence dodging Nameless patrols. Until that day – that miraculous day – finally arrived, when a human ship – was seen roaring across the sky, ending their nightmare.

"I followed after your group or at least I thought I did," Damien said as he gently touched her cheek. Since the fleet returned I've been looking for you."

"You got here just in time then," she whispered. "A hospital ship arrives tomorrow. I'm transporting to Earth – no room on Landfall for useless mouths."

Survivors were still being found. Most of the population of the planet that had survived had done so by getting as far into the wilderness as they could. Thousands, tens of thousands, were still out there. The fleet didn't have the means to airlift them back and could only do supply drops. For those who had reached the refugee centres, there was no easy future. With the planet's infrastructure devastated, there were months and years of work ahead for the traumatised survivors. Those who could not work would be returning to Earth, while those who could, would remain. In neither case would there be a choice.

"They can do amazing things these days with prosthetics and regrown tissue," he started to say before trailing off as she squeezed his hand with the only one she still had.

In the chamber the holo pad began to glow and everyone stood as the Council members appeared.

"Please sit," President Clifton said as her hologram stabilised, giving them a moment to do so before she continued. "Admiral Lewis, welcome back and may I extend both my personal congratulations and those of the people of the United States. All of us owe you and those you commanded a tremendous debt of gratitude."

Lewis nodded his acknowledgement.

"Now, Admiral Wingate, moving onto business. Your report, please."

"Thank you," Wingate replied with a nod. "Council members, firstly I can confirm with a high degree of certainty that as per earlier reports, the Nameless have now completely left our arm of the galaxy. Furthermore, scouts that have reached Earth since the Home Fleet departed the Spur have confirmed that the Nameless are evacuating the system destroyed by the Phantom task group. Those scouts have also observed activity in other systems on the Nameless side of the Rift and it would appear the Nameless are fortifying their border."

"I by no means disparage the efforts of the fleet but this is an unsatisfactory peace," said Prime Minister Layland.

"Yes sir, we have a peace without a treaty, armistice or even ceasefire," Wingate replied. "In essence, the war is over only because they cannot reach us."

"Nor have we stripped from them their ability to wage war," Lewis said forbiddingly.

"How then can we be sure that they will not return, a month from now or six months?"

"Eventually sir, I regret to say I believe they will," Wingate replied. "On a fundamental level, the Nameless believe that our very existence makes us a threat. Unless that changes, it is impossible to see any way by which we might meet them halfway. But in the short term I believe they cannot. Their fleet suffered massive losses attempting to break the Home Fleet at the Spur. Additionally, now that we have proven our ability and willingness to destroy a world" – several council members winced at that – "it means that we have demonstrated we are the very threat they so fear. Finally, while they can go round the Rift at the expense of both time and effort, by contrast we can cross it relatively easily. Thus, what remains of their fleet must be retained in home defence. They will rebuild and fortify, but so will we."

"Unsatisfactory," Clifton agreed, "but far better than what we could have hoped for eighteen months ago."

"Yes indeed, Madam President," Wingate replied. "We stand on one side of the Rift and they glare at us impotently from the other."

Lewis and Wingate walked down the corridor away from the Council chamber, in the latter's case, perhaps for the last time.

"Still absolutely determined to retire, sir?" Lewis asked.

"Absolutely. And you could still refuse, Paul. The Council can't actually force you to become head of the fleet."

"And I'm sure quite a few of them would be glad if I did turn it down," Lewis grunted. "But I'll take it, at least for a while. There's too much to do. Being a bona fide saviour of humanity opens a lot doors and, more importantly, treasuries.

"I'll only give the fleet three more years, though," he continued. "Laura is trying to put Science Fleet back together again but she wants to let younger backs take up the load as soon as possible, then for the pair of us to spend our last years somewhere warm, an idea that I'm already finding very appealing."

Lewis smiled briefly to himself before adding: "Three years will be enough to get the work started on the Rift Line. After that, better for the old to make way for the new."

"The diplomats are already seeking rapprochement with the Aèllr and Mhar," Wingate said. "The Aèllr are convinced that the Worms are a threat and if they go round the Rift, it takes them straight into the Confederacy."

"So old enemies become new friends. Another good reason for the old to take their baggage and go," Lewis replied. "We stood alone once and won when we should have lost."

Wingate smiled and nodded. Currently, the Rift Line really only existed in name. Fortifications would need to be built and infrastructure to support it. Already ship designers and intelligence officers were attempting to evaluate all the lessons of the war, and beginning to incorporate them into the next generation of warships. It was a project that would take decades, but when would it need to be completed?

"Peace in our time, the war to end all wars: that's always the promise but we can't offer even that lie. Someday they will cross the Rift," Lewis said abruptly. "In the clear up we found a working example of one of their gates and they must have got versions of our jump drive. Given time, they will cross and they won't make the same mistakes. This is our poisoned gift to the next generation."

"Fifteen years at least, fifty years at most," Wingate commented almost whimsically. "That's how long we've given the next generation to prepare."

They'd reached the main entrance to the building. Wingate paused at the top of the steps and looked up into the sky.

"You're right Paul. Here we are at the end of one war and

already planning for the next — a poisoned chalice indeed. In imperfect solution in an imperfect universe, but what we did was our best."

THE END

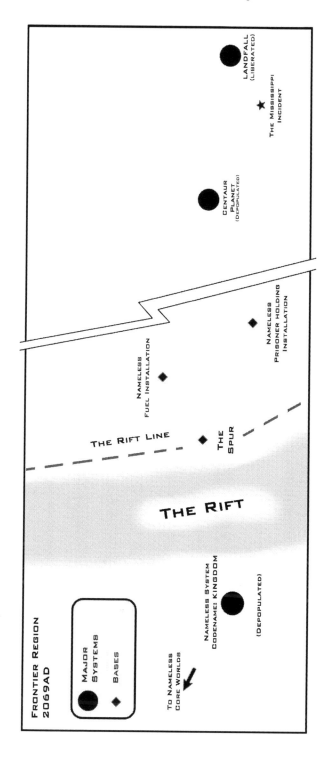

Glossary

Aèllr: Carbon based oxygen breathing mammalian life form. First intelligent alien life form encountered by humanity.

Aèllr Confederacy: Located approximately coreward of human space, a political union of the eight major and six minor planets occupied by the Aèllr race. Population: 32 billion (approx.), Government type - democracy.

Baden Base: Battle Fleet instalation located at the edge of the Landfall system. Its destruction is generally considered to mark the beginning of the Nameless War.

Battleship: Large gun armed ship, carrying heavier armour and guns than any other category of vessel. In human service this vessels frequently serve as fleet flagships.

Centaurs: The human designation for a pre-interstellar spaceflight species now considered extinct. Believed to have been destroyed by the Nameless.

Chaff: Standard passive counter measure, aluminium strips which give false returns or swamps radar systems. Chaff bursts are usually deployed by rocket.

Coms (Communication) Laser: Low powered lasers used for communications at short range (up to 70,000 kilometres). Standard feature of all human starships, coms lasers transmission can not be jammed.

Contact War, The: Humanities first interstellar conflict, fought against the Aèllr Confederacy. Largely fought with Earth's solar system the conflict ended inconclusively with the Treaty of Mars. Battle Fleet was founded during the early stages of the conflict.

Cruiser: A category of vessel that can be loosely defined as the largest ships to be built in significant numbers. This classification is given to the workhorse of every fleet.

Dryad System: Human controlled solar system close to Mhar Union and several of the Tample Star Nations. Dryad Two is borderline habitable and has large Zillithium deposits.

EMD, Emergency Message Drone: Missile sized drone equipped with a one use jump drive and a small transmitter. EMD's are for the vast majority of ships the only means of communicating across interstellar distances.

Fire Control: A ship's weapon control systems.

Governing Council: Political leadership of Battlefleet. The council is composed of rotating eight members, two from each continental block.

IFF, Identify Friend or Foe: Identification system designed for command and control. It enables military and civilian- interrogation systems to identify aircraft, vehicles or forces as friendly and to determine their bearing and range from the interrogator.

Jump Drive: The system used to travel between star systems. Not technically a faster than light drive but allows a ship to generate an artifical wormhole between two points in Real Space. The drive may not be used within the region around a planet or other large spacal body known as the Mass Shadow.

Jump Space: Term given the region within a jump conduit through with space vessels pass.

Landfall System / Planet: Human controlled system. Initially called Fortune, the system is now largely known by the name of its principal planet. An Earth-like body, Landfall has been conquored by the Nameless.

Lazarus Systems: Collection of systems which automatically reroute power and command signals around damaged connections, allowing human warships to remain functional with even severe damage.

Light Speed: 299,792,458 metres per second.

Local Control: Targeting systems built directly onto each gun mount. These systems are a back up measure should a ship's main Fire Control be knocked out. They lack both the sensitivity and accuracy of main fire control.

Mass Shadow: The 3 dimensional area surrounding a planet or large spatial body that prevents a vessel from making transit into or out of Jump Space. The size or 'depth' of a mass shadow is proportional to the mass of the spatial body generating the shadow.

Mhar: Carbon based oxygen breathing mammalian life form. Third sentient race to be encountered by humanity. Technologically inferior to humans in most respects. Relations between Humanity and the Mhar are friendly. Government type: centrally planned democracy.

Nameless, The: Interstellar capable species about which almost nothing is known due to their hostility to all other sentient life. The Nameless appear to exclusively favour missile armament and use a form of jump drive different from that of any of the other known races.

Plasma Cannon: Standard anti ship weapon used by Battlefleet and the Aèllr Defence Fleet. Light plasma cannons as carried by destroyers are effective out to 60,000 kilometres, cruiser scale weapons to 100,000 kilometres. Heavy plasma cannons as carried by battleships ships are effective out to 130,000 kilometres. Plasma Cannons will not function in atmosphere.

PO, Petty Officer: Non-Commission Officer.

Point Defence Guns: Active defensive system designed to protect a ship from fighters, missiles and small astronomical hazards. Standard feature in both military and civilian vessels, although military vessels will carry significantly more point defence guns.

Railguns: Projectile thrower which uses two charged super conductor rails to accelerate metal projectiles. Used principally as secondary armament on Battle Fleet battleships and cruisers.

Rating: Lowest rank of fleet personnel, equivalent to an army private.

Real Space: Conventional Newtonian space.

Red line, The: Standard terminology for the outer edge of a planet's Mass Shadow, thus the closest to a planet that a ship can make transition in or out of jump space.

Scram: To shut down a nuclear reactor rapidly in an emergency.

Silent Running: A state in which a vessel powers down and reduces all emissions to avoid detection.

Skipper: Unofficial term for officer in command of a vessel. As such can apply to officers of virtually any rank.

Tample: Carbon based oxygen breathing life form with both Lizard and Insect characteristics. Broken down into seven separate and competing. Star Nations the Tample were the second sentient race to be encountered by humanity.

Author's Postscript

So, here we are at the end of The Nameless War and for me the end of a project going back ten years. The funny thing is that this wasn't the story I originally intended to tell; that story fell foul of a dead hard drive and failure to back up my work. Instead of attempting to reconstruct the lost text, I chose to move on to the story of an encounter at the edge of known space between an alien vessel and an aged starship called Mississippi. But with the story complete (and this time backed up) I found myself curious to see what the implications of this encounter would be.

With the first book of the Nameless War completed, I began to serious consider publication. I was lucky with my timing, self publishing was really starting to get under way and I was able to join a new wave of writers who were able for the first time reach a mass audience. Along the way I've made some mistakes, have had to learn a lot of new skills, as well as find new uses for old ones. I would to thank again Sorcha for her encouragement to hit the big scary button marked publish. To Phil and Peter for letting me bounce ideas off them for years on end. To Jan and Ray for their editing. To Anne for that stupid idea that was actually a very good one. Thank you to my parents who have supported me in all things.

I would like to finish by thanking you the reader, for your support, your suggestions and yes your criticisms. I thank you for giving me the opportunity and motivation to explore and expand the Battle Fleet universe and hope I will hear from you in the future.

Edmond Barrett
September 2014

The Last Charge

Also by this author

The Nameless War Trilogy
The Nameless War
The Landfall Campaign
The Last Charge

Coming Soon
Ships of the Fleet Volume One - Battleships

Printed in Great Britain
by Amazon

66172115R00253